THE STRANDING

A.L. NELSON

Trigger Warnings (which can also be spoilers): Please note that the author is trying to help, not harm, and is doing her best without being an expert in medical, psychological, or associated professions. Some of what this book covers that might cause unintended reactions include: aerial vehicle crash, human death, kidnapping, physical fights, guns, cheating, and divorce.

Copyright © 2020 A.L. Nelson, All Rights Reserved
All rights reserved.
ISBN: 9798577223472

Cover designed by Kennedy Nelson. No part of this publication may be reproduced, distributed, stored in, or introduced into any information storage and/or retrieval system, or transmitted in any form or by any means, including electronic or mechanical methods, photocopying, recording, or otherwise, including any hereafter invented, without the prior express written permission of the author.

The Stranding is a work of fiction. The story, all names, characters, dialogue, and incidents portrayed in this production are fictitious and a product of the author's imagination. All incidents, dialogue and characters are products of the author's imagination. No identification with actual persons (living or deceased), places, buildings, and products is intended or should be inferred.

Dedication

I would like to dedicate this book to my son. I originally wrote the story four or five years ago, when my son was young. He helped me work out the details of a crash scene using one of his toys (you'll know which toy when you read that part of the book). He proved very knowledgeable for such a young kid!

Acknowledgements

I'd like to recognize the efforts of my husband. He keeps the household and the family together while making it possible for me to carve out time to write. He's also my first critic and strongest supporter.

One

My stomach lurched, shifting location dramatically from my brain to my feet and back again. At least, that's how it felt. The turbulence might force me to use the barf bag I kept so firmly clutched in my left hand. No doubt people everyone would hear the bag begging for mercy if not for the ear-splitting screams going on. The armrest held fast against my death grip. I didn't trust the ability of the seat belt alone to handle the job of keeping my body where it belonged.

Another jolt, another sickening drop. Surely, the ocean wasn't far beneath us by this point. There could be hungry sharks below. That'd be just my luck.

The next jarring sent my long ash brown hair into a deeper state of tangles. The heavyset older woman beside me clutched a rosary, knuckles white, praying aloud. I put a hand on her forearm between lurching motions, hoping to comfort her. A few minutes before, I'd typed out a text to my husband, telling him I loved him and our daughter, and said goodbye. Maybe my phone would survive a plane crash and my family would know I'd been thinking of them.

A sharp motion to one side then back again popped the overhead storage bins open, sending an assortment of belongings onto the heads of those occupying the aisle seats, who cried out, some sustaining minor injuries resulting from the impact with hard luggage, raising the total number of wounded. Oxygen masks dropped in front of us from above, creating a fresh wave of panic.

The co-pilot announced we should ignore the masks and hang on, because we were almost out of it. The conditions made it difficult to believe him. Perhaps the worst thing was watching through the window as the wing on my side of the plane cavorted about independently from the body of the aircraft with each shudder.

On top of everything else, in under an hour I'd be airborne again, in a helicopter. Provided I managed to live through the current rollercoaster ride. Why did I ever agree to this? I must have lost my mind, like I might lose my lunch. Or the contents of my bladder. A dream career wasn't worth my life.

"Dear God," I whispered, "please save us, or take us quickly. Some of these people won't be able to make it through another drop like that one, including me."

The aircraft gave another shudder, leaving everyone waiting for plane parts to separate like a jigsaw puzzle. But no accompanying drop came this time. After nearly a full minute of sniffles, whines, and moans, disbelieving passengers took it all in. We waited, either for more tossing or to simply drop out of the sky and be blown into a billion tiny bits upon impact with the water.

It didn't happen. The day remained beautiful and sunny. Cottony clouds cast dark blue shadows on the surface of the ocean beneath. And dry land swung into view in the distance as the plane made a gentle turn. The landing gear thumped as they descended from the belly of the aircraft, as designed. My feet longed for solid ground.

"Everything's under control now, folks. We'll be landing in just a few minutes. Hang in there. Medical personnel will be meeting us at the gate," the co-pilot reported in a thick accent, repeating the same in two other languages.

"Thank you, God. And please, let this be the one and only terrible experience I will ever have in the air, for the rest of my life," I whispered. Fulfilment shouldn't be difficult, considering in a week I'd be home and never go on anything that went higher than a porch swing again. People weren't meant to fly, just as my husband always said.

I combed my fingers through my hair and fanned at myself and my grateful seatmate, using a crumpled magazine. At least I had something dramatic to write as part of the article I was here to research. The next step in the process involved touring islands, which should prove relaxing. What could possibly go wrong with that scenario?

I stopped in the shade of the small airport building I'd just checked in at, backpack strapped over my shoulder. There were three helicopters parked on the asphalt ahead. I must have lost my mind, ready to go through with leaving the ground behind again.

"Hello ma'am. You must be Savannah Dalton. I'm Dave Rodgers." Dave had just emerged from the building behind me.

My mouth gaped open almost enough for me to fit my fist inside. He was perfect if a woman liked tall, dark, and devastating, with a manly voice to match. The man was overloaded with more than his fair share of the wow factor: muscular, dark hair and eyes, olive skin, and a small scar on his forehead that dipped into his left eyebrow, only serving to add to his rugged sex appeal. As if he needed more. He extended his hand while revealing the most likeable smile I'd ever seen in my entire life.

"Hey. You're the pilot?" I shook his hand, hoping my palm wasn't too sweaty and that he didn't notice. I should have wiped it off on my pants first. I was amazed at my own ability to form words. Let alone that they came out correctly and were audible.

"Yes, ma'am, that'd be me. I've already got your photographer strapped into his seat. He's quite a character. Have you known him long?" Dave led the way toward one of the three machines.

"I've never met him. He came highly recommended by a friend of mine at *National Geographic*. She made the arrangements." I swiped away a trickle of sweat from beneath my hair before it found its way down my back. I didn't want to look sweaty and nervous around Dave, even though I was. The temperature had me overheated almost as much as Dave did. I attempted to cool off a bit by flapping the front of my shirt as we walked. It was a lovely chartreuse color, but white would've shown perspiration less. Who could've expected a situation like this? At least I'd pulled my hair back.

My focus shifted to the helicopter he angled us toward. It looked like it belonged in a museum. "How long old is your helicopter?"

"She's got some years on her, but I keep her in top shape. She flies like a dream. You'll have the best flying experience of your life."

I hoped his idea of a dream wasn't different from mine. The nightmare I'd just gotten off of popped into my head.

"You aren't afraid to fly, are you?" he asked, opening a rear door. It creaked. Naturally. I should've expected the helicopter would be an antique.

"I've never been in a helicopter before. And I just finished a scary airplane ride less than an hour ago. It was the most frightening experience of my life."

"But it landed in one piece." He helped me into my seat after tucking my backpack into a compartment under the seat ahead.

"You heard?" I took note of the full-sized first aid kit squirreled away in the netting on the rear of the seat ahead and wondered if there were barf bags inside.

"It came over the radio while my friend Ryan and I were getting the chopper ready. A bunch of sick and injured passengers on the outskirts of the tropical cyclone—that's a hurricane back in the States. It intensified faster than expected. We'll finish up and get back here before there's a problem in this area."

"Are you sure?" My eyebrows rose.

"Positive. Your pilot was either overconfident or behind schedule. He should've diverted his course. I'm sorry you had such a rough trip. You guys hit some bad turbulence."

"We did." This guy should be on television or in a movie or have a modeling career. There must be dozens of women falling all over themselves to be near him at a moment's notice. I'd move here and be one of them if I weren't happily married.

I was happily married, right? Surprisingly, I needed to give the idea a moment of thought before confirming. More or less, anyway.

The air temperature had to be about five degrees hotter around Dave. Maybe more like ten. If I focused on him, he'd provide enough distraction to get me through anything this flight could throw my way.

"You weren't one of those sick ones, were you?" Dave asked.

"No." His hand touched my shoulder fleetingly, sending my internal body temperature skyrocketing.

"You should be proud of yourself, going through what you did right after a meal was served and not getting sick. We just might make a flying ace out of you yet." He flashed perfect white teeth.

The word *wow* kept going through my mind. At least the thought stayed in my head. Didn't it? I wasn't sure.

"Impossible. After I get home, I don't think I'll ever fly again as long as I live."

"You'll change your mind after flying with me. I promise I'll take good care of you." He patted my shoulder reassuringly.

"I'm going to hold you to that." I smiled and he returned it, strapping me in.

My seatmate was a tall, thin man with salt and pepper hair pulled back into a ponytail at the nape of his neck. His eyes were gray, and mirrored aviator sunglasses hung from one of a multitude of pockets in his vest.

"I would let you sit up front for a better view, but I'm hauling an extra passenger." He motioned to the seat ahead. "His name's Ryan Buckley, a friend who came for a visit after...what, Ryan? Two years now?"

Ryan turned, briefly acknowledging my presence. "Hi, it's good to meet you. And it's been fourteen months, not two years, Dave. You need to check a calendar out here in the boonies occasionally." Ryan was a nice-looking guy, lean but muscular, and probably around my age, with close-cropped light brown hair, blue eyes, and a pleasant smile.

Dave winked as he closed my door and gave it a slap.

"Hey, Ryan. I'm Savannah Dalton." Shockingly, I remembered my name. Dave had me in such a daze it could've easily been forgotten.

"Savannah's a pretty name." Ryan put on dark sunglasses.

"Thanks." My eyes were locked on Dave as he climbed in.

"For a pretty lady," the photographer said in a French accent. "I'm Alphonse Boudreaux. Pleased to make your acquaintance." He extended his hand.

Alphonse was supposed to be an up-and-coming nature photographer. When I shook his hand, he gave mine an exaggerated kiss, then started working his way up my arm.

"Hey!" I pulled my hand away and grimaced, while he laughed. Great choice of photographers. Maybe I needed a new friend at *National Geographic*.

Ryan slid his sunglasses farther down on his nose to send the photographer a threatening stare. Alphonse caught it and returned to rummaging around inside his camera bag, chuckling to himself.

Dave started the engine, and the rotors spun obediently. I wondered if it was too late to change my mind. My little voice told me this was a bad idea. Maybe worse than the trip that got me here.

As the helicopter lifted, I gripped my seat, both side and front. The material proved itself up to the challenge. Going straight up was a foreign sensation.

I'd gone along with the trip because my friend made it sound glamorous. Tropical islands, adventure in a beautiful foreign country, the potential for a fascinating discovery. An important magazine assignment would benefit my burgeoning career, and this was a giant of the field, *National Geographic*.

"I see you're married." Alphonse pointed to my left hand. "I'm married myself. But I wouldn't let my wife go off without me, especially to a romantic, tropical getaway. Of course, I go off without her all the time for my work. Do you have any kids?"

"Yes, a daughter. She starts middle school in the fall."

"I have two girls, but mine are twenty-four and twenty-three. I love them so much. But I love my job, too. I get to take photographs for a living because my wonderful wife makes lots of money and wants me to be as happy as I make her."

"That's nice." Beyond my window was ocean, making my stomach nervous.

"The woman who arranged everything said this article might be a feature story. I've had cover shots, but never with *National Geographic*. This is a wonderful opportunity."

Concentrating on the views outside was difficult with the conversation taking place inside. But it was taking the edge off the queasiness.

"Do you just write freelance articles, or do you also write books? You might get famous doing that, like what's his name? Patterson, James Patterson."

"I've thought about it, but I've never tried. Even if I did, I'd never have the following of James Patterson. No one does."

"He's been at it a long time, of course," Alphonse said.

"Is it hard...writing, I mean?" Dave asked, angling his head back to me, flashing that amazing smile.

"It's great, but it's part time. I teach high school geography for a living. What about flying? That seems absurdly complicated, remembering what all those buttons and switches are for. How long have you been flying?"

"Flying is my lifelong passion. I flew in the Coast Guard for fifteen years before I gave that up to start my own business out here. The Coast Guard was where Ryan and I met. Mostly now I fly tourists around. It's exciting to be contracted to assist on a big story for *National Geographic.*

"Speaking of which, I've been wondering about something. How do you manage to write such interesting articles? When I signed on, I researched you...and you, Alphonse. It helped me understand what the two of you might be looking for. But for the life of me, I don't understand how people write like that. Did you study to be a writer?"

"No, my major was geography, so my work focuses on nature. But speaking of careers, while I have the opportunity, I'd like to thank both you and Ryan for your service."

They smiled, Dave adding a thumbs up.

"If you want to know the truth, photography is harder than either of your jobs. I love it and would never want to do anything else, but everyone thinks it's easy. Just push a button." Alphonse shook his head emphatically from side to side.

"So, what else is there besides pushing a button?" Dave interjected.

"It's quite involved, more so than you'd expect. You must consider lighting, shadows, weather, and a whole host of technical issues with equipment. Plus, you end up taking hundreds of photographs just to get one image that works its unique magic."

I turned away to stare through the window at the ocean. There were several islands of diverse sizes and shapes nearby and more on the horizon. Alphonse continued actively engaging Dave in conversation.

Ahead, Ryan glanced over his shoulder, pointing to the ocean and a group of distant islands. I nodded and continued searching for one to match the description related by an early explorer in an obscure

7

newspaper article from around the turn of the twentieth century. Dave was here to fly, Alphonse to photograph. My assigned task was attempting to rediscover something lost, nicknamed Shark Tooth Island.

After somewhere around four hours, during which time we made a pit stop to refuel and relieve ourselves on a seemingly abandoned, inhospitable-looking island outpost, Alphonse called to the pilot. "This looks like a good spot for some photographs. Circle it for me. What do you think, Savannah? Even if we can't find the island you're looking for, we can document the effort."

I had been completely lost in thought. Following Alphonse's gaze, I noted the heavily wooded island on his side of the helicopter. It wasn't the largest we'd seen, but it held interest, with a wide, sandy cove, the water shallow, and a lovely turquoise. It held promise to at least pass for Shark Tooth Island. I nodded to Alphonse in agreement and took the next logical step in his idea. "And we might still be able to get it published. Maybe not the cover, but you're right. What we're doing will make for an interesting story."

Trees roofed the majority of the island, sloping from towering cliffs to sandy beaches. Flocks of birds scattered from one cluster of trees to another as our helicopter passed. A narrow streak of water spilled from inside a grouping of rocks on a steep hillside. It splashed gleefully as gravity took it, disappearing into more rocks some twenty feet below. There was no pool, meaning water collected underground before ending up in the ocean.

Beach encircled the entirety of the island, except on the north end. There, the topography ascended mightily above the ocean. At the foot of intimidating cliffs, there was little room for a beach. Large, jagged rocks jutted defiantly from the ocean's angry surface. Frothy, furious waves crashed over them, the surf rolling in and out. The ominous water in-between was a deep, dark blue, sloshing back and forth. It was spectacularly treacherous.

"That's scary-looking." I glanced to Alphonse.

"It's gorgeous!" Alphonse countered. "And a perfect match for what I've read in that old newspaper article."

"That's what I was just thinking about that cove we passed over. It's worth exploring." We flew away from the violent cliffs to reconnoiter. The rest of the island was peaceful and lush, the ground often hidden amongst the dense vegetation. Bright, tropical flowers grew on trees and on bushes in the understory.

"There're some coconut trees over that way." Dave pointed but I didn't know enough about tropical trees to spot them amongst all the rest. "And I saw bananas. Banana and coconut trees produce pretty much year-round out here."

"There're probably edibles there. No people though?" Ryan asked.

"Small and remote for that," Dave said. "What's next, Savannah?"

"Let's go up a bit, so I can get a look at it from above, to see the overall shape."

"Yes ma'am." The helicopter rose smoothly, circling.

My eyes noted details, working it out. "I think I see it...no, I *know* I do. It's got a cove almost totally closed off from the ocean and the whole island is shaped like a giant shark tooth. This might be it!"

"I see it, too!" Ryan caught the excitement from me and Alphonse.

"I don't know...I've seen lots of islands in my travels that could pass for a shark tooth," Dave said with reluctance, piloting the helicopter toward the more pointed end of the island. "We'll come back tomorrow if you want and land so you can verify the rest. Good luck with that, by the way. I'll hover you over the water, but I won't go in there with you."

"What do you mean by that?" Ryan asked.

"It's supposed to be a major gathering spot for sharks. That's from the old report, from back in 1901. And I'm not getting paid to dive with sharks. They can send in a scientific expedition for that." My swimming skills were decent, but I wouldn't risk a shark encounter for any amount of money.

"I think these cliffs are the most interesting part of the island for Alphonse and me. What do you say, Alphonse? All set back there?" Dave asked.

"All set; ready to open up!" Alphonse responded.

Open up? What did that mean?

"Let me hold her steady for you. Okay, go ahead," Dave hollered over his shoulder, the helicopter ceasing its forward progress to hover over the steep jungle terrain near the cliffs.

While I'd been talking, Alphonse had fastened straps to the harness he wore, attaching himself to steel cables, one above the door and the other by Dave's seat. Next thing I knew, he'd disconnected his seatbelt, pulled a handle, and slid the door open. Loose strands of hair from the long ponytail swirled all about his face.

As did mine, poking at my eyeballs. I hadn't expected this. The door was wide, freaking *open*. Using both hands, I tried to rein in my hair, not to mention my fear. "Is this safe? Having the door open, I mean?"

"Yes, ma'am. We'll be fine, don't worry. It's safer to do this in a helicopter than an airplane. Some people remove the doors altogether," Dave yelled back.

That must've been intended to reassure. Hopefully, the meal on the jet was too far through my system to be thrown up now. Although from the sensations in my stomach, I could be wrong.

"Is this a good spot or do you want me to find something else?" Dave chimed in.

"This is great, Dave!" Alphonse called out. "Circle the island again; then go lower for a close look."

"Will do!" Dave hollered back.

The helicopter rotated smooth as silk, taking us around the perimeter of the island. This part was enjoyable, away from those cliffs. Alphonse alternately snapped images and shot video. The plant life formed a near-impenetrable jungle, hiding away deep, dark secrets. I couldn't help wondering what those secrets were.

Dave returned to the cliffs for that up-close look Alphonse wanted. In several locations there were deep crevices inviting exploration. Some of them appeared to be caves; but the long, narrow overhangs cast shadows, limiting visibility, and generating doubt. A simple trick of shadow and light, most likely.

"This is great! It's what I live for!" Alphonse exclaimed, jubilant.

THE STRANDING

Dave's helicopter lifted to the peak, shifting to hover thirty feet above the treetops. The branches swayed as if in the throes of a hurricane from swirling air currents generated by the helicopter's rotors.

"Here's a good view for you!" Dave hollered with obvious enthusiasm.

The helicopter tilted at a sharp angle then, as Dave rotated the machine in a circle, which had me focused on not screaming. Alphonse released a loud whoop of delight, and Dave let loose a big belly laugh. He eased up on the angle but continued to swivel the machine as my photographer leaned out as far as he could get.

The harness was all that kept Alphonse from falling to his death as we hovered over the absolute edge of the cliffs. He braced himself with one knee against the arm of his seat as he snapped away. His work here would be incredible.

Dave maneuvered higher and back toward the trees, periodically tilting the helicopter at an angle for a shot or two. Alphonse was exposed to the violently swaying treetops, my window showing sky.

How could this even be possible? Weren't we defying the laws of gravity enough already, just by flying in this thing normally? When would he stop angling us over? However many photographs Alphonse had taken, it was bound to be enough. We should be done here.

As if reading my mind, Dave called back to Alphonse. "Okay, that's it. We've got enough fuel to get us back to the halfway station. We've already been gone longer than I filed on my flight plan for the entire duration of the trip, and we've still got to get back. We've deviated way off course at your request, too, Alphonse. That was a big no-no, so we've got to get going. Plus, there's a brewing cyclone out there to consider. We'll be flying back in the dark as it is. Might get a little dicey, all things considered."

"Wait a minute! There's something down there. I see...something. Take us a little closer, Dave!" Alphonse insisted.

"What is it?" Dave asked, glancing down through his side window at the trees below us, easy to do as he tilted the machine again.

"I don't know." Alphonse lifted his camera and resumed snapping images at a rapid pace. "I think maybe it was..."

Dave began angling the machine slowly back toward level, even as he was craning his neck, trying to spot whatever had gained Alphonse's spellbound attention. We were partway to level when he uttered a sharp expletive, and Alphonse screamed.

"Oh my God, get us out of here! *Go!*" Alphonse yelled.

It was already too late.

My head turned toward Alphonse quickly, but it was hard to see past him. Then I caught a glimpse of what had thrown them into a panic. Birds. Dozens upon dozens of seagulls funneled up from the jungle in a nightmarish apparition. Death reached for us from the dark depths of the jungle on black-tipped wings.

Everything happened fast after that, yet to my terrified mind it seemed a slow-motion, frame-by-frame series of events. It had to be happening to someone else. It couldn't be me.

The birds flew straight up at us out of the treetops, as if from a genuine calling. One collided with Alphonse as he threw up his arms to block it. As he screamed and thrashed, his camera went into free-fall, shattering into bits as it bounced off the rocky ground at the base of the tree line. The remains sailed in an arc over the cliffs, headed for the crashing waves far beneath.

The raucous cries of the birds filled the air as they continued moving skyward, too close to change up their flight paths to avoid us. Bits of blood, feathers, and bird parts rocketed around the helicopter as the birds repeatedly struck the aircraft. The helicopter was beset with massive tremors. Dave's muscles bulged and his facial muscles tensed as he pulled it higher and straightened the listing machine before it tilted too far. It was becoming too difficult to control. We lurched radically to the opposite side.

The engine made a loud shrieking noise, akin to the birds. Thickening smoke swirled in the air. We screamed in horror as the engine died and the blades slowed their spinning, giving up the struggle, unable to keep us airborne as their spinning slowed. We plunged to the earth like a very large, very heavy rock.

The first impact to our pitching aircraft was with the top of a tall tree. Alphonse let out a yelp, cut short as the branches shoved their way inside with us, splintering glass the birds hadn't fully shattered themselves. The helicopter ricocheted off the tree, spiraling toward the ground, completely out of control.

Two

The force of the jolt from striking the top of the cliff, upside down, was inconceivable. Even though Dave had me strapped in securely, the insides of my body jostled like a shaken soda, that when popped open would spew its contents into the air. The collision crushed the cabin's interior by multiple inches and the windows on my side took on the appearance of overlapping spider webs.

The momentum of the impact rolled us over, the pilot's side ending up against the ground. The giant metal bird was now in an uncontrolled slide, scattering rocks and dirt into the air as its metal form scraped with a voluminous nails-on-a-chalkboard screech across the rocky terrain, shoving debris ahead of it. One of the blades ripped free and became airborne, somersaulting away. Those remaining careened into the rocks, generating vivid sparks as they sliced into the cliff in a vain attempt to perform their job.

The skidding machine jolted to a sudden halt, leaving us on our side at the brink of the precipice. A loud creaking sound came from the body of the aircraft as it rocked back and forth like a massive seesaw. When it finally ceased moving, utter silence hung thick in the air, along with rising dust and smoke.

Beyond Alphonse, the broken windows of the helicopter stared straight down into the roaring blue and white maw of the ocean's crashing waves. Alphonse drooped from his straps, outside the helicopter, over the abyss, twisting aimlessly in the air and streaked with blood.

The acrid smell of smoke seeped into my mind. Was there a fire? Were we on fire? Panic welled inside me at the thought. Was escape from the metal tomb even possible?

Dave's head slumped against the remnants of his window, shattered from the encounter with the birds, the tree, the rocks, or all of it. Red was smeared all around, but I couldn't tell if it was from Dave or the damned birds. He wasn't moving.

"Dave..." My voice croaked, barely making a sound. I cleared my throat to try again. "Dave? Dave!"

The helicopter made a creaking sound, internally this time, so I stopped calling out, attempting to identify the source instead. Movement ahead caught my attention. Ryan was conscious, struggling with his seatbelt.

As he succeeded, he called out. "Dave! Dave–buddy!" Ryan braced himself against gravity as he reached an outstretched hand toward his friend, but another strange sound came, this one from outside.

Ryan immediately ceased his movements. He realized it; just as I had. Our precarious balance on the edge of the cliff was beyond unstable. We peered, first through the opening Alphonse hung from and then behind us. The length of the machine, from the tail to somewhere shy of the center of the rear compartment where Alphonse and I were, was positioned over the drop-off. The front portion of the aircraft, somewhere around half by volume, was resting on solid, though uneven, ground. But just barely.

The fulcrum point of the craft rocked us back and forth slowly, teetering between life and death. The weight of the people onboard made all the difference. If Ryan got out with Dave, the helicopter would fall into the ocean, taking Alphonse and me with it.

Ryan's wide eyes met mine. I was well beyond petrified, realizing my predicament. Alphonse remained slumped, unconscious, or dead. If he was alive and awoke, then began to panic...

"Savannah, I want you to listen to me." Ryan's words came out soothing but strong. "I want you to very slowly and carefully remove your seatbelt."

"No. I can't do it. It'll make me fall." My words were clipped, sharp. It was difficult to catch a deep breath when looking past Alphonse.

"No, you're not going to fall. Remove your seatbelt and then climb up here with Dave and me. We need more weight up front. If you don't come up here, then I'm going to have to go ahead and get Dave out and there might not be time for you and Alphonse.

"The helicopter could shift and go over the side. You don't have a choice. You have to do exactly as I've told you." Strong, reassuring...an anchor.

My eyes closed for a silent prayer. Lord, I know you didn't save me from that jet to kill me in a helicopter on the same day. That wouldn't make any sense. I opened my eyes and stared into Ryan's. The blue of his shone with determination.

"Don't look down. Keep your eyes on me. Reach over and unfasten your harness. Keep your feet and your other hand braced wherever you can find a spot, so you don't fall out past Alphonse. If you do, I might not be able to catch you in time. Now come to me. You can do it."

I nodded, wondering if he saw the terror on my face. I slid my right hand along the strap until I came to the buckle, then pulled my body upward with my left hand to ease the pressure on the harness. I swallowed, taking a deep breath as I released the buckle.

The weight of my body obeyed the force of gravity as my feet struggled unsuccessfully to find a grip on the perpendicular floor. It was too much pressure for my left hand to work against as Ryan's seat shifted unexpectedly, loosened by the crash. In less than a heartbeat I knew what was about to happen.

My fingers slipped from the swiveling seat edge and I dropped, screaming, before Ryan lunged forward to grab a fistful of my shirt near the collar. His grip gave me time to secure my stance. It was difficult to move, since the interior of the helicopter wasn't meant to be used as a ladder, but I found footholds as I stepped up.

"That's a good girl, keep coming...you're almost here. You can make it."

Each movement was accompanied by creaking and groaning noises. Ryan stood directly in front of me now, clamping a hand firmly over mine, the one that had landed again on his seat, for lack of anything else to grab onto. Then I stood in the cockpit.

"Stand on the edge of Dave's seat so you can balance yourself. There, that's it, you've got it." Ryan said. "Now, I'm going to push my door open and help you climb out."

"But what about you and Dave? And Alphonse? I thought you needed my weight up here so you could get them out?" My questions piled one on top of the other in a flurry of panic.

"I'll get them, don't worry. The first thing I'm going to do is get you to a safe place. Come on."

"But Ryan…"

"No. Haven't you ever heard of ladies first? That's how I was raised and it's too late to change now, so let's go. Watch yourself and try not to get cut on anything." He turned away to press with all his might against the crumpled door. "I don't need you up here; I need you to add weight to the part of the chopper that's over the land."

After several shoves and heaving groans from a red-faced Ryan, metal gave way against metal. With another firm, steady thrust, the top hinge snapped, and the door crushed back.

"Okay, give me your hand," he insisted.

When I reached up, he locked his hand steadfastly over mine, providing stability as he pulled me toward him. Once there, he pushed me up and out through the gap. On my hands and knees, I balanced myself on the side of the helicopter.

"Now what?" I asked.

"Get off and away from the helicopter in case it goes over."

"What? I can't do that. I won't leave you here. Besides, I'm supposed to help hold it down. That's what you said." If Ryan and the others went over, what would I do on my own?

"I lied. You don't weigh enough to do that. Get out of here. Go on!" He turned away from me, picking his way to Dave.

Instead of complying, I stayed put, watching. Noting the blood, my mind turned to the first aid kit resting in the pouch attached to the rear of Ryan's seat. We'd need it for Dave, and Alphonse, if he was still alive. My backpack had been jostled out from where Dave had wedged it under the seat, now in reach of my outstretched fingers. It held a big bottle of water and some food. I leaned in as far as I dared and slid my hand along the material and into the pouch to fish around. I successfully withdrew the first aid kit and tossed it and the backpack out behind me without looking, slinging the objects well beyond the helicopter.

While I'd been rescuing the supplies, Ryan had checked Dave for a pulse, then removed the harness and the headset, kicking back a part of the console that had Dave partially pinned in. With that barrier aside, Ryan tugged mightily at Dave until he had him nearly upright, pressed against the seats. Dave groaned with volume then, as Ryan coughed on the accumulating smoke.

"Pass him up to me," I ordered. Focusing on the plight of someone else, someone helpless, let me put aside my fears.

"What in the hell are you still doing here, Savannah? I told you to get clear!" Ryan peered up at me.

"I don't listen very well."

"Good thing for Dave, I guess. He's gained a few pounds since we were in the Coast Guard. Knowing him, he's bulked up on more muscles." Ryan grimaced, pushing and pulling the limp form toward me.

I took Dave under the arms and heaved. It took a tremendous amount of effort. My being slight of build didn't help. Ryan was above average in height and thankfully strong. Between the two of us, we extricated Dave from the cockpit.

After some tugging and wriggling, I had him perched parallel to the bottom edge of the helicopter, his head resting in my lap. His moaning increased. I leaned over his head and made soothing noises like I'd done for my daughter when she was a baby, while caressing his cheek.

"No time for that right now, Savannah. Get your feet on the rocks, then pull him down with you. He's too big for you to carry, so you'll have to drag him. Make sure you don't stop until you're both clear of the skids. And stay away this time; don't come back."

"What about you?"

"I'm going after Alphonse."

"What if the helicopter falls when Dave and I get off?"

"Make sure you take good care of him for me. He's my best friend, like a brother." His eyes teared up.

It was a good bet Alphonse was dead already. There was no need for Ryan to die, too. I didn't know anything about medicine beyond applying a peel-and-stick bandage. How could I possibly take care of Dave on my own? What if he was hurt even worse than it seemed? What would I do then?

"Ryan, please! Don't leave me with Dave all alone! I can't do this. If you go after Alphonse, you'll fall with him and the helicopter. He's probably dead already. You know it's true!" My eyes were wide with fear.

"Everything will be okay. Now go on, Savannah; you can do this. Get out of here and I mean it."

Slowly, carefully, I lifted Dave's head and slid out from beneath him. My legs hung along the underside of the helicopter. I was reluctant to drop, fearing I'd tip the balance. There was no option, though. When I slid off, the big bird creaked and groaned, but stayed put.

Reaching up, I tugged at Dave, sliding his body until his legs hung over the side. He dangled from the helicopter for an instant before slipping over. The idea had been to slow the descent of his body, but Dave was a lot bigger than me. The plan ignored the laws of physics. His head slumped forward against my shoulder as he dropped, overbalancing me.

Gravity set me heavily on my rear, followed soon after by the back of my head as it struck the rocks. My eyes closed as the world spun for a moment. The weight from Dave's body on top of mine, pinning me down and preventing my chest from rising and falling brought me out of it. It took effort to roll over with him, putting me on top.

I scrambled around to squat and get ahold of Dave from behind. His solid build, the loose rocks, plus me moving backwards, made our progress slow. Teeth gritted, I tugged us to safety, a step at a time.

Rocks crunched underneath the weight of the helicopter. Ryan's movements must have caused the machine to shift. Once Dave and I were well clear, I laid him down. He'd ceased moaning.

A different sound at the cliff's edge instantly raised the hair on the back of my neck. A glance showed the metal hummingbird shifting in slow motion toward the ocean, its balance irretrievably gone.

"Ryan!" I screamed in a massive wave of panic, bolting for the helicopter, darting beneath a skid. In a desperate, vain effort to alter the balance with my weight, I leapt upward, throwing myself onto the side by Ryan's open door.

His arms jutted out from the smoke, flailing around, grabbing for anything. My hands became that anything, stretching forward to reach him, then pulling backward to brace myself against an object that had begun a terrifying descent. I caught sight of Ryan's head, followed immediately by his shoulders.

The flightless metal bird slid away as Ryan leapt to the ground. He lifted me unceremoniously off my feet by wrapping his arms around me. He vaulted forward, spinning, and ducking us between the skids like a football player as the helicopter pivoted over the cliff. We slammed to the ground, with me wrapped in the cocoon of Ryan's body.

As we lay together on the rocks, I shut my eyes against the sound of the metal as it crashed into bits from a single, explosive blow against the side of the cliff, followed by a final impact somewhere beneath. Ryan held my head against his own, both of us in horror at what must have happened to Alphonse below.

We rose together. Afraid of what we'd find, we approached the edge of the cliff to glance over. Ryan blocked me with his outstretched arm, preventing me from moving too near the absolute edge of the drop off.

The helicopter was smashed almost beyond recognition, teetering again. This time on a huge, angular rock jutting out from the ocean. A massive wave roared over it and the upside-down helicopter swayed toward the cliff, nearly tipping. When the water receded, the powerful force of the drawback cost the metal bird its equilibrium. It sank, vanishing in the dark blue depths.

A radical change had come to our lives, and the end of Alphonse's. He had been so excited by the photographs and he was taking. Then there was his family. My eyes filled with tears for them, my body shaking from shock. Ryan took me in his arms, holding me tight, turning me away from the scene. But I'd glimpsed tears in his eyes, too. I pressed my fingers into his back as I cried, releasing some of the fear and grief.

"We're okay, Savannah. It'll be okay," he whispered into my hair.

After a minute, Ryan ended the embrace. He angled my head, forcing me to meet his gaze. His eyes narrowed as he studied my face, rubbing a thumb across my right cheek. "You've got a little abrasion on the edge of your cheek. Doesn't look serious."

"I'm okay. It doesn't hurt. Your left arm is scraped up." I rubbed my hand along the bicep, smearing bits of blood.

"I'll be fine, too. We both got a little cut up on these rocks, that's all. We can wait. I need your help with Dave, okay?" He gently brushed at my tears with his fingertips.

I sniffled, nodding.

"Good girl." He held my hand as we walked to Dave.

Ryan kneeled beside his friend and checked his pulse, then lifted each lid to check his eyes. "I wish we had medical supplies."

"Oh, wait—we do!" Fretful scanning found one of the items—my backpack. It was wedged in amongst rocks, freed without much effort. I threw it over one shoulder, darting around in search of the first aid kit, finally locating it at the edge of the jungle in some brush. I ran the objects to Ryan.

"Where did those come from?"

"I yanked them out from behind your seat and Frisbeed them clear while you were getting Dave."

He sent me a grateful smile. "Good thinking."

Ryan opened the first aid kit and began working on treating the worst of Dave's injuries. The kit was a large one, but there still weren't enough bandages for his wounds. I handed over a spare tee-shirt, which he ripped into bandages. Once we'd done all we could, the realization hit me—we needed to carry Dave down the hillside, through the jungle.

"Do we need to move him, like down to the beach maybe? Should we wait until morning since it's getting late?" I asked. Ryan should be the one to decide.

"Ideally, we need a litter. But making that'll take more time than we've got to spare. The sun's going down and clouds are building on the horizon. We're too exposed up here in case of a storm, especially if there's lightning." He nodded to the horizon.

There was indeed a line of dark clouds in the distance. The west held the glowing sun, heading for a day's-ending dip in the ocean. The light would fully abandon us in less than two hours. Neither of us could think of a quicker way to accomplish the daunting task than the conventional. Stuffing in the first aid kit, I shouldered my backpack and moved to Dave's feet.

"Ready?" Ryan asked, kneeling by Dave's head.

"I'm ready. I might need to take a few breaks along the way, though."

"That's okay, we'll make it." He nodded before cautiously lifting the upper body of his friend as I raised his legs. Ryan walked backward wherever we were forced by terrain or vegetation to travel single file. It happened often in the tangled jungle.

Dave remained unconscious as we descended the hillside. Little light passed through the dense canopy; just enough to see by. When the trees thinned, we were on the gentler incline of a broad hillside. We were forced to go out of our way by sporadic, rocky outcrops and elongated clusters of trees, lush with undergrowth. We passed the waterfall we'd viewed from the air as we made our way down, but there wasn't time to stop.

Once we reached the bottom of the hill, the lower jungle vegetation was sparse compared to the backside of the cliffs. My arms and back were breaking from the strain, but the light to show us the way was all but gone. The sun had to be well below the horizon.

The relief when we reached the open sand was palpable. We placed Dave carefully before daring to drop for a rest. I dreaded having to go any farther, but after a cursory examination of our surroundings, I knew we had to. The reach of the tides on this island were unknown to me, but we couldn't risk remaining here when there was a wide beach not far away.

"Savannah, I'll stay up tonight to watch Dave and take a nap once the sun comes up. You go ahead and get some sleep."

"We can't stay here. This beach is too narrow. There's seaweed all the way up here near the tree line. That means the tide could come up this far. A storm could push it even higher."

Ryan glanced around. "You're right. I didn't notice. My thoughts were occupied with Dave, I guess."

"We need to move him farther down the beach, to the south. It's a lot wider there. We don't want to have to scramble to get him away from the ocean at the last minute. That could force us back into the jungle in the dark to avoid the water. Let's rest a little while and then get going again," I suggested.

"Are you sure you can make it?"

"I have to. Dave needs me." I didn't dare mention the depth of my concern about his condition.

"Okay then." He paused a moment before continuing. "Listen, I didn't get the chance to thank you back there. Your help was much appreciated; even though you didn't do what I told you to."

My gaze shifted away.

"There's no way I could've gotten Dave out of there on my own. And I might not have gotten out of the helicopter in time myself if not for you tugging on me. Knowing you were putting your life on the line for me was an excellent motivator if I needed one. I think you may have even helped get me out a second or two sooner. Seconds made all the difference."

"Glad I could help."

His demeanor changed to one occasionally shown by my father. "From now on, though, I fully expect you to do what I tell you to do, when I tell you to do it. I know what I'm talking about, Savannah. We're in a potentially dangerous situation here with a lot of unknowns. You're to listen to me and react quickly, without question. Do you understand?"

My elbows rested on my knees as I released a loud sigh of resignation. "I'll try. That's the best I can honestly do, Ryan. Sometimes I act on instinct; I can't help it." At first, I thought I'd made him angry, because he didn't respond right away.

"Fair enough. I might be dead right now if you hadn't done your own thing and come over to help pull Dave and me out of that cockpit like you did. We owe you our lives."

"Then we'll call it even. You saved mine, too. I couldn't have gotten out of the helicopter on my own." Panic would have grown in me, robbing me of precious time to get at the helicopter's jammed door. If I could have avoided falling to my death past Alphonse, that is. Unlikely.

The waves rolling in relaxed me. If we weren't in such a traumatic situation, I could fall asleep. The sand was soft and warm, the air humid, just the way I liked it. But sleep had to wait for a safe area. If there was one.

Three

Boisterous seagulls fighting over some scrap of food awakened me. The sun had risen, peeking between gray clouds. After multiple good, hard blinks to help release the dehydrated contact lenses from my eyeballs, it all came roaring back.

The events from the day before were obviously not a terrible nightmare; they were an even worse reality. We were stranded on a deserted island. People didn't get stranded on deserted islands anymore, did they? Wasn't there too much technology in the world for that? Of course, if the Malaysian airliner with over two hundred people onboard vanished despite all the people and technology searching for them, what would become of three insignificant souls trapped on a remote little island?

I sat up to look around, wiping sand from the right side of my face and arm. Sand had wedged its way into the grooves of scratches on my cheek, which stung when I brushed at it. Every muscle hurt; even breathing hurt. And thinking.

Half the surface area of the ocean was composed of whitecaps, the waves rough, churning. Seagulls took turns stealing a large mollusk of some sort from each other. One flew off with it, while the rest endeavored to peck it away in midair. Finally, it was dislodged from a beak to plop into the ocean, too deep for the birds to attempt retrieval. They flew away, reprimanding each other.

They were entertaining to watch, but they altered our lives for the worse yesterday. Realizing the birds were fighting over breakfast reaffirmed the fact that we were stranded alone, with no restaurants or grocery stores. There was no telling what kind of food we might be able to discover to hold us over until rescue. I recalled talk of fruit trees yesterday in the helicopter.

We could naturally eat fish if we could figure out a way to catch them. Neither the first aid kit nor my backpack came equipped with a fishing rod. Not to mention bait.

The primary concern remained Dave. Last night, I had asked to lie between Dave and the ocean in case the water should somehow manage to make it this far, even though it wouldn't. Ryan had readily agreed, wanting to plant himself between us and any threats presented by the jungle's as-yet unknown inhabitants.

He was gone now, no telling where. Hopefully, he was scouting for food or fresh water. If there was no potable water here, we'd all die within a few days.

What Ryan didn't know was that I had breakfast bars, peanut butter crackers, and little pouches of trail mix in my backpack. That was one of the reasons I'd snatched it from the helicopter before it fell into the deep blue oblivion. There'd been too much going on last night to remember to tell Ryan about the food.

Scooting over, I got as close to Dave as I could without touching him, so I wouldn't wake him. Although, considering that the brash seagulls in proximity to us a minute ago didn't wake him, I doubted my touch would. His breathing was shallow. Hopefully, he'd awaken soon and feel better. I looked forward to getting to know him while we were stranded. I rested my hand on his shoulder and gave it a squeeze but there was no response.

Rescuers would surely arrive before too much time passed. They were no doubt searching for us. We'd be found and they'd get Dave to the nearest hospital. Then he'd be okay. Survival would be a definite for a tough guy like Dave.

Staring into the sky, I noted the sun, watching as it crept higher and higher, working warm rays to our location in between the clouds. Tracking shadows cast by the trees let me guestimate when we'd need to move Dave, to keep him in shade. That should be sooner rather than later.

Sunlight wouldn't penetrate far in the jungle. Even though the breeze would be minimized, it would be better to keep Dave out of the sun. As long as there were no threats posed by wild creatures lurking within, like snakes, Dave would be safe. There couldn't be anything else around, because what would a large predator eat on this island besides us? And birds, which were in abundance, akin to a bird sanctuary.

Rustling noises grew. I squinted, peering into the jungle, seeing nothing. Clearly, this had been a bad time for Ryan to leave Dave and me alone. If a wild animal was stalking us, I had no weapon to defend us with. A hasty scan of the immediate area revealed nothing useful. I scrambled to my feet, stepping over Dave to block whatever was coming.

I didn't spot Ryan until he was close. Relief swept through me. He held something in his left hand, like long clusters of grapes.

"You're awake. How're you feeling? Does your head still hurt?"

"Not too bad. What's that?" Food took precedence over pain. My mouth watered.

"They're called sea grapes. They're ripe enough, even though it's a little early in the season, I think. There were masses of them growing all over the place. I could be wrong about that, though. These were the ripest ones over where I was searching. No doubt there's plenty more in most every direction. How's Dave?"

"No change. He's breathing steady, but he hasn't made any sounds or opened his eyes or anything." I returned to my post beside Dave, wrapping my arms around my knees.

"He'll be okay. He's a tough guy. It'll take more than a bang on the head to keep him down. Here, you go ahead and help yourself, I've already eaten enough. I'll sit with him if you want to stretch your legs. Take a strand of grapes with you and go for a short walk.

"My next step is to hike deeper into the interior, as soon as I can find a big shell to bring back water in. Hopefully that waterfall we saw yesterday is potable. Potable means we can drink it without getting sick." Ryan sat near Dave's head. It was simple to see the worry he attempted to mask.

"I know. I'm a geography teacher. Ryan, I have some water, a big bottle of it." I retrieved my backpack and placed it alongside him before standing. "I also have some food. It won't last us forever, but it'll help."

He'd unzipped the main compartment and withdrawn the water by the time I'd finished speaking. He smiled up at me. "You're right, this'll help. We'll ration your bottle until I see if the water on the island is good or not."

He cracked open the lid and handed it up to me. I took a sip before passing it back.

"Drink more than that." He extended the bottle to me again.

"No, I'm fine. I'll be eating your grapes. They'll help quench my thirst. You go ahead and drink what you need."

Even though I didn't know him well, the look he gave me let me know I might be pushing my luck with him. He took a quick chug, screwed the lid back on and returned the bottle to my backpack.

"Aren't you supposed to be sleeping now, Ryan? Last night, you said you were going to take a nap after the sun came up." My hands were on my hips, trying to appear stern. He gave me such a warm smile I couldn't maintain my demeanor.

"There're more important things to take care of first. I'll sleep later, plus I got some rest last night. You don't need to worry about me, just yourself. Okay?"

"Okay." I retrieved a string of grapes before walking ten feet away, following the edge of the trees. When I spotted a small opening in the vegetation, I stepped into it. The rebuke was swift in coming and quite a bit louder than necessary.

"Savannah! Get out of there!"

The return to the beach came on instinct. Had he found something scary in the jungle he hadn't shared yet? "What is it? What's wrong?"

"Where do you think you're going?"

"I was going to find a comfortable, shady spot where we could move Dave to. I figured he shouldn't be out in the sun. The sun will be shining right there where Dave is within a few hours."

"That's considerate of you, but I'll handle that myself. We don't know anything about this island. I want you to stay out on the beach where I can see you until I've had a chance to check out this place thoroughly, or unless I'm with you. Understand?"

"Yes, I get it. I'll be right back then." I turned again to the trees.

"I thought you said you understand?" The reprimand came fast.

"I do. But I need to go to the bathroom." My bladder needed to be relieved and Ryan had too much focus on exerting his presumed authority over me.

"For you, the bathroom is out here on the beach." He jabbed a finger at the sand.

"What?" He had to be joking.

"You heard me. I already told you I don't want you in there and why. You'll relieve yourself out here in the open, on the beach."

"You can't be serious." Even as I uttered the words, I knew he was.

"Yes, I am. Look, Dave's unconscious; I'll turn my back, and the birds don't care. Now go ahead. When you're done, you can go for a little walk if you want to, like I said before. But don't go out of my sight. When you look back here, if you see me waving at you it means you've gone too far, and you need to come back without hesitation. Understand?"

Wow. This would get annoying, fast. If there weren't any dangerous wild animals, what was the problem? "Yes, I understand." I walked away, shaking my head. At least he cared. And he seemed like a nice person. He made me feel safe, which was vital for my sanity at the moment.

The sand beneath my bare feet was comparatively cool, shaded by the tree line. I walked another ten feet before scooping out a little depression with one foot, placing the grapes on the sand nearby. As I was about to lower my pants, I glanced back toward Ryan and saw him watching me. Seriously? He was probably thinking about Dave, zoning out, not being a pervert or anything. Still, though...

"Turn your head!" I hollered. He was prompt in complying, throwing in a wave of his hand.

I didn't like not having toilet paper to wipe with; dripping dry took a lot longer for a woman than for a man. Once I'd finished, I raked a little sand over the spot, retrieved the breakfast, and continued my stroll, brushing the sand from each grape before devouring it.

The first one was a wakeup call. Each sea grape contained a large seed at its center. I always bought seedless grapes in the grocery store, so seeds hadn't even been a consideration; I could've cracked a tooth. I spit the seed toward the jungle and consumed the remainder of the grapes with caution. They were tangy and refreshing. Of course, my hunger would've made a leaf from a tree taste good right about now.

Using seawater, I rinsed my hands, my cuts and scrapes stinging from the saltiness. But I managed to remove the sand that had been embedded inside the little grooves. A glance in Ryan's direction had him waving his arm through the air. I must've wandered farther afield than he was comfortable with, so I returned to him.

But I took my time and made sure to meander a little, studying the ocean and sky, examining a couple of shells. Ryan would be leaving me with Dave while he explored, after all. I decided to keep that complaint to myself. He was certainly more qualified than me to handle any traveling in those jungles. We were going to need water soon in this tropical heat. It wasn't something that could wait.

When I reached the two men, I decided to send Ryan on his way. The sooner he left, the sooner he'd get back. I didn't care for being left with no one to talk to. I tended to be talkative, but it passed the time. Maybe I could talk to Dave while we waited. It might help him wake up.

"I'll stay with him now. You can go ahead if you want. Why don't you leave me with a breakfast bar and a pack of trail mix while you're investigating? You should take the water along in case you need it. You'll do better if you use the pack to carry water rather than having the bottle in your hand."

"Don't need it. You'll need it more than I will, especially if Dave wakes up before I get back."

"Okay. You should at least put some trail mix in your pocket, though." He might end up being wrong about needing water. Hopefully, he wouldn't pay too steep a price for it if that happened. It wouldn't be easy for me to find him if he collapsed somewhere along the way. And I'd have to leave Dave unattended.

"I'll be fine. I know what I can and can't eat. Speaking of which, you be sure to stay out here on the beach near Dave while I'm gone. And don't eat anything except what's in your pack, or more grapes."

"Okay. Please be careful."

"Try not to worry. I'll be back before the shade you're in is gone." Turning away, he was swallowed up by the jungle.

The sun had nearly reached Dave. My body was squished up

against his side, both to block the encroaching light from Dave and because I didn't need to be in the sun too much myself. Getting a sunburn would only add to the unpleasantness of the situation.

Not long afterward, sunshine warmed my lower back. It was filtered through the clouds, but I still didn't want Dave exposed. It would be impossible for me to move Dave alone as sore as my body was. But I might be forced to try.

Using a gentle touch, I applied a little balm to Dave's lips. "You don't want to wake up to cracked lips, now do you? Don't worry, there's no color to it. I don't like to use much makeup myself when I'm traveling." I returned the tube of balm to the side pocket of my backpack and gave him a loud sigh.

"So, Dave. When do you plan to wake up? You need to hurry, you know. What's that? You want to know why? Well, I'll tell you why. It's because you haven't had water in a long time and it's hot and humid out here. You need to drink some water, so you'll stay hydrated. Plus, you need to tell us where you're hurting. That'll help us make you better. Speaking of that, you also need to wake up for Ryan. He's worried about you."

"Yes, I am."

I emitted a squeal and nearly jumped clean out of my skin. "Ryan! You scared me half to death! Don't sneak up on me like that or I'll tie a bell around your neck!"

He grinned.

"It wasn't funny." Surely, he could tell by the expression on my face or the hand clutching at my chest that I meant it.

"I'm sorry, Savannah. I had no intention of trying to scare you. I was eavesdropping on your conversation; it was nice. I like that you're talking to him. I'll make noise next time."

"You'd better. I'm serious about that. I don't like being scared or having people jump out at me. It's a big phobia of mine. I despise haunted houses, by the way."

"All right, I'll remember. I promise I will. And no haunted houses, not ever." He plopped down next to me, chuckling for a moment. "Now how's Dave doing?"

"No change that I can tell. We'll need to move him now. Sun is good for making vitamin D, but he doesn't need too much exposure. I started talking to him while you were gone to see if maybe that might make a difference."

"Did it?"

"Not yet. I wish I was a doctor or a nurse or something."

"Yeah, me too. I wish there was a hospital on this island, or maybe a telephone that functioned all the way out here, or a big cell tower."

"That would be perfect. My cellphone is in my pack. It still works, thanks to the case protecting it from all the banging, but there's no signal, no bars." I bit my lower lip. "I checked Dave's bandages while you were gone. His bleeding stopped."

"Has it? Well, that's a good sign. Speaking of bleeding, I never did patch up your cheek. Why don't you let me take a look at it?"

"It's fine. Thanks, anyway. How about your arm?" My worry over Dave grew by the hour. It would be good to have a different focus, even for a few minutes.

"My arm is fine, just some minor scrapes. Let me look at you."

"Nothing's wrong with it. When I was down at the ocean after I ate your sea grapes, I rubbed the dried blood and bits of sand off my face with the water." A glance showed glowering eyes. "What? What's that look for?"

"You should've let me help you."

"Why? You're not a doctor. Are you?"

"No, I'm not. But we had some medical training in the Coast Guard. Now let me look at you."

Clearly, the man was ridiculously stubborn. I sighed with deep resignation. "All right, already. It's just a scratch." My head stayed still, but he clamped my chin in his grasp to make sure I didn't move. He explored the wound, poking and prodding with his fingertips. Then he turned my head to look into my eyes.

"Come with me." He rose, striding confidently into the hazy light.

I followed. It was something to pass the time. He did the exact same things in the brightness that he'd done in the shade. I glanced to the increasing clouds. No more direct sunlight today, most likely.

"I want you to follow my finger with your eyes. Don't move your head, just your eyes," he instructed.

He moved his forefinger in various directions, and I made sure to watch it closely, so he'd be satisfied and leave me alone. It was like a science experiment. When he finished, he walked around me in a circle, arms folded across his chest, studying me.

"What're you doing now?"

"Relax, I'm just checking you out."

It would be a better decision to give him the benefit of the doubt, because he certainly must've meant that in a medical sense rather than anything else. At least this was keeping his mind off worrying over his best friend. I could put up with it and cooperate a little longer.

"Now, I want you to walk away from me, in as straight a line as you can. Go until I tell you to stop."

"How should I walk?" I put my hands on my hips and cocked my head to one side.

"What?"

"How do you want me to walk?" The teasing was intended to add levity to the situation. He needed to lighten up. It shouldn't be long before rescue arrived. We'd all make it.

"I don't know...walk like you usually do."

He didn't get it. Maybe he was serious all the time. That would make for some boring days. As I walked away, I hoped rescue would come soon, or that Dave would wake up today. Dave was a lot more fun to talk to than Ryan.

If I gave too much thought to the seriousness of our situation, I'd get depressed, or cry, or both. I didn't want to do either.

"Okay, stop and come back to me now."

When I turned, I put my hands on my hips again. "How do you want me to do that? Do you want me to walk like I just did, or can I improvise this time?"

"Improvise? Savannah, this is serious. I want you to walk like you normally do."

I let loose another sigh. He was no fun at all. I walked back as ordered. He rested a hand against my cheek and gazed into my eyes.

"I think you're fine. And you've got about the prettiest brown eyes I think I've ever seen. There're flecks of orange and mahogany brown in them. Did you know that?"

That comment had me pulling my head back in surprise, brow furrowed. "That wasn't very doctor-like."

"I'm not a doctor."

"It looks like you're the closest thing we've got to one. So, mind your bedside manners."

I moved past him, returning to Dave's side. He was pale beneath the tan. One of my hands rested on one of his, my fingers curling around to slowly stroke his palm, attempting to illicit a reaction, a flinch, something. My other hand lay on his shoulder. "Come on, Dave. Wake up. You can do it."

There was no response.

"By the way, the waterfall is drinkable, Savannah." Ryan had followed me to Dave without my noticing. "Not bad tasting, either. And so far, I haven't suffered any ill effects from drinking it."

"Okay, that's good news." I remained focused on my charge.

"Maybe you should keep talking to Dave. He might wake up for you. I know I would."

I glanced up in surprise, but Ryan was walking away, farther out onto the beach to stare at the ocean. The waves were angrier than they'd been earlier that morning, smashing onto the beach with a flurry of foam. What Ryan had said was too weird for me. "Come on, Dave. Please. We need you."

Four

At the point in the dream where the helicopter crashed, it startled me awake. Sleep seemed impossible without the accompanying nightmare, over and over.

There was dark sky above and sand beneath. The resounding slap of the waves as they hit the shore confirmed my location, along with the unsettling, constant roar emanating from far beyond the furthest whitecaps. No stars or crescent moon lent their faint illumination tonight, blocked by an abundance of clouds and vegetation. The wind blew hard enough to keep the jungle air moving, tree branches and palm fronds swaying. Before noon, we moved Dave a few yards inland, in case of high surf. If there were mosquitos, they wouldn't be able to feast on us tonight considering the windy conditions. So far, we'd been lucky on that count. It would serve to add to our plight; like the sunburn I'd continue trying to avoid.

Hunger strove to overcome reason. The sea grapes that were accompanied by the bland tasting interior part of some palm Ryan cut out for our dinner with his pocketknife didn't hold me long. It took effort not to think of cheeseburgers or pepperoni pizza, with extra cheese, extra pepperoni, and mushrooms. Those thoughts had me drooling a little.

Ryan was a gray form in the dark, but I knew he was asleep because of the snoring. I placed a hand lightly on Dave's chest and felt the shallow rise and fall. He should've awakened by now, surely. I leaned over him, placing a light kiss his on cheek. I lay back then, my head on my arm, staring at Dave. My other hand rested on his shoulder.

"Please, Dave," I whispered.

The next morning dawned, but the approximate time was indiscernible. Everything had a dull cast to it. Staring up through the trees at the sky showed gray. The slapping palm fronds gave a steady whistle from the wind blowing through them. When I pushed up to check on Dave, Ryan was gone.

"We've got a problem," Ryan's voice sounded out behind me.

It made me jump again. "Geez, Ryan! You promised me you weren't going to do that anymore!"

"I'm sorry, I forgot. Here, maybe this'll make up for it." He handed me a huge, roasted crab, still warm from a fire.

"Oh wow! Where'd this come from? Do they have take-out all the way out here?" The delectable aroma overwhelmed my olfactory senses.

Ryan sat, chuckling, his own crab in hand. "I caught them at the edge of the surf. They were hung up in some seaweed. A third one got away."

I tore off a leg and cracked it open. After a deep sniff, I smiled and let my teeth grab some of the succulent meat and pull it in, where the sweetness melted on my tongue. "Oh my God, this is incredible. You're completely forgiven."

He smiled in return. "That's a relief. I'm glad you like it."

"Like it? This is amazing. If the rescue helicopter were to land on the beach right now, I'd tell them they have to wait until I've finished eating first."

"You do realize they'd let you bring it onto the helicopter with you, right?" He inhaled a mouthful.

"Oh. Yeah, I guess they would. I'm just trying to pay you a compliment, that's all."

"Ah. In that case, thank you."

"Wow. The only thing that could make this better is if Dave woke up. Or if someone came to rescue us so we could get him to a hospital. Maybe they'll come for us today."

Ryan swallowed his bite, staring at his crab without getting more, even though the meat was hanging temptingly from the claw he held. "About that, Savannah."

"About what?"

"Rescue. They're not coming. Not for a while, anyway."

"What makes you say that?" My stomach tightened with the affirmation to come.

"Well, there's a storm brewing out there and it looks to be a big one. The seas are too rough, and the wind is too strong. They couldn't risk flying or taking a boat out in this kind of weather. I'm sorry."

I thought about his news for a minute before responding. "That's okay. I kind of figured this was coming yesterday. The ocean was already tumbling, and the wind was picking up. What do you think it is?"

He glanced down at his crab again before looking at me. "I think it might be a hurricane."

"That's my theory, too."

"How'd you come up with that?" He looked surprised.

"Geography teacher, remember? One of the classes I teach is earth science, which includes climate and weather. Plus, I grew up in Savannah. I know what the cloud formations of tropical systems look like, how they move. I watched them coming in all day yesterday, plus there were the effects on the ocean. All the signs were there. The one my plane flew too close to must've shifted course again to bring it in our direction here. The last forecast I saw had it moving farther to the north. They did expect it to stall sometime yesterday, though. I must've slowed down and something else kicked it in the head, sent it this way."

Ryan didn't speak.

"As soon as we've finished eating, we're going to have to find shelter of some kind to protect us from the hurricane. We can't be out here in the open like this," Obvious, but I said it anyway.

"All we can do is go deeper into the jungle. We can't build a real shelter right now; there isn't time. Besides, it'd blow away."

"I have an idea." It's likely all we had. Hopefully, he'd concur.

"Let's hear it; I'm open to anything."

"We'll need to get Dave back to the hill. It's our only chance."

"We can't shelter at the top of the cliffs, Savannah."

"I'm talking about the hill, not the cliffs. There were lots of rock outcroppings on that sloping hillside on the way down here. Some ledges might be large enough to shelter under. We won't have to worry about a tree falling on us there."

"Okay. That's not bad at all. I think we should check around the waterfall first. It's about halfway up the hill and there're several overhangs nearby. I didn't take the time to check them out; I was too busy with the water and getting back here to you and Dave."

"That sounds good. We'll need to get up as high as we can."

"Storm surge?" Ryan finally pulled the crabmeat from the claw.

"Just in case. I'd prefer to be well beyond the thirty feet above sea level mark, but higher would be better. I saw the reports on this system when it was a tropical depression; it was on the news right before my plane left the states. There's no telling how strong it's gotten since then. I remember Dave saying it'd become a cyclone."

"Let's go ahead and finish our breakfast. Then we'll load up and go."

It was with great relief that I helped Ryan place Dave on the ground. All I could do was watch as Ryan arranged his friend to his liking. He positioned Dave safely out of the storm's reach, against the rear wall.

We had carried him all the way up in a driving rain without breaks. I couldn't count the number of times I slipped and went down on my knees. We were pelted by an outer band of the cyclone. The worst was yet to come.

Getting down on all fours, I crawled in across the stone surface and leaned back against the rocky side wall with a sigh. The stone was, well, hard. The temperature of it retained a warmth just below that of the air. There was room for Ryan to sit near me at the back corner, by Dave's head. For now, though, he had planted himself near the overhang, which afforded a good view of the building weather.

The deep shelf of rock over our heads appeared to be mostly embedded in the hillside. More of the rock formed a side wall that was likewise fixed in the ground. That was where I settled, while the opposite side and front were open to the elements. I closed my eyes and waited for my breathing to slow from the exertion, feeling the water streaming off my hair, my clothes, my skin.

The weather was delaying our rescue, in a foreign country, no less. Most likely, they didn't care much for Americans anyway. Most of the world didn't, it seemed. By the time the storm departed, any rescuers might have resigned us to our fate. I couldn't cry with Ryan around. There was no sense in depressing someone else.

"Here, Savannah. Take a good drink. We've got fresh water nearby. After you've had enough, we should try and get some rest." He passed me the water bottle.

I took several long drinks and returned the bottle to him. The steady sound of the rain lulled me to sleep, until my head slipped over to one side, which startled my eyes open. The waking nightmare continued.

For a few minutes, I occupied myself watching the rain. The water flowing down the hillside above us made dozens of miniature waterfalls in its cascade over the irregular lip of our shelter. The sound of the rain made me drowsy again, but I couldn't locate a good spot for my head to prevent it from slipping and waking me again.

Ryan crawled over to sit beside me. I hadn't even noticed he was still awake, over by the entrance where he'd been reclining on his back. Without a word, he tugged my head over to rest against his shoulder. I snuggled up to him and closed my eyes, falling asleep almost immediately.

The passage of time was impossible to judge since I'd been asleep for a while. A break in the rain had come and the sun shone through the clouds, giving momentary hope. Then the brightness switched off. The rain came again in sheets, blowing almost sideways, but still away from the overhang's entrance. There was almost as much white on the surface of the broiling ocean as deep bluish gray. The location gave a view that would be prized by a homebuilder if they didn't mind extreme isolation.

Ryan's head was braced in a sturdy spot and he snored lightly. I watched Dave as he breathed and wondered how much longer this could go on for him. I wished so desperately I could turn back time. I decided to move myself over and lie parallel to Dave but at an angle, with my head in Ryan's lap. That awakened him, and he stroked his fingers through my hair. The sensation lulled me into a deep sleep.

When my eyes fluttered open, the sun shone on the wet ground beyond our little shelter. My contacts felt as though they were permanently adhered to my corneas, in desperate need of eye drops. I sat up to rub the arm I'd been lying on and saw Ryan giving me a sympathetic smile.

"Is something wrong?" I asked.

He placed a hand on my cheek. Tears filled his eyes, his words choked as he forced them out. "Dave didn't make it through the night."

My eyes widened in disbelief. I turned with a start to check behind me, not believing him. Dave was still, his face peaceful. "No," I muttered, scrambling over to put a hand on Dave's heart. The beating had ceased, the shallow rise and fall of his chest was no more.

What was a person to do? I'd never experienced anything like this in my life. The only dead bodies I'd seen were those belonging to distant family members or relatives of friends. No one I'd known personally. Both sets of my grandparents passed before I was old enough to miss them.

I hadn't known Dave well at all, or long. Yet, I knew I owed him my life. His skills were almost certainly what kept us from plunging over the cliff. We all could have died there. He sacrificed himself to save us. There was no doubt of it in my mind.

Overwhelming sorrow stunned as my vision blurred with tears I didn't know how to control.

"Savannah." Ryan's hand touched my shoulder.

Shunning the physical contact, I shook my head repeatedly, backing out of the sheltering rocks in a scramble. Once clear, I walked a short distance away and stared down at the jungle, swiping angrily at the tears with both hands.

A few seagulls flew overhead, their raucous cries piercing the air. I glanced around my feet and spied a fist-sized rock, torn loose from higher up by the tremendous rains. I picked it up and gave it my best shot, hurling it at the birds and missing them by a wide margin, of course. They were out of reach and my aim was poor. "I hate you birds!" I screamed at the top of my lungs.

Ryan stepped in front of me, pulling me close to him for a comforting embrace. "It's okay, Savannah. They might not even be the same birds. And it wasn't their fault. They didn't destroy themselves on purpose to try to kill us. You and I are still alive and I'm going to make sure we stay that way. We'll be okay. It'll all be okay. I promise."

I latched onto him and cried until there was nothing left. My body was an empty husk. I took a small step back from Ryan, but he kept an arm around my waist and wouldn't let go. He wiped at my tears with his free hand. After a minute, I raised my gaze to his red, puffy eyes.

"Where should we bury him?" I whispered, not recognizing my own voice.

"He'd prefer to be as close to the sky as possible, but we can't dig through rock. That means we're going to have to carry him back to the beach. We'll bury him near the tree line, nice and deep in case of more storms. You let me know when you're ready."

"I'll never be ready, so we may as well do it now."

"Are you sure?" He wiped at both our tears.

"Yeah, I'm sure." I lead the way back to Dave, feeling lost and numb inside, devoid of hope. Dave deserved so much better than this. It was wrong.

I crawled in first, stopping by his head to gaze at his face for a moment. I leaned down and gave him a kiss on the cheek. "Thank you for saving my life, Dave. I'm so sorry this happened. You didn't deserve this."

Ryan rested a hand on my lower back. "It wasn't anyone's fault, Savannah. But you're right, he did save our lives. He was an amazing pilot. Go on and back out from under here. I'll put the backpack on and pull him out. Then you can take his feet, okay?"

"Okay." I retreated to stand near the entrance to wait for them.

Five

Dave and I waited in the shade, me keeping watch while Ryan dug. He'd found several good-sized shells washed up on our wide beach, thanks to the cyclone. They proved useful for digging, plus they'd be good for hauling drinking water later. Our campsite was shifting to the hurricane refuge by the waterfall since we no longer had to care for Dave. It made sense.

I didn't want to think about any of that. My sorrow ran deep but I didn't know why. Dave did save two of us on that flight, but I didn't know him. Perhaps his death had frightened me, leaving me feeling exposed and vulnerable. There were lots of ways to die, especially when there were no doctors around to heal you.

Ryan's sky blue shirt, rolled into a sweaty ball, sailed up and over the side of the hole to land at the base of a tree. I would offer to help, but I knew he wanted to do most of the work himself. Or so he claimed. Most likely, he was being chivalrous. And he said Dave shouldn't be left alone, that he deserved nice company.

After several more minutes had passed, it dawned on me that the digging had ceased. The quiet inside the hole persisted long enough to concern me. I crawled to the edge and peered over to see Ryan lying spread out at the bottom, his eyes closed. His chest, shiny with sweat, was moving with his breaths, so at least I could tell he was alive.

"Ryan? Are you okay?" It took everything in me not to jump into the hole to check for myself.

His eyes popped open, providing me immense relief.

"Yeah, Savannah. I'm fine. I stopped first to measure the length then I thought I'd take a little break. There's no breeze in here, but the sand's a lot cooler. Did I worry you?"

"Yes. You scared me for a second there."

"I'm sorry."

"It's okay. Are you sure you don't want me to dig for a while? You have to be worn out."

He sat up, rubbing sand from his hair. "That's okay, Savannah. I can make it. I'll take a nap later. Besides, I'm done. What do you think?" Ryan climbed out, rubbing at his lower back as he stretched.

"It looks fine to me." It was unpleasant to think about what that hole was about to be used for.

"All right then. You take his feet for me; brace them so they don't just fall over the side. I'm going to go ahead and slide him in."

"Okay." I got into position.

Dave's body had stiffened a bit. For a moment, my stomach rolled with a wave of nausea. But I held myself together well enough to assist Ryan. He needed me and I wouldn't let him down. He arranged Dave in the hole, then told me he wanted to be alone for a few minutes to say goodbye. He gave me a boost up to the top.

"Don't go far," he warned.

"I won't." I walked away, farther than Ryan would've liked but he was otherwise occupied and wouldn't notice.

There was a spot in the jungle where I'd seen large, lovely red flowers blooming while watching Dave one of the times Ryan was exploring. It was the sole time I'd gone into the jungle against orders. This trip made it twice. I selected four of the flowers and broke them off with a length of stem attached. The blooms were tattered, but usable. Then I returned to the gravesite. Ryan had already climbed out, his hands on his hips as he scanned the area. A tongue-lashing would likely descend upon my arrival.

"Where were..." he began with a harsh edge to his voice, but he stopped when he noticed the flowers. His eyes were again red and puffy, his cheeks moist.

"I had to get these for him. It was the least I could do."

"I understand. Thanks, Savannah. I didn't even think about that. Good job."

Smiling, I stepped forward and placed the flowers in the shade at the base of a tree. Selecting the most perfect specimen, I sat on the edge of the grave and then wriggled forward until I dropped the remaining distance. I moved carefully around Dave's body and straddled his chest to lay my flower on him, tucking it into his shirt a bit to hold it in place once the sand came in. Tears fell as I stood over him, leaving wet spots on his shirt. I swiped at my eyes and turned away, struggling to maintain my composure as I returned to the edge.

Ryan took my hands and pulled me out. We stood on the side for a minute, staring at Dave in silence. But I knew something needed to be said. Otherwise, it wouldn't be right. I closed my eyes.

"Dear Lord, I know you've already taken Dave's soul up to live with you in Heaven. I saw the rainbow you sent this morning, just for a few seconds, while Ryan was pulling Dave's body out from the shelter under the big rock. I'm sure that was a celebration of his homegoing. He was a brave and wonderful man who risked his life in the Coast Guard and again for us here. We're going to miss him so much." I teared up again, my voice breaking.

It took a few seconds to recover. I inhaled deeply and cleared my throat before continuing. "God, please help Ryan in dealing with his grief over the loss of his friend. And I pray that you will lead rescuers to us soon. Be with those we've left behind and help them to be comforted while they wait for us to come back to them. Amen."

Ryan took my hand, giving it a squeeze. "Thank you, Savannah. That was perfect."

Tears streamed down my cheeks. Ryan did his best not to cry. He released my hand to kneel beside the grave. He gathered a fistful of sand, held it up to the sky, then closed his eyes, tossing it into the hole.

His body hunched over then, heaving repeatedly. I moved over and knelt beside him, putting an arm around his shoulders. "Ryan, please let me do this part. Please. I'd like to help. Please." It would have been wrong for Ryan to be the one to cover his friend in sand.

Ryan nodded, standing. "Thanks for that, Savannah." He retrieved his shirt and stepped into the sunshine, staring at the ocean.

Deep sobs racked my body with each scoop of sand as I covered his face, which I left for last of all. That act made it so final, so real. I used the two big shells to scoop sand into the grave. The task was emotionally draining, only made easier once Dave's body was hidden from view.

I remembered the time I buried a bird once. I'd found it dead in the backyard of my home, back when I was seven years old. I'd gone into the shed and gotten my mom's gardening trowel. I dug it a nice hole a few inches deep at the foot of a deep pink peony. I'd wanted him to have beautiful flowers for his grave and shade from the sun. I'd carefully laid it at the bottom and stretched out its pretty little brown wings so it could fly in Heaven. As I put in each bit of dirt, I had cried. And cried even more when it was over. This was so much worse, by an incalculable magnitude of order.

It took a long time to complete the job. I stopped periodically to pat the sand down, firming it over him. That part was hard on me, too. It felt disrespectful, even though I knew packing it helped to protect Dave's body.

The entire process was exceptionally challenging, both physically and emotionally. When I'd finished, the sand was in a smooth, well-packed mound. I laid the three remaining flowers across the top of the grave and sat to rest, my clothes sticking to my skin, the sweat rolling off me. My body bordered on shaking from the exhaustion.

Ryan sat on the sand, hugging his knees. The strong breeze off the ocean ruffled his open shirt like a kite. Occasionally, he wiped at his eyes. The two men must have been close friends indeed. I'd have to give him some time before asking about it.

A thought occurred to me, and I darted into the jungle, leaving Ryan to grieve. A diligent search turned up two good candidates, sturdy branches lying on the ground, one much longer than the other. I gathered a good length of vine, cutting it loose with a sharp rock, dragging it along behind me as I returned to the beach.

Ryan didn't appear to have moved since I'd left for the jungle. I sat next to the head of the grave to work. Using the rock, I struggled with the branches, carving grooves into them to help stabilize my project. The crosswise branch was a different type of wood and proved more stubborn. Once I finally got a dent in it, I decided it was sufficient to do the job. I had already pinched my thumb on it twice in the effort. The next task was to strip the vine of its tough, leathery leaves and weave it around and around to make a cross capable of withstanding the winds with regular tending.

Using one of the shells, I dug down near the head of the grave. It wasn't easy because the sand near the surface had less moisture and cohesion. That made it slide back into the hole over and over, frustrating the living daylights out of me. When it was finally done, I placed the long end of the cross into the hole and backfilled with sand, patting it down firmly. I mounded even more around the base, patting that down, too.

Enough time passed that I needed to check on Ryan. He seemed to have stopped crying. When I reached him, I simply sat beside him in the identical position he was in, scooting over until our arms brushed. After a minute, I leaned my head on his shoulder. He responded by resting his head on mine. We remained that way until my neck grew stiff. But I held the position because it seemed to comfort Ryan.

In one quick motion, he turned his head to kiss the top of mine and interlaced our fingers, standing, helping me to my feet. "Dave was a happy guy. He wouldn't want us sitting around mourning him like this all day. Let's go for a walk."

A quick glance over one shoulder toward the grave had him frowning, changing up the course of our walk, and releasing my hand. I hoped he wasn't upset by the appearance of the grave. I trailed along after him, stopping a few feet away, biting my lower lip, prepared for a tongue lashing. After all, I didn't know either of them well. Dave may have had a different religion...or none.

Ryan turned to me, the trace of a smile on his lips. "Thank you for this, Savannah; it's wonderful. You did an amazing job." He came over to hug me.

"You're welcome. I was glad to do it."

"You must be tired."

"I'm okay. My work was easier than yours." I conjured up a smile for him, though it was difficult to force and weak in nature.

He kissed my cheek, rubbed my shoulders, and somehow managed to return my smile. "Let's go for that walk. Then we'll find something for dinner."

<hr />

We sat side by side near Dave, stretched out to relax after dinner. The short stroll we'd taken ended up shorter than imagined; we were worn out. We'd eaten heart palms and sea grapes, the sole meal we'd had all day, but we hadn't had appetites before.

The waves rolling up on the beach weren't as violent as this morning, but there were still loads of whitecaps on the ocean. The conditions were bound to be too rough for anyone to risk the kind of far-flung search required to locate us on this remote island. That had been Ryan's contention, anyway.

The sun rode low in the sky, making for a stunning sunset. The colors were vivid, the sunbeams slicing through gaps in the clouds to create an amazing visual display, blasting rays of brilliant orange alongside deep blue-violet. We watched in awe as the colors faded.

A long string of pelicans flew past, skimming above the water's surface, which reflected a soft orange sky glow. A flock of seagulls passed in the opposite direction, higher than the pelicans, but this time not uttering a sound. It was almost as if they were showing reverence for the dead.

Ryan had scarcely spoken all evening, so I remained respectfully quiet. I wondered what was going through his mind, how he was feeling. I drew in the sand with a stick to keep myself busy, to give him privacy, alone time. In my experience over the years, guys seemed to prefer that at a time like this.

My husband didn't share his feelings. He was the stoic type, always trying to be the strong one. When I had emergency surgery after an auto accident, Sam showed no fear. He was strong and confident, whenever he'd been by my side during those few days. He never shed a tear, telling me I'd be fine, that he wasn't worried. I missed my family.

If this crash hadn't happened, I'd still be on my mission of discovery in this part of the world. I wasn't due to leave for home until the day after tomorrow. I wondered if Sam even knew yet. There was a good chance he didn't. He and Samantha might be blissfully unaware of the situation, thinking the lack of communication was due to the cyclone.

I sincerely hoped that was the case. It was better for everyone to be worried about a brushing blow from a cyclone than for them to believe me lost at sea, deceased. I shook my head; there was no need for that line of thought.

My focus needed to be on the present, on myself and Ryan. No point in worrying about something I couldn't control. Sam and Samantha would be fine, no matter what happened to me.

Closing my eyes, I took a deep breath, releasing it quietly. I attempted to rise, but before I could, Ryan extended his arm across my lap to block me.

"Where're you going?"

"I was going to wander aimlessly for a little while and give you some time alone. I thought you might like that." Might as well be honest about it. The truth often slipped out before I could even make myself think of using discretion instead, or a blatant lie.

"No. I'd rather have you beside me. I'd worry too much about you if you weren't here. And I like having you around, Savannah. You're making me feel better." His eyes were liquid, melting my heart. He had already lost so much.

"In that case, I'll stay." I gave him a smile, but he didn't reciprocate. "If you decide there's anything you want to talk about, you let me know."

"Thanks. One of these days I will."

"Okay."

We sat in silence until the sunset glow had drained from the sky. A sliver of moon was visible from time to time through the clouds as they drifted past. My eyelids were growing so heavy I couldn't keep them open, or stop yawning, having to turn my head aside to avoid having Ryan notice. The gusts of wind rustling through the trees were generating enough of a commotion to block most noises, but the sounds made me sleepier.

Ryan wasn't ready to talk; he simply needed my presence. So, I laid back on the sand, rolling over onto my right side. I fell asleep almost instantly.

The next morning, I awoke to the sound of seagulls again. Sometime during the night, I'd rolled over, closer to Ryan, my head on his upper arm. His other arm lay across my hip. He was soundly sleeping, his eyes twitching periodically with dreams.

There was no way to know what time he finally managed to let everything go and lie down to sleep. He needed his rest, but my muscles were exceptionally sore from yesterday's labor and needed movement to encourage them to loosen up. Slowly, I sat up and removed his arm from my hip, resting it on the sand. I stood to pace nearby, strolling to the cross, where I stretched. Ryan stirred.

"Good morning, Dave," I said. Ryan sat up and looked my way. "Good morning to you, too, Ryan."

He sent me a warm smile. "Good morning, Savannah. Good morning, buddy."

The greeting to his friend widened my smile. "How about if I go find us some sea grapes for breakfast and you stay put this time?"

"No, that's okay. You stick around with Dave; I'll get it."

"Ryan, when are you going to stop being overprotective of me? There aren't any dangers around here. I can go gather sea grapes just as easily as you can."

His expression grew stern. He stood, brushing off sand as he approached. "As long as you and I are trapped on this island, I'm going to be overprotective of you. I won't stop, so you may as well get used to it." He leaned in to give me a quick kiss on the cheek before heading off into the jungle.

"What am I going to do about him, Dave? I sure could use some advice. I wish you could tell me what you know. He was your friend, after all. I guess now he's mine, too. That makes me a lucky woman."

The weather conditions were comfortable, almost cool. A spurt of rain came in a brief band, sending me for cover beneath the trees. I watched it pass, noting the sky. Strange, but the air felt drier than one would expect in the tropics, despite the rain band. The long gray line of clouds swept by, clearing out the sky.

Ryan returned soon after with heart of palm and green bananas.

"Ryan, instead of sitting here with Dave to eat, I'm going to go for a short stroll along the water, since the air feels nice and it's still early. I won't be out long enough to get sunburned. Plus, the sand's wet now and I'd rather not have a damp spot on the back of my pants when I get up."

He laughed, a loud, quick burst like the rain band. "Okay, that sounds like a good idea to me. Let's go."

"Oh, you don't have to come; I'll be fine by myself." I hadn't even considered that he might accompany me. "I'll be out there where you can see me." I indicated the area of choice. "In case you don't want to go, I mean."

"If I didn't want to go, I'd tell you. Now let's go for that stroll. Here." He passed me some palm. "We can munch on breakfast while we walk."

The ocean remained rough, understandable after the close passage of a cyclone. The waves curled into tubes as they rolled in, slapping the sand with a resounding boom. Where they formed far out beyond the shallows, they grew to something like fifteen feet before the wind blew their foamy tops back out to sea.

"And me without my surfboard," Ryan commented as we approached the edge of the water's reach.

"You're a surfer?" I didn't know why that surprised me. Maybe because he seemed more conservative than that.

"I used to be, occasionally. I haven't done it since I was a teenager."

"I've never done it at all. I've never had the desire to learn. Were you any good?" I bit into breakfast.

"Not bad, I guess. After this many years, I'd probably fall off and break a bone."

"I'll bet it's like a bicycle. You'd pick it back up fast. And I'm sure you'd do great. You look very athletic."

He smiled and we walked in silence, eating.

"What're you thinking about?" Ryan asked, raising his voice to be heard above the breaking waves.

"Nothing much. Just silliness. The thought occurred to me about how sometimes people talk about wanting to be stranded on a deserted island."

"I think most everyone talks about that from time to time. I know I've done it myself."

"I have, too. I know I'll never talk about it again, that's for sure.

Not like it's a game. The reality sucks." I nibbled the banana he handed over.

"It does, especially the way it happened to us." He glanced toward the grave with a heavy swallow. "So, what is it that you would've brought along if you'd known this would happen?"

"How many things am I allowed to bring?" A diversion would take Ryan's mind off Dave, with the added benefit of helping us get better acquainted.

He gave his rule some thought. "Let's limit ourselves to one."

It needed to be something good, under the circumstances. "Okay then. Could my one thing be a person?"

"Sure, why not? Let me guess; you'd bring your husband."

"No. I'd bring the world's best doctor...for Dave."

A dark cloud passed over Ryan's face and I realized I'd said the wrong thing. He watched where he placed his feet before reaching out to take my hand firmly in his own, giving it a gentle squeeze.

"Thank you, Savannah. That was a thoughtful choice. All I came up with was bringing a spear gun to catch fish with, or maybe a sack full of hamburgers."

"Hey, those would be good, too."

"Right." His brow furrowed as his gaze shifted to the horizon.

"No, they would. Seriously. After the doctor saved Dave's life, we could eat hamburgers. We'd be hungry."

"You're a nice person, Savannah."

"I screwed it all up, Ryan. I didn't mean to make you feel bad." I bit my lower lip. I guess I didn't help him after all.

"You didn't screw anything up. You did fine."

"Okay, since this seems to be getting messed up, I'm going to take charge of the game and it's all going to go as I say. So, I'd bring a doctor, a specialist, and you'd bring his bag full of instruments and medicines, because he'll need those to work on Dave. A doctor isn't as good without those things."

Something else occurred to me. "And the doctor would bring the big sack full of hamburgers, and Dave would bring a spare helicopter, fully gassed. So, after Dave was better and we'd eaten our fill of hamburgers, Dave would fly us out of here. How's that?"

Ryan chuckled. "That sounds just about perfect to me. Like you."

"Let's try something different," I suggested. "If you could travel anywhere in the world, where would you want to go?"

"Anywhere in the world? Well, I've always wanted to visit Australia. Wide open spaces, big cities, kangaroos. One of these days, I'll get there," he conveyed with confidence.

"That's a good one. I'd like to go there, too."

"Then I'll have to take you with me." He gave me a pleasant smile.

"That'd be nice, but more than Australia, I want to see Egypt. You know, all the typical tourist stuff, like the pyramids and the museums. I'd have to use my dream trip there instead."

"That's an interesting choice. And when you asked the question, you neglected to set up any rules. So, that means I can take this in any direction I want to, the way you did with the deserted island question."

My left eyebrow rose sharply.

"First off, you and I will be traveling together. We'll go to Australia and Egypt. That'll be the vacation of a lifetime. We're both going to need to take at least a month off from our jobs, though. I'm planning on us spending at least two weeks in each country. We're going to have so much fun. What other trivia questions can you think of?"

"I don't know about trivia, but why don't you tell me your favorite food?" The plan was working better than I'd hoped. "Is it hamburgers?"

"No. I'm a steak man. But I do love hamburgers. What about you?" We turned to walk back, staying near the water.

"Seafood is my favorite."

"Lucky for you, huh? In a way, I mean." His smile faded.

It took me a second to realize it. There was a dark side there, certainly unintended. "I guess so. Those crabs were fantastic. When I lived in Savannah, my friends had a dock and used a crab trap to catch them. Do you think we could try making a crab trap somehow?"

"We can. That's a great idea. What do you say we go work on one now? It'll take some time to build it right. Then, we'll have to figure out how to bait it."

"You have to have food in order to catch food," I noted.

"Yes. Palms and grapes aren't on their menu. We're going to need some meat. If we can catch a fish or even another crab, we'll use the leftovers as bait for the trap."

I found myself getting excited about the prospect, though it was more the idea of having something productive to do. "How about this? Why don't we explore the interior of the island some more, starting right now? Maybe while we're doing that, we can collect materials for a crab trap–*and* for a fish trap! That's how we can do it!"

"Well, maybe, Savannah. Don't get your hopes up too high. It won't be easy to build a fish trap either. But what might work for catching fish is a spear gun, like I was talking about before."

"But we don't have a spear gun. How would you build something like that?"

Ryan thought for a quick moment. "I can make the next best thing. The spear part of it'll be easy enough. Then, I can swim out past the shallows and skewer something for us to eat. We can use the leftovers as bait."

"Okay, that sounds good, I guess. I don't like the part about you going into deep water, though. That's a long way from shore, Ryan."

"It'll be okay, come on." He shifted our direction toward the jungle.

"But what if something bad happens to you while you're all the way out there?" The worry over him doing something he hadn't even done yet begin to fill my mind.

"Nothing bad will happen, don't worry."

"That's not very reassuring, because it's not realistic." He wasn't going to be able to brush this off. Not with me.

"How do you figure that?"

"We've already had a lot of bad things happen to us. Things highly unlikely to happen to *anyone*."

"That's true, but I'm thinking we've used up a lifetime supply of bad luck already."

Clearly, the man wasn't a realist. Maybe he was trying to avoid frightening me. It was too late for that.

Six

Ryan set out first thing the next morning in search of spear candidates. We hadn't had much luck yesterday, but we managed to construct a halfway-decent fish trap from branches and vines. My job was to check how well it held up. Our expectations were low. Good thing.

Hands on hips, I strolled leisurely toward the water, stopping a few feet from the reach of the waves and a thick layer of seafoam. The ocean remained rough, with an abundance of whitecaps. The wind whipped the dry sand around like a fog, stinging at my bare feet and ankles. The sky was clouding over, their structure familiar. Yet, the overall situation was odd.

A variety of birds flew about in search of a meal, even with the clear approach of a big storm. Pelicans dove with limited success. Seagulls joined them in trying to scoop up small fish near the surface. Bits and pieces of our trap lay scattered around the beach, some out bobbing on the ocean. Waves shoved additional fish trap debris ashore.

While I studied the area, Ryan walked up and handed over a long strand of sea grapes. "Those pelicans are doing lots of diving. Are they catching anything?"

"Not much. The seagulls aren't having even that much luck with the slim pickings. The fish seem to have gone into hiding."

It took a moment to realize Ryan was staring at me. "What?"

"That's what I was going to ask you. You look like you're trying to solve a puzzle or something."

"I am. Look at the water and sky."

He studied them. "A storm's coming."

"That's what I was thinking. But the winds have me wondering. After a hurricane passes, the air's usually still. There's never any wind for relief from the heat. I'm thinking we may be in for a second system, following along the general track of the first, maybe feeding off it, maybe stronger than the first, or passing closer. After the first cyclone came that little dry slot that cleared things out for a few hours yesterday. And then in the afternoon, well before sunset, clouds started building back in. Judging from the pattern of the clouds and the ferocity of the wind, both of which seem to be coming in bands, I'm thinking a cyclone."

He studied the ocean for a long moment. "Maybe."

"Well, at least we know where we can go for shelter. Let's take some sea grapes with us this time. And we can eat the food I've got in my pack."

"That works for me. But I'll harvest more food from the palms that went down in the last storm. There weren't many of them in that one since we only took a glancing blow. I found coconuts on the ground, along with green bananas, passion fruit, and papayas. We need to gather up everything we can find. If this cyclone is bad and hits us head on, we could find ourselves with nothing to eat here but whatever fish I can catch with the spear I haven't even made yet. We should save your food."

"That sounds like a plan."

"Do you want to come along and help me? I can teach you how to get the good stuff out of those palms."

"Yes, I'd like that, thanks." It was nice to be included this time. "What about your spears? Did you find some straight pieces that'll work for you?"

"Yes, I did. They're up by Dave, along with all the edibles I could carry. Working on the spear will give me something to do while we wait out the storm. We'll pack some fruit in your backpack and carry it with us. Then, we'll come back down and do it again."

"And we'll need some sharp rocks or shells for you to whittle with. Maybe we can make a new and improved fish trap while we're at it." I began retrieving as many of the components from our original attempt as I could find on the way back to Dave. "We've got our work cut out for us. We'll need to gather more materials for the fish trap on our way to the shelter. These leftovers won't be enough."

The supplies we'd gathered were under the big rock outcrop that we sheltered in before. There was more room this time since Dave wasn't with us. I'd much rather have our quarters cramped.

Ryan wriggled in backward, cradling two large shells filled with water from the swollen falls. He found good spots on the uneven rock floor to wedge them into so they wouldn't spill. "Let's drink these first. We'll use the last of your bottled water if we're trapped in here by lightning or high winds for too long."

"All right. Are you ready for your palm innards?"

"Palm innards? That sounds gross, Savannah," he chuckled.

It was good to hear him laugh. "Well, that's technically what they are."

"That's not the technical term for it."

"Maybe not, but that's what it is. And I made you laugh."

He turned his head to study the splatter of raindrops he'd managed to beat into the shelter. Then he looked back at me with a slight smile. "Thanks for that."

"You're welcome." I handed him a chunk of palm, working on my own.

"I can't believe how much you cheer me up. I don't know what I'd do without you," he said.

"Same here," I responded from where I reclined against the rear wall. "Why don't you sit at the back of the cave-port with me, Ryan?"

"Okay." He stopped mid-crawl. "Wait. What did you call it? A cave-port? What in the world is a cave-port?"

"This is. It's kind of like a carport. You know, a roof, a floor, and a couple of sides, but made out of rock, like a cave."

"Is that a real word or did you make that up?" His eyes narrowed as he ceased his approach again to stare at me.

"I made it up, just now. What do you think? You have to admit it's accurate." I gave him a mischievous grin. I wanted to make him smile, or maybe even laugh again. He needed it. My focus was on him, putting aside my own fears, my need to see my family again. We needed to help each other get through this. Besides, I enjoyed his smile.

Ryan studied me for a moment before shaking his head, smiling as he crawled the rest of the distance to sit beside me. "You're something else, Savannah Dalton."

"Is that good or bad?" My eyes narrowed and I raised one of my eyebrows, but the skepticism act failed to stick.

"It's good, believe me. Of all the people in the world I could've been stranded with, I got the cream of the crop."

I beamed. "What a coincidence! So did I. We haven't known each other long, but we've been through a lot together. You're a good friend, Ryan."

"Fair enough. Eat up and then we'll work on our projects. And after this storm goes, the weather's bound to clear up. We can gather a bunch of the big palm fronds that'll have gotten blown down and spell out a message on the sand with them. I read an article about some people who got stranded a few years ago and they did that. They wrote out the word help, I think. We could do that, too."

A glimmer of hope. "Okay, that sounds great to me. Thanks, Ryan. They're bound to find us soon—well, after the cyclone goes away. My husband and parents will be trying to find me. What about you, Ryan? Who'll be looking for you; a wife, a girlfriend, parents?"

"I have a girlfriend named Laura. We've been together for, let's see, eleven months now, almost to the day. I wanted her to come out here to visit Dave with me, but she had a big project at work and couldn't leave. She's a computer engineer with a federal defense contractor.

"She won't be missing me yet. She's probably figuring I'm out having a good time with Dave. It'll be a while before she recognizes there's a problem. Then she'll try to reach me and check around online. After that, she'll contact my folks and they'll all try to find me. My folks will fly over here. They're kind of hands-on people."

"Good, I'm glad to hear it. The more people searching for us the better. Somebody's bound to find us. All we need to do is wait for this cyclone to blow by. Then we'll spell out a message and wait for our rescue to come." I took another bite of the palm, wishing I possessed a fraction of the confidence I attempted to project for Ryan's benefit.

The next morning, discerning the sun had risen came from the fact that it appeared less dark outside. The rain poured, making it hard to see past the edge of the overhang. And that was when you caught a momentary break in the curtains of water coming over the edge above.

I drank a couple of sips of water. I didn't want to consume much because I already needed to relieve myself. Instead, I munched on more palm and a few sea grapes as I tried to judge how far away my eyes could pick out details of the terrain past the deluge. Visibility was perhaps as far as forty feet, the distance shrinking as the rain came down harder.

Not bad under the circumstances. That was the side view. The wide front had become a massive waterfall.

"Morning," Ryan mumbled from next to me. He blinked heavy lids.

I glanced down into his blue eyes and smiled. "Good morning."

"How long have you been awake?" he asked, sitting up, running a hand over his short hair.

"Not long. If it doesn't slack off soon, I'm going to have to go out in that mess. I can't hold it much longer."

"Hold it? Oh, sorry. I get it. I need to go, too. I guess we'll both get soaked."

"At least we'll be clean."

He gave me a quick smile and lifted his shell for a drink. "We can set these out beyond the overhang here and they'll fill up with rainwater fast."

"That's a good idea. We won't get as wet as if we had to go to the waterfall."

"You know I wouldn't let you go to the waterfall in these conditions, don't you?" He placed the shell on the floor.

"Yes, I know. I guess I'm lucky you're going to let me go out to pee."

"If I could find a way around that, I'd take it."

"Well, all this talk about waterfalls and rain has done it for me. I can't wait anymore. I'll be right back." I got on my hands and knees, crawling to the edge, getting splashed with a fine spray of water that bounced off pretty much everything. Nothing like what would be coming.

"Wait a minute. I'm going with you. You're going to stay near me the whole time, and don't worry, I won't look." He crawled up beside me.

"Okay, let's go then." We squatted on the balls of our feet.

Ryan took ahold of my hand and intertwined our fingers before clamping down so tight it hurt a little. "The water's running down this hill pretty fast. Look at the bottom."

There was a massive rush of water forty feet below us. It ran off fast to the west and was so wide it gave the island the appearance of having been split in two, lower jungle and hills. I couldn't discern the depth, but I didn't care for the looks of it.

"The rain is sheeting off the hill quick. If you lose your footing and I can't hold you, you'll be swept away from me in a heartbeat. You don't let go of my hand, no matter what happens, until I let go. Understand? Not unless I fall. If I do I expect you to leave me and get to safety."

He was deeply serious, so I nodded affirmatively. I took a deep breath.

"Okay, let's go!"

We moved into the elements, making our way judiciously toward the grove of trees nearest us, where the ground was relatively level and the wind partially blocked. Each step squished and splashed. Rain pounded like thousands of tiny rocks, while the high-pitched background whistle of the wind stirred an instinctive fear and made hearing anything else difficult. We stopped in the middle of the grove.

"Right there!" Ryan yelled over the wind, pointing to a spot on the ground at my feet.

I could barely see, but I nodded in acknowledgment. The rain poured into my eyes, as did the rivulets cascading from my sopping head and the leaves of the trees we stood under. I did my best to avoid inhaling it. A person could drown by simply turning their face to the sky.

It didn't take long to finish what I set out to do. Then began the struggle to pull up my soaked pants once I'd managed my underpants. Suddenly, Ryan was in front of me. He grabbed my pants on both sides and tugged them up faster than I could, then zipped and buttoned me as I held the bottom of my shirt out of his way. He reclaimed my hand and led the way back to the cave-port.

Water drained off both of us in sheets as we sat, our breaths coming fast and heavy.

"I'm sorry about that, Savannah. I just wanted to hurry up and get us out of there and back under here where it was safer. I don't make a habit out of dressing or undressing women. Not unless I'm dating them at the time." He sent me a quick grin.

"That's okay; I was having trouble. I appreciate the help."

"Anytime." He grinned again, handing me a string of sea grapes to munch on. "Let's try to avoid drinking water as much as we can until this eases up some. And help me keep an eye on the flow of water down there. Some of it could be from storm surge."

"Okay." It didn't look any worse than when we'd set out for the trees, but that could always change, especially if there was storm surge. And it didn't look to me as though we were at the storm surge part of the cyclone yet.

It should be nearly impossible for the ocean to push all the way to our shelter, unless the eye passed over us and we were hit with a massive surge. My guesstimate was that the cave-port sat fifty to sixty feet above sea level. If forced, we could make our way through the jungle above our backs, which led to the cliffs. The top had to be another seventy feet up. It wouldn't be an easy climb if we had to make it in the middle of a cyclone.

We munched on sea grapes as I squeezed water from my hair, Ryan observing. It was good to have him to help me and keep me company.

"Savannah's a nice name. How did you get it? I mean, I know your parents gave it to you, but why? Was it because of where you were born?"

That was random, but at least his mind was off our troubles. "The latter. My mom grew up near Savannah and her family went there a lot; she loved it. Have you ever been there?"

"No. What's it like?"

"It's beautiful...one of the most beautiful places I've ever seen. You should consider adding it to your list of places to visit. I'll make sure I come along to give you a personal tour. It's an old city, but well planned. The heart of it was laid out in a grid pattern to have what they call squares, which are small parks. They're famous for those. They have horse-drawn carriage rides through the main part of the city and trollies, too. It's along the Savannah River, where it empties into the ocean.

"My parents were both born there, got married there, and now they live there. That's where I was born and raised. I got married there, too. I go there every chance I get. I'd live there in a heartbeat if I could." My enthusiasm was getting the better of me, so I stopped for a breath.

"Why can't you?" Ryan tossed leaves he'd stripped from a vine into the rain, where they washed downhill too fast to keep up with.

"My husband can't tolerate the heat and humidity, plus he has an important job near Washington, D.C. that he won't leave. Even D.C. gets too hot and humid for him in the summer, so we take a few weeks in July every year to visit his family in Vermont. That's where Sam's from."

"Vermont has to be hard on a southern girl."

"There's nothing wrong with Vermont. It's a beautiful place, just not my thing. Way too much snow for too much of the year. After those few weeks are over, I'm ready to get back to D.C. Except that the traffic and noise is always a culture shock after the peace and quiet. At Christmas, we always go to Savannah to stay with my parents for a few days. They're in a small condo near the river."

"It's too bad you couldn't reverse that and spend more time in Savannah during the winter and less time in Vermont during the summer."

"Sam might be willing to do that for me. But my schedule isn't as flexible as his and he refuses to fly, so we drive everywhere. There wouldn't be much time left from driving to spend in Vermont for

Christmas. As it is, our daughter sees more of my parents than she does Sam's."

"What about you? What do you do for a living?" Conversation was a good distraction.

"I'm a software engineer."

"Oh, wow. That sounds like an interesting job."

"It has its moments. When I was fresh out of school, I created software programs for a fast-growing startup. I wasn't there long before I went into the Coast Guard. I've been working with a defense contractor for two years now."

"Is that how you met Laura, at work?"

"Yes, we work for the same company, although the campus is huge, and it was pure chance we came across each other. We met at the company cafeteria during lunch one day."

"That's great you found each other. She must be pretty special."

"She is. I'd planned to propose when I got back from this trip. My plan was to propose to her *on* this trip, originally. Dave told me about this romantic little spot, and we had everything all set up. But then she decided she'd rather stay behind and work on her project. She's angling for a promotion. Her career is extremely important to her. Lucky for me she's also anxious to get married."

"It's a good thing she didn't come. If she'd been with us on the helicopter, who knows what would've happened to her. This way, she's alive and well."

"You're right about that. Do you always turn things around to look on the bright side and cheer people up like this?"

"I try."

"You succeed, all the time. At least you do with me. Your parents should've named you Sunny."

"My dad called me Sunshine, until 2003."

"What happened in 2003?"

"Those Disney pirate movies started."

"The ones with Captain Jack? I loved those...he's the coolest."

"Yeah, well, my dad loved them so much he gave me a nickname from the movies."

"And what nickname was that?" He grinned, anticipating.

"Savvy. Captain Jack said it all the time. It supposedly means understanding or wisdom. That's what my dad always says, anyway. He hasn't called me by my real name since. He says Savvy is a derivative of Savannah, or close enough for him, anyway. It was an excuse…he's totally obsessed with pirates."

"Most people love pirates, especially since they don't have to experience them in real life. Savvy. I like it. Do you mind if I use it?"

"Sure. Most people call me Savvy; it started back in college. My husband doesn't, though. He says it isn't an appropriate nickname for a woman. Sam has never been a big fan of nicknames, pirates, the beach, or any of that. He loves snow and Christmas. So does our daughter—she takes after her dad more than she does me."

"My parents prefer cooler weather, too. And my sister. I'm the weird one in the family. So, what's your daughter's name?"

"Samantha."

"Whose decision was it to name her after your husband?"

"His. He decided he only wanted one child, so he wanted her named after him, which was fine with me. I already miss her. Back when I was pregnant, a friend told me I'd find out what it felt like to have my heart walking around outside my body.

"I didn't understand until I held Samantha and they took her from me to the other side of the room to weigh her; she was crying the whole time. Then they took her out of the room to clean her up and all. I had already made Sam promise to follow them everywhere they took her and not let her out of his sight. Even though I knew she was safe, and Sam was with her, it was still like a part of me I needed desperately was gone—my heart."

"I've never heard it put like that before. You make it sound special to be a parent. I guess I've never given it that much thought. I'd like to have one or two someday."

"You probably will, with Laura. Then you'll understand."

"Provided she says yes."

"She'd be insane not to."

He gave me a quizzical look. He reminded me at that moment of a puppy I'd had a long time ago, who'd run off into a neighborhood pond and came out soaked, dripping, apparently surprised I'd been so happy to see him.

"I haven't known you all that long, but you're a terrific guy, Ryan."

"Thanks. Listen, we'll get out of here; I don't want you to worry about that. I know you miss your family and I'm sure they'll be scared once they realize you're missing. If I was your husband, I'd go crazy. And I'd never stop looking until I found you."

"Thanks, Ryan." My cheeks reddened, so I turned my attention to the opening of the cave-port, and the new waterfall. "I hope they find us before the storm washes us away."

"They will and we won't."

The wind shifted directions, blowing rain into our shelter, splattering us. It also drove the water pouring over the top of our cave-port inside in sheets. The space was only eight feet to the back at its deepest point, so there was nowhere to go to escape it.

I grabbed the backpack, moving it against the rear wall, hunching myself over it in an attempt to keep it dry. It held the remnants of the first aid kit, in addition to everything else. The rain pounded against my back, until Ryan blocked it by placing himself between me and the rain, hugging me from behind, resting his head against mine.

"Hang in there. It'll be doing this for a while yet."

"Thanks, Ryan."

"You're welcome, Savvy." He leaned over my shoulder to give my cheek a quick kiss.

This was going to be a long day.

Seven

The sun had risen by the time we were able to leave our shelter. Most of the clouds were still around, the winds were gusty, and our clothes had yet to dry. Ryan carried out an armload of wood we had sheltered from the rain to use for a fire. Provided we found food that needed cooking. The thought made my stomach growl.

We moved warily down to the base of the steep hill that was home to the waterfall and the cave-port. We paused to look up at where we'd been, fortunate to have such a sturdy refuge. Palm fronds of varying shapes and sizes, along with tree branches and stripped leaves, carpeted the ground everywhere in layers. Building materials were plentiful.

"We could embellish the cave-port, Ryan...maybe add to the sides with palm fronds."

"That's a good idea, Savvy. This is the time to gather palm fronds, that's for sure."

"The first thing I'd like to do is work on that message for help." I surveyed our surroundings.

"Then that's the second thing we'll do. The first order of business is to get something for breakfast."

"You're right. I'm starving."

"Come with me and we'll see if maybe we can get lucky with another crab. Or maybe the storm's brought something else in. Otherwise, we'll scrounge up some fruit or go back to the cave-port for the stash we've got there."

"Sounds good to me." I followed as he led us to the beach, wading carefully through wide, slow-moving ribbons of water. A carpet of seaweed nearly obscured the sand.

"Hey, I just spotted breakfast. Right over there." He dropped the firewood and pointed down the beach, at the edge of the water. "Stay here unless I call you. I'll be right back."

He returned a couple of minutes later, at a jog, a big grin on his face. "This guy's huge, isn't he?"

"I've never eaten a conch before. How do you cook them?"

"First of all, I'm going to let you guard him while I build a new fire pit. It won't be easy because even the wood we took to the shelter to keep dry got a little damp, not to mention the wet sand. Keep your fingers crossed. After we eat, we'll gather armloads of seaweed and dry it. That stuff can store for months. It isn't the tastiest food we can find, but it's easy to get at right now and it keeps well."

"I'll give it a try. But what do you mean by guarding the conch? He's way too big for a seagull to carry off."

"I meant, don't take your eyes off him for too long. He'll walk away." Ryan placed the conch on the sand near my feet, grabbed a sizeable half-shell, and set to work constructing our new fire pit. We'd also need to replace the mound of sand over Dave, as the top had been pulled away, the remainder noticeably sunken. I intended to volunteer for that on my own, for Ryan's sake.

While keeping an eye on the conch, I gathered a multitude of weedy wisps stuck in nearby vegetation or amongst the heaps of seaweed. I held them tightly in my grasp by one end, allowing them to blow in the ample wind and dry out. I had large bunches in both hands, totally blown dry by the time the fire pit was prepared.

"Here's some kindling." I handed it to Ryan.

"Hey, that'll help a lot. Go ahead and arrange our damp wood on here with your fire starter while I go see if I can find anything else we can use."

"All right." Once I'd gotten everything ready, I retrieved the conch, which had made amazing progress since Ryan put him down for me to watch. The shell he lived in was gorgeous, but heavy. I placed him near the fire pit to wait.

When Ryan returned with brushy material, he began his efforts to start a fire under less than ideal conditions. His attempts to block the strong gusts with his body needed help, so I planted myself up against him to widen the wind barrier.

Once the fire was going, I left Ryan with the conch for my next assignment. I walked around, sorting through chunks of seaweed, thinning them out, and then spreading them all around, twisting the strands around a tree limb or weighing them down with a branch or rock so they wouldn't blow away. By the time the conch was cooked,

I'd covered the area immediately around us in seaweed.

"Come on, Savvy. That's enough for now. We'll gather more after we eat. Bring a handful over here and we can eat it with the conch. It doesn't have to be dry for that."

I did as he asked, sitting beside him. "Don't you think I've collected enough? Unless it loses a lot of its volume by shrinking as it dries, that is."

"It does, so we should take advantage of the opportunity and prepare as much of it as we can. It's a windfall. We could use something to alternate with the palms and fruit to give us some variety. I found more coconut and banana trees with green fruit still hanging on them, so we'll have those to eat, as well as some other things I've come across in my searching. Some of the fruit that blew off got lodged in the underbrush, so things aren't as bad as they could've been after a cyclone like that one.

"I'm going to start spear fishing at least once a day. We'll experiment with building different kinds of fish traps, too. And crabs. I didn't forget about your love of crabmeat."

His grin faded as he took note of my expression. My disbelief bordered on anger. He glanced down at the warm chunks of roasted conch in his hand and passed them over to me. I took them but didn't attempt to eat.

"You're talking like we're going to be here for a long time...maybe the rest of our lives."

"I just think we should be prepared, in case rescue never comes," he spoke the words softly, staring at the slices of conch roasting over the fire.

"Never comes? Are you kidding me? We're going to be rescued. How could you even say that?"

"Savannah." His eyes spoke of patience.

"No! I won't listen to this. It's crazy talk. They're coming for us. They're probably going to find us today, in fact. The storms are gone, and they'll be able to fly again. As soon as I've finished my breakfast, I'm going to clear the rest of this part of the beach and spell out the word help, nice and big. And then I'm going to go do it on the other side of the island. You can go ahead and keep gathering seaweed if you want to. I'm going to get us out of here."

"Savannah, I didn't mean we wouldn't be. I only meant it's *possible* we won't be, and we have to keep that in mind. When we've finished eating, I'll help you with the rescue message. I'll help you until you're satisfied. But then I'm going to spread out more seaweed to dry. Every bit I can get my hands on. It'll help us survive."

There was compassion in his eyes. I had to remember both of us were under a great deal of stress. He'd left loved ones behind, too. Plus, he had to bury one. I took his near hand in mine and rubbed it.

"I'm sorry, Ryan. I know you're right. And I know you're working hard to keep both of us alive. I'm grateful for that, really I am. I lost my temper for a second there. I thought you were giving up."

Ryan pulled my hand to his lips then and kissed it, one corner of his mouth turning up a little. "I know. It's bound to happen from time to time, provided we're not rescued, of course. Which, we will be. Everything will be fine. I don't want you to worry about anything. Now eat your conch while it's still warm. I think you'll like it."

We made it back to our shelter ahead of a straggling rain band from the cyclone. The wind roared again, bending the tops of the trees as it whistled and shoved its way over and through. The coast wasn't clear for us quite yet, it would seem.

It had been a lot of work, marking the island with two giant help signs. I had joked that even a commercial airliner might be able to see the last one we made. When we walked back by Dave's gravesite, we stopped to finish cleaning it up and smoothing the sand I'd piled up earlier. And we repaired the cross, which was substantially askew. It was nothing short of a miracle that it hadn't blown or washed away.

Ryan hauled a huge bundle of plant material up the hill with him, arranging it to his liking on the floor of the cave-port. "Okay, give it a try."

I crawled over to lie down at the back wall. The rock had been well-padded, several inches deep. "Hey, this is nice. It's much better than the bare rock. That cut off my circulation. You did a great job making us a bed. Thanks, Ryan."

"No problem; it helps me, too. I'll bring in more tomorrow to make it thicker and softer. The sun is on its way down, so what do you say we go to sleep early? I'm worn out."

"Me, too. That's a wonderful idea. Come on, Mr. Fixit." I patted the spot next to me.

Ryan crawled over, stretching out on his back and releasing a loud sigh. Almost immediately, he began snoring. It amazed me how fast he fell asleep.

Sleep eluded me, thoughts of what Ryan had said playing over and over. It had never even crossed my mind that we might never be rescued. Not until now. I hadn't allowed myself to think about it, trying to remain positive. I couldn't be without Samantha. The world seemed suddenly far away and uncaring.

―――

At first light, I awakened to find I'd snuggled up next to Ryan during the night. We were facing each other, with him breathing across the top of my head. His right arm was slung casually over my hip. He stirred, sliding his hand over my rear to pull me even closer against him. Then he kissed my forehead and nuzzled his nose to mine. He must be immersed in a dream.

"Hmm, good morning," his words slurred, trying to push away from the world of dreams.

"Good morning." I removed his arm from its resting place and watched him. "How about if you let me go gather some plant material for breakfast while you stay here and sleep some more? You worked so hard yesterday. I'm sure you could use more rest."

"You're sweet, but you know the answer to that without me having to say it. Besides, I've slept enough. But if you want, you can stay here and keep resting a while longer. I'll get breakfast and bring it to you. It'll be breakfast in bed. How does that strike you?" He propped himself up on one elbow, reaching out a hand to pull a few blades of grasses from my hair.

There was little he could have said that would've surprised me more. A little independence. "Wow. Okay. That would be great, Ryan. If you're sure you don't mind, that is."

"I don't. I should start showing you a little freedom. This shelter is our home for now and you're perfectly safe here. There aren't any wild animals that could pose a threat to us and we're the only people on this island. Plus, I won't be gone long. Go back to sleep if you can; I'll wake you up when I get back." He got himself onto all fours.

"I'll try. Thanks, Ryan."

"No problem. I'll be back in about a half hour; longer if I find more crabs." He winked before backing out. When he stood, he stretched and checked the surroundings, studying the skies, the terrain, everything, before walking away.

He was a wonderful protector, despite the suffocation. It was a good thing he wanted me to be with him most of the time. It was terrible being trapped on an island, but at least I had companionship. Nice companionship at that.

Since my eyes were feeling dry, I opened the backpack and removed items until I found the small bottle of eye drops. Conservation mode had me applying only one drop per eye, with the knowledge rescue could be multiple days distant. But then, as there were just two additional pairs of contacts with me, I could use as many drops as I wanted. My glasses would take the duty after that. I plopped in a second drop for each eye, making them feel much better.

As I repacked, I couldn't help noticing a pack of peanut butter crackers had gone missing. I knew how many I brought with me. It didn't matter how many he ate. Ryan was keeping me fed. If he wanted all the crackers, trail mix, and breakfast bars I brought on this trip, he was welcome to them.

When I withdrew my deodorant, I hesitated. That should be conserved. And I should offer to share it with Ryan. We should also share my travel toothbrush and sparingly use the tube of toothpaste I had. Once a day was all we should aim for, again, to be conservative. I reached in to feel around for the objects.

Instead, my fingers touched something sharp. Reflexively, my hand whipped out. I studied my fingertips, but they weren't cut. I couldn't think of anything I'd brought that would feel like that, until I remembered my nail trimmer. But it didn't feel like the sharpness of a trimmer. It felt more like a tiny, sharp rock. I had no idea what it could be, aside from an actual rock.

One by one, I removed each and every object in my backpack, taking stock of their condition. The nail trimmer was secure in its plastic case. Nearly everything was out.

Lastly, I withdrew my glasses case, and immediately noticed how light it felt. A stomach-churning sense of panic gripped me. Not wanting my fear to become reality, I opened the case in slow motion to find it empty. Oh my God. My glasses couldn't be broken. Please, no. Everything else was out of the pack. Peering inside, I found my glasses, the frames twisted and snapped at the bridge and the tiny side hinges missing.

Hands shaking, I crawled from the cave-port with the backpack. Exposed to the sun, there was no reflection from the lenses catching the light. They were gone. I dumped the remaining contents onto the roof of our shelter. Sparkling bits of shattered lenses spilled out like tiny diamonds, catching the early morning beams. Not only were the lenses destroyed, but they were smashed to the point of being useless. There wasn't even one segment large enough to utilize for a semblance of an eyepiece.

What would I do now? The contact lenses I'd been wearing twenty-four hours a day would need to be exchanged for new ones in something like a week. Probably the most I could reasonably expect out of the other pairs was three weeks each if I was lucky enough.

Meaning seven weeks was all I had remaining of my sight. Without manmade correction, I wouldn't be able to see. Over and over I tried to convince myself everything would be all right, that rescue would come before my contacts were gone. Seven weeks. I took several breaths to calm down before crawling back into the shelter. I replaced the contents of my pack, my mind not on the task.

Laying down didn't bring sleep. I worried about myself and how I'd ever survive without my vision, even with Ryan helping me. I knew he'd continue taking good care of me, the way he'd already been doing.

My worry shifted to Ryan then. What if something happened to him out there while he was trying to be considerate and let me sleep? He might be working to catch a crab or a fish or something. What if he went into the water and didn't pay attention? What if a shark came? There were poisonous creatures in the ocean, too. I had to stop being lazy and find him. We needed to stay together.

Before I knew it, I was racing down the steep hillside, not considering the risk of a fall. At the bottom, hesitation set in. Something didn't seem quite right. Turning, I checked back up at the cave-port to study its surroundings. What was it? Did I see or hear something out of place when I crawled out?

Everything looked the same, but it wasn't. If we weren't rescued, it never would be again. My world was collapsing.

I ran for the beach and didn't slow until the ocean became visible between the trees. Emerging onto the beach, I immediately scanned the water for Ryan.

According to my watch, it was five twenty-three. Which, it wasn't. My watch must have given up the ghost during the torrential downpours. I removed the now-useless instrument, dropping it to the sand.

No human head popped up from the ocean. I continued the vigil until it had been too long for him to have held his breath. I pressed my hands to my temples. Where could he be? He wasn't in the water. He must've gone inland, gathering plant material instead, or fresh fruit. I jogged into the jungle, searching the last place he'd been using to gather the palms. It didn't look like he'd been there. From our conversations, the plants bearing sea grapes were scattered around the island. That meant Ryan could be anywhere.

"Ryan!" I cupped my hands around my mouth to project my voice. "Ryan! Where are you?" The vegetation muffled sound so well he wouldn't be able to hear me. I stopped to study the palms. There'd been no activity in at least a day.

"Ryan!" I screamed, bolting forward through the vegetation, jumping fallen trees, and shoving past branches with large, leathery leaves. When I stopped to catch my breath, I decided to think like a sensible person, rather than someone who'd lost control of themselves. Whenever you were lost, you should stay put and wait to be found. I needed to get back to the shelter, back home. Ryan would go there, expecting to find me. He'd go crazy if he didn't find me there. It might be too late for that already.

On a deep breath, I ran. Ahead, Ryan called out.

"Savannah! Savannah!" Ryan yelled, the panic in his voice unmistakable.

As I reached the base of our hill, Ryan emerged from a grove of trees near the shelter, tearing down the hill toward me, not decelerating until he neared. As he skidded to a halt, I threw my arms around his neck. He hugged me, burying his face in my hair.

"I was so worried about you, Savannah. I've been searching everywhere. You scared me half to death." He pulled his head back to study me. "What happened? Why'd you leave the shelter?"

"I went looking for you because I was worried. You're all I've got. We need to stick together, all the time from now on. I'll never leave your side, I promise." My head dropped to his chest, his heart pounding beneath my cheek. He must have been running hard, just as I'd been, and just as afraid.

He kissed the top of my head. "That sounds like a plan to me, and I'm going to hold you to it. Nothing short of an injury will stop me from taking you along from now on."

"But that's not going to happen. We won't get injured, because we'll always be together and we'll protect and help each other," I said.

"That's right. Always." He rubbed his hands over my back, and I lost it, breaking down into deep sobs. "Hey, there's no need to cry. You didn't get hurt, did you?"

"No." It was difficult to get the words out past the cascade of tears. "I was so afraid something had happened to you. Like maybe you'd been eaten by a shark or something. Please don't go deep in the water. Promise me."

"I promise." He wiped at my tears. "I won't do it. We'll find another way to catch our fish. We'll start working on making a new trap today. How does that sound?"

"Good." The waterworks didn't stop, though.

Ryan's brow furrowed. "What is it? There's something else, isn't there?"

"Yes. I was getting something out of my backpack, and I found..." I didn't want to make it real by saying it out loud.

"What? What did you find?"

"My glasses. They've been broken all to pieces; tiny little pieces! I don't know what I'm going to do!"

"It'll be okay, Savannah. I didn't even know you wore glasses. You haven't used them here on the island yet, so you must not need them much."

"I'm wearing contact lenses...disposables. The pair I have now will have to come out before much longer. I have two other pairs with me. I'll be able to wear those for about three weeks each. Then it's all over with."

"What do you mean, it's all over with? You'll be fine. So what if you can't read a newspaper? We don't have any reading material anyway. Or do you need them to see far away?"

"I need them to see *everything!*"

"Everything?"

"Yes. I'm almost legally blind. Seven weeks from now, what's going to happen to me? What am I going to do, Ryan? How am I supposed to function without my sight? How am I supposed to survive?" My words piled on top of each other as the panic refreshed and the sobs returned.

"Hey, hey, now...take it easy. Everything will be okay. You'll be okay. I'll take care of you, I promise. I won't let anything happen to you, Savannah. You'll be fine. I'm right here. I'll never leave you." His voice soothed as well as his hands on my arms.

"Do you promise?" His image blurred through the tears.

"Yes, I just told you that. I promise you. I'll take good care of you, always."

"But what kind of a life is that for you? You're going to spend every day, maybe for the rest of your life, taking care of me."

"I don't mind helping you, honey. It's certainly preferable to slowly going insane living on this island all alone, like in that Tom Hanks movie with his soccer ball. I'd much rather have you here with me, whether you can see or not. I mean, if I could, I'd wish both of us off this island and safe at our homes. Or that we'd never flown here in the first place. That way, Dave would still be alive." Ryan's voice trailed off.

There was no need to see his face to know he was sad. I gave him a heavy sigh. "I'm sorry."

"What do you have to be sorry about? It isn't your fault your glasses got broken; accidents happen. It isn't your fault we're stuck here. It's just the way things worked out, that's all. Life just threw us a serious curve ball. We'll deal with it. We'll be okay. Everything will be okay. I'll make sure of it." He kissed the top of my head a couple of times and held me tight.

Eight

After breakfast, we made our way to Dave. The area of greatest shallows we'd seen around the island's perimeter had been here, in the cove. It turned the water to turquoise. It was a nice spot for Dave, too. The area around his gravesite provided shade for us as we sat with him.

I'd brought along a fresh red flower. Fresh was a relative term. The flower was fresh in that it was intended to take the place of the three originals that blew away in the storm. That's where the whole fresh thing fell apart, much like the flower itself. The storm had torn away most of the flowers on the island, blowing them to kingdom come. This one was in sad shape, but at least it was a replacement for what was lost.

"Ryan, I have an idea. I was thinking maybe instead of flowers for Dave's grave, he might like shells."

Ryan turned, quizzically. "Shells?"

"The flowers fade away...or blow away. A shell would be more permanent. I was thinking about the conch shell over there, the one you fixed us for breakfast yesterday. It's big and pretty."

"That sounds like a good idea."

"Okay," I said, pleased he concurred. I retrieved it and positioned the shell on the grave as if it were a headstone. I buried a little in the sand for stability. "How's that? Do you think Dave would like this? Should I maybe start a collection or something?" The words came in a rush.

"It's fine, Savannah. I'm sure he likes it. And I'm sure it makes him happy knowing you care so much. You're a special person. You're always thanking me for taking care of you. But you do just as much for me, and I don't think you're fully aware of it. You're the best companion I could have ever hoped for. You make me laugh and smile and keep my spirits up. I'd be getting depressed by now if not for you. You're thoughtful, too, even to someone who's no longer with us."

"He's with us in spirit." While I believed in the words, I knew Ryan needed to hear them out loud.

"You're right, he is. We shouldn't keep waiting because the water will just get hotter, since it's shallow. It might already be uncomfortable as it is, considering the air temperature." He stood, me following suit, heading for the ocean.

I stopped at the water's edge where the wet sand proved to be slightly cooler than the dry. "I've always heard saltwater isn't good for your clothes."

"What does that mean?" He stared at me with wide eyes. "You think we should go in there naked?"

My mouth fell open. "No, of course not. But we could strip down to our underwear and leave our clothes on the beach by Dave."

Ryan's eyebrows shot up as he hesitated. "I guess that would be all right. If you're sure you're comfortable."

"Yeah, I could do that. It's pretty much a swimsuit anyway." I forced a smile, made easier by Ryan's unease. I unbuttoned my shirt, removing it as I returned to Dave. It was a bikini, nothing more. Reasonable.

Once I reached Dave, I removed my pants. After rolling my shirt, I wrapped my pants around it, tucking the clothing carefully into a shrub so nothing would blow away.

On my return trip to the ocean, I strolled by Ryan on his way to strip down and leave his clothes behind as I'd done. His shirt was already off. I smiled, averting my eyes, running a hand through my hair as we passed. My reaction must have been subconscious; I wouldn't have done it on purpose, surely.

This wasn't high school. It was a blatantly flirtatious move on my part; me, married to someone else. Ryan smiled politely, but I'd caught sight of his head tilting to check out my backside as we passed. That was okay, fair was fair. I'd noticed his muscular physique from a distance when he'd been unlikely to detect where my eyes were gazing.

Sam had given up maintaining such muscle tone about a year after the wedding, like a lot of married people. He was still sexy in his own way, and I missed him. Guilt set in. I needed to maintain my composure. Sam and I had plenty of problems, but I'd be back with him one of these days.

The farther out onto the sand I went, the easier it became to clear my mind of those thoughts. The sand was soft underfoot, but my feet burned from the heat of it. My walk turned into a jog.

"Hey, wait for me! Don't go in past your ankles until I get to you, Savannah." He waved as I glanced over my shoulder. The water lapped at my ankles, providing scant relief from the heat.

There weren't many fish in this part of the shallows, certainly nothing large enough for a meal; they were merely baitfish. Several shells lay scattered about, mostly broken pieces. The sandy bottom was relatively featureless, aside from some deeply rippled patterns created by wave action.

"Okay, let's go," Ryan came up from behind to clasp his hand snugly over mine.

"Ryan, you don't need to hold onto me, I'm fine. Thanks anyway, though."

"All right, then. But stay close to me." He planted a kiss on my cheek as he released my hand, moving ahead. "Shuffle your feet with every step. Walk where I do in case there're any stingrays hiding in the sand."

"Yikes. I hadn't thought about those." I should've thought of it; I knew better.

"They're probably not out here. It's too hot for them. They should be in deeper water."

"I'll stay right behind you, just in case." Now there'd be paranoia about stingrays. As if I needed another dangerous sea creature to worry about, especially when Ryan came out here alone. I wouldn't be of much assistance to him from the shore. And once my contacts were gone, it'd be unlikely he'd bring me into the water for fishing. But I'd still need to bathe unless he made me use the waterfall instead.

We continued a fair distance out before the water reached my waist. The waves broke farther beyond, where the water was a deeper blue, giving the illusion of being cooler. Tempting.

"Okay, Savvy. You swim first while I watch. We'll keep it to a short swim today since the water's so warm. Next time, we'll go in a few hours earlier, so it'll be cooler."

Nodding, I swished my hands through the water before pushing off to swim away. It was like a giant bathtub, my body deciding to revel in the warmth, as achy muscles soothed. I made a gradual turn toward Ryan, ducking my head under the water a couple of times to douse my hair before reaching him, then stood to wipe at my eyes as he smiled, his eyes sweeping over me.

"Now it's your turn." I couldn't help noticing how every part of him visible beyond his briefs was in amazing shape. No doubt the parts hidden from view were amazing, too. My eyes shifted to the horizon for a moment, taking a deep breath and gathering my thoughts. What was wrong with me?

Sam was at home, worrying about me, missing me. At least, I hoped so. There were doubts in me about that. I hung my head, regardless.

"Thanks. I haven't seen a sign of any trouble at all." He rested a hand on my arm before sliding it away.

He performed a little dive and swam under the water for what seemed too long. It was impressive to watch someone hold their breath the way he did. It must have been from his time in the Coast Guard. When he returned to me, he circled a couple of times, one hand sticking straight up out of the water over his head, making me laugh.

"What's so funny?" He wiped the water from his eyes, only to have more run down from his hair.

"You. You're so silly. Let's go before a real shark comes. I'll race you." I tore off with my short head start, spurred by the scorch of the sand once I got clear of the water.

Ryan blew past me before I got halfway there. We stood in the welcome shade near Dave, catching our breath. Ryan put a hand on my shoulder as he leaned in to give me a long, slow kiss on the cheek. I closed my eyes, a quiver running through my belly.

"Here, let me get your clothes out of there for you." He carefully withdrew them so they wouldn't snag on twigs and branches.

We dressed and sat down to munch on sea grapes, watching the birds flying by until the sun invaded our territory. That had us retreating to our shelter. Higher and shaded inside, it caught a better breeze and cooled our sweat-sprinkled skin.

The day was hot, as usual. I had taken to calling our adventure *The Stranding* in my journal. It would be the title of a book, provided we were rescued someday. Ryan had decided to go off spearfishing in deeper water for dinner, beyond the shallows. It was late afternoon, but still early enough to avoid worrying so much about sharks.

His reassurances didn't stop me from being unhappy about the decision, which had come after he'd promised he wouldn't do it. He claimed we needed protein. In my opinion, he craved a challenge. I leaned back where I sat by Dave.

Two of the fish traps we'd worked so hard to make over the past weeks had fallen apart and floated away. Our latest version was intact, but empty. I'd told Ryan I preferred eating fruit, but he insisted on trying to catch a fish. We'd been working on a crab trap, too, but needed bait.

I rubbed at my eyes, straining to see farther than was possible. The three weeks per pair got stretched out a little further than that. Only a few weeks remained before they were pushed beyond their limits, leaving me all but sightless and useless. I should have packed additional contacts. But I hadn't expected to be marooned, or to have my glasses smashed to bits.

"Again, Dave, I wish you were here. Maybe you could figure out how to build a better fish trap so Ryan wouldn't be risking his life out there. Or maybe you could convince him not to go in the first place. I tried. He thinks he has to do it for me, but he doesn't.

"I'd eat the palm or anything else for every meal for the rest of my days to keep him safe. I'm so afraid of something happening to him out there. We said we'd be together all the time and never go anywhere alone." The ocean beckoned.

"While he's out there, he could need me, and I wouldn't know until it's too late. We're supposed to be together, so we will be. I warned him about this already anyway, Dave." I stripped to my underwear before jogging across the searing sand to wade into the hot water.

I waded out to where the water lapped at my shoulders. I stopped, watching for Ryan. He hadn't come up for air in a while, but he could hold his breath for a ridiculously long period of time.

As I waited to catch a glimpse of him, I glanced back at the grave, although I wasn't sure why. A funny feeling had come over me, almost as if Dave was watching. Most likely, it was the thought of having to dig one of those on my own, to bury my friend and constant companion in. It wouldn't come to that.

Ryan would never come into the ocean alone again. If he tried, I'd go with him. The thought of my life potentially being in peril, especially once I lost my vision, would stop him.

To my great relief, Ryan's head broke the surface of the deep blue as I watched, shielding my eyes from the glare with one hand. He faced the ocean horizon, sliding his arms through the water to rotate his body until he aimed toward the shore, and me. He lifted his hand as if to wave, the empty spear in his grasp. No fish yet.

But he didn't finish it, his wave. Instead, he lowered his arm to the water. He continued staring at me, angling his head to peer beyond me, or around me. What was he doing? Was he looking at Dave? I remembered how I'd had a strange feeling about that myself, even though I'd never believed in ghosts.

Without any indication as to why, Ryan plunged forward, disappearing from my view. Still watching for him, I spotted the distant shadow of his body and then Ryan himself as he entered the beginnings of the shallows I stood in, where the turquoise water was deepest, at a dozen feet. I stood halfway between him and the shore.

Ryan swam toward me like a torpedo, as if he were in a race. A panic welled up in me. There must surely be a shark in pursuit of him, the way he swam. Instinctively, I took several steps backward. A shark. Why else would he be swimming so fast?

Why else, indeed? There wasn't anything coming along behind him, no shadow in pursuit, no fin breaking the water. It gradually dawned on me. Ryan was coming to my defense. There was indeed a shark, but it was after me, not Ryan. An indescribable horror welled up inside me.

THE STRANDING

Nine

Slowly, not wanting it to become a reality, I turned to see the large creature swimming smoothly through the water toward me. He was a lot bigger than me. While I'd been focused on Ryan, the shark focused on me. My eyes widened with the realization of the impending attack, or exploratory strike to be followed by an attack.

My muscles stiffened in terror as I watched the fin slicing first through the edge of the water's surface and then higher up into the air. The creature would be here in seconds. Ryan couldn't possibly make it in time. I'd have to save myself.

Instincts flew well ahead of my brain, which was paralyzed with fright. I rotated my body to face my fate, forcing patience, waiting for it to come close enough. A foot away, summoning every ounce of courage and survival instinct I possessed, I emitted a guttural yell, thrusting forward in my best attempt at an arching dive.

Essentially, I fell on the shark.

My body struck the top of it, my chest impacting the side of the creature next to the dorsal fin. As the collision occurred, I lifted my feet up high to clear the water and avoid having them become a target for the creature's mouth. That resulted in my knees smacking the snout. The blow for me was rough and jarring. The shark diverted course in a split second, thrown for a loop at the unexpected assault. Its tail flipped aside, slapping me as we passed.

Recovering, I swam with all my might toward shore, expecting at any moment to feel one of my feet embedded in the creature's sharp teeth. But the bite didn't come. I glanced back once, enough to catch sight of the shark. It had turned its attention to Ryan.

My response came without a single thought. Reversing course, I swam toward Ryan before coming to the realization that reaching him in time was impossible, just as he'd been unable to do for me. Nor did I have any way to help. I had no weapon.

I stopped swimming and stood. The water bobbed at my waist. Mentally running through everything I'd ever heard about sharks, there was only one thing I could think of doing that could possibly help. I had to try. I'd do anything to save Ryan's life.

I pounded my hands furiously against the surface of the water, attempting to gain the shark's attention by making it think I was injured. It had reached Ryan, too interested in its new target to take any notice of me. Ryan stood in water nearly to his shoulders, rotating his body with the shark, using his spear to keep the creature at bay.

The shark circled, uninterested in anything else. I hadn't fooled it with my splashing. Don't let Ryan die. The injury ploy didn't work, so what else was there? Injury needed blood. I remembered sharks were able to detect a miniscule trace of blood in the water for some incredibly ridiculous distance. I reached through the water to grab a piece of broken shell.

It took repeated gouging of the sharpest edge across the inside of my left arm near my wrist to cut through the skin. It wasn't deep, but the blood came freely regardless, producing more than I'd hoped for in the warm conditions. I immediately submerged it in the water, swirling it around, slapping the ocean's surface with my right hand. Come on stupid shark, come on! Come and get me already!

The shark circled Ryan once more before suddenly switching course to make a beeline for me. I never imagined he'd come that fast. Wide-eyed and stunned, I dropped the shell, dove into the water, and swam in a panic toward shore.

This time, the shark was coming and wouldn't stop for anything. I should've gotten closer to land before carrying out the plan. The thought of not making it filled my mind. The adrenaline surging through my body did its best to get me there, though. My arms and legs propelled me faster than I thought myself physically capable of going.

The shore seemed unattainably distant. I had to reach a shallower depth before the shark reached me. As that depth neared, swimming became difficult. Instead, it was time to run.

Scrambling to my feet, I began a race for my life, through water that slowed my movements. Glancing over my shoulder, the fearsome foe was there. Close. But he'd soon be running out of water, just as I was running out of time. The question was which would come first.

The creature was on me. I made a desperate leap forward to escape the jaws. My feet tangled, taking me to my knees. The shark got hung up briefly by the shallowness of the water and the ridges of sand. That didn't stop it, which came as a potentially fatal surprise. The creature seemed intent on reaching me somehow, struggling mightily, the strong body finding traction as he snapped his jaws toward my nearest leg.

Screaming in terror, I swung my leg clear to crawl forward in the struggle to escape; panic had me getting in my own way. The shark twisted his body repeatedly, thrashing, making progress in his approach. I shoved up and ran. A glance over my shoulder showed a change. The shark wasn't trapped; instead, he flailed about, attempting to reorient himself toward deeper water. Ryan was in deeper water.

Ryan was close, pursuing the shark. The creature performed a massive flip of its body to reverse the heading. That placed Ryan directly in its path, too focused on catching the shark before the shark caught me.

Reversing my own course, several running steps gave me momentum to lunge forward. The intention was to fall on the shark again. Instead, my hands brushed at the body.

Operating on raw instinct, I latched on as I dropped, digging my fingernails in, by the tail. To the large fish, it must be like an annoying nibble. Still, the shark jerked his body sideways toward me, his tail flipping free, knocking me onto my side.

The jaws snapped in my direction, as he pivoted to face me. Yet again, I'd succeeded in gaining his attention. This time, we faced each other, my head above the surface, pulling in a breath of air as I assessed my latest predicament. On my haunches, I retreated.

My attention was taken by Ryan, as he splashed toward the shark, covering the last few feet between himself and the creature at his best speed. In his hands, he held his spear, high over one shoulder. In a single swift arc, he thrust it into the center of the shark with all the force he could muster, piercing the body.

The shark thrashed violently, raising an underwater sandstorm, penetrated by a puff of red shooting into the water, above and below. I struggled to get clear in the shock of the moment. Ryan moved quickly, yanking me up, tugging me backward.

He stood in front of me, off to the side, his hand reaching back to touch my heaving stomach, keeping track of me, and preventing any forward movement. The creature struggled to rid itself of the spear, but without success; nor could it gain traction to swim off. Its movements slowed, ceased.

Ryan turned, wrapping his arms around me, pinning me tightly to him. A moment later, he eased back enough to meet my gaze. He glanced at my mouth before leaning in with a fast strike.

The kiss was long, our mouths open. Frantic, forceful, and passionate. His mouth on mine exhilarated, activating nerves I didn't remember having. I let go, accommodating, surrendering control. His fingers commanded, holding me tighter as his tongue slid into my mouth, caressing mine. The hardness of his body made its desires known.

A hot shudder welled up inside then passed through me, ripping into every ounce of flesh along the way. I thrust my body hard against his, wanting that closest of contact between a man and a woman. One of his hands slid low on my back, pulling me in closer. The hand slipped lower still as my heart pounded.

In that moment, I had never needed any man more. I wanted Ryan to carry me away and never, ever let go. I ran my hands over his muscular shoulders and into his hair, forcing his lips into an imprisoning lock against mine. His kiss enveloped me, shutting out everything else.

Ryan broke the kiss, giving us both an opportunity to gulp in oxygen, but leaving me hungry for more. Our eyes remained locked on one another as he rubbed his thumb tenderly across my lips and over my cheek, sliding around to lock onto the back of my neck. I tilted my head, parting my lips to meet his, stretching myself up to reach what I wanted. This kiss was more deliberate, more sensual, slow, and probing, his hands moving over my body, raising my internal temperature until the vision of catching on fire entered my mind.

It took more time than it should have for clarity to come to my mind. I remembered I awaited rescue. I remembered my husband, the man who had never made me feel this way. I turned my face downward to break the moment building between us before it became something even my moral compass couldn't stop. That *something* was exceptionally close.

Ryan kissed my forehead, releasing his grip. He turned to drag the shark's body closer to shore, but it wasn't much farther than where the creature died. I tried but was almost no help at all.

"Bring me my knife, Savannah," Ryan ordered, without looking up.

I jogged to Dave to retrieve the implement from where Ryan left it, returning to him to hand over the knife. "Here you go."

Ryan glanced up as he took the knife, muttering a hasty thanks. He set to work cutting up the shark; swishing a piece in the water to rinse off blood and holding it out to me. I reached for it, but he pulled it away, dropping it in the water, forgotten. He stabbed the knife into the shark and left it there as he stood.

"Show me your arms." His face wore a question mark.

I did as he asked, knowing what he'd seen. It was a simple matter to tell when he found it. He turned my left wrist to examine the cut.

"What happened? Did the shark bite you?" His words came fast, his brow deeply furrowed. His finger rubbed the injury tenderly, exploring it.

"No. I did it. I cut myself with a broken shell."

"Why did you do that?" He was perplexed, not putting the pieces together.

"I...I needed blood to lure the shark away from you."

"You're kidding me, Savannah. What were you thinking?"

"I had to. It was all I could come up with at the time. And it worked," I wrapped up a quick defense.

"It almost got you killed. I don't ever want you to do anything like that again and I mean it. I've got a piece of cloth in the pocket of my pants. Go get it and bring it to me so I can wrap your arm."

I nodded affirmatively, leaving him to his work. I retrieved the strip of cloth and took it to him. He gently rinsed my arm with saltwater, kissed the cut, then wrapped it carefully.

"I can't believe you did that for me," he said in a voice that didn't sound strong anymore and eyes that brimmed with tears.

"I'd do anything for you, Ryan."

He kissed the palm of my hand and let me go. "Please don't ever put your life in danger for me again."

"But you'd do it for me in a heartbeat. You already did."

"You said you'd do anything for me, Savannah. Staying safe is what I want you to do for me. I'd do anything in this world for you, but you have to stay safe. For God's sake, please. Now, go on up by Dave and get a fire going if you can while I cut more meat. I'll leave it sitting here in the water until you get everything ready."

He didn't look at me while he spoke. His words were clipped, an edge to them as he jabbed the knife into the shark with a rough motion. I took a few steps backward, not understanding, until I realized he had no intention of meeting my gaze. There was little point in remaining, so I left to set up the fire pit.

After dressing and gathering materials, I made a decent fire before returning to Ryan for chunks of meat. The portions of shark were skewered and positioned to hang over the fire. I returned twice more for additional meat to roast. When I left him, he was cutting up more to use for an attempt at making jerky, and as bait for attracting crabs or fish.

Later that evening, after gorging ourselves on shark steaks, we watched the stars emerge, one by one. The fire had died out. A second one, farther out on the beach, was where the jerky cooked, a long, slow process. It was glowing, the way he'd said he wanted it. Ryan seemed focused on the expanse of twinkling stars overhead, lost in thought.

The same flowed through me. We'd hardly spoken a word to each other. Things were awkward since we'd kissed. There was a profound attraction that had been growing steadily between us, but I thought I'd be able to control myself. There was a measure of guilt to be carried, even though there'd been extenuating life and death circumstances involved. But I had to make sure it didn't happen again.

Perhaps the biggest problem was that there was more than a mere physical attraction involved. I'd been waiting all these weeks for rescue so I could resume the life I had before. But now I wondered if that could happen after what Ryan and I had been through. My feelings for him were deeper than I'd ever imagined they could become.

The events and time spent with Ryan had changed me. In such a short time, my connection to him had grown stronger than I'd ever felt with Sam. I had no idea how to forget about Ryan, to let him go, how to deal with it all. Yet, I had to be ready. Not to forget about him, but to let him go. We would be rescued at some point, after all.

"Ryan." My voice boomed after the sustained silence.

His head turned to me, his fingers stretching to brush against mine. "What is it, sweetheart?"

This wouldn't be easy. "We need to talk about what happened between us, after the shark."

He looked away at that, his smile faded, his fingers sliding from mine. He sighed audibly in the darkness, illuminated by a quarter moon. "I know."

"Hey, it's okay, you know," I said. "We were caught up in the moment. We've grown close to each other; it was natural something like that might happen after nearly being killed."

"I still can't believe you did that, Savvy."

I slid closer to him. "We saved each other. It's what we do now. We take care of each other—we have to. But you have to promise me you'll never go into the deep water again; not for any reason."

"I won't, I promise." He rubbed his hand along mine.

"I'm going to make sure you keep it this time, too. If you ever go out there again, I'll be right behind you, just like today." I sat up, glaring in the moonlight.

"Savvy, before long you won't be able to see *where* I go." He put a hand behind his head.

"That won't stop me. Don't you go thinking for a minute that it will." He had to be made to understand how serious I was.

"It'll be too dangerous for you. You'll get yourself killed,

Savannah."

"Then it's up to you to make sure I *don't* get killed. I'll do whatever it takes to keep you safe, Ryan," I said firmly as I stood, my jaw set. I wiped the sand from my backside, my hands moving to my hips then.

"I guess that means no more spearfishing. I'd never do anything to purposefully put your life at risk." He sat up to poke at the warm rocks, the glow gone. He scooped in a few handfuls of sand and stood, brushing at the clinging sand. "Let's get back to the cave-port before it gets any later. We both need a good night's sleep after what happened today. And we need to get back here early to keep the seagulls from stealing our jerky."

We left the meat, concealed by branches and palm fronds, and made our way along the familiar path to the shelter, silent the entire way.

Ten

Ryan yawned, fingering his beard as the sun rose over the ocean. We were next to Dave, as was the case most mornings. Ryan had tossed and turned a lot during the night; I hadn't slept much myself. I couldn't stop thinking about everything that happened yesterday.

"Are you close to your parents?" I asked, for want of conversation.

"Yes. You?"

He didn't seem in a talkative mood. "Very much. I miss them. I used to call them at least once a week. And I got them to where we could video chat and text."

"That's excellent; mine don't use video chat, but they text. They live in Gilroy, California, same as me. In fact, they still live in the house I grew up in. The real estate prices there are crazy. My sister and I inherited our grandparents' home when they passed. It's a bungalow in an up-and-coming neighborhood; I bought out my sister's half interest in the place and I've been renovating it on weekends and holidays. When we get out of here, I'll show it to you." He hesitated then. "You'll visit me, won't you?"

I'd been trying to find something innocuous to discuss. I hadn't considered that the conversation might take an unexpected turn. I swallowed before answering. "Naturally. Like you'll visit me someday. We'll go to the National Mall in Washington and see the museums."

The silence returned for a couple of minutes.

"Do you think your husband will let us see each other? Would he let you fly out to California to spend time with me?"

"I honestly don't know, Ryan." That hadn't even been on my radar.

"I wouldn't."

The words shocked me. "You mean you wouldn't trust me?"

"I'd trust you. I wouldn't trust *him*, the other guy. The man you went through so much with. Life and death situations change people. Not to mention us having been alone together for so long. And there's no telling how long it'll be by the time we're rescued." Ryan paused to clear his throat. "But don't worry; they're going to find us any day now. Don't lose hope."

"I won't." But it had already begun to come over me, reality seeping in around the edges.

"I'll check the traps. Crab would be a nice start to the day, wouldn't it?"

"Yes, it would," I drug up what passed for a smile. "Always is."

He removed everything except his boxers and headed toward the water.

"Give me a wave if you've got something and I'll start the fire," I said to his back.

Ryan threw me a wave over his shoulder. "I'm sure we'll have something, using that shark for bait. Go ahead and get everything ready."

His first action came in taking a big run at the seagulls feasting on the shark carcass at the edge of the water. They scattered, complaining about the disruption. Ryan left them, angling to where we'd left the crab trap in the shallows.

He was bound to be right about the bait, so I prepared the fire pit, arranging everything in time for Ryan's wave. I returned it before entering the jungle for firewood. After today's breakfast, we should venture in together and stockpile a sizeable supply on the beach, maybe enough to last us a week or two.

The jungle held its own unique sights and sounds. The leaves and flowers had made a substantial recovery since the last cyclone stripped many of them nearly bare. Indeed, they were in overdrive, the hurricane having ramped up the production of flowers and fruits in case the parent plants were to die from the stress brought on by the storms. Our food pickings had been slim for a while, but enough survived that we did, too.

Small birds and butterflies flitted about in search of breakfast. The jungle teemed with life. Today though, for some reason I couldn't discern, the hair on the back of my neck stood on end as I reached beneath a dense shrub for a piece of wood. The sensation was so strong, I abandoned it and headed out of there fast.

The ocean was visible through the trees close to the exit I sought, but something unexpected on the path made me stop.

What are *you* doing in here?" I asked the seagull. "I hate you.

Seagulls, I mean. Maybe you're not one of the guilty ones, but then again, maybe you are. You or your kind killed people, you know. Dave was a good person. He didn't deserve to die. Neither did Alphonse. Why don't you go away, before I ask Ryan if seagulls are edible? I'll bet you are. You probably taste like chicken. I like chicken." I glared at it, hoping to cause it fear.

The bird remained in my path, looking up at me with blatant curiosity, and perhaps innocence. Seagulls didn't live in jungles, right? So why was this one here? I'd have to ask Ryan. This was strange. A second one flew in, landing near the first.

Cautiously, they approached me, passing off to my left, disappearing into the dense vegetation behind me, where I'd felt so unnerved. It made no sense. Perhaps they were a mated pair with a nest in there. Still, it was strange. Was it even nesting season?

My hair stood on end again, or still. It was inexplicable, instinctive. Something was wrong and I needed to get into the open, to the beach. Shaking my head, I emerged from the jungle as Ryan came along, crabs in hand. They struggled to pinch flesh for a chance at a drop to freedom in the sand.

"Hey, it looks like the trap worked. They're at least as big as those first two you caught right after we got here." My glands salivated at the sight.

"Yeah, it worked great. I hope you won't get tired of crab. The trap was packed with them. I threw the little ones out, but there're still enough big ones to keep us happy for the next few days."

"I'm certainly up for it."

As the crabs cooked, I decided to ask about my curious interaction in the jungle. "Ryan, while I was in the jungle gathering wood for the fire, a weird thing happened."

"And what would that be?" He poked at the roasting crabs with a stick.

"Two seagulls flew in there. They landed on the path right in front of me. They stared at me and then walked on by and disappeared into the underbrush."

He stopped what he was doing to look at me. "Seriously? You're right. That is weird." Ryan's forehead creased.

"That's what I thought."

"I wonder what they're doing in there?" He stared past me, into the jungle.

"Could they have a nest, maybe?" It was the only explanation I could think of.

"I suppose so. But I don't know for sure. As soon as we've finished eating, let's go check. Maybe I could fix us eggs with a side of crab for breakfast tomorrow. How does that sound?"

"Oh, wow. That would be great! You run the best restaurant you know. I think you missed your calling."

"I'm glad you approve." He returned to monitoring the crabs.

After consuming the crabs with a side of seaweed, we went into the jungle in search of seagulls. "They were right here."

"Are you sure about that?" He sounded skeptical.

"I am. Look, over here. You can see their tracks." I pointed to the spot.

Ryan kneeled. "I see. It looks like you weren't imagining it after all."

"You thought I was losing it, didn't you? Like Tom Hanks."

"Maybe." He grinned up at me.

"That's not funny," I responded, placing my fists on my hips.

"Yes, it is." He stood, patting my shoulder. "Let's follow them."

"Straight through there." I motioned toward the dense brush.

"Yep, that's where the tracks lead." Ryan hesitated, rubbing a hand through his hair.

"So, what are you waiting for?" I asked. It was unclear to me why he'd halted, studying the barrier ahead. I figured he would've simply plowed on in.

"Hey, I'm a gentleman. Ladies first." He gestured toward the undergrowth with a bow, stepping aside.

I raised an eyebrow. "Really? After everything you've done to protect me all this time, you think you're going to get me to believe you'd let me walk in there ahead of you?"

He laughed at that. "Okay, okay. You've got me. I'll go in and you wait here."

"No way. I'm going with you. I want to see this for myself. It's cool to have a mystery to solve, especially since it's not life-threatening."

"Suit yourself," he said, leading the way in.

"Do seagulls build a nest or are they one of those birds that lay their eggs in the sand? I know there're some coastal ones who do that, at least back in the United States."

"They make real nests, as far as I know, anyway. If there's one in here, it might be hidden. This is odd behavior. I've never heard of them walking into a jungle before. They tend to hang around in large groups when they nest for the whole safety in numbers thing." Ryan lifted the low-hanging branch of an overgrown bush.

"It's strange that they weren't afraid of me. They marched right past me, like they were being called or something. Could their eggs have hatched, and they heard their chicks chirping?" I peered under a mass of vegetation, unwilling to stick my hand in it. No telling what might be in there.

"Maybe they haven't seen people before, so they aren't afraid. Maybe they were intrigued by you."

"Maybe." My trepidation grew by leaps and bounds, even though Ryan was with me. Something didn't seem right.

Once we were in even denser vegetation, we searched with greater caution. Ryan checked low for a nest while I studied tree branches. The seagulls themselves seemed to have vanished. We explored with no luck.

Then I found something I wasn't looking for. "Dang it! I walked right into a huge spider web. Please come over here to check me and make sure I don't have a spider on me, Ryan."

As he approached, he shook his head, grinning.

"I couldn't help it, you know. It wasn't my fault," I said in self-defense. "It's dark in here with all these plants. It's hard to see a spider web without the light to hit it exactly right."

"I know. Turn around for me, nice and easy, so I can take a good look."

I did as he asked me to, rotating slowly to give him a chance to examine me everywhere. I despised a spider crawling on me, or even the thought that there *might* be one. And the sticky, stubborn webbing was providing me with lots of those thoughts.

"Hold still for a second and let me check through that soft, silky hair of yours."

He ran his hands through my hair as I continued wiping the web from my face, arms, and shirt. Even when there couldn't possibly be another shred remaining, more of it became readily apparent whenever I moved. I'd be feeling this one long after it was gone. And good luck on sleeping soundly tonight. It would never happen. Ryan lifted my hair in one hand to run his fingers across my hairline.

"Now I know how a fly feels." It was impossible to keep my feet in one position.

"Try to hold still for a minute, Savvy."

"This is so gross." My anxieties spread to other parts of my body.

"The spider web or me?"

"You silly man! The spider web, naturally. Are you sure he's not on me?"

"Relax, I'm still searching. Like you just pointed out, it's kind of dark in here."

"You need to hurry up; you're taking too long. This is freaking me out. My skin is crawling. I'm scared he's on me."

"Hey, I'm not going to go too fast. I'm taking my time on purpose. You can't rush something like this. I have to be thorough. You don't want to risk me missing it, do you?"

"No, of course not." I gave him a few more seconds, which was fast approaching all I could tolerate. "Maybe I should go jump in the ocean."

"What if he gets an air pocket and he's still on you when you come out? Or maybe he'll bite you for revenge when you try to drown him."

"I can't take this anymore!" I knew he was trying to be funny and put me at ease, but his manner of doing so wasn't working. I shoved past him to run back to Dave, where I began stripping off my clothes, managing to stop myself at my underwear.

"Whoa. This looks like a much better idea, Savvy," Ryan commented as he followed me, beaming.

"Okay, now check me, out here in the sun." I backed away from him until I stood fully illuminated by the sunlight, extending my arms out of the way.

"I know you're married and all, Savvy, but I check you out every time we go swimming. That body of yours is killing me. You know that don't you?" His eyes were moving all over me, slowly taking in every inch of me now that I'd given him permission.

"Just look for the stupid spider, please." I lifted my hair for him.

"Okay, okay. I'm playing with you, you know."

"Play later, after you've made sure he's not on me. I hate spiders."

"I'd never have guessed. Just try to hold still this time."

"I'll try, but it won't be easy." My feet remained jittery, and not just due to the sand's temperature.

He walked around, looking me up and down, lightly trailing a hand along the bare skin of my abdomen as he went. If I weren't so concerned about the spider, I'd be experiencing a completely different sensation. In fact, both fear and excitement flooded through me simultaneously. Why did I have to be stranded with such a good-looking a man? But the attraction between us had developed over time and through surviving shared experiences.

"I don't see anything, but I'll need to explore your hair for a little while." He hesitated, eyes narrowing in thought. "You don't feel anything inside your underwear, do you?"

"Oh my God! Why did you have to say that? I wasn't kidding when I said I hate spiders, Ryan." I dropped my hair, my arms slapping to my sides just before my fists clenched.

"I know you weren't. It was just a concern. We don't know anything about the spiders here. I have no idea if any of them might be poisonous."

"Great. More information I didn't need to hear right now. Check me, then."

"What do you mean?"

"You know what I mean. Check me."

Ryan had moved to stand in front of me, his eyebrows shooting up with surprise. "Are you serious?"

"Yes, I'm serious."

His mouth fell open. "Well, okay. You do realize I don't have anywhere I can go for a cold shower after this, don't you?"

"Come on, Ryan. Be serious."

"I *am* being serious. It astounds me that you can't figure out how badly I want to be with you."

"Okay then. Never mind, I'll do it myself. I'm sorry, I guess I wasn't thinking." I turned away and immediately felt his hands on my back.

"Hold still for a minute. You can't check back here. I can do it, I promise. Lift your hair for me."

I did as he asked, moving my hair clear. Ryan ran his fingers past my shoulder blades and under the straps of my bra, down to their ends. He paused to run a finger over the hooks. A strong shiver ran through me as his fingers slid forward, brushing the edge of my breasts.

His head lay near mine, his warm, rapid breaths blowing on my neck. He delivered a delicate kiss to my right shoulder. My resolve shook.

His fingertips leisurely descended my back, raising my heartrate. Then they slipped into the top of my underpants. He lowered them, running his hands up along my hips and down over my rear, caressing it far more than the simple search for a random arachnid intruder called for. I closed my eyes, feeling my control fleeing.

I'd allowed my excessive fears to take over without giving the idea any logical consideration. Over the time we'd been here, I'd done my best to ignore that I was stranded on a deserted island with an attentive, attractive man, his appeal growing by the day, if not the hour. And I had to go and *ask* him to fondle me. Was there a brighter woman than me, anywhere? I doubted it.

"Okay, Ryan, thanks. That's good enough," I sputtered, pulling up my underpants as I took a step away from him, as his warm breath made the first hint of contact where his hands had just been.

"What about your front? If I was a spider, that's where I'd go. There're lots of interesting places to crawl up inside of…"

I cut him off. "I don't think he could get into my underwear anyway. It's tight enough to keep insects out, I'm sure." I reached down and readjusted the undergarment. "I should've thought of that in the first place instead of panicking. And I think I should examine my front on my own. Thanks for checking, though." I didn't dare turn around. I couldn't let him see the expression on my face. If he did, he'd know how close we came.

"You're welcome. Let me know if you change your mind. I was looking forward to inspecting the rest of you, considering how sexy your backside is," he whispered in my ear, his lips lightly brushing over. His hands rested on my hips. "You're absolutely incredible. Do you know that?"

I couldn't take it anymore. I closed my eyes, leaning into him, my heart hammering. "Ryan."

"What is it, baby?" he whispered so softly I almost missed it.

His lips nuzzled my earlobe before he kissed his way down my neck, then along my shoulder. My body pressed against him as his hands slid around to a position low on my abdomen. He hooked his fingers inside the top of my underpants as a deep sigh escaped my lips of its own volition. It was too late; I'd lost whatever control I'd fooled myself into thinking I had. I wanted him desperately.

At that moment, the unruly squawking of seagulls, accompanied by the snapping and crashing of vegetation came from behind us. Startled, we both turned to look back.

"Get down!" Ryan shoved me to the sand, covering me with his body, as a pair of agitated seagulls emerged from the jungle, aiming for our heads.

"Shit!" Ryan exclaimed angrily.

"What was that all about?" I asked, alarm creeping into my voice.

"Stay here and get your clothes on, fast," Ryan ordered, leaving me as he arrowed into the jungle.

I dressed quickly and waited for his return, pacing. Several minutes passed as fear and nervousness vied for my attention. The jungle revealed nothing beyond green and shadow. Spooky could be justifiably added to that description. Pacing became a coping mechanism. When Ryan emerged from the darkness to the beach, I nearly tripped over my own feet as I ran to meet him.

"What was that all about?" I asked. "What did you find?"

"Nothing. Those birds were in the jungle, like you said, where they don't belong. And then they came out of there like bats out of hell, like something was after them, like they were scrambling for their lives."

My eyes widened and I retreated two slow steps backward. "Do you think there's some kind of an animal in there, maybe something we haven't seen yet? Did it try to catch the seagulls?"

"I don't know, Savvy. If there was one, I didn't find it. But this doesn't make any sense. There's a trail of broken vegetation leading away from here to the north, like something took off out of here in a hurry. I don't think you and I made all that mess when we were searching for those birds, but we might've. I'd like to follow the trail, but I'm not taking you with me and I won't leave you here alone." He glanced over his shoulder into the jungle.

My eyes followed his gaze.

"One thing I know for sure is that you're not to go in there alone again. Not for any reason. Not even for a little firewood near the edge or a flower for the grave. Do you understand me?"

"Yes. I understand. I won't do it, don't worry." A deep stab of primal fear chilled me to my core. "What's going on around here?"

"I don't know. Maybe it was nothing. But until I find out for sure, one way or another..." He didn't offer to finish his sentence.

"I kind of wish we had a gun right about now," I said.

"Yeah, me too. I'll carve a couple more knives and show you how to use them. And I'll make you a spear of your own. Until then, you'll stay by my side at all times, no matter what. At least until I'm comfortable we're not in danger. Like I said, it was probably nothing," he added when he saw the fright etched on my face, my body trembling. He took one of my hands in his and I clasped my other hand over it. Even the hurricanes weren't as frightful as this.

"Let's go back home, Savvy. I'll get my spear while you grab the jerky. That'll be for lunch, with seaweed. It'll keep us in a safe, defensible spot. We'll come back for more crab for dinner way before it gets dark. We'll be more careful with everything we do for a while, until I've figured out what we might be up against."

Eleven

A few days passed uneventfully. There'd been no trace of any sizeable animals, at least not along our regularly traveled paths. We were careful to stick to those religiously. I'd grown concerned that if there were potentially dangerous animals around, they might try to dig up the grave. I hadn't shared my worry of that with Ryan. It made one less thing for him to fret over.

I'd been sitting outside the cave-port since I woke up. I made sure to stay close by, so that Ryan couldn't help but see me as soon as he opened his eyes. There was no point in throwing him into a panic. He worried about me so much already.

We hadn't spoken about how close we came to making love on the beach the other day. I was grateful for that. Ryan had been hyper-focused, constantly on the alert ever since, more concerned with our safety than anything else. He didn't sleep much at night, preferring to watch over me while I slept. During the daytime, he'd take a nap or two, but still wasn't getting anywhere near enough sleep.

"I wish you wouldn't come out here without me, Savvy." Ryan's sleepy, reproachful, voice sounded behind me as he crawled out.

"I'm being careful to keep a close lookout. Plus, I have my knife with me." I held up his latest wooden carving so he could see it. He'd made the handle so that it fit my hand perfectly, with a curve at the end to help it wrap around and stay in my grip more securely.

He stood, surveying the terrain while he stretched. "I'm glad to see that, but I still worry."

"I know you do. Do you think we'll have more crabs for breakfast today?" I turned my face up to him.

"You're changing the subject. Besides, aren't you tired of crab by now?"

My eyebrow rose as a smile played about my lips. "Is that even humanly possible?"

His lips curved to the sky. "Probably not. Let's go see what we've got." He grabbed his spear and led the way down the hill.

"You need more sleep than what you've been getting. Maybe you could take a long nap after breakfast. I'll keep watch and wake you up for lunch."

"I'm fine, Savvy. You don't need to worry about me. Why don't you tell me about your daughter instead?"

That surprised me. There hadn't been a lot of extraneous conversation since the seagulls nearly knocked us down in their escape from the jungle. Those birds had been frightened out of their minds.

Like me.

"She looks like her dad, dark hair and eyes and I think she's going to be taller than me. Sam's a big guy. She's smart, too, and older than her years. She's constantly surprising me with her observations on people or the world."

"I don't know anything about the kind of man your husband is, aside from the fact that he's obviously got good taste. And he's the luckiest man on the face of the earth and probably has no clue about it, the good-for-nothing..." his voice quickly trailed off, leaving me with a frown.

Ahead of me, Ryan continued mumbling in an angry whisper. He shook his head sharply from side to side, as if to clear his thinking. "Anyway, I'll bet we'll find something nice for breakfast. Good thing we like fruit since there's so much that's ripe just now."

"I'd have starved by now if not for you, Ryan. Thanks for that."

He took my hand as we reached the bottom of the slope to help me over the edge. "You're welcome. I'm glad I'm here to take care of you. I owe you my life. You saved me from going over the cliff with the helicopter."

"Like we've said before, Ryan, we saved each other then."

The day passed slowly into a long, sleepless night, as I thought about Ryan's cross words for Sam. There were issues plaguing my marriage, or Ryan and I wouldn't have come so close to making love. I'd wondered lately about the inattention from Sam, almost as though I were a friend rather than his wife. I wished I was home so we could talk things through. Instead, I was left wondering about what kind of future we might have, should rescue come someday.

"So, what's the first trivia question for today, Savvy?" Ryan asked jovially as he crawled from the cave-port to sit beside me.

Concerns about a potentially vicious wild animal were gone now, after more than a week with no indications of any kind of threat. Ryan slept through the past night soundly. But his question struck a nerve, and I wasn't sure why.

"Trivia question? Am I your entertainment director, Ryan?" I asked with a note of irritation.

He hesitated. "You're not mad, are you? I was kidding. I like the questions you bring up. They help pass the time."

"The whole reason for them is that I don't like sitting around in silence all day and it helps me get to know you better."

"I understand that. I like getting to know you better, too. I want to learn everything there is to know about you, Savannah."

I gave him a skeptical glance before focusing my attention back to the jungle below, rather than responding.

"Hey." He nudged my arm playfully with his shoulder. "Are you all right? I honestly didn't mean anything by it."

"I know you didn't; it's okay. I'm feeling kind of moody right now. I don't want to talk about anything." I hesitated, trying to sort out what was going on in my head. "I'm going to go down to the beach and sit by Dave for a while. I'll see you later."

"Wait a minute." He grabbed my arm to stop me as I attempted to rise. "I don't want you going off anywhere alone, you know that. In fact, a week ago we agreed on it."

Instead of allowing the situation to escalate, I decided to try explaining. "Yes, but I'm not going into the water. I'm going to sit and watch it. I need to be by myself for a while. I have to."

"What do you mean, you have to? You might want to, but you don't *have* to. And I'm not going to let you. Tell me what's going on. I'm worried about you, Savannah. You look sad."

"I guess I am sad. I want to go off by myself and think. I enjoy watching the ocean. It soothes me. And I like talking to Dave. I realize he doesn't hear me and that he can't respond, but..."

"That's right, he can't. But I can. I'm here, right here with you, Savannah. It's just the two of us and we need to lean on each other. There's no way in hell I'm letting you out of my sight when you're like this, so you can forget it. If you want to go off someplace alone, you'd better tell me what's going on inside that head of yours." He released my arm, standing. Clearly, he meant to physically prevent me from going.

"Ryan, in a few days, I'll have to remove my contact lenses. It'll leave me all but blind for the rest of my life if we're never rescued. I'm sorry, but you can't possibly understand what that means for me. I'm not even sure I understand it fully." I stood slowly.

"I'll be defenseless...and useless. And then there's my emotional state. I won't get to watch the waves breaking, or clearly see a sunset, or sunrise, or look at the stars. I love looking at the night sky; I always have. I won't even be able to tell where I'm putting my feet when I walk, or see what I touch, or the expressions on your face. I'm going to miss seeing your face most of all."

"Your vision's going to be impaired, Savannah...badly, I know. But you won't be blind." He rested a hand on my shoulder, rubbing it.

"I wish I could make you understand, but I can't. There's no way for you to...*see* what it's like." A tear rolled down my cheek and I angrily swiped it away. "I'm going to go down to the beach now, alone. In fact, for the next day or two, I'm going to do what I want, when I want. It's the last of my independence. After that, I'll be totally reliant on you for absolutely everything. I'll see you later." I stormed off, and he let me go.

I hadn't even realized all those feelings and fears were bottled up inside. I'd been focusing on something far more pleasant, getting to know Ryan, instead of thinking about my vision and the massive loss approaching. It hit me fast and hard, leaving me adrift and alone and I didn't know what to do.

When I reached my destination, I stood by the grave rather than sitting, to see the ocean better. "Dave, I wish you were still here. I wish you'd made it. I didn't know you all that well, but I liked you. And to have such a great friend as Ryan is, you must've been a wonderful person.

"I'd sure like to hear your advice right now. I feel like I'm losing my mind. I don't know how I'm going to survive without being able to see. People do it every day, but not on a deserted island in a foreign country. I've never been through anything like this before.

"Ryan will take good care of me, I know that. I couldn't think of anyone better. To be perfectly honest, I don't know that even my husband would be as attentive and as good at taking care of me as Ryan will be. In fact, I'm sure of it. But what kind of a life is that for him? He didn't sign up for any of this."

"But if I could have, I would have."

I turned to see Ryan striding over to me. He wrapped his arms around me and pulled me close for a bear hug. It started me crying. I didn't want to, but I couldn't seem to stop it. Ryan held me, rubbing my back, patiently waiting. Once I'd gotten ahold of myself, I tried pushing away, but the enveloping grip remained too tight for that.

"I'm not going to let go of you, not ever," he whispered in my ear.

I returned his hug, realizing I didn't want to be alone after all. "Thank you. I'm sorry for how I acted. I'm upset and afraid. I wasn't thinking about how lucky I am to have you in my life." I nestled my face up into the base of his neck and applied a quick kiss there.

"That's funny. I was just thinking that I'm the lucky one out of the two of us."

All I could think was that Ryan was one of the best men on the planet. He was my friend, my provider, my protector, and despite hoping for rescue, I wanted more. But both of us were with other people. I'd never be able to make myself forget about those kisses, or the rest of it.

"How about we go find out if we're both lucky enough to have caught a fish in our latest trap?" I smiled, pushing back from him while taking his hand in my own and tugging. "Come on, let's go see."

He chuckled as we strolled toward the ocean.

Dawn was on the verge of breaking. I'd been lying still so I wouldn't awaken Ryan. I'd been watching him as the light in our cave-port home had grown steadily brighter, determined to memorize his face, every feature, every detail.

That way, once I removed my contact lenses, I wouldn't have to get awkwardly close to see him. I'd be able to see him in my memory instead. As I studied him, I couldn't help smiling. He looked so peaceful when he was asleep. His beard contained a little wedge of gray over his chin. It was difficult to see, though, amongst the blond that had grown in much lighter than the hair on his head.

Without thinking about it, I reached out and stroked his cheekbone with my fingertips, barely touching his skin. His eyelids fluttered open at my touch. He smiled warmly, taking my hand in his to lift it to his lips for a tender kiss. This man was easily the best friend I'd ever had.

"Good morning, Savvy. Did you have trouble sleeping?"

"A little, not too bad."

"Why didn't you wake me up? I told you to wake me up if you couldn't sleep," he admonished gently, rubbing my hand, and kissing it again.

"I know, but I didn't want to disturb you. I enjoyed watching you sleep."

He smoothed my hair back from my face. "You never disturb me. I want to help you. What did you do, lie here and stare at my face all night?"

I smiled. "No. I went outside."

"Where'd you go? You know I don't want you going off anywhere alone." He was instantly worried, upset about something out of his control and long since over.

"I didn't go anywhere. I sat right outside, a couple of feet away. I wanted to watch the stars one last time. There were meteors, too. It was kind of like they were a parting gift, just for me. It was great."

He sighed in obvious relief. "I wish you'd woken me up, so I could've sat with you. You're not alone in this, Savvy. I'm always here for you."

"I know that, I honestly do. Listen, could we talk about this later?

Right now, I want to watch my last sunrise. Will you come with me?"

"Of course."

Ryan crawled out first, me close on his heels. We stood together, Ryan's arm around my waist, watching as the horizon brightened. There weren't any clouds, so the sunrise was ordinary, which was perfect. I'd still be able to see future ones that had clouds to color. Birds flew by, searching for food. The newly risen sun glinted brilliant beams off the ocean, the waves and swells sparkling like they'd been sprinkled with thousands of diamonds.

"Are you ready to go foraging for breakfast like these birds are doing?" Ryan asked.

"Yeah. I'm hungry."

"Let's go see what we can find then."

As we walked down the hill, Ryan pointed out places where he was going to have to be extra-careful of with me, starting tomorrow. He was worried about me experiencing a dangerous spill that might result in injury.

"This is a tricky spot. Hold on for a second and we'll try it out."

He hopped down to the small, rocky bottom of the hill. Above that was a twelve-inch vertical drop. Yes, twelve whole inches. How would I ever manage it? His concern made me smile.

"From now on when we get here, I want you to wait and let me go first. Then I'll lift you down. When we come back, I'll lift you up from behind. How does that sound, Savvy?"

My head was already shaking slowly from side to side as I chuckled. "Ryan, you won't need to help me this much. It's a foot."

"So, you mean you'll be able to judge the distance correctly and navigate it safely in both directions, all without being able to see clearly?" Granted, I'd only known him for a couple of months, but he *had* to be wearing the most skeptical face he possessed.

"It would be helpful to have you guide me going down. But you don't need to carry me around or anything like that. I'll be able to do most of it on my own, including this. Honest. I want to do as much of it as I can. I need to."

He fisted his hands on his hips and issued a particularly loud sigh, staring at the ground. He turned his face up to me then, exasperated.

He was overprotective of me before this. I should have expected him to ramp it up.

"Savannah." It wasn't spoken as a question. It was more like a statement of fact. His voice was flat, and he made the name sound heavy.

He didn't call me Savvy. And he used my name as a sentence. From my time growing up, and from being a parent myself, I knew immediately what that meant.

"I would much prefer to carry you everywhere for the rest of our lives than to risk even the most remote chance of you breaking an ankle, or even stubbing your toe. I don't happen to care about your sense of decorum or pride or your concern for my wellbeing or anything else. I am completely unwilling to take a chance on letting *anything* happen to you *ever*. Do I make myself clear?"

That was harsh, in my opinion. Yet, I would have said the same to him if our roles were reversed. As he was speaking, a grin blossomed on my face...I couldn't help it.

"Did you find something I said funny?" Judging from his expression, I'd say he was the opposite of amused.

It was hard to rein in my smile sufficiently for a response. "No sir, nothing at all."

As he reached a hand up to me, I hopped down beside him without accepting the assistance. I popped up on my toes and gave him a kiss on the cheek. "You are so very sweet."

I proceeded into the jungle, with Ryan close behind.

An hour later, we feasted on a small, yet plump, fish. Our latest fish trap finally worked. Our hopes for dinner would be realized; the shark meat had attracted a continuing bounty of crabs.

"You are such a wonderful cook," I told him, licking my fingers.

"Thank you. I'm glad you approve of *something* I do."

Clearly, he remained upset, so I didn't respond. After my last bite, I walked to the ocean to rinse my hands and mouth. Then I stood with my arms crossed, staring at the surf.

Ryan walked past me a moment later to swirl his hands in the edge of a lapping wave. He remained there, allowing them to drip dry as he took in the horizon. He was probably worried about me even more than I was. My problem would add to his responsibilities, but he'd never let me down, not even a little.

I had to say or do something to break the tension between us, but I didn't know what. I couldn't come up with anything effective or meaningful, so I positioned myself in front of him. Then I put my arms around his waist and hugged myself close. He immediately returned the gesture.

"I'm sorry, Ryan. I keep thinking about tomorrow. I like who I am, even though I get on your nerves sometimes. But I know that starting tonight, I'll be a different person. I'm scared."

He rubbed his hands along the length of my back. "What do you mean, you'll be a different person? Just because you can't see well, it won't change who you are."

"It *will* change me. Not only will I miss a lot of things around me, like the sunsets, but I'll be timid, afraid to do anything, even take a step. And I won't be able to help you much anymore. Of course, I've already been relying on you for almost everything anyway, so I guess that won't be much of a change after all. I don't contribute my fair share as it is. And I'm sorry about that, by the way." I hung my head, feeling guilty and self-centered.

He lifted my chin to force me to meet his gaze. "You contribute plenty around here, Savvy. Even if you didn't lift a finger to help me—which you do, by the way—you give me back more than you obviously realize you do. I've already told you that. Your companionship means everything to me. You cheer me up or make me consider things I otherwise wouldn't or even make me laugh. You give me a reason to keep going, a reason to get up in the morning."

"You're the best friend I've ever had in my whole life, Ryan."

He smiled, but it was forced. I wondered if I'd said something wrong. He swallowed noticeably as he looked over my head out to the ocean, his smile fading.

"So, what else do you want to do today, Savvy?"

"How about we walk to the other side of the island and back? We haven't checked on the help wanted sign over there in the past few days."

He chuckled good-naturedly. "Okay, let's go then. You're the boss for the rest of the day. We'll do whatever you want."

We had a leisurely crab dinner. There were far more in the trap than we could eat, so we tossed the little ones and left several big ones munching happily on the smelly shark remains. They'd make a great breakfast in the morning.

We sat together and watched the sunset from the hillside above our cave-port. The stars were beginning to reveal themselves. It was silly, but I made a wish on the first star.

"Did you make a wish?" Ryan said, obviously noting what I'd done.

"Yeah." I leaned back against my hands.

"So did I." He smiled, resting his hand on top of mine. "It'll be okay, Savvy. Even if they never find us. We'll be okay."

That made me think of a question. "Ryan, how long will they keep looking for us? I mean, when will they give up?"

"I don't know. Your husband could fund a private search if he's got the will and the money."

"He doesn't; the money, that is. We do all right, but we're not rich."

"The authorities..." Ryan hesitated. "Why don't we talk about something else?"

There was a long silence. "They've already stopped searching, haven't they?"

He leaned over to kiss my temple. "Yes, most likely...a good, long while ago at that. I'm sorry, honey."

I nodded my head. "I figured maybe they had. Still, that doesn't mean someone won't find us in the future, by accident if nothing else. I have another question, though. What about...when will they declare us dead?"

"Legally? Around seven years. That's the norm, anyway. Sometimes they make exceptions to that rule."

"Wow. So, Sam will have to wait seven years before he can remarry? That's not fair."

"I would've thought you would prefer him to wait for you."

"I would, except...we've had a lot of problems over the past few years. It seems to just be getting worse, not better. But if they don't find us, he deserves to be happy. And I'd like for Samantha to have someone, you know, a mother she could talk to." I lowered my head and sniffled. I didn't want to start crying, especially with what was about to happen.

"Hey, don't go getting all down on me. Sam doesn't deserve your time or sympathies anyway." He kissed my cheek again. "We'll help each other through this. We're lucky, Savvy. We have food, shelter, and fresh water. We'll make it until we're rescued. You'll see your daughter again."

"And each other."

"What?" One eyebrow rose.

"We also have each other." I managed a smile.

"Yes, of course we do. Always." He nuzzled his head against mine. "Are you ready?"

I took a deep breath, releasing it slowly. "Yes. It's time. I've postponed it as long as I can." I reached up and, one at a time, removed my contact lenses. They'd been irritating my eyes for the past couple of days. It was a relief to have them out. I held them on the palm of my hand and let them blow away in the breeze.

"Are you all right?"

"Yeah...I'm okay. I'd give almost anything to have my glasses to wear. When I was a kid, other kids bullied me because of my glasses, especially as my eyesight got worse and worse and the lenses kept getting thicker and thicker. But I wish I had them now."

"I know you do. I wish you had them, too. Kids can be vicious. I was bullied. They must have stopped harassing you when you started wearing contact lenses, though, right?"

"Yes, they did. But you were bullied? How could a guy like you have been bullied?" The combination of fading light and lack of good vision eliminated Ryan's expression.

"A guy like me?"

"Yeah. You're wonderful. I couldn't imagine anyone I'd rather be stranded with, or just spend time with under normal circumstances. You're strong, smart, brave, and the nicest, most thoughtful guy I've ever met in my life. And you're attractive."

He smiled and turned away, as though embarrassed. "Thanks, Savvy. When I was a kid, my body decided to have a little fun and make me a late bloomer. I was short and small in stature until I got into high school. Then I started working out, plus I experienced a big growth spurt. I went from being picked on to being accepted. The thing is, I'd already figured out I didn't care to be accepted by that group. They weren't the kind of people I wanted to hang out with. I didn't fit in all that well because of it, but there are more important things in life than fitting in. I did a lot better with friendships in college."

"Good. I'm glad to hear that." Even that probably had its difficulties. Always did for everyone, as they worked on figuring out adulthood and real life.

"By the way, what does that even mean, you think I'm attractive? Does it mean you can look at me without feeling nauseous? I'm okay to look at? I won't break any mirrors?"

"Geez, Ryan, of course not! It means you're a good-looking guy. I happen to find you handsome."

"Thanks. You haven't said anything like that, so I've been wondering. And then the opportunity presented itself, sort of, so I decided to go fishing for a complement to see what you'd say. Every time we were out anywhere together, the women always preferred Dave to me. Every time—all of them. It was usually like I wasn't even there. He was a popular man, but he never took advantage of anyone because of it. He had a big heart and was the best person I ever knew. Until now, anyway."

"Thanks, Ryan. That's sweet."

"Come on, let me help you up. It's bedtime." He stood and braced me as I rose. We made our way slowly to the cave-port, a few feet beneath us. It made me more nervous than I'd imagined, moving in the dark, unable to see my feet or where I put them.

"Watch your head," he cautioned, placing a hand on my back as I crawled inside. The ceiling was a foot above the top of Ryan's seated head at the rear wall. Up front, it was closer to three feet above. Crawling presented little risk.

"Okay, I'm in," I said. Using the back wall as a reference, I positioned myself and laid down on my back.

Ryan followed me in to lay on his side, facing me, his head propped on his hand. "Is there anything I can do to help you relax and go to sleep? How about a back rub?"

"No thanks, I'll be okay. I just need some time."

"Let me know if you change your mind. And be sure to wake me up during the night if you need me for anything at all. I mean that, Savvy." His tone left no room for doubt.

"I know you do."

The details in the rock above me were blurred out. Of course, it was nighttime. Tomorrow, in the daylight, would be the real test. I'd need to relearn a lot of things I'd taken for granted in my life. I sighed, more deeply than I'd intended, and tried not to think about it.

"Come here," Ryan ordered in a deep, firm voice.

"What?"

"I said, come here. I want you to lay your head on my arm."

"But your arm will fall asleep."

"Why don't you let me worry about that? Now come on. Remember, I know what's best for you and I'm in charge now."

"You are?" I smiled.

"Yes, I am." He responded with a broad grin, patting his arm.

"Okay. I think I like you being in charge. Or at least thinking you are."

He laughed at that. "Everything's going to be fine."

I scooted up against him before turning onto my side. I laid my head on his arm, which was more comfortable than the vegetation he kept bringing in for us. I kissed his bicep and closed my eyes. He placed a long kiss on my forehead. The fingers of his other hand gently stroked my hair, over and over, until I fell asleep.

Standing outside, I inhaled deeply of the refreshing, early morning air, the world totally out of focus. I stretched in preparation for our brief journey to the beach for breakfast. It wouldn't be crab today. I smelled rain on the air, and it was cloudy. Ryan had already helped me get to our bathroom area and back.

He handed me my knife. "You stay right here, Savvy. I'll be back soon."

"You're leaving me here by myself? Why can't I come? We're not supposed to go anywhere alone, remember?" I wished for good eyesight to see his expression.

"Just stay here and relax, Savvy. I want you to take it easy today."

"Why? Because I can't see anymore? Because I'm useless to you now? Because I'll slow you down?" My arms were crossed resolutely over my chest. How could he treat me this way, after everything we'd discussed? I frowned, pursing my lips.

Ryan put his hands on my shoulders. "No, my sweet girl. I want you to stay right here so I'll know you're safe. There's a storm building out there, so I need to move fast, and I don't want you exposed. Crawl back into the cave-port and wait for me. I'll be back with breakfast before you know it." He kissed my cheek before heading down the hill.

The situation angered me, but I returned to our cover as a rumble of thunder sounded in the distance. He would've taken me along if there weren't any storms to worry about, I realized.

Regardless of the lightning threat, I remained at the edge, watching for Ryan's return. The back wall was about eight feet farther in, so there wasn't much difference. Besides that, our shelter wasn't fully enclosed, being partially exposed to the elements. The third side had been constructed from tree branches and palm fronds and was holding up well, but it would prove insufficient to certain elements. If lightning struck the shelter or near it, I'd be a goner regardless of where I sat.

So far, there'd been only the one clap of thunder. Despite my badly flawed eyesight, I'd be able to detect a flash of lightning, even from a distance. I decided to risk a rebuke from Ryan by inching forward a little more, to watch for lightning better. Not that Ryan could hear me if I yelled for him. He'd be in the jungle gathering food, rather than collecting on the open beach or in the water. Those areas were too dangerous in a storm and he was smarter than that.

Strange, though. I could swear I'd heard something, like footsteps on the roof of the cave-port. But that was impossible-Ryan had gone down the hill. I would've noticed his blurry shape moving if he'd come back up the hill. Plus, he would've hollered for me to get farther back inside as he passed. Could it be a large bird walking around up there, like a seagull?

It all made horrifying sense as a large man dropped heavily from the roof to land directly in front of me. Startled, I gulped in a huge quantity of air as my body jerked reflexively. I let loose the loudest scream I'd ever issued in my life. Instantly, even with my blurry vision, I knew this man wasn't Ryan.

The clothes covering the large man's leathery, heavily tanned skin sagged, and the wind blew his unwashed stench into me. His salt and pepper hair and beard were unkempt, long, dreadlocks. His bared teeth were deeply stained. He was a wild man, a fearsome stranger.

Twelve

There was nowhere to go for escape. I scrambled madly into a backward crawl. The man crouched low and reached in for me. That's when I realized I'd dropped my knife, somewhere. I kicked viciously at his arm and face. He succeeded in grabbing one of my feet around the ankle. My other foot landed squarely against his forehead.

"Son of a bitch!" he yelled but didn't release me. Instead, he dragged me out.

I had no weapon and there was nothing for me to latch onto in my attempt to prevent him from removing me from my home. I hauled most of the bedding out with me. On the edge of the ground at the base of the cave-port, my knife rolled under my fingers. I stretched out and grabbed for it.

The man took a fistful of my shirt collar with one hand, my right wrist with the other. With a yell, I swung my left hand, clutching the knife. It caught him across the chin, slicing it open to let the blood flow. He drew back but grabbed me again before I could escape. He took my left wrist and slammed my hand onto the ground until the knife was dislodged and my hand was wracked with pain.

"No! Ryan! Help me! Ryan!" I screamed at the top of my lungs.

We struggled, but he was larger and stronger. The man drew his right hand back in a fist. The explosion of blinding pain when he punched my face was worse than I'd imagined such a blow could be, but I'd never been hit by anyone before. Despite the white flashes dancing before my eyes, I attempted to crawl away, crying.

The stranger forced me flat against the ground and sat on my back. The weight of his bulk crushed me. Breathing was nearly impossible, but I used up what breath I had remaining in me on one final scream. Large hands stuffed a cloth in my mouth then. He followed it with a gag tied behind my head, pulling it tight.

My hands were bound together at my back so tight that my hands went numb. The vine he used was so taut it pinched my flesh. He yanked me roughly to my feet, pulling me alongside him, forcing me to climb the cave-port hill, headed for the big one, the one our helicopter crashed at the top of. Ryan and I rarely went into that jungle. The walking was difficult, especially with my head still spinning from the blow of his fist.

We entered the thick growth of the steep northern hillside and made our way higher and higher. The climb was nearly vertical in some places, made more difficult by the fact that the bindings around my wrists made me unable to extend my arms for balance, or use my hands for grasping. The lack of clear vision didn't help, either. I stumbled often but didn't offer the man any trouble. My fear and disorientation had me compliant.

And I wanted him to think my submissive behavior would continue. Ryan would return soon. He wouldn't leave me alone for long. If an escape attempt was timed right, I might be able to reach Ryan, or get to where he'd be able to see me.

How did this happen? Where did he come from? Who was he? What was he going to do with me? Ryan, please. I need you.

At a particularly steep portion of the ascent, I decided it was time to change things up, since my head had straightened itself out and the stars before my eyes had faded.

"Climb!" he ordered brusquely, pushing me ahead of him.

The next foothold was nearly two feet, straight up. He was forced to let go of me in order to step up after I did, which he seemed to be finding difficult. His attention was on the ground.

Memories of an old self-defense class I took in college rushed back to me. Already at a slight angle to him, I shifted my balance imperceptibly to my left foot and pivoted to deliver a jabbing kick with my right. My foot landed directly across his face.

Yelling out in pain, he sailed backward heavily to the ground, grunting upon impact. I leapt from the two-foot vertical drop, narrowly missing my captor's legs. I managed to stick the landing with a bobble.

I ran, plunging through the jungle, essentially unseeing. Large leaves slapped me across the face and a tree branch spotted too late to avoid took me down, but I regained my feet quickly, fear overcoming pain.

Behind me, I heard the man crashing haphazardly through the

vegetation in pursuit. I was faster and more agile, but those qualities couldn't overcome my disadvantages. Moving fast made everything a lot worse, and more dangerous.

That was what cost me the most, in the end. I emerged from between the large, broad leaves of two bushes to find a drop-off I could neither see nor negotiate. I issued a muffled scream past the gag as I plummeted, the land disappearing from under my feet.

When it reappeared, the jolt from the impact was seismic. My body tumbled, over and over, gaining momentum, completely out of control, striking a multitude of objects on my way down. Waves of pain radiated with every collision. The blow from my head impacting the trunk of a tree, my body wrapping around it, ended the rolling.

Staring at the surface in front of me revealed tiny cracks and crevices in the smooth bark of a tree. Up close, my eyes worked well. My mind didn't function well enough to reason it out. Why was I looking at the bark of a tree? Then the cracks became squiggly and blurred into a foggy nothingness.

Once, as a child, I'd gone into the church bell tower to watch the large bell as it was rung. My friends and I placed our hands on the side of the bell immediately after it was struck. The vibrations in the metal transferred easily into our bodies from that simple contact.

My head felt like that now, vibrating from waves of pain jabbing throughout my body. There was no recollection of what had happened. I didn't understand and was hesitant to open my eyes, but I did, albeit slowly. There was little illumination to see by. Was it day or night? Where was I?

My chin rested against my shoulder, while the side of my throbbing head leaned against something firm, unforgiving...rock, relatively smooth. Why couldn't I make my eyes focus? Repeated blinking didn't clear my vision. Then I remembered it was gone. Ryan was supposed to be my eyes.

Where was he? Oh, right. He went off to get us some breakfast.

And there was a storm coming, so he left me behind at the cave-port for shelter.

That was when the terrifying memory shattered my world. Ryan left me alone and someone found me—a stranger, a man. All this time, there was someone else on the island. Or did he perhaps come to the island on a boat? His intention wasn't rescue. Why would he kidnap me?

The intruder in my world...I ran from him through the jungle. Until I fell. What happened after that?

There was a sound here, something familiar. I listened for voices, for thunder, but instead heard a pattern of rumbling, booming, that didn't sound like thunder. It was something altogether different. Where was the storm? That was why Ryan left me alone in the first place. Alone and all but defenseless.

Where did the stranger go? Was he nearby? Where was I?

It was difficult and painful, but I had to look around to make sense of my surroundings. My head felt heavy and large. What was this place? It appeared I was inside...something. The air was thick and stale. It might have been a small room or cave. Discerning which of the two was visually impossible, although from exploring with my fingers, it felt like the same surface as the floor continued up and into the wall. Ryan and I would have discovered a structure before now. So, it must be a cave, a well-hidden one.

Ahead of me were straight lines of dim light, two long verticals and two horizontals, that must be caused by a door leading to the outside. And the ocean. The surf pounded. The sound of smashing waves was what I'd confused with thunder earlier. I needed to figure out the situation before my kidnapper returned. There had to be a way to escape.

My head still rang, but it eased as the minutes ticked by. My arms ached from strain and my wrists were sore, still bound behind me. Calling for help was impossible, due to the cloth in my mouth. There might not be anyone around to hear my cries anyway. I hoped Ryan was alive and free.

Wherever and whatever this place was, I needed to find a way out of it. My attempt to rise was ended by a sharp increase in the level of pain in my wrists. The sound of metal clinking against metal resulted when I moved. Pulling forward met with resistance, so I used my fingers to explore. A large, metal loop was bolted into the rock wall, while a length of chain extended from the loop to my wrists. The vine used to restrain me had been replaced by metal chain.

I was a prisoner.

Terror struck my heart. Where was the attacker? When would he return? Why did he come after me? Ryan was my sole hope of rescue, but I was someplace we hadn't known about.

Unless there was a way to escape on my own. I set to work on the metal around my wrists, but there wasn't much slack, preventing my hands from slipping out, no matter how hard I tried. The next step was to pull against chain and the loop in the wall. My best effort, accompanied by a deep growl, got me nowhere. Neither object gave any indication of giving way. The skin beneath the shackles felt on the verge of splitting open, so I ceased my struggle.

Instead, I leaned my head against the rock wall and remembered how comfortable it was in the cave-port with the bedding Ryan brought in for us. Not to mention the pleasure of his company. He was so thoughtful and took such good care of me. Did I ever even thank him for any of that? Did I ever say it out loud? I wanted another chance to say it to him. I'd never known a better person in my life than Ryan Buckley.

Along the wall to my left were stacks of wooden crates, stretching from floor to ceiling, far higher than my head if I were standing. There was writing on them, appearing as dark smudges to my eyes. The other walls were barren.

I minimized my breathing for a moment to listen. A seagull cried repeatedly not far away and there was the ongoing crash of the surf. Those things weren't what I wanted to hear. My goal was listening for the approach of footfalls. There were no indications of another human, not even the sound of Ryan's voice calling to me. I listened for a long time, but his voice didn't come. There was only crashing, mind-numbing surf.

It occurred to me then that the worst could have happened, that Ryan might've found this place in his search for me and the stranger may have injured or killed him. Or the stranger may be hunting Ryan.

I closed my eyes tight against the images flashing through my mind, needing to center my thoughts. I couldn't afford to lose focus. I had to be ready to seize any chance to escape or even kill the man, if an opportunity presented itself. There had to be a way.

There was nothing to do but wait as I tried to ignore the pain and fear.

As I awakened from a nap, I became aware of tiny, incessant splashes on stone caused by water dripping from multiple sources around me. It was likely due to the morning storms, leaving rainfall to trickle through porous rock or fissures. Too bad none of the leaks were close enough to reach with my mouth.

Pain and thirst blocked my thoughts. I hadn't had any water since dinner the night before. I strained at one of the tiny, dripping streams. My tongue stretched as far as it could reach, but that was a few inches too little, the proximity teasing.

Water seemed to be everywhere I wasn't. There was the near-constant symphony of splashing drops in-between the roaring crashes of waves. Everything reminded me of being parched.

Periodically, seagull laughter bounced around for a minute or two and then waned. Not far beyond the door. The sounds of the ocean and the seagulls were much louder here than at the cave-port.

I missed my home on the hill and its breezes, and Ryan. Ryan most of all. Where could he be?

As time passed, I wondered why no one came. My thirst grew, along with hunger. Pain was everywhere. Dried blood covered part of my forehead, and along the right side of my face.

Periodically, I reminded myself to maintain concentration. The lines of light around the door faded, signaling the approach of nightfall. That's when my lack of normal vision wouldn't matter so much. If the kidnapper didn't have a flashlight, we'd be approaching equal. Except that he was bigger and stronger. And even though I kicked him good twice already, he was still functioning. I doubted he was hungry or thirsty, either.

The island wasn't all that big. Ryan was bound to have passed by already in his search for me. Wherever I was. The thought of what Ryan's absence could mean filled me with an all-consuming fear. I wanted to be free but not at the cost of Ryan's life.

Where could the two men be? The lines of light were gone now, so it must be nighttime. I decided to sleep to prepare for whatever tomorrow might bring. But I dozed fitfully, my head propped in a wide groove in the wall.

Any sound, real or imagined, startled me awake. There were a few large insects in the cave with me, which brought on a high level of discomfort as they skittered about. I tried to meditate, but I didn't know how, so I prayed. It calmed me a little. Mostly, I tried talking myself out of my fears. Morning would come, eventually, as would my captor.

After a decent stretch of sleep at the end of the night, the barest hint of brightening came into the cave. The sky must be clear to admit this much illumination, compared to the day before. That would mean the storms were gone, so maybe it would be easier for Ryan to find me. Again, I tried to study my surroundings, but without the benefit of correction, my eyes showed me little more than yesterday.

I was lightheaded, whether from hunger, thirst, or the head injury, although the pain had lessened. Hunger had me shaking, thirst had me yearning more for water than freedom. The walls of my bladder were stretched tight, already at maximum capacity. Relieving myself was the priority if I were to be given a choice. My bladder wouldn't hold much longer, that was certain.

Judging from the light, it must be somewhere around seven or eight o'clock. Inside, the air was heavy and moist. The place smelled of rotting wood and decaying metal. The slightest of breezes were permitted entry around the fringes of the door, the sole access point

THE STRANDING

to the outside world.

Right when I decided there was no alternative to peeing in my pants, a crunching sound came, like footsteps on loose rock.

I held my breath as I listened, waiting, heart racing. The sound drew closer, and my parched throat managed a rough swallow. A shadow fell across the sunlit lines at the door and there was the sound of metal on metal, a door being unlocked with a key.

My heart moved into my throat and my aching muscles stiffened in dread and preparation. It might be preferable to die of thirst chained to the wall than for that man to give me food and water. Assuming that was what he was coming for.

If only this could be Ryan. Even though I doubted it, I held out hope. Until the door swung open, revealing a large form looming in the doorway. I pressed myself tight against the wall, as if I were able to become a part of it, disappearing from the man's sight and reach.

My captor left the door open, admitting a broad beam of daylight. The outside appeared exceptionally bright to my squinting eyes. Fresh salt air wafted in on the wind, blowing at my hair and renewing my spirit. After all, I was still alive; and life meant hope. The cave, now easier to survey with the addition of so much light, wasn't much larger than I'd thought it to be the day before. It could hold perhaps as many as a couple dozen people, all lying down at once, if the boxes were gone.

The scruffy man shuffled over, his bare feet slapping across the smooth rock. He settled himself in front of me on his knees with a groan. I squinted for a marginal improvement in my vision. The man's large frame was gaunt, the clothes tattered and dirty, like his scabby skin. Yellowed hair was restrained at the back of his neck by something I couldn't see into a long ponytail. His lower face and neck were concealed by a lengthy, tangled, graying beard and moustache with strong yellow tints. His eyes were cold and brown, already dead.

In his hands, he held a rusty can with a peeling yellow label, and a dark, plastic bottle. He placed the can on the floor along with the bottle. He pulled the spit-soaked gag from my mouth, dragging it across my chin, to leave it hanging around my neck. The inner cloth was next, which he threw against the nearby wall. I opened and closed my mouth repeatedly, then worked my jaw from side to side. There was pain from where he'd punched me in the cheek, enough to make me wince.

He retrieved the plastic bottle, popped the top of it, and held it to my lips. Squinting, I saw a drop of clear liquid at the tip, sparkling like a shiny diamond in the beam of sunlight.

"Take a drink." His voice was raspy, as if unaccustomed to speaking.

I sucked down the water greedily as he squeezed the bottle's sides. The taste wasn't great, but I didn't care. Once I'd drained half of it, he placed it on the floor.

The can was retrieved next, along with a bent metal fork from his front shirt pocket. He stabbed the instrument into the can and produced something I assumed to be edible. When he dangled it closer to my face, the fat slice of peach dripping with juice became discernable. My mouth salivated uncontrollably at the sight of it. Peaches. I'd loved those as a kid; fresh, Georgia peaches. We looked forward to them with anticipation every year.

"Open up," he ordered.

Mimicking a starving baby bird, I took the peach in my mouth obediently. Although the flavor had grown bland and metallic with age, I swallowed it with gusto after a single chew. He proceeded to feed me the entire can, slice by slice, and held the can up afterward to allow me to drink the juices. He followed it up with the remainder of the water. Both my thirst and hunger had been relieved, but I wondered what might be coming next.

He set aside the can and bottle, licking the fork repeatedly, eyes closed. The behavior repulsed. After wiping it on his shirt, he replaced it in his pocket. If I could find a way to get my hands on that fork, there were a number of places I'd like to stab it into. Over and over.

"What's your name?" he asked hesitantly.

"Savannah Dalton."

"Savannah," he repeated slowly. "That's a pretty name."

I declined to respond, uncertain of what to say, afraid of causing trouble either way.

"I said, that's a pretty name." His voice carried a sharp edge to it.

Clearly, my choice of tactics had been incorrect, so I responded quickly. Maybe it would benefit my cause to engage him in conversation. "Thanks."

He grew silent, staring at the floor. There was no way to be certain if I'd answered suitably this time. Considering my circumstances, it wouldn't hurt to try something else. "Who are you and why have you brought me here?"

"I'm Douglas. You're here to keep me company."

"Do you mean you live here all alone?"

The response came in a quick nod.

"That's terrible. What happened?" It was important to gather information. And maybe befriend him at the same time. He'd likely gone mad here, alone on this island. There was no telling what might help me escape.

"Some other time; I'm in a hurry."

"Douglas...do people call you Doug?"

The reply came in a snap. "No. I don't like Doug."

"Oh, okay then."

"You gotta go to the bathroom?"

I swallowed the dread, my voice squeaking. "Yes, please."

His movements were uncoordinated as he rose. "You make sure you keep your mouth closed, all the time, and don't even think about giving me any trouble or it'll go bad for you."

"I won't. I promise I won't." He had to believe me. I intended to scream for Ryan at the top of my lungs as soon as we were outside, assuming that was where we were going. Ryan had to be searching for me. If he happened to be nearby, I'd do my best to give him every chance to hear me. Not a great plan, but it was all I could come up with.

Douglas's eyes narrowed as he stared at me, as if trying to read my thoughts. "I don't trust you. Hold still while I put the gag back in."

"No, please don't do that," I begged.

My plea fell on deaf ears. He pulled the handkerchief over my chin and into my mouth. The corners of my lips wanted to cry out in pain. Most importantly, the gag would prevent me from calling out for help.

"If you do anything wrong out there, the results will be your fault.

Everything bad that's already happened on this island is all your fault anyway," he cautioned.

My fault. What did he mean by that? How could everything bad be my fault? I hadn't done anything wrong.

Douglas moved to the wall behind me, producing a handful of keys from his pocket, the pieces of metal jingling as he fumbled with them. I held perfectly still, anxious to be free of the chains, even temporarily. The clicking sound as he unlocked my bindings was music to my ears, a welcome sense of relief as they dropped to the floor.

He took a crushing hold of my hand, yanking me to my feet to pull me outside into the morning sun. There was no need to see the deep red marks on my wrists to know they existed. He didn't seem to care.

The brilliance filled my eyes, making it difficult to see anything for several seconds. I shielded my vision from the sun with my free hand. As my eyes adjusted, the blurry view terrified and I recoiled from it, emitting a loud gasp despite the gag. I stepped backwards into Douglas but didn't care. In front of me was the sight I'd seen from the top of the cliffs when the helicopter had gone over, carrying Alphonse to his final resting place. Even without the capacity to see well, I knew without a doubt where I stood–the most petrifying place I'd ever been in my life.

We were on a narrow ledge in a steep, rocky landscape with crashing ocean waves far below. Above us was an overhang, jutting out from the steep walls well enough to conceal most of this ledge from anyone who might be peering down from the top of the cliffs. My heart plummeted with an overwhelming sense of absolute despair.

"Pull your pants down and go in the hole; make sure you hang yourself over this depression, so I don't have to clean up your mess. Don't try anything, either. I'll have to hurt you if you do. You behave yourself and pee quick so I can get you back inside. I've got more important things to do."

I nodded anxiously and did as instructed. I wondered about the rush but couldn't ask because of the gag. The bathroom area made control easy for him. The ledge here was less than three feet wide and

I hovered over a carved-out depression with a big hole in the middle of it. My eyes perceived the distinct colors of both the sand and rocks on the beach below and the ocean through the hole. The repeated crashing of large waves stoked my fears.

Douglas kept a closer eye on the tiny strip of beach off to the east than on me. There wasn't a possibility of getting past him. Even if I were able to do it, I had no idea how to scale the cliff. I'd never be able to see the pathway to freedom, let alone navigate it successfully. That meant my options were sorely limited. Once finished, I pulled up my underwear and pants quickly.

He turned at the sound of my zipper and snatched my wrist, leading me back to the cave. The entrance was through a short, narrow tunnel. The overhang at this end of the ledge was substantial and from the angle of the sun, the projecting rock cast the entry to the cave into deep shadow beyond the morning hours. That left it well concealed from view atop the cliffs and likely from below as well.

My sole hope for salvation withered and died, carried over the edge by the winds to crash into the ocean below, just as the helicopter that brought us here had done. Ryan would never find me.

We were about to step into the tunnel when we heard it, somewhere on the cliffs above.

"Savannah! Savannah, where are you?" Ryan's haggard voice sounded out as my heart skipped a beat.

Douglas stopped to glance upward in clear surprise. He recovered himself quickly and tightened his grip on my wrist in his efforts to drag me into the tunnel.

I pulled against him, attempting to force my way past. I tugged with desperation at the gag with one hand. It was impossible to escape, but the gag gave enough to enable me to yank it down.

Douglas picked me up around the waist and carried me inside as I kicked and thrashed against him, screaming for Ryan. Once inside, he shoved me hard to the floor and fastened the chains to my wrists. He reattached and tightened the gag and without another word, collected what he'd brought in and scampered out, making sure to close and lock the door behind him.

I shut my eyes and prayed for Ryan's safety. Douglas either went after him, or he'd position himself somewhere, waiting for Ryan to come this way. I shouldn't have yelled out for him, fearing it might result in his death.

But Ryan didn't come.

Thirteen

Later that afternoon, as the light lines around the door began to diminish, Douglas paid me another visit. I had no idea what to expect after our scuffle earlier. He wore an angry scowl, his eye sockets hollowed.

He placed the water bottle on the floor with a thud and unlocked my bindings, leaving the gag in place. He pulled me roughly to my feet and escorted me outside. The sky had turned pink as the sun dropped. It had been something like thirty-six hours since I'd seen Ryan.

Douglas jabbed a finger at the hole and spent the time alternately looking both above and below. Ryan must still be out there somewhere, alive and well. That filled me with gratitude.

Once I finished, Douglas returned me to my cave cell and chained me to the wall. I made no attempt to give him any trouble this time. He roughly removed my gag, retrieved the water bottle, and held it over my head. When I opened my mouth, he proceeded to squirt a stream onto my face.

Caught by surprise, I closed my eyes and lowered my face, so the water ran down my chin, where it streamed down my neck and into the front of my shirt. I shook my head as I coughed and tried to blow the water out of my nose.

"This is your first lesson. When you misbehave, there will be repercussions. Never forget that. The punishment can be severe if called for. Everything that happens, both to you and your husband, is all up to you. Every time. And anything bad that happens is your own fault, Savannah. You just make sure you never forget that.

"Now, open your ungrateful mouth."

I opened again, feeling there was no other choice. This time, he squirted the water repeatedly into my mouth, so fast it made me choke. But I had to keep drinking, not knowing when I'd get more; and my body was dehydrated.

When the bottle was half empty, he climbed to his feet, taking the water with him, and went to the door. It was getting darker, barely enough light to discern the movement when he turned toward me.

"This was all your fault. The rest of your punishment is no dinner. Maybe that'll give you enough to think about for tonight. Behave yourself tomorrow and you'll get two meals. Cause me problems and you'll starve to death. Your life makes no difference to me. You'd do well to remember that."

He slammed the door shut and locked it, leaving me alone in the dark with the scampering insects for unwelcome companionship. My body began to shake, accompanied by a flood of tears.

The next morning, I monitored the light at the door closely. I needed to relieve my bladder again. Where could Douglas be? I'd have to ask to go more frequently. If he wanted to give me food and water once a day, that was okay, but managing the wait for a trip to the bathroom area was difficult.

As I watched, the tell-tale shadow fell across the cracks around the door. Douglas unlocked it and entered. The first thing he did was remove my gag. There wasn't any food or water for me. It must be a continuation of my punishment from yesterday.

"Douglas, please, I can't hold it this long anymore. I have to go to the bathroom so badly."

"Okay but hurry up. And keep your mouth closed this time or I'll gag you again. Your husband isn't anywhere around. He's searching for you on the other end of the island now." Douglas unlocked the chains and took me outside.

As I watched him, he exhibited antsy behavior. Instead of standing in one spot like yesterday, he paced like a caged animal, scarcely paying me any attention at all, so focused was he on the terrain above us. Ryan must be nearby, despite Douglas' claims to the contrary. Dear God, how I hoped that was true. It was tempting to call out for help, but I knew it would go badly for me if I tried.

I believed punishment would result. But of higher importance than punishment for me was Ryan's safety. The risk for both of us was high and the results could easily be like yesterday, or worse, should I yell for help. Even if Ryan was close, he still might not find me. Yet, Douglas might find Ryan.

So, I kept quiet and gave him no trouble when he led me back inside. He shackled me to the wall, and I complied. Cooperation made more sense to me.

"If you don't make any noise and behave yourself like you did just then, I won't have to gag you when I take you out every time. If your husband finds our hiding place, I'll have to kill him, and it will be all your fault. It's up to you whether he lives or dies. You make sure you remember that.

"Are you smart enough to remember all these things I'm telling you, Savannah? Are you? I wonder about that. You don't look very smart to me and you certainly didn't act smart yesterday. Your husband will end up paying the price if you mess up." He left, locking the door.

I closed my eyes as I leaned back into the wall. How had my life gone so terribly wrong? And what kind of life was it? The thought of living out my days with Douglas as a companion sent tears down my cheeks. And had me trying to think of a plan to avoid such torment.

Somewhere around noon, my captor returned. He unchained me and deposited a small handful of stale saltine crackers on the floor in front of me, along with a third of a bottle of water. I'd been so hungry and thirsty my head felt light again. I dove on the crackers like ants at a picnic, my face low to the floor. That way, finding every tiny crumb was doable, with my eyes closer to the source of the pitiful sustenance.

Douglas watched me curiously. Maybe I was a human guinea pig for him, or a temporary distraction. He stayed with me for only a few minutes this time. It didn't take long to scarf down the crackers, including every tiny crumb, after which he led me outside. He didn't look at me even once, craning his neck to search all around. Ryan had to be near.

After Douglas chained me to the wall, doused my face and throat with the water bottle, and secured my gag, he left, never having spoken a word. I pondered what a wretched existence I had, unable to believe Ryan hadn't found me. Realistically, there was no way he could find me. Yet, my fantasies had him accomplishing the feat, every time.

If I were able to see clearly, it might be possible for me to free myself. Considering that impracticality, I needed to create a backup plan, like befriending Douglas, convincing him to let me go. It was all I had, aside from the last resort, one that smacked of complete desperation.

Early in the evening, Douglas paid me another visit. He brought water and another can of peaches. It made me wonder if he was feeding me just enough to keep me alive and weak. I liked his silent treatment even less than the meager rations. It made him scarier, not having any idea what he might be thinking.

Once I'd eaten, he took me to the bathroom spot. He didn't seem nearly as anxious this time, but he still watched both above and below.

After my restraints were on, I decided to ask him some questions before he could reapply my gag. It might prove beneficial to get him talking and humanize myself for him, which might make him less likely to harm me. I'd heard about that technique once or twice, anyway, with no idea if it was true. There wasn't much to lose.

"Where do you stay at night?" I asked.

He flinched, almost as if I'd swung my arm at him instead of words. After the extended silence, even my own voice sounded rather loud.

"There's a second cave, next door to this one." He gestured to my right.

"Does it have a door, too?"

"No, it's open, but camouflaged. I like the outdoors. I like this island."

"How long have you lived here?" A long time, judging from his appearance.

"Almost ten years now."

Shock filled my voice. "Ten years? What happened to you? Were you shipwrecked?"

"No. I picked this spot and my brother and I hired a crew of locals to carve out these two caves. We brought in enough canned food to last me a long time, a lifetime's worth. And I've got other supplies.

"My cave is nicer than this one. It's bigger and more comfortable. I even have a cot with a pillow and a blanket. Once your husband gives up looking for you, I'll take you over there with me. You'll like your new home. You and I will be good company for each other."

The thought of that appalled me, but I set it aside to focus. And at least he'd just let me know Ryan was still free and alive. "Where's your brother?"

"He left me here." He shrugged.

"Why did he do that?"

"Because that's what I asked him to do. It was our plan."

I frowned. "I don't understand. What if something happened to you? Why would you want to live here, stranded and all alone?"

"Because I don't like people. My brother does. I'm the oldest, so I was supposed to inherit the family business and the fortune right along with it, but I wasn't interested. My brother always wanted it and everything that goes along with it–that whole lifestyle. I don't have proof, but I think he may have tried to have me killed once, so he'd inherit everything. The man is bloodthirsty, like dear old dad.

"Me? Not so much. I like simple things: the ocean, the breezes, and everything about the tropics, but not people. It worked out exactly right for me. My brother has more money and power than he can handle, thanks to our agreement. But that's what he wanted. If he screws it up, it'll be his own fault. I warned him about it, more than once.

"My brother and I searched for a long time until we found this place. He helped me set everything up. We faked my death and when we were sure everybody believed it, he brought me out here. He left and I haven't seen him since.

"That's what I wanted. If I end up having made a poor decision in coming here like I did, that'll be my own fault. I knew the risks and I was willing to take a chance. I didn't walk into this not knowing what I was doing. Except for the arrival of you and your friends, of course.

"It's nice and peaceful out here. I can do whatever I want, whenever I want, with no one to answer to for anything, ever. No one has bothered me here, either. Not in all the time I've been at this place. Until you, that is. You and your friends had to go and crash your infernal helicopter into my island and try to ruin everything for me."

"Do you own this island?"

"No, but it's mine just the same. I have possession." Douglas scratched absentmindedly at his beard. He sat close enough for me to make out his hands, his fingers. The nails were long, thick, and yellowed, with enough dirt and grime underneath them to plant seeds.

"Your brother never came back to check on you?"

"No. I didn't expect him to. We weren't close or anything. We both got what we wanted."

My brow furrowed as something occurred to me. "Why didn't you come and help us when we crashed? We could've used your help."

"I was hoping all of you would die. When that didn't happen, I took matters into my own hands."

"What do you mean by that?"

"I went down to your house while you and your husband were out on the beach. My house here is better than yours, by the way. Even with the changes I watched you and your husband make to it. There's no comparison. Mine is easily superior.

"When I went to your house, I checked through what was in the backpack. Those are some nice, fresh crackers you brought with you. I'm going to have to go down there and get some more. I should've brought peanut butter crackers myself when I moved here, but it never occurred to me. That makes it my own fault. Do you want me to get some for you, too, Savannah?"

"No." Then I gave the idea more consideration. If he went down there and took food, Ryan might notice and get suspicious. Maybe Ryan would even see Douglas when he grabbed the food. "I don't like the crackers so much. I like the bags of trail mix. It's healthier for you. You can take whatever you want out of there. My husband doesn't like any of that food and never goes in the backpack for anything. That's why there's still so much food in there. He prefers his food fresh."

"Then I'll bring you trail mix."

"That would be nice. Thank you." So far, so good.

"You're welcome. But you have to do your part."

"What's my part?"

"You'll have to stay quiet." He paused, frowning at me. "I can't trust you yet."

I needed to do something to convince him otherwise. "I can understand that. I promise to behave, but you should put the gag on me while you're gone. It'll make you feel more comfortable."

Even my bad eyes were able to discern the surprise that came over his face.

"When do you think you're going down? I'm looking forward to that trail mix." That was a mistake. Eagerness would bring suspicion. I shrugged my shoulders and threw in a yawn. "But I can wait until you decide the time's right. It's no problem. I like those peaches you've been feeding me. I've been missing those since I got here. They've always been my favorite fruit. Could I keep having more of them, please?"

"We'll see." His tone carried his mistrust, his words coming slow.

I decided to share information with him that he might already be aware of and observe his reaction. "Speaking of seeing, you should know I can't see. I mean, I can see, but not very well. My glasses got broken by accident."

"I know. I thought they belonged to your husband, since they were kind of manly. You should've gotten some that were pink or had flowers or something feminine like that. Then it never would've happened. That makes it your fault they got broken. I could tell from looking through them that the prescription was strong. I thought your husband wouldn't be able to see without them. I'm sorry for what happened; I didn't know they were yours."

"What do you mean, you're sorry?" Where was he going with this?

"I broke them on purpose because I thought they belonged to your husband. I wanted to leave him vulnerable, so I could take you away from him easier. As it turns out, he left you alone when you couldn't see, so I didn't need to kill him. My plan was to end his life while he couldn't see well enough to defend himself. It surprised me when he left you, with you being vulnerable and all. He shouldn't have left you, but I'm glad he did. And now he's without you, which is his fault."

I experienced an all-consuming anxiety that Douglas had wanted, and maybe still did want, to kill Ryan. I had to try to manipulate Douglas, to shift his focus to me. "That's okay, even though you've hurt me. I forgive you."

"Hurt you?" His eyes narrowed.

"It broke my heart when I found my glasses. I knew I'd never see the details of another sunrise or sunset. They're always so pretty with the intricate patterns of the clouds. And I'd never be able to see the stars at night. I've always loved looking at the stars–since back when I was a little kid. I know all the constellations in the northern hemisphere and a few in the southern. Plus, there are comets or meteor showers to watch. It hurts me very deeply that I'll never see any of those things again."

His mouth gaped open, as if dumbfounded. "I'm sorry, Savannah. I didn't know. Like I said, I thought those glasses belonged to your husband. I wouldn't have hurt you like that on purpose."

"But you *have* hurt me on purpose. You took me away from my husband. I love him and I need him. Please don't do anything to hurt him. I'd rather you hurt me instead."

He drew back. "I don't want to hurt you. If you cooperate and your husband doesn't find us, I won't kill him. How does that sound?"

"If you promise not to hurt him, I'll cooperate."

"Maybe." He left me then, uncertainty written on his features. But he didn't put the gag in place.

I watched the door until the light faded away. Ryan must be so terribly worried, probably thinking I fell off the cliff into the ocean. Eventually, he'd give up searching. Please, Ryan. Please don't give up on me yet.

The next morning dawned bright, pouring in around the door, but there was no sign of Douglas. I decided to wait instead of yelling for him, even though my bladder complained again. You'd think it would be getting used to this kind of abuse by now, but that wasn't the case.

It was nearly midmorning by the time he came. He surprised me with a bag of trail mix, plopping it onto the cave floor beside me casually. He released me from the chains and sat nearby, legs crossed, with a pack of peanut butter crackers and his bottle of water.

I rubbed my sore wrists that were red and raw before I began to eat. It was a delicacy to my taste buds, plus I was hungry, and the trail mix was fresh enough. The pumpkin and sunflower seeds cracked between my teeth as I munched. In between bites, I attempted to strike up a conversation. "Thank you for this, Douglas, it's a real taste treat."

"You're welcome."

"I didn't think you'd go this soon. But I'm glad you did. This is so good." I held the bag out to him, even though I was starving. "Do you want some?"

He gave me a surprised look. "No thanks."

"Where was my husband? Did you see him? Is he okay?"

"I guess so. But he must miss you. When I saw him, he was out on the beach, sitting beside the other man's grave, staring out at the ocean. He cleaned up the grave first and straightened the cross I watched you make that day."

"How long have you been watching us?" It was a frightful thought, reviewing the things he might have seen if he had made voyeurism his hobby.

"Since you've been trespassing on my island. I saw how you saved yourself and your husband from that shark, too. Watching you when you did that was how I decided I wanted you to move in up here. I figured we'd be friends and maybe... Well, you seem like a nice lady."

"Thanks. But why didn't you just let us know you were here? My husband and I would both be your friends. My husband's a wonderful man. He's kind-hearted and generous; the best person I've ever known in my life." There was nothing but truth in my words.

My heart ached for him. Even with Douglas here, I was all alone in the world. But I desperately missed Ryan's companionship. I cared for him more deeply than I'd imagined.

"No. I told you I don't like people. And I only trust women. Your husband would never trust me; not now. He's bound to be angry and I'd have to keep a close eye on him all the time. He'd try to kill me for bringing you up here."

"You don't know that for sure. I could talk to him."

"No. There'll be no talking to him. None! This whole situation is entirely your own doing. It's all your fault, Savannah."

I decided not to argue the point. Silence reigned in the cave for several minutes as we continued eating. Douglas made a satisfied sound after swallowing each cracker. I doubt he'd gotten even one tiny crumb in his scraggly beard. He licked his fingers, smacking his lips; then the two of us shared his water. Not something I wanted to do, but with the depth of my thirst, I'd have done almost anything for a drink.

"What was it that brought you and your friends all the way out here to trespass on my island, Savannah? I don't like trespassers. I told you I moved here to be alone."

"I'm a part-time freelance writer–magazines and sometimes newspapers. I came out here, kind of on assignment for *National Geographic*, to look for an island that was written up in an old newspaper article. I had a photographer with me, to take pictures for the story. It had a good chance to appear on the front cover of the magazine." My voice trailed off to a whisper. It sounded so petty in comparison to the magnitude of the losses. Douglas watched me but didn't offer any comments.

When the food was gone, he took me to the bathroom area. After leading me back inside, he stuffed the handkerchief in, reapplied the chains, then left.

Again, I sat alone in the dimly illuminated cave. I needed to ramp up my efforts to befriend Douglas. It might be the only chance of escaping.

Douglas returned in the late afternoon but didn't speak. I'd need to be cautious in what I said in the future, since his fuse was short.

After my trip to the bathroom, Douglas pushed me to the floor of the cave near the chains. The landing was hard, but I refrained from issuing a complaint. As difficult as it was for me to admit to myself, I found his brief visits preferable to isolation. I'd never been good at being alone, especially when that solitude came with being imprisoned in a dark cave. My imagination ran to frightening places.

Skittering insects I couldn't see made it worse. They must be sizeable for me to hear them in between the crashing of the waves. When Douglas was around and with daylight streaming in, they hid away somewhere.

My captor sat in front of me, reaching for the open can he'd brought with him.

"Douglas, did you know there are bugs in here? Can you see them? My eyes don't work well enough for me to see them." Perhaps he would show some sympathy.

"What bugs?" His words were clipped, irritated.

"I don't know. I can't see them, but I can hear them running around in here whenever you aren't with me. I think they're afraid of you. Maybe you could find them and get rid of them for me? They've bitten my ankles a few times; plus, I have a bad phobia about bugs...especially spiders."

"I know. I saw you that day, too."

"What day?" As I said the words, the image surged into my mind. He had seen me closer to naked than I'd ever want. "Oh, out on the beach, with my husband."

"Yes." He stared at me, not offering to elaborate.

I wished I'd never brought up the topic. I'd be much more comfortable not knowing he'd ever seen me like that. It made me wonder what else he'd seen. I diverted my thoughts immediately. Where they headed was terribly unproductive.

"You can't hear spiders, you know."

"You're right. I guess these must be something else, then."

Douglas stood, moving around to search for insects. There were so many nooks and crannies in here, it would be impossible to find a bug trying to hide itself away. He didn't spend much time in the attempt.

"You know, you shouldn't panic from spiders the way you did that day. You scared my seagulls, and I couldn't calm them down."

"Your seagulls?"

"They followed me from my home here. They were paying me a visit in the jungle while I watched you and your husband. They follow me around like loyal pets. They're my babies. I had a little treat for them, but you scared them too much. You didn't talk nice to them, either.

"I almost decided against bringing you up here because of it. You shouldn't allow yourself to get so upset that you use bad language; especially not when you're talking to my babies. I don't like that, Savannah."

He glanced around the cave once more before plopping down in front of me. "I don't see anything. Those bugs won't really hurt you, anyway. If you're hungry and they come close enough, you can eat them."

My face undoubtedly reflected my revulsion. "I don't think I could ever do that."

"Then you might starve one day."

"Maybe. But that would only occur if something happened to you. You've been taking good care of me. Thank you for that, by the way." Compliments could work wonders sometimes, even if not genuine. I needed to make sure he couldn't tell the difference.

"You're welcome," he said hesitantly.

Maybe I'd laid it on a little too thick. I should do a better job next time.

"How do you manage to get up and down those cliffs, Douglas? My vision is blurry, but it looks like it's straight up. I just don't get how anybody can do it. You must be agile and a good climber. I tend to be clumsy." I despised giving him compliments, even if it helped my case.

"It comes natural to me. I've always been a good climber. My brother and I made sure the path to get down here from the top was difficult for an intruder to discern. I'm the only one who should be using it anyway." He straightened his shoulders. "Are you a climber, Savannah?"

"No, I'm not. I've never cared for it. I prefer flat ground, where you can see things coming. You know, if something bad happens to you, like say, you slip and fall off the cliff, what'll happen to me?"

"You won't have to worry about eating any of the bugs. There wouldn't be enough of them for you to live off of. Besides, you'll die of thirst long before you die of starvation. You won't have a problem, the way I see it. You'll only make it a few days at most. And part of that time you'll be off your rocker. Then you'll die."

"And that doesn't bother you?"

"Why should it? Your being here is your fault, remember?" He reached over to retrieve the can he brought in. He jabbed the fork into the contents and withdrew a half dozen green beans. One slipped off, splashing into the liquid inside.

"Open," he ordered.

I did as he instructed and consumed the beans. He fed them to me almost faster than my throat could swallow them. Clearly, I'd upset him again. I must choose my words better, to keep him on my side, allowing me to stay alive until Ryan found me.

Yet, from what Douglas said, Ryan had already given up searching. Not that I blamed him. I'd never blame him for anything. I missed him so much. In my sleep, I dreamed of him, of the two of us together again, laughing as we ate freshly roasted crab.

Douglas brought more crackers and trail mix with him the next morning. He sat, opened his crackers, and popped one into his mouth with obvious delight, keeping my trail mix in his lap. Hopefully, he had removed all the food from the backpack. Ryan was bound to notice the missing food at some point. Maybe he'd start searching for me again once he noticed. If he didn't assume I'd eaten it. That thought hadn't occurred to me before. My grand plan, ruined.

I swallowed and tried to ask nicely, considering how he'd seemed angry the day before. "Douglas, whenever you're ready, I really need to use the bathroom, please."

The hope was in me that Ryan might be out there somewhere, still searching since more food had been taken. And maybe, just maybe, he'd be in the right place at the right time and see or hear us, somehow.

My endurance for captivity wore thin. I hated being near Douglas, but I hated the nighttime even more. Feeling the insects crawling on me, biting, and chewing, was all but unbearable. The restraints made it difficult to thrash my body well enough to shake them off.

Douglas didn't say a word. He simply stopped eating for a moment to take me outside, then brought me back when I finished. He still hadn't given me the trail mix yet. He ate while my chains and gag were both off. It was wonderful to feel even that bit of freedom. I spent the time stretching in place and rubbing my swollen, bruised wrists, being careful of the scabs. Not long afterward, the cry of a seagull broke the rhythm of the smashing waves.

"One of my babies is back, begging for food again. Seagulls are such great company," he commented with a chuckle.

"Seagulls are your babies?" Being alone for as long as Douglas had been, it was understandable he considered the birds as close company.

"A lot of the ones on this island are my babies. They come when I call them, and sometimes when I don't. They'll even follow me if I go into the jungle. Seagulls don't usually go into the jungle, but mine are special. Their voices are all a little different from each other; no one else can decipher the subtle differences, only me because they're mine. I love seagulls."

"I hate them." The words snapped from my mouth before I thought of using self-control. The friendship idea didn't seem to be working and I'd grown impatient.

"Why? How could you hate them? How could anyone hate them? They're such funny creatures. They always make me laugh." He wore a big, toothy grin.

"Not me. Not anymore." My words were clipped.

"Why?" he asked, clearly puzzled at the thought, sliding the trail mix over to me.

"I hate them because they made our helicopter crash. They killed my friends and stranded me here. I have a daughter I'll probably never see again."

His mouth dropped open, eyes widening. "I didn't know you had a daughter. If I'd known, maybe things would've been different." He paused, storm clouds passing over his eyes as his lips pursed. "You never should've come here in the first place! Everything that happened was your fault!" he yelled.

The reaction startled me, so I drew back in response, dropping the bag of trail mix I'd just opened. "What're you talking about?"

"My seagulls were killed, too, you know."

"Your seagulls? What do you mean *your* seagulls?"

"This was your fault, you know—all of it. Their deaths are on your conscience, the men, and my seagulls. If you hadn't come here, none of this would've had to happen. Then your daughter would have her parents to grow up with. How old is she?"

"Eleven. What are you talking about with the seagulls?" My suspicions grew.

"One of those men in your helicopter. He saw my seagulls."

"I don't understand. What're you talking about?"

"I had a big cage I'd made myself out of trees and vines on the jungle side of these cliffs. That's where I kept my seagulls. I dismantled it after you and your friends crashed. It was empty anyway, and I couldn't risk you finding the cage and searching for the person who built it. Those birds were mine!" He slapped his right palm against the stone floor. "I raised them from the time they were babies. They didn't deserve to die like that! You did it! It's your fault!"

The ghastly scene coalesced in my mind: Alphonse spotted the birds in their cage. That was what he witnessed, right before we crashed; a giant cage where none should be. Douglas saw Alphonse leaning through the open door, taking photographs, and set the birds loose upon us. "Do you mean *you're* the reason we crashed? You did that to us *on purpose*?"

"I had no choice. He saw them…he saw my babies. He was taking pictures to show the world my paradise and my babies. If you knew about the cage full of birds, you'd know there had to be a person taking care of them. You'd report me and people would come looking. They'd find me. I couldn't take a chance on that happening. No one can know that I'm here, and alive. The sacrifice had to be made. It had to be made for *me*."

"You released them, knowing they'd fly straight up into us?" It was so difficult to believe the words, let alone the action.

"Of course. I had to protect what's mine. I had to eliminate all of you. It was your fault, Savannah! You changed everyone's lives. You did this to us!" He fumed where he sat for a moment then scrambled to his feet in anger, grabbed a fistful of the back of my shirt, my hair caught up in it as he dragged me backwards. I cried out and reached back to flail uselessly at his hand. He reattached my chains and stuffed the gag into my mouth before storming out with the food.

I sat there, stunned by the news. Tears rolled down my cheeks and were absorbed, as my sobs were, by the handkerchief in my mouth. Now I knew what happened, and the reason. Why did I ever decide to do it? Why did I make the senseless decision to take this trip and destroy so many lives? Douglas opened the cage, but he was right. It was my fault. I killed Alphonse and Dave. It was me.

Fourteen

Late in the evening, Douglas came for me. Everything that had happened since I arrived in the tropics was for no good reason. Douglas was a psychopath and a murderer. But I'd been his full-fledged accomplice. We were both guilty but me more so than him. And I hated him for giving me that knowledge.

He released me from my bonds and my gag before half-dragging me to the bathroom area. I stumbled once and he yanked me back to my feet. After I finished, he took me inside.

"Drink some water and eat the rest of your food." He motioned to the water from this morning that he'd left behind in his hasty exit. He dropped a pack of fresh crackers and a bag of trail mix on the floor.

"This was your fault, Savannah. You make sure you remember that. Everything was your fault. There wouldn't have been any deaths if not for you. *You* killed them."

I kneeled and picked up the bottle, drinking several quick swallows, only enough to quench my thirst. Then I returned it to the floor where it had been. I stood then, returned to the wall, and sat on the floor, fastening the cloth in my mouth, and tying it in place at the back of my head. I put my hands behind my back to wait but didn't look at him.

Douglas stared at me for a minute or two without speaking or moving. Then he lumbered over to chain me to the wall. He collected the food and water. His form was difficult to see in the growing darkness, but I knew he was standing in the doorway, staring at me again. I focused my attention on the nearby wall instead, until the door closed and locked. It was then I allowed my rigid body to slump.

If only I'd never come here. My sorrow for Alphonse and Dave overwhelmed me. I said a prayer before sleeping, a prayer for Ryan. Then I asked for patience, strength, and forgiveness. And lastly, for a quick, merciful death, even though I knew I didn't deserve one.

As I dreamed, Dave came to sit with me, to tell me everything would be okay. Happiness had come to him in death, just as it would for me.

The next morning, Douglas showed up bright and early to take me outside. But it wasn't bright outside. A misty rain fell. It was appropriate, the atmosphere matching my mood. Once back inside, Douglas motioned me to sit in my regular spot. He chained me to the wall, like usual. I winced in pain from the cracks in my scabs caused by the metal carving at my wrists.

The shackles felt relatively smooth, but the chains were rough, likely due to age and rust. The memory of the year of my last tetanus shot was lost somewhere in my mind, not that it mattered. Whatever resulted, I deserved it. Samantha had her father, so she would be fine. My sole hope was for Ryan's rescue, or at the very least for his long life, sound mind, and good health.

"Open your mouth." The words were sharp and loud, like the crack of a whip.

I behaved for him. He fed me more green beans, though only half a can. I missed the peaches but didn't ask about it. What I received was keeping me alive and that was something to be grateful for. Or maybe not.

"You must be carrying around a lot of guilt, Savannah."

"What?" I asked, swallowing the last forkful of beans.

"Don't talk with your mouth full; it's rude. Didn't your parents teach you any manners? I guess they didn't teach you much of anything, though, considering what you've done here."

"Yes, sir."

"Let's wash down those beans." He squirted the liquid into my mouth before I was able to fully ready myself.

Some of the water streamed down my chin, along my throat and into my shirt. He didn't wait for me to catch up, squirting my face gleefully. I caught little of it in my mouth as I coughed and ended up with additional water squirted onto my face for it.

"Oh, you've made a mess of yourself, Savannah." Sarcasm wasn't his strong suit.

"I'm sorry. It was coming out too fast for me." More coughs came over me.

"Are you blaming me for your mistake, like you blamed me and my seagulls for killing your friends? After all, we both know that was your fault, right?" he yelled.

I hung my head, the guilt washing over me. I shouldn't let Douglas get to me with his accusations, but there'd been a seed of doubt in my mind ever since the crash. My captor had provided sustenance for it to grow. "Yes," I whispered, shoulders slumped, head nodding.

"Good, I'm glad to hear it. That's progress. At least you're capable of admitting your guilt. I want you to spend the rest of the day considering what you've done to all of us. You've caused an enormous amount of damage and hurt so many. And there was no reason for any of it, now was there?" His voice lilted, bordering on upbeat.

"No. I'm so sorry." A flood of tears came, releasing a wave of guilt and pain.

"Good. You should be sorry. You need to think about the lives you've destroyed, every day, all the time." His voice hardened. He left then, leaving the gag off.

The tears wouldn't stop. The guilt weighed on me, impossible to bear. I knew Douglas was the one who caused the crash with his damned seagulls. But there was plenty of blame to go around, more than enough for me to have a share. Maybe even the lion's share. Definitely that.

I'd give anything if I'd never come here in the first place. The entire series of events would have been interrupted. Alphonse and Dave would still be alive. Ryan would be engaged. I would be with my husband and daughter. Nothing was worth this. Nothing. What had I done?

My mind overflowed with the hopelessness of my situation. Ryan would never come, his efforts at searching obviously over. There was nothing I could do to rescue myself. I didn't have the clear eyesight or energy, the strength or spirit to attempt an attack on Douglas, to gain the opportunity to run away. Even if I did and was successful, there was no logic in it. How could I ever manage to find my way off this cliff in my condition, before being stopped by Douglas?

That left only one solution. I'd have to end the torment by jumping. The more time I spent thinking about it, the more appealing the idea became. Yet did I have the right to the mercy provided by a quick ending? Alphonse got that, sort of, but he was innocent. Poor Dave hung on and fought for a while, even though he was unconscious. My death might even come faster than Alphonse's, leaving no time to reconsider, not that I ever would. I said a quick prayer, for strength to do the task.

When Douglas came to give me a bathroom break around noon, my dejection didn't give me the courage to look at him. He unchained me and led me outside. The skies were cloudy, but the rain had stopped. Everything was still wet and dripping.

Here it was...my opening. I'd be free from the overwhelming sense of remorse, something beyond my capacity to endure any longer. After I'd relieved myself, I pulled up my pants. I took two steps toward Douglas, along the edge of the precipice, then pivoted to my right and stepped into the air beyond the ledge.

The panic-provoking absence of solid ground beneath my right foot and the beginnings of my fateful fall proved more terrifying than I had imagined. Death would come at my own hands. But I was releasing myself, setting my soul free. And Douglas would fail.

The sensation of falling was abruptly interrupted by Douglas. He grabbed me around the midsection and flipped me around, slinging my body into the cliff, near the cave entrance. The impact was worsened by my weakened state and emotional overload. Both my shoulder and the left side of my face were scuffed up, burning like fire. He took me by the arm, forcing me back into my prison cell as I cried.

"You idiot! What did you think you were doing? That was very foolish of you, Savannah! And very selfish."

"S-selfish?" I stammered, teeth gritted, as I attempted to control my sobbing and catch a breath.

"Yes, selfish. Don't you think those people you killed deserve to have you wade through a period of guilt? You need to spend time wallowing in it. You need to break. My father broke me once. I thanked him for it later."

"Break?" What did that mean? Was I not following the proper procedure for a suicide? Were there rules? I never knew there were rules.

"That's right. You need to be broken to rebuild your life. I'm breaking you. Trust me. I know what's best for you. I'm all you've got."

He reattached the chains with care this time, giving me additional slack thanks to a longer length of chain. It still wasn't enough to allow me to lie down, but it was better. He left my gag off, too.

"Goodbye, Douglas," I said softly as the door closed, not knowing if he heard me or not.

Everything in me was broken already. How much more could there be?

Douglas gave me only a small amount of water that evening, a couple of meager swallows. There wasn't any more in the bottle. And he brought me no food. He released me from the chains and led the way to the bathroom area. This was the first time he hadn't kept a hold on me as we walked. I didn't question it, just followed obediently, head down, shoulders slumped. He had emptied me, left me defeated.

As I relieved myself, I decided it was better to go hungry than ask about the lack of nourishment. It would be even better if I stopped talking altogether. It got me into nothing but trouble.

I finished, then buttoned my pants and zipped them up. When I turned to Douglas, his proximity startled me. And he was staring at me. He had always given me privacy before. But then, he had always seemed preoccupied watching for Ryan.

Somehow, I knew we'd reached a turning point, a bad one. It suddenly felt as though a heavy object sat on my chest. Dread filled me.

He stepped forward, gently taking my hand. "Let's go inside my room. I want to show it to you now. I think you're ready."

All my fears of Douglas, simmering since my capture, surged forth as I found what little strength and life-force I had left, hidden somewhere in the deep recesses, even from me. It was impossible to go into that cave with him, no matter what rebellion cost. I yanked my hand free from his and screamed at the top of my lungs. *"Ryan! Help me!"*

Douglas struggled, attempting to hold me tight and clamp a hand over my mouth.

I bit him for it, drawing blood I could taste. *"Ryan! Ryan!"*

Douglas tripped me up, sending me hard to the rocky ledge. Pain radiated outward from the left side of my face and body, again. He sat on my back the same as when he originally captured me, a lifetime ago. He gagged me, tying the handkerchief so tight I would have begged for mercy if I'd been able to speak. The skin at the corners of my mouth split apart, blood soaking into the cloth.

Taking both my hands in his, he dragged me, face first, into my prison cell. Inside, I flailed against him, using everything in me, but it was no use. He overpowered me, reattaching my chains. Not that I expected any other outcome. Yet, it was a release; at least now, he'd leave me be.

He stepped back then, staring at me, his breathing labored. Everything I'd been trying to build with him was gone. But I didn't care. The knowledge that I'd never see Ryan again had me preferring that Douglas kill me.

Please, end it. End me.

Nothing was happening. It must be that I needed to encourage him to do it, so I threw myself against the chains as they tore at my wrists. My attempts to reach him caused the monster to take a step backward. I gave an extended, growling yell of rage and frustration, muffled by the gag. Douglas retreated another step, leaving soon after.

My sanity was departing. And maybe more than that. But what difference did it make? I'd already lost absolutely everything that mattered, including my freedom. I lost my family long ago and irretrievably in this isolated place. I'd lost two companions. What mattered most of all was the loss of Ryan. I never told him how important he was to me. I never truly imagined how much I would miss him. I always thought he'd be there, that there would always be a tomorrow.

The realization of how wrong I had been was unbearable. I gave a muffled scream from the burden of the knowledge of loss I had suffered.

Fifteen

It was early morning when Douglas returned. Neither a container of water nor a can of food was in his hands. I'd figured he wouldn't show up at all. After taking me for a bathroom trip, he secured me roughly to the wall and left without speaking.

It was just me and the bugs. One of them crawled on me, apparently as a coordinated distraction, while the other bit me. I didn't have any slack in the chain for upper body movement, although I did kick one of them off. It thudded against the stack of boxes. The little creatures had to be cockroaches. They'd likely feast on me once I died, if not before.

As a little girl, my father once helped me collect insects for a science project. We put them to sleep in a way the teacher had called merciful. Yet, I wondered about that as I watched them scramble madly around in the jar, searching for an escape. Then their movements had slowed to twitching and eventually stopped altogether.

There had been guilt in me then, both for capturing them and for ending their lives. Who was I to decide whether they lived or died? It was even worse when I had to stick a pin through their bodies to mount them on a board. I labeled each of them carefully, using my best handwriting. But what was a label to a bug? Was it like a headstone? Was that what they would have wanted if they could've chosen for themselves?

I found myself wondering if I should name these little companions of mine. What name should one give an insect, especially one that would end up consuming you? This would require some serious thought. It had to be fitting, after all.

My captor didn't return until late afternoon. He took me out for the obligatory bathroom break then reattached me to the wall, removing my gag. The corners of my mouth were torn from the continual torment of the restraining cloth. In addition, the side of my face and my chin were swathed in dried blood from being slammed to the rocks, then drug across them. Not that I cared.

He withdrew a small pill bottle from his shirt pocket, unscrewed the lid and grabbed me by the hair, yanking my head back at a sharp angle.

"Open your ungrateful mouth. This is your fault—all of it!"

When I hesitated, he violently shook my head from side to side, jarring my brain against my skull, so that I opened my mouth. Instead of pills, there was water, but only a thimbleful. He laughed and let go of me. He replaced the gag nice and tight then walked out, locking the door.

I didn't understand. There'd been the trickle of water. Was he trying to tease me, tempt me, or let me know he was ready to kill me? Perhaps he wanted to watch me die slowly. That made the most sense. It was what I deserved.

How long would that take? Didn't it take a few days to die from thirst? Perhaps I should perform the last science experiment of my life and count the time it took for me to succumb. I'd need to keep track in my head, since I couldn't write on the cell walls. That was what would be hardest since my brain wasn't working right anymore. Was that what happened to a person who killed someone? Did the guilt cause them to go insane?

My thoughts turned to Ryan. Because of me, he'd be stranded here, all alone. Well, not quite. Hopefully, he'd never encounter Douglas. The report Douglas had given me was that Ryan was sitting by Dave, and that was a few days ago. The missing food from my backpack had obviously gone unnoticed. He hadn't come for me. Maybe he had figured it all out for himself, that the death of his best friend had come at my hands. Maybe he'd decided I wasn't worth saving.

My grand plan had utterly failed. With luck, my captor would leave me here to die of thirst. That was about the best I could hope for. It would be a quicker, more merciful death if he tossed me over the side. I screwed up the attempt to do it myself so badly yesterday that I doubted Douglas would give me another opportunity.

Perhaps I truly deserved a slow death after the terrible things I'd been responsible for. I waited for sleep that was fitful when it came, interrupted periodically by visits from my insect pals.

The next day, I had just decided Douglas must have left me to my fate when he returned around midday. He released me, pulling me roughly to the bathroom area, leaving my gag in place. Once I'd relieved myself, he took me back. There was no food for me, which was to be expected. But he repeated the thimbleful of water from his damned little pill bottle.

"You just remember it didn't have to be this way. It's your fault—everything, everyone. The deaths happened because of you!"

He locked me away again and eventually I managed to doze. My dreams were frightfully unpleasant.

It was a relief to awaken from the world of nightmares, although the world of reality was equally disagreeable. Judging from the strips of sunlight, it must be afternoon. My only company was my multi-legged pets. At least one of them had transitioned from biting to chewing on me experimentally, not that I'd noticed much. Still, it wasn't nice of them, in my opinion. After all, when I was hungry, I hadn't eaten them. It made me glad I hadn't yet gone to the trouble of giving them names.

My captor arrived as I contemplated the misbehavior of my little companions through the pain of a terrible headache. It had been growing since the day before. My lips were dried, cracked in multiple places. If there'd been something capable of making me smile, the cracks would've split open. As it was, the blood at the torn corners of my mouth had dried, sealing the gag to my skin, resulting in free bleeding when Douglas yanked off the handkerchief.

There was still no food, but at least there was fresh air and sunshine to stumble out into for a couple of minutes.

Douglas was clearly impatient with my efforts. My body had weakened dramatically, and when I attempted tasks requiring dexterity, such as fastening and unfastening my pants, my hands shook. My body lacked coordination. There was a miniscule amount of dark urine to be squeezed out. My body was shutting down.

That realization was as close to being happy as I'd imagined myself capable of since the kidnapping happened. It meant this lousy excuse for an existence would soon be finished. That was something to look forward to. At last, there was an end in sight.

Douglas chained me to the wall. The torment with an insignificant amount of water and the blame game came again, as expected. I didn't give him a response, so he left. I said my prayers, begging for protection from harm for Ryan, a long and healthy life for Sam and especially Samantha, and forgiveness for myself, for the terrible things I'd done. Every time I asked for forgiveness, it made me feel better, whether I deserved it or not. I knew God forgave me, regardless of how selfish I'd been, or how much sorrow and pain I had brought to others.

Douglas returned sometime later. He took me out to the bathroom area, but this time there were only a few dark drips to excrete. It was difficult to remain upright, let alone walk, due to the dizziness and nausea. My feet stumbled. Douglas allowed me to fall to the rocks repeatedly, then yanked me as close to upright as my body would get.

Once chained to the wall, I waited for the miniscule amount of water. This time, though, he changed things up. He slipped the gag under my chin and ordered me to open my mouth for the water, which I managed through tremors. Instead of pouring it into my mouth, he spilled the contents onto my face. He dropped the bottle on the floor and walked to the doorway, chuckling to himself. He left the gag off.

"This was all your own fault. You can take that pleasant thought to your grave. None of this would've happened if not for you. I'll throw your body over the edge once you're dead. It'll be a burial at sea, and food for my babies." The door closed and the lock clicked.

This was truly the end, yet so unnecessary. I handled the entire encounter poorly the other day. I might've survived. At least, some part of me might have survived. But it was impossible for survival to have been worth the cost.

As I contemplated my impending death, I realized my perspiration had stopped. It surprised me, considering the humid, stuffy conditions in the cell. My body shook and my thoughts grew increasingly incoherent.

I wondered where my insect companions had gotten to. Maybe they were resting. They'd return soon enough. They always came back, always hungry. That was okay, I wouldn't mind.

Ryan would soon be resting for the night, back in the cave-port we'd shared, or on the beach by the decomposing body of his best friend, the brother he never had, the one I'd taken from him. I wondered if Ryan missed me. Maybe he was glad to be rid of me. Maybe he wished I was dead already, the way I did.

I missed Ryan desperately, though. I wanted to see him again, just one more time. My head slumped back against the wall, sending me into the world of dreams, where life was better, where I was happy and in the arms of the man I loved. I was in Ryan's arms.

My head slipped, awakening me with a start. The nausea had faded, replaced by an increase in the dizziness. The pain in my head made me want to scream. There was an unfamiliar sensation around my wrists.

It was difficult to see my surroundings because it was so dark. Then I remembered what happened to me. I had blissfully forgotten the change in my life for a moment, and the approaching end of it.

Carefully, I listened to figure out what had roused me. Did I hear a longed-for sound? Could it have been Ryan's voice calling to me?

After a few minutes, during which my hopes deflated like a pricked balloon, I realized there was nothing. It had been another disappointing dream.

My situation remained the same. Ryan still hadn't come for me. Crying was something I'd always disliked, mostly since Sam disapproved of it but he wasn't here to make me stop. No one was. It wouldn't stop, even though the dehydration mostly prevented actual tears. The dejection overwhelmed.

Once I'd given up on the sobbing, the quiet in the prison cell became noticeable. The weakness in me was worse, much more so than yesterday. I hadn't believed it possible. Today was likely going to be the end of the torment. That thought pleased me. There was only a little more time remaining to endure. My body slumped forward, my head inches above the floor. It was too heavy, unmanageable to lift. My thoughts were disorganized and nonsensical.

There had to be a way to get my spirits back up. I shouldn't surrender, I needed to fight back. Ryan would tell me to fight, to remain confident and positive.

So, I should see what I could do about that, perhaps thinking of things that made me happy. I liked being close to the ocean and breathing in the humid, salty air. What else was there to like about this place? I did have food and water for a while, but those were gone now. I missed those canned peaches. Longing for just one more filled me momentarily, until I thought of how much more I'd rather have water.

What else? My tiny pets? I wasn't sure about that, though. They weren't grateful for the company I provided them with, nor the munchies. I'd stopped kicking at them when they bit me, even though I didn't enjoy being bitten, or the feeling of them scampering over my ankles, trying to crawl up my legs from inside my pants. Yet, the stinging pinch of the bites let me know I still clung to life. It served as a not-so-friendly reminder in case my delusional mind forgot.

And sometimes I did forget, especially whenever Dave visited. When he came last night, his voice gave away his presence. This morning, it was more; I saw him, too. It was spooky at first, talking with a dead person. It startled me into thinking I had died. Not yet, he'd told me.

He was so sweet to me. He even tried to remove the chains, pulling so hard it felt as though my hands were going to come off. The attempt made me cry out from the pain, and the frustration from failure. The wet stickiness of blood running down my hands made Dave try again, but there wasn't enough blood to lubricate the cuffs, to allow them to slide over my hands.

Dave had cried, telling me he was sorry. Since he couldn't free me, he told me we'd have to wait until the end. Then the chains wouldn't be capable of holding me anymore and my captor's power over me would be at an end. No more torment.

When Alphonse had visited, he blamed me for taking him away from his beloved family. I hadn't even known most of the people who'd come earlier, but they blamed me, too. Some of them scared me. They bared their teeth and hissed and threatened me, telling me I would pay in the afterlife. As if a slow death wasn't already enough for me to suffer through, not to mention the weight of all that guilt.

Dave would be back later. When the end was nigh, he'd be with me, to take me by the hand and escort me all the way. I would miss Ryan, but Dave said I'd be happy on the other side, and that he'd stay with me for as long as I needed him.

It was easy for me to understand why Ryan had been so upset to lose Dave. The man had been such a great friend, always thinking of others. I looked forward to the end, not as afraid as I otherwise would've been. I wouldn't be subjected to any more agony, plus I'd be with my friend Dave. It couldn't come soon enough. A labored breath shuddered in my chest.

Something had awakened me again. At least, I supposed I was awake. Maybe it was nothing but dreaming about being awake. Life had grown quite challenging to make sense of.

Earlier, there had been many people in my cell with me; dozens of them. Yet, it hadn't seemed crowded at all. We had talked and laughed for a while, but in the end, each of them had told me they weren't allowed to set me free. They told me my predicament was all my own fault, just as Douglas did. Even Sam blamed me. I had made the decision to come here in the helicopter. It was my fault Samantha would grow up without a mother. It was my fault Alphonse and Dave were dead. And if Ryan was murdered by Douglas, well, that would be my fault, too.

The door to my cell was being unlocked, snapping me out of my self-rebuke. My captor was returning to dole out more torment after all. I should've known...it was too good to be true. That was okay though, I deserved it. Everyone knew that.

Could he possibly have water with him? Had he decided to give me a second chance? I didn't care about that anymore, though. Did I? Come to think of it, maybe I'd like to have that thimbleful of water. Yes, if only he was bringing me some water. Please. I'd never been able to imagine a thirst like this before.

The door opened, slamming against the wall. He rushed toward me, shoes pounding on the rock. I let my head sag; there wasn't strength to keep holding it up any longer. Had I been holding it up? Probably not, at least, not much. He knelt beside me, placing a hand on my shoulder.

"Oh my God. Please, you can't be dead; I can't be too late. I've got you now, Savvy. You're safe. I'm so sorry this had to happen to you." Ryan gently stroked the hair back from the side of my face so he could see me. I angled my head to peer up at him, although it barely moved, was incapable of moving.

"Ryan? Is it really you?" I mouthed the words, my dry, scratchy throat unwilling to allow words to escape my mouth.

"Yes, it's really me. I'm sorry it took so long to find you. But I finally did it, after all that searching. I found you."

"You found me?"

"Yes, I did. I've been searching for so long. It wasn't easy. The path leading down here was hidden. I almost didn't find it. But we can talk about that later. Right now, I need to find the keys to unlock these chains around your wrists. Where are the keys?"

"I'm so glad you're here."

"Me too, but I need you to focus. You need water and I have to get you out of here. I need to know where those keys are. Can you tell me, Savvy?"

"Douglas. He has them."

"Douglas? Is he the man who brought you here and chained you up?"

"Yes. He always has the keys. They're in his pocket." I remembered the jingling when Douglas walked. Where was he? Was he coming?

"Oh, no." Ryan's face fell.

"What?"

"We were fighting, and I threw him over the cliff into the ocean. His body was swept away."

My eyes struggled to widen sufficiently through the realization. "But...the keys."

"It's all right, Savvy. We don't need the keys anyway."

"We don't?"

"No, we don't," he smiled at me, still stroking my hair, just the way I liked it.

"Why not?" My confusion deepened.

"Because I can't let you leave here. This whole situation is your fault. You know that. You killed Alphonse and Dave. I'll never be able to forgive you for killing Dave; he was the best friend I ever had in my whole life. I couldn't have loved that man more if he was my brother. Goodbye, Savannah. I do love you, though. I always will."

I did my best to cry. The pain in my heart was excruciating, the worst pain ever. With great effort, I raised my head enough to beg Ryan not to leave me in prison. A tiny, single tear rolled down my cheek. I licked at it with my swollen, cracked tongue, thirsty for the moisture. I wanted to ask Ryan to forgive me, but he was already gone, the door closed and locked.

My head slowly drooped back to where it had been. Sorrow might break my heart enough to take me faster than the dehydration could. At long last, the relief of death was coming over me.

Sixteen

Footsteps. Dave was coming for me. My ears didn't detect the metal-on-metal of the door being unlocked until the very final click. There was a slight creaking as the door was pushed all the way back to thud against the wall. I opened one eye, a tiny slit. I didn't possess the strength to lift my head.

Dave was accompanying me on my final journey. I knew he wouldn't let me down. He hadn't wanted me to be afraid or alone. I hoped I'd be allowed in Heaven, even though I'd been such a terrible person. I still believed, still had faith. Dave was in Heaven. He said he was happy there. All the pain was gone. Oh, how I longed for that.

The light of the moon shot across the floor in a broad beam, illuminating me. It must be a full one. I'd always liked full moons. It was appropriate to die in the light of one. My time was finally up. I could feel it; the lessening of the awareness of pain, the bluish glow around me, and Dave's voice calling to me, from somewhere off in the distance. He was coming to escort me to the other side. At last, a friendly, forgiving face.

Grooves from the carving of this shelter were brought out by the angle of the moonlight. My head hung slumped to the floor from its own weight, bringing me close enough to see the details. In a few minutes, I'd be dead, just as everyone wanted, so what did grooves matter? I was getting what I deserved.

My captor was welcome to throw water in my face again if he wanted to. It meant nothing anymore, especially after that heart-wrenching rejection from Ryan. I closed my eye. I already knew everything was my fault. I didn't need to hear it from Douglas again. My spirit was about to leave my body, my breaths nearly gone.

"Savannah...oh my God! Savannah, can you hear me?" the voice asked in a panic.

Ryan must have come to say goodbye, to pay me a second visit. Maybe he had forgiven me and wouldn't break my heart this time. Perhaps Dave was with him. Even though Dave's death was my fault, he'd been so nice to me, so forgiving. Was that yesterday? His voice rang out, calling my name.

"Savannah. Savannah, please no. Dear God."

Fingers pressed at my neck. Was Ryan going to choke me for killing his best friend? His hands moved to mine as keys jingled. When the chains were unlocked, my body collapsed the remaining few inches to the floor of the cave. The impact didn't register. Only the release of pressure.

The force against my wrists, tearing at my flesh, ended. My body was shifted away from the wall and rotated to put me on my back, arms at my sides. It was such a welcome treat to be able to stretch out.

Wasn't this how your body was positioned for burial after death? Did I die? I didn't even notice. There wasn't a bright light. Wasn't there supposed to be a bright light. Had that been the moon? Was Dave here to help me, preparing my body to be left behind?

My head was gently raised, nestled in the crook of an arm. A finger came into my mouth, attempting to part my lips. The delicate skin over them tore and blood trickled out. A thimble-sized amount of water soon followed. At least he didn't throw it into my face the way Douglas did. It swirled around my mouth and cascaded down my throat. It felt welcome, yet foreign, to my insides, dried up like a long-forgotten sponge left out in the sun.

Why was he doing this? I didn't want water. It would only serve to postpone the inevitable. I was ready to go, wanted to go. Why couldn't Ryan simply let me die? It was finally my time.

His fingertips caressed my cheek. "What in the hell did that monster do to you?"

After a brief hesitation, more water came and more still, each time with a pause in-between. A hand gently caressed the side of my throat to encourage a swallow. When a larger gulp was given, it made me cough, sending most of the water back out, spilling from the side of my mouth to moisten my neck and shirt. The coughs racked my body with spasms of unwelcome, additional pain.

"Come on, sweetheart. Swallow for me. You can do it." He kissed my forehead. "Please, Savannah. Open your eyes. I won't let you leave me. God, I love you so much."

Ryan was still with me. He sounded so frightened. He'd be okay though. He'd get used to living alone if he hadn't already. Dave was here, somewhere. His comforting presence filled the cave. He came back for me, just as he said he would. Dave swore he didn't blame me for what happened. He was the only one.

He'd also promised to find a way to make Ryan feel better once I'd gone. I was nearly there; another minute, or a few more breaths. Maybe Ryan would bury me beside Dave, even though it was my fault Dave was there in the first place.

"Here, try a little more before we go." He poured another dose of water into my mouth.

He must have decided to take me to Dave after all. It was such a lovely, peaceful spot for a grave. The beach had always been my favorite place. I hoped Ryan would make me a cross like the one I made for Dave. And maybe I'd get a big, pretty shell for a headstone, too.

Ryan lifted me into his arms to take me to be buried next to Dave. That would make me so happy. Ryan could visit both of us every day. I had missed him so much. The three of us would be back together.

My head was lifted slowly from the ground again, but not far. There was scarcely any sensation of motion since it was performed with such delicacy. Water flowed into my mouth. After a pause, it happened another time, and another.

It was as though I was gradually awakening from a terrible nightmare, yet what would the reality be like? Was my captor giving me more of the teasing sips of water? Was he trying to bring me back so he could torment me further? How much was enough to pay for two lives?

There probably wasn't enough in all the world for that.

I fought to open my eyes. When at last I managed it, the world was as out of focus as before but brighter, and the air was fresh. A hand clasping the little brown pill bottle swung toward my mouth.

"No!" I croaked. I succeeded in my panic somehow to turn my head away as the bottle touched my lips, spilling the liquid across my cheek and down my neck. I struggled to move out of reach, but my legs wouldn't work, and my arms and hands were just as uncooperative.

An arm tightened around my shoulders, holding me firmly in place. "Savannah! Savannah, it's me, Ryan. I've got you, you're safe now. You're safe, honey. It's okay. You're going to be okay. Take it easy, please. I need you to drink water. You have to."

I couldn't believe my ears. Surely, it was another delusion. Or could both of us be dead now? If that was true, Dave should be around. Where was he? He promised.

Still, there was a chance. "Ryan?"

My head was lowered to the ground. The surface was hard but had the crackle of old vegetation for a cushion. Ryan smiled, leaning close, allowing me to see his face better.

"Savannah." His fingers softly stroked my cheek, over and over. He leaned down and gave my torn, swollen lips a feathery kiss. "I'm right here. I'll never leave you again."

"Ryan." My whispered voice cracked; a tremor of relief passing through me.

"Shush, now. Don't try to talk. Just lie still. I'm going to lift your head up again to give you more water. You need more. I want you to drink for me, okay? You have to."

He lifted my head higher this time, sitting me up so I leaned against his chest. He tried using the little brown bottle again and I turned my head away, refusing him. "No."

"Savannah, you have to have water. You're badly dehydrated. You're not going to make it without water."

"Not that," I murmured.

Ryan held the bottle out to study it for a moment before setting it aside. He held up my water bottle and I allowed him to put it to my lips. After several sips and more coughing, he stopped, lowering my head carefully.

"I'll give you some more in a minute, okay?"

I nodded. He sat staring at me. Since I couldn't see his expression,

I turned my head away from him to the rear wall of the cave-port. I recognized our home but maybe it was my mind playing tricks.

If it weren't, that meant Ryan had found me somehow and rescued me from prison, from death. My thoughts fell immediately to my captor and I faced Ryan, my eyes wide. I forced my hand to reach out to him. It couldn't get quite all the way there, trembling badly and dropping between us. He took it in his own hands, lifting it for a kiss.

"Douglas. Where?" My whispered voice asked urgently.

"Douglas? Who's Douglas?" He kissed my hand again, closing his eyes to savor the contact.

"The man."

"Oh. You don't have to worry about him ever again, Savvy. He's dead. I killed him."

"You did?"

"Yes. Of course I did. You don't have anything to worry about, I promise."

"You promise?" This was too much to hope for. It couldn't possibly be real. This must be another delusion, the sweetest one yet. I didn't want this one to ever stop.

"Yes, sweetheart. I promise. I'll never let anyone hurt you ever again as long as I live—no matter what. It's time for more water." He lifted my head.

Seventeen

Sunlight announced a brand-new day had begun, like it or not. Part of me didn't want to move. Nighttime was scary, with everything so dark. Of course, a few things helped last night. The moon was a couple of days past full, providing illumination most of the night. No more chains restricted my movements—I'd been set free now, my captor dead in my place. Then there was Ryan. I laid there with utter assurance that he was between me and anything beyond the cave-port that might attempt to do me harm.

Without rolling over to check, I knew he was there, his soft snoring a reminder. He hadn't gotten much sleep since Douglas had taken me and had worn himself out with searching. I still couldn't believe we were back together. For a while, I'd been convinced it would never happen; that I'd never be blessed with seeing his smiling face again.

Yet, here I was, by the grace of God. By the persistence and skill of Ryan, without a doubt.

A sizeable insect scurried around beneath the bedding, the sound audible, near my head. I rolled over and pushed up on my elbows, squinting as I tried to make out where it was.

My ears told me better than my eyes. The vegetation movement was nearly imperceptible, but the scratching noises gave its location away. It broke from cover, scampering for the entrance and unconfined spaces beyond. It could have been the same kind of insect as that in my cell, although I never saw them. They didn't like daylight. I did.

Ryan's eyes popped open. He followed my stare before grabbing a nearby rock, flattening the creature just as it scurried into the low swath of greenery beyond our cave-port entrance. "There. It's gone now. I'm sorry, Savvy. It didn't scare you or bite you, did it?"

"Why did you kill him? He wasn't hurting anything. He followed me here from my cell. He must've missed me." Thankfully, I couldn't see the squished body.

"What? Savvy, it couldn't have followed you all that way. And it was a bug."

"He wasn't just a bug to me. He was my pet, my friend."

"Your what? Pet?"

"I had a couple of pets. They looked like that one, I think." I shuffled my feet in the bedding as I realized my reaction was leading to an actual conversation, something I didn't want. And this was one likely to cause me a measure of trouble. I bit my lip and stared at the dead vegetation under me.

Ryan propped himself up with one arm to study me. "I want you out in the sunshine. I'm going to check the bedding for any more of them."

He rolled over a couple of times until he was out, then helped me join him. "After you tell me about these so-called pets of yours, I'll pull the bedding out. It's time for fresh plants anyway. Here. Sit right here. I don't want you standing for long until I've gotten some breakfast into you."

Parking myself where directed, I watched him settle in front of me, both of us cross-legged. He would think I'd gone crazy. Maybe I had.

"Okay, tell me about the bugs, Savannah."

Rather than searching for the expression on a face I couldn't see, my gaze shifted to the blurry ground in front of me. "He kept me chained to the wall almost twenty-four hours a day. And alone, most of that time. I could hear insects—big ones—scampering around in the dark. It was scary at first. They'd always run away and hide from the light. You know, like whenever the door was open. When it was closed, they'd come out to play, and eat.

"The first time they skittered across my ankles it startled me and made my skin crawl. I screamed, but there was the gag, so it didn't matter. Nobody came to help me." From the corner of my eye, Ryan's body seemed to shift, and I heard his sigh.

"Anyway, I shook them off and kicked at them, but they kept coming back. They always ran back, skittering across the floor to me, like something out of a nightmare. I heard them coming for me from different directions in the dark." I paused for a sob, but regained control. That memory had me thinking that maybe the bugs weren't so nice after all; certainly not well behaved.

"They probably wanted the food in the storage crates, but I think it was all in cans, so they couldn't get to it. They could get to me, though. At first, they bit me a few times, but nothing serious. Not until later, at the end there, when I was dying." I absentmindedly rubbed my fingers over the darkened, swollen areas on my lower legs as I spoke.

"Those insects were my only company, until the others started showing up to talk." I ceased rubbing my legs and looked up slowly. That was a slip-up I hadn't intended to make. I shifted my gaze fast to the dark splotches on my pants.

Ryan had taken them to the waterfall to try to get some of the blood stains out. I'd watched him work for a while, until he had to give up. I knew they wouldn't come out; he did, too. But he'd needed to try. He hadn't wanted me to wear the reminder.

"What others?" Ryan asked.

"Others? There were no others," I lied.

"You just said there were."

"Oh. Well, that was a simple mistake on my part." I'd be damned if I'd tell him the rest. He'd know I'd gone crazy if I told him about Dave, not to mention the other people. I wasn't crazy. They were there—including Dave. There was no way I'd ever discuss that, not with anyone. Other people would think the same as Ryan would. If I was crazy, that was my business.

"Was it?" His head tilted to one side.

"Yes," I whispered.

"Why don't I believe you?"

"If you don't believe me, that's not my problem." I began pulling at strands of vegetation in front of me, then tearing them into pieces.

"Savvy." He sighed. "We can talk about that later. But those pets of yours were bugs, not pets. I know you're aware of that, at least on some level. You're a little confused right now with everything that happened to you. You don't need to be upset that I killed a bug. It wasn't one of yours. It couldn't be. Those ones deserve to be dead, too, for chewing on you like that. Damn it." Another sigh came, heavier than the first, and he ran a hand through his hair.

"I'm so sorry, Savvy. God, I'm sorry for what you went through up there. I wish I could take it all away for you, but I can't. I can listen, though. I want you to talk to me. You need to tell me what happened up there, for your own mental health and so you can get past it. I can help you. I'm not going to press you, not too much, anyway. Not right now.

"But bugs aren't your friends or your pets, okay? Can we just agree on that one thing?"

"Sure." The word came out reluctantly, without meeting his gaze. I didn't know that I believed him, or if he believed me.

"Come on, let's get some breakfast. I think you're strong enough to walk at least part of the trip today. And I'm not leaving you alone while I get it, either. We're all out of food, so we have to head out and find something. Drink this water first, though—all of it." He handed me a shell, filled with water.

Once I'd finished, he helped me to my feet and we walked, one of his hands firmly clasping mine, the other around my waist. "Can you talk to me some more about something, anything?" He busied himself helping me over rocky parts of the terrain so I wouldn't stumble.

I pursed my lips, staring at the ground I traveled over in response.

He gave me a minute, waiting patiently. "You don't have to talk about the kidnapping right now, Savvy. We can talk about anything you want. You need to talk, though. It's unhealthy for you to keep everything bottled up inside. It'll tear you up, mess you up, and I care too much about you to let that happen."

We'd reached the bottom of our hill by that point and I pulled my hand out of his when he stopped. He glanced to my hand and then my face before hopping down.

"I know you didn't want me helping you here before, but I'm going to do it anyway, at least until you've regained your strength."

He placed his hands on my waist and lifted me down. I moved my hands quickly to his shoulders for balance since I immediately felt unsteady. My feet touched the ground as he lowered me, but we didn't let go of each other.

There was so much fear in me, fear of talking about what happened to me, of Ryan forcing me to relive it. But the joy, the thrill beyond comprehension to be with Ryan again, to have my dream come true, was worth anything. I leaned forward, sliding my hands down his chest to wrap them around his waist, hugging him to me, as best I could manage in my weakened state. He rested his head on top of mine and let loose a deep sigh.

After a couple of minutes, he leaned back, lifting my face to his, applying a kiss to my forehead. "How do you feel? Are you tired? Do you need to rest?"

"All the above." My breaths were coming fast, my pulse racing. Physical activity was a challenge in my current condition.

"Then how about I carry you to where I'm planning to grab our breakfast?"

"That works for me," I managed the slightest of smiles, which he returned in much greater measure, positively beaming.

He scooped me up and carried me to where he intended to gather food. Cautiously, as though I were terribly fragile, he placed me on the ground.

"Now, you sit right there while I work. How about sea grapes this morning? Or are you tired of those?"

"No. They're fine."

"Okay then. They're good for you, too. We'll work on expanding the menu as you get better. Bananas will be a good next step." He harvested a couple of long strands of sea grapes while he talked to me.

"This'll give us enough to cover the day's munchies. You'll be able to get more rest if we don't have to go anywhere else to collect food. But if you're up to it, we'll come back down here in the afternoon. I'll grab this coconut, too. That'll be our dinner in case you're too tired to forage.

"Tomorrow or the next day, we'll try three square meals and see how you do with that. Provided that your system can handle processing everything well enough, that is. Speaking of that, I'll need to check you over once we're back home."

I smiled at his chattering. It was obvious how excited he was to have me back. I watched him, trying to focus on his words.

"I'm going to use you as my shopping cart." He laid the grapes across my lap, smiling. He added a large coconut next, pulling the strands of grapes around the base to hold it steady. I rested one hand on top, while the other slid around his neck as he lifted me again, still wearing that smile.

～∽～

On the eighth day after my rescue, Ryan decided to give in, allowing me to leave the cave-port for something besides food-gathering. Even though our little home was open on the front, it still felt too confining, too much like the prison cell. It was difficult for me to be comfortable in it when I awoke. Plus, it was the place where my ordeal had begun.

I sat on top of the hill, a few feet above our cave-port. My arms surrounded my knees as my eyes, unseeing, took in the vast blue blur of the ocean. There was no way to know how much time had passed, but it was late afternoon. The day was heavily clouded, casting a muted pall over the landscape. Ryan wasn't far away, sitting off to one side of the cave-port, staring out to sea.

My mind had suffered a dramatic change. I'd lost control earlier in the day, when Ryan left me sleeping in the cave-port to get fresh water to go with breakfast. I had awakened and he was nowhere to be seen. I'd curled up in a fetal position and cried, screaming for him. He had come running, assuring me he'd been in sight of the cave-port the whole time, but it took several minutes before he was able to calm me down, before it sank in.

So, he made sure to stay where I saw him all the time now and promised to wake me before going out for water or even to relieve himself. Maintaining proximity might be due as much to his fears as mine.

He carried an abundance of guilt, obvious even to someone with impaired sight. He shouldn't feel guilty. Douglas might have killed Ryan to get to me if he hadn't left me alone that morning. I was well-acquainted with remorse like what Ryan was going through.

It must be time to go, because Ryan was coming my way, near enough for me to detect his movement out of the corner of my eye.

"Savannah, it's time to get dinner," he called.

Ryan was careful to let me know he was approaching whenever my head was turned, to avoid startling me. I appreciated that. Being startled was the last thing I needed. I pushed up to meet him.

Even if it was hard for Ryan to see, there was gratitude in me for my life, not to mention my freedom. And in equal measure came the warmth and comfort of being back with him. But things between us weren't the same. Everything had changed.

We still had affection for one another, but there was a gulf in-between. I craved alone time, time to adjust, to think. But I needed him nearby. Even when one of us was relieving ourselves, Ryan talked. The subject didn't matter, just that I could hear his voice, occasionally responding so he heard me, too.

"Here. Take my hand, sweetheart."

He extended his hand, and I took a firm grip, like a lifeline, as always. We cautiously picked our way down the hill. Ryan kept ahold of me in case I should experience a misstep, like I'd often done since coming home from my prison ordeal. Today was better, as my physical coordination had improved.

"In a couple of days, I'm going to try to catch a fish. I think your system will be ready for it by then. Maybe even sooner than that." His tone was upbeat.

"Okay," I responded.

"Here, let me go first and then I'll lift you down."

Ryan said that every time we reached the bottom of our hill. It was the way he'd said things would go at this spot before I removed my contact lenses that evening. He had identified this area as one where he'd need to help me, and I had rejected the idea. I regretted treating him badly. He'd been trying to protect me.

He hopped down, turned, and put his hands around my waist, while I put mine on his shoulders. I enjoyed the sensation of him lifting me down; a feeling of safety and comfort came over me. When my feet touched the ground, we hugged one another. I made sure we did that every time. We were developing a routine, twice a day, while he gathered food.

This marked a first for me since the kidnapping: the third meal in a single day. He said my improvement was noticeable, that I'd gotten stronger and my body needed exercise, along with more food.

He rubbed my back, momentarily resting his head on mine, as usual. Then we began our slow trek into the jungle in search of fruit and palm innards. Ryan had taken to calling them that, as I had done what seemed like so long ago. He used everything he could think of to make me laugh or smile. It didn't work often.

I tried to give him at least a quick smile from time to time. Things between us were awkward, regardless. He felt guilty while I was stunned, as if I had a steep hill to climb but I couldn't even figure out how to crawl.

"Hey, how about these? Do you think you could hold onto them for me? They're kind of heavy; you may not be ready for that much weight yet. Just let me know." He pointed to a bunch of what must be sea grapes, from the form and color of the blur.

"I can do it; for a little while, anyway." The sea grapes were nearly all ripe and ready to eat. It was a double strand, having grown tangled around each other.

Ryan sliced the clusters free from the plant and handed them to me, waiting to let go until I had them secure in my grasp. "There you go, you've got them." He smiled brightly at me, like a proud parent to a young child. "You stay here, and I'll get some palm innards from that one over there. And it looks like we've got a few ripe bananas on the ground."

I watched as he worked. He must surely be growing tired of this food by now. "Ryan, why don't you go ahead and put a fish trap in the water? You could eat it without me, you know."

He seemed surprised I initiated conversation. I hadn't done that since the bug discussion. I hadn't wanted to talk much...about anything. Still didn't.

"I can wait, Savvy. I want to take care of you. You're all that matters to me. You have to know that."

I nodded and he returned to his gathering. When he'd assembled more than enough food, he came over and took my hand, lifting the grapes from me.

"I can carry them a while longer, Ryan."

"That's okay. You just focus on where you're putting your feet." He led me carefully back to our little home.

After we'd finished eating, I sat staring out from the back wall of the cave-port.

"Why don't you come and sit up here with me?" Ryan patted the bottom edge of the entrance to the cave-port, giving me an encouraging smile.

"I don't want to." I shook my head repeatedly, frowning. How could he suggest such a thing?

Ryan crawled over to me instead. "Why not? You've always liked sitting up there for the breeze and the view."

My stomach tightened. "That's where I was sitting the morning I was kidnapped, while I waited for you. Douglas dropped down in front of me from the roof. It was so completely terrifying. I don't ever want to sit there again."

Ryan kissed my cheek and put an arm over my shoulders. My stiffening body resisted his efforts to comfort. I ignored him, continuing to stare out ahead.

"He's gone now, Savvy. He's not coming back. And there was no one else–it's only us. I've checked, everywhere."

"I know. You told me." My voice was emotionless.

"It doesn't help, does it?"

"No," I whispered.

"You need to tell me what happened up there. I want to help you, but you have to let me in."

"No. I don't want to." It was my fault anyway, I wanted to add. That would bring more questions. I didn't want more questions.

"All right; for now, anyway. You're going to have to tell me about it sometime. You can't go on like this. You're not the same person you were before."

"Of course not. How could I be?" I still didn't look at him.

He sighed, pulling my head over so it leaned against his shoulder. I cooperated for a minute to placate him before straightening to shun the physical contact. He removed his arm from my shoulders, staring out with me in silence.

THE STRANDING

The sound of distant thunder awakened me, and I took stock of the situation. I faced the back wall of the cave-port. It took me a minute to review everything in my mind. I became aware of the weight of Ryan's arm where it laid over my hip.

Gently, I lifted it away, placing it on the bedding at my back. I sighed softly, trying to keep quiet until Ryan awakened. Yet, I must have disturbed his sleep by moving his arm. He rubbed along my shoulder and down my arm. I tried to force my muscles to remain relaxed, but I couldn't. I shifted my body to lie on my back, so he'd stop. Instead of telling him to leave me alone, I decided to be civil to the man who'd saved my life. "Good morning."

"Good morning, Savvy." He didn't smile, seeing my expression.

"Could we stay here and eat leftover sea grapes for breakfast? Because of the storm, I mean." There was no way I'd let him leave me here alone, ever again. Not that he'd try.

His hand touched my cheek, a soft caress. "Of course, if that's what you want."

"That's what I want." The comfort of his touch was confusing. I wanted him to touch me and yet I didn't. But there was no need for displays of affection. I killed Dave, after all. I didn't deserve any fondness.

"Okay then."

He stroked my cheek with his fingertips. I noted his expression of concern since he was so close to me. He slid his hand over my chin. I turned my head obediently, knowing he wanted to check on my healing, just like every day.

"I don't think you're even going to have a scar from this one on your forehead. Hopefully, the ones on your cheek and chin will be the same." He rubbed his fingers across my face so tenderly I could barely detect their presence. But there was a definite tingle that followed them. The fingers slid to my mouth. "These cracks on your lips and at the corners are better, too. You're a good healer."

Next to come were my wrists, so I held them up for him to examine. He ran a finger over them and their rough scabs, before bringing each to his mouth for a kiss. He had removed the gauze last evening. He placed my hands back at my sides. Then, Ryan propped himself up on one arm, rubbing a hand across my midsection, stopping at my stomach. I arched my back to raise it, allowing him to slide my shirt up to my ribcage. This had become more of our routine.

Using a soothing touch, he rubbed his hand over my bare skin, occasionally pressing down. His fingers slipped slowly past the waist of my pants, continuing to press, checking to see how my intestines were readjusting to food and water. His fingers reached down farther this time, to the edge of my triangle. All the while, his eyes remained fixed on mine.

He'd checked me every morning and evening since bringing me home. This was the first time since then that I'd felt something stir deep inside me at his touch, so low on my abdomen. Not pain, but the beginnings of something else. I knew what that sensation meant. But I didn't deserve him.

"That feels much better than yesterday. Now comes the pinching," he warned, removing his hand from my pants, and lowering my shirt, covering my exposed abdomen. He took a bit of the skin on my arm between his fingers and released it, watching the recovery time.

My eyes saw well enough to watch the smile spread across his lips. He was such a wonderful man. And I was so deeply in love with him.

"Hey, that's great. I think we can put a stop to the pinching. The rest of it, too. You're getting better so fast. I'm proud of you."

That made me smile, a genuine smile. "It's all because I've got the world's greatest doctor."

"Now you're talking nonsense." His smile was replaced by a raised eyebrow.

"No, I'm not. How many times would I be dead by now if not for you?"

"Don't talk like that. You've saved my life, too." He tugged and smoothed at my shirt.

"Maybe." I had nothing but doubts on that.

"Don't sell yourself short."

It was all my fault we were here; everything that happened. He knew it, but he was too good of a person to say the words out loud. "Ryan, thank you for saving me the other day; from Douglas, I mean.

I don't think I've said thank you."

"You did. You just don't remember."

"I did?"

"Yes. And you're still welcome. Let me get those grapes for you." He sat up to retrieve the sea grapes left over from last night.

"How did you do it?"

He stopped. "Do what?"

"Rescue me. What happened? How did you find me?" It wasn't an easy thing to ask and might not be easy to listen to. That didn't stifle my need to know.

"You're ready to hear that story?"

"Yes, I think so."

"All right then. I can't tell you how badly I wish I could turn back time, Savannah. I'd never have left you. When you were kidnapped, I was too far away, and the surf was crashing, and the wind was blowing. I didn't hear anything. I'm sure you must have screamed for me. Didn't you?" There was definite dread in his words and tone.

"Several times. Until he gagged me. He drug me out of here, then punched me in the face and almost knocked me out. He pinned me down so he could tie my hands behind my back and gag me."

Ryan was distraught and his voice came out broken. "That tears me up inside. I knew you must have cried out for me to save you. And he hit you? Damned monster. I'm so sorry, Savannah. I should've waited until the storm passed so I could take you with me. I'd give anything in this world if I'd waited."

He turned away to stare outside, his jaw rigid. I put a hand on his and my touch startled him. "It's okay, I know."

A kiss was applied to my hand before he laid it on my stomach to remove the contact. "No, it's not okay. We promised each other that neither of us would ever go off anywhere without the other. You even reminded me of that. And I broke that promise. I let you down. The first time I did that, you were very nearly eaten by a shark. This time..." He swallowed hard and averted his eyes again. He couldn't finish it.

"Ryan."

"No, Savvy. You could've been killed. You almost *were* killed. You were right at the edge when I found you. I can't believe you made it back to me from that. I'll never forgive myself for what happened to you, not as long as I live. I almost lost you; for days on end, I did lose you. Those were the worst days of my life. I swear to God I'll never leave you again, not ever."

"I won't leave you, either." But if rescue came, what then? I doubted my ability to survive without him in my life.

He gave me a forced smile. "Good. Then we've got nothing to worry about. You're getting better all the time and I'm never going to let anything bad happen to you ever again as long as I live."

"Ryan, you can't do that." There was no realism in what he said. A bad step on the hill was likely for me, considering all the embedded rocks. The fact that my eyesight was uncorrected was my own fault. I should have bought pink glasses. I've never cared much for pink.

"I can and I will."

"You can't control everything. I could be struck by lightning or develop cancer or take a bad step on the hill..."

"Stop. Don't say things like that. Nothing bad is ever going to happen to you."

It was pointless to argue with him, as determined as he was. "Okay. Nothing bad is ever going to happen to either of us. How'd you find me?"

After a deep sigh and a pause, he continued. "When I got up here with breakfast, I saw where you'd pulled most of the bedding out. My first thought was that someone or something had drug you out of there, kicking and screaming. I couldn't believe it. I panicked. But then I remembered that in all our time here, we hadn't seen any traces of other people or of animals large enough to take a human.

"I yelled for you, checking all around for a clue as to where you went. But there was nothing, aside from the bedding and some blood. That terrified me. And I found your knife, the one I made you, with blood on it. Then the rain started, washing away any clues that might've been out there. I searched anyway–everywhere. I yelled for you all day, until I grew hoarse.

"After that, I wandered around the island over and over, calling for you. The fear of losing you terrified me. I figured you were lying somewhere in a ravine or something, unconscious. You needed me and I couldn't find you. I've never felt such fear in my life.

"The worst thought I had was that you'd gone up to where the helicopter crashed for some reason, and you'd fallen off the cliff into the ocean. I ran up there and searched for you. I couldn't find you, but I went up there other times, too. I must've been so close to you. I didn't know; if only I'd known." He stopped to scrub his hands over his face.

"Anyway, I kept searching. I turned this damned island upside down, but I couldn't find you anywhere. My heart was broken. I almost lost it.

"One morning, I sat with Dave, thinking, and talking it over with him, like I'd seen you do. I'd always thought it was sweet whenever I caught you talking to him, but I hadn't been able to bring myself to do it before then. Talking with him helped get me back on track. It was impossible for me to give up on you.

"Later, at the cave-port, I wracked my brain to think of where you might've gone. That's when I noticed leaves from a vine that grows here, the ones we've been using to make our traps with. Those leaves are tough and leathery, and the vine is a good substitute for rope. I don't use those vines in our bedding, and they don't grow in this area, just in the deep jungle. The ones we'd used to strap the branches and palm leaves together for this extra side wall were still in place. Besides, I'd stripped the leaves off them down in the jungle where I collected them, so I didn't bring in leaves with them. I surmised that someone could've used more of that vine to take you captive. It was all I had to go on and the theory fit with the bedding being pulled out.

"That meant I had a chance to get you back, rather than the other option I'd dismissed already, that you'd been taken as a meal for an animal. I knew I needed to search for an unknown person on this island instead. While it was possible someone had taken you away by boat, I had to give the island another try.

"The next morning, I prepared to head out again. I pulled some items out of your backpack because I wanted to haul water and the first aid kit in case you needed them if I found you. When I repacked, I noticed the food missing; all of it. You and I hadn't eaten that food, which meant someone else did. I knew then you were most likely still on the island, somewhere. All I had to do was find you.

"I set out a methodical grid search pattern. I eliminated the southern two-thirds of the island, which included our hill. There weren't any places where someone could hide away with you in those places, plus I'd already covered it thoroughly. The southern jungle wasn't as dense as the northern one. I decided to focus in on that area, especially the cliffs. He had you someplace where I couldn't see you. Those cliffs were the only logical possibility.

"On the way up, I found a few recently broken stems in the jungle up on the highest hill, leading to the cliffs. I couldn't find any traces from that point, though."

"He was carrying me," I inserted.

"What?"

"I broke away from him and I ran. I did good for a minute or two. I tried to reach you, but I couldn't see so I fell down a steep slope and hit my head on something, or a bunch of somethings, as I went down. I remember running, but that's about it. Not much of anything after I hit my head. I must've passed out. Douglas would've carried me from there because I woke up alone, chained to the wall in the cave."

Ryan had closed his eyes, his teeth clenching. I waited until he was ready. "Then what happened?" he asked softly.

"I screamed for you once, without thinking. Douglas had taken me out to use the bathroom. I heard you while we were out there. You were yelling out my name and it sounded like you were close, maybe near the top of the cliff."

"I thought I imagined hearing your voice once or twice while I searched in that area. I guess it wasn't my imagination after all. It gave me hope, regardless." He ran his fingers through my hair, shifting it from where it had slid across one eye.

"I turned this island upside down, but it never occurred to me to look closer at the cliffs that first day. It should have. I could've saved you from so much of the pain and suffering you went through." His voice broke again. He wiped away tears from both eyes, growing silent for a minute.

"What did you mean when you said you screamed for me without thinking?"

"I had to keep quiet. I made a deal with him to protect you. He told me that if my husband found us, he'd kill him. Kill you."

"He thought I was your husband? Did you tell him that?"

"No. He assumed, and I didn't correct him. He'd been watching us the whole time since we crashed here."

"God, how I wish it was true." He paused a moment to trace his finger over my lips. "You made a deal with that monster to protect me?"

"Yes. He wanted to kill you, so you'd never find us at the caves. I had to behave so he'd leave you alone."

"If he'd come after me, I could've killed him sooner. I would've forced him to tell me where you were, and then killed him, Savvy. He couldn't have taken me down; he didn't have a gun and I'm stronger than he was. You should've encouraged him to come for me." He hung his head.

"I couldn't do that, Ryan. I couldn't take that chance. Keep going with your story, please."

He sighed heavily. "Late in the afternoon of the third day on my new search pattern, I saw him. I managed to catch a glimpse of the top of his grimy head when he walked out of his cave. He disappeared under an overhang to the west and came back again less than a minute later, zipping up his stupid fly. Both caves were so well-camouflaged by that damned overhang that I missed them before. I missed them from the beach and from the top of the cliffs.

"The instant I saw him I knew what'd happened. When he went back into what I later found out was the cave without a door, I started examining the area around the cliffs until I found the pathway down to the ledge. I waited until the sun went down and the moon came up before going in. The full moon gave me plenty of light to see by.

"I got ahold of the bastard while he was sleeping. I woke him up with my knife at his throat. I wanted him to know he didn't win...that I'd found him and you. I wanted him to know why I was killing him. I didn't know if you were dead or alive or what he might have done to you. All I knew was that he took you...that was enough.

"After I killed him, I found the keys in his pocket and got you out of that damned cave. When I first saw you there in the light of the moon, I thought you were dead, Savvy." Ryan's eyes teared up. He stopped talking because his voice was breaking, again.

I slid closer to lay my head in his lap, hugging one of his legs. He stroked my hair, over and over, for a long time; until my stomach growled.

"Come on, we'd better get some food in that belly of yours. It's a good sign that you're getting hungry on a regular basis. Sit up so you can eat for me."

I did as he asked. He took such good care of me, without asking for anything in return. More than once during the past few days, Ryan had said he loved me. I clearly heard him say it, even when he probably thought me to be unconscious or sleeping. Now that I'd returned to a state of relative normalcy, at least physically, he was more reserved. He exhibited patience, hoping I'd find my way to him. It might be too late for that.

Later that afternoon, I waited while Ryan divided a roasted fish that had blundered into an empty trap in the shallows. He made lots of small talk during the meal, even though I added little to the conversation. The chasm separating us seemed insurmountable. I didn't know how much more of his perseverance I'd need.

At times, I hovered on the borderline of deep depression. It was partially due to the loss of hope in rescue. But mostly, it was a holdover from the kidnapping.

Douglas' voice remained in my head, telling me everything was my fault. I knew he had mental issues and that he was angry and trying to control and manipulate me. But a part of me was convinced Douglas had been right. I knew I should let go of the guilt, but it refused to leave me.

Divulging what I'd done was unthinkable. Ryan would tell me it wasn't true, even though it was. I didn't deserve to be alive when others had died.

"That was delicious, Ryan."

He smiled while scooping sand over the remnants of the fire. "Good. I'm glad you liked it. Hopefully, we can catch another one of those fish sometime soon."

"Let's go make a new crab trap, Savvy. I have an idea for how to improve on our old one. You can help me gather the materials and then we can sit with Dave while we work on it. We'll use the remains of our dinner for bait."

"Okay." Sitting with Dave was more difficult now. The lesson Douglas taught me was a hard one. It was harder yet to realize what kind of a person I was, deep down inside. Douglas was dead, but his words lived on. Just like with Dave. Dave was in my head because of me. I guess Douglas was, too.

Eighteen

Ryan laughed at a story he'd related about Dave. He hadn't laughed since my rescue. "Look at those seagulls. They can't seem to get along." The two birds dove at one another.

"Speaking of seagulls, there's something I need to tell you, Ryan."

"What's that?" He glanced to me.

"It's about Douglas. He was a hermit. He chose to live out his life on this island, alone, isolated from the rest of the world. He never wanted to be around other people. But then we came. He was afraid of us.

"He had a huge cage full of seagulls in the jungle, essentially behind his caves. When Dave's helicopter hovered there, that's what Alphonse saw. That's where the seagulls came from. Douglas released them to try to crash us on purpose. He knew Alphonse had seen his birdcage and that the secret would be out. People would find him."

Ryan was near enough for me to see his deep frown. "He was responsible? He killed Dave and Alphonse? And he almost killed you. He tried."

"Yes." I didn't want to extend the analysis any further. I didn't want him to know that it was my fault, too. He might hate me then—forever, just as Ryan undoubtedly hated Douglas even more now than he already did.

"Damn him." Ryan looked at the grave, then out to the ocean. He stood and walked several yards away. It startled me when he suddenly gave a deep yell, hurtling the stick he'd been using to dig in the sand.

"I'm so sorry, Ryan," I whispered. "And I'm sorry for what happened to you, Dave. But I know you forgive me. I remember you telling me that when the end was coming for me, in my prison cell. You're such a good person." I stretched out on the sand and lay my head on my arm, up alongside the very edge of the grave.

"I wish I could change everything for you. I almost wish I'd never been born. But then, my sweet child never would have existed."

"Savvy, are you okay?"

I glanced toward my feet to see Ryan standing there. "Yes."

"Do you need to go to sleep early tonight?"

"No. I wanted to talk to Dave for a second." There was an exaggerated sigh as Ryan ran a hand through his hair. I'd frustrated him again.

He sat where he was before, extending a hand to me. "Come on, Savvy. Sit up."

I did so, reluctantly.

"I wish you'd talk to me the way you talk to Dave."

I scooted over as he tugged me close. His arm slid around my shoulders to lean me in, putting my head against his. "It's time to gather food for dinner."

"I'm not hungry."

"What's wrong?" He placed a hand on my forehead, and I turned away. "What's going on with you, Savvy?" he asked again.

"Nothing. I'm just not hungry, that's all." If only Dave could climb up out of that hole.

"Don't tell me it's nothing and expect me to believe that. Something's going on with you and I want an explanation–right now, Savvy. You've been like this since I found you. You can't keep it up. You're going to break."

"Let me break then!" I yelled at him, flashing back to Douglas' words. I scrambled to my feet, took a few steps backward to give myself room, then executed two running steps forward to jump over the foot of the grave. Now I was in the open, where Ryan couldn't block my escape.

"Savannah! What do you think you're doing?"

It was a given, without looking, that he'd come after me. A half a dozen strides toward the ocean was all I managed before Ryan stopped me. He blocked my path, taking hold of my arms.

"You're not going to do this, Savvy. Whatever *this* is, I don't care. I'm not letting go of you until you tell me what's going on. I mean it."

I refused to meet his gaze. Thoughts popped into my head that I'd never experienced before. So much guilt. Everything that happened; it was all because of me. The weight of it, the burden of the lives lost, was becoming unbearable. I couldn't keep it in, nor could I share it with Ryan. If he hadn't found me in time, this would be over with.

"I want to walk to the ocean, by myself. I want to be alone for a few minutes. That's all."

"You've been telling me how you don't want to be alone, ever again. You have a panic attack if you think I'm not close enough to you. You don't laugh and barely smile anymore. And you want me to let you walk into the ocean?"

"That's not what I said."

He lifted my chin to study my face. "Your eyes are different since the kidnapping. Everything about you is different. You need to tell me what happened—all of it, Savannah. You have to. You can't keep this up. Let me help you, please."

I attempted to wriggle free. I needed to sit by Dave, alone, and talk to him. He understood. He didn't blame me for what happened, even though he should. "Let go!" I yelled.

"What's wrong? Tell me, Savannah."

"No! I said let me go!" My anger and frustrations were building so that I wanted to strike out at Ryan, to force him to let me go.

"Where are you going to go if I do that? Where?"

"I want to sit with Dave." I ceased struggling, my body going stiff in his arms.

"Dave? What the hell is it with you and Dave, Savannah? He's gone! He's not in there—not the part that counts, anyway. Listen to me—he's gone. You know that. Why is it that you can't talk to me? I'm right here. I'm not going anywhere."

My expression hardened and I stepped back quickly, yanking my arms free and screaming at him. "No! You can't help me! You can't! No one can—stay away! Leave me alone!" I spun around him and continued toward the water.

My mind, my sanity, was slipping away from me. The situation couldn't go on much longer. Ryan was right—I needed help. After less than a minute I stopped, collapsing to the sand, my hands pressing my temples as the conflict in my mind raged. I hugged my knees as I cried because I didn't know what else to do. And those terrible thoughts screamed in my ears.

Ryan lifted me from the sand and carried me, but I didn't open my eyes and couldn't stop crying. He sat beside Dave, holding me in his lap, keeping me tight against his chest, stroking a hand over my hair. I loved it when he did that. I didn't deserve to be treated this well. I should be in that hole in the sand instead of Dave.

"I could use some help here, Dave ol' buddy. You know, those magical powers of persuasion you have? How about helping me out here?" He kept stroking my hair, then started to cry. "What do you need, sweetheart? Tell me, please. I'll do anything to help you, Savvy."

Why did he have to be so good to me? The sole explanation was that he hadn't figured out what I'd done. When he realized it, he'd hate me. I still remembered what he said to me in my prison cell that first time he came to rescue me. He ended up blaming me for Dave's death. How could he not?

I found my voice then. "Why do you care? Why are you so good to me all the time?"

"I love you, Savvy." He kissed the top of my head. "I love you."

I pressed my face into his shoulder. I knew it. I knew he loved me. I just needed to hear it with all the turmoil churning through me. Taking a deep, shuddering breath, I made a choice in that moment, to fight back against Douglas' voice in my head. I grabbed Ryan's shirt in my fists and held on tight. "Don't let me go, whatever happens. Please, Ryan," I cried in a choked whisper.

"I won't, I promise. I'll never let you go, Savvy. I'll never let you go." He hugged my head against his chest and held me.

There was only one way to do this. If I didn't let it out, it would eat me up inside. "It was my fault. It wasn't Douglas. He didn't kill them—it was me. I did it."

"What?" Ryan released my head from the hug, before applying his fingers to my chin to turn it, making me face him. "What're you talking about, Savvy?"

I pushed at his hand and turned away. I couldn't face him. "Douglas. He figured it out. He told me it was all my fault. He said that every time. He'd bring me a thimbleful of water in his little brown pill bottle, just enough for me to taste it. I knew he'd decided to kill me then, to watch me die slowly.

"There was no more food. My body was shutting down. It was easy enough to feel it. The dehydration cracked my lips first, and then my tongue; it even felt like the insides of my throat were going to split open from the lack of moisture. I had muscle spasms, a terrible headache that wouldn't go away, and I couldn't think straight anymore.

"Twice a day he came. The last time, he poured the water onto my face instead of letting me drink. Every time he came, even from right after he first took me, he told me it was all my fault—everything bad that'd happened to us. He said it every time I saw him.

"And he was right—it was my fault. It was because of me that we all came out here in the first place. That makes it my fault that Dave and Alphonse were killed. And I knew that if Douglas killed you, that would be my fault, too. Even my own death from Douglas, that would've been my fault. It was because of me that my daughter would grow up without a mother. None of it ever would've happened if not for me. I killed them. It was all my fault."

Ryan waited, but for what I didn't know. Was he going to tell me he hated me now and leave me? Would he kill me for what I did? He could kill me if he wanted to, but I didn't want the man I loved to hate me.

"You can't blame yourself for any of that! Douglas was a crazy-assed monster. He tortured you and planted thoughts in your head while he did it, to make it worse for you. If I'd known he did that to you, I would've cut him up into little pieces before I killed him. Damn it." He hesitated for a moment. "If there's anyone to blame for this besides Douglas, it's all of us."

"What?" I shifted my gaze to his. He wasn't lifting the weight. Douglas had been crazy, though. Ryan was right about that much.

"You're not to blame for any of us coming here. You can't think that. You were simply doing your job, following a dream. Your friend was the one who booked the flight with Dave in the first place. Are you blaming her? She also hired Alphonse. Should we blame her for that, too, since Alphonse was the one who wanted to hang around long enough that he saw those birds?

"Speaking of him, doesn't he get a share? There's plenty of blame for him in all this. He was the one who kept pushing and pushing Dave to fly this way, farther out from other islands. And all so his career would soar. When we got here, if he hadn't been obsessed with taking so many damned pictures, we wouldn't have been in the area for him to see the birdcage. And he was the one who wanted Dave to hang near those cliffs, where Douglas kept his seagulls.

"We can blame the seagulls if you'd like. They flew straight up into us. Of course, they'd been prisoners all their lives. That was their first taste of freedom. I'm sure they didn't kill themselves on purpose.

"And there was me. I made the decision to listen to Dave and come out here for a visit. You didn't force me to do it; we didn't even know each other then. I'm also the one who decided to fly with you and Dave that day. I didn't have to; Dave gave me the option. And I didn't try to stop him from listening to Alphonse and continuing to fly farther out. I was too busy talking with him, enjoying our time together.

"And, we have Dave. He knew better than to leave his prescribed course, but he did it anyway. He stopped along the way to refuel us so we could fly longer at Alphonse's insistence, but he didn't notify anyone over the radio that our flight plan had changed. There was no one where we refueled to have notified the authorities about us either, obviously. I helped Dave, so I know that for a fact. Those people had gone to seek shelter from the approaching cyclone.

"I even asked Dave about letting someone know we were there, but he said we'd be fine, that we wouldn't be out much longer. I didn't press the issue, but I should have. Do you want to blame me? Or maybe me and Dave, together?

"We probably would've made it back to the airport, if not for Douglas and his birds. But then again, who knows? Something else could have easily gone wrong somewhere else along the way, especially with a cyclone growing stronger and getting closer than predicted after we'd left the airport. Something could've gone wrong while we were over the open ocean with no land around. Think about it, Savvy."

Everything he'd said was right. It wasn't my fault. It wasn't entirely on me. The torment I'd put myself through had been unnecessary. Was I that weak of a person, that susceptible to persuasion? How could I have allowed those thoughts to build?

I closed my eyes and released a pent-up sigh. The weight rolled off me. Ryan lifted it.

He studied me closely, his gaze settling on my mouth. He leaned forward and kissed my lips, soft and gentle. It was a brief kiss, enough to let me know he cared about me and didn't blame me for anything. I threw my arms around his neck and held on tight. He buried his face in my hair, nuzzling his way in. His warm breath blew on my ear. We stayed that way for a long time, holding each other.

Nineteen

I'd been slack about keeping up with my journal, not writing anything in months. Not that there'd been anything of significance to note.

The days ran together. We kept track of time by marking the caveport's back wall, but we eventually gave up on the effort. I still missed my family, but I'd come to accept the likelihood I'd never see them again. Ryan had become my family. Not in a husbandly way, but he filled a huge role in my life just the same. And I knew he wanted more, that one day it would come.

He diligently provided our food. It would be easy to complain about the monotony of the days, but we didn't. We made the best of the situation, noticing a rainbow in the sky, or the silly actions of a seagull, or a school of fish leaping from the ocean to avoid a predator. Most of those things were beyond the abilities of my eyes to see well, or at all. But Ryan described them in such vivid detail, I easily pictured them in my mind's eye.

On this bright day, I sat by Dave while Ryan checked our traps. The wind blew the scent of salt into my face as the cries of seagulls filled the air. I relaxed, my toes digging into the warm sand.

Dave's voice startled me. He stood beside the grave, chuckling as he watched Ryan. It had been so long since I'd seen him. He smiled my way, plopping down beside me in the sand. The oddness of a dead man talking to me, seemingly alive and well, not to mention clearly in focus, escaped my notice after the initial shock.

"He's a good guy, you know, Savvy."

"Yeah. The best there is." It was good to see Dave again. But why now, after all this time?

"And he's in love with you." Dave studied me, then nudged my arm.

After a pause to stare out at the ocean, I responded. "I know."

"Do you also know you'll never find a better man as long as you live?"

A smile played about my lips as I watched for Ryan. "I know that, too."

"So, what're you waiting for?"

"I don't know. I guess I keep thinking about my husband."

"Your husband isn't here, and he never will be. Ryan is. And if you'd met Ryan before Sam, Ryan would've been your husband instead. You know that's true."

"You're right about that. I wish we'd never been trapped here and especially that you hadn't died, but I'm so happy to be with Ryan. And I do love him. I love him so much I don't have the words to express it."

"That's obvious, except maybe to him."

"But if we're rescued..."

"Why dwell on something that may never happen? You very nearly died, Savvy. For a while there, I thought I was going to have to take you with me to the other side. I'm glad I didn't have to. You're too young for that and I don't know how Ryan would've survived without you. He loves you, maybe more than he loves himself. You two were meant to be. You've been given a rare opportunity." Dave looked out to the ocean and back.

"What do you mean?"

"You found a man good enough to share your life for a while and you married him. You had a beautiful daughter together. But now you've managed to find, in all the people of the world, the man who belongs in your heart. Other things got in the way, but now you've found him. Don't ever let him go. Love like the two of you have is too precious; and life is too short."

I glanced from Dave to Ryan. He was coming our way. The waves of heat from the fire pit in front of me made his blurry form shimmer and dance.

"Can you tell if he has crabs, Dave?"

No response came. I glanced over to find Dave gone. My head drooped. That was the only time I'd seen and spoken with him since the cave. It made me wonder if I'd seen our dead friend because being free and with Ryan again was a dream and I still dwelt in the cave, imprisoned. Flashbacks came over me sometimes, despite the comfort and reassurance Ryan provided. The awful nightmares came sometimes, too.

I closed my eyes to relax and reason with myself. A cloud must have passed over the sun because the environment grew darker, my skin cooling. I opened my eyes to the darkness of my prison cell. My hands were chained, and the roar of the ocean waves surging back and forth set a bleak tone. Seagulls laughed at me.

No! This was too much. I couldn't take it anymore. I began to cry in dry, heaving sobs as I called out for Ryan. He'd been so close. He rescued me.

"Savvy! Savvy wake up. Savannah!"

I gradually came to realize I'd been dreaming. A nightmare was more like it. Ryan knelt in front of me as I sat up, attempting to catch my breath and stop crying. He wrapped his arms around me and held on tight, kissing the top of my head.

"It's okay, honey, it's okay. You're safe. I'm right here and I'm not going to let anyone hurt you, remember? It was just a bad dream, that's all."

Being back in the prison cell had been horrifyingly real. I found myself uncertain of which was the true reality. "Are you real? Is this real?"

"Yes, I promise you. I'm right here and you're not a prisoner anymore."

My brain tried to sort it all out. I had to pick one to believe in. The choice in front of me was far too pleasant to give up, making my decision easy. It didn't matter if Ryan was real or not.

A few nights before I removed my contact lenses, Ryan and I had lain on the hillside, spending time stargazing and watching for meteors. We counted thirty, but some were probably double counted between the two of us.

Tonight, we experimented. Ryan described everything he saw in the night sky with as much detail as he could fathom. I attempted seeing through his eyes those things I'd been missing.

"You paint a wonderful picture, Ryan. I think your version is better than the reality."

"You're exaggerating."

"No, I'm not. You even describe the subtle colors of the stars and meteors, like I taught you, only better. And you trace the trails of the meteors for me by naming off the constellations they pass through so I can imagine it in my mind. Besides, I like hearing your voice."

"I aim to please."

"And you succeed."

He chuckled a little, almost to himself. I reached over to put my hand on his, knowing what would come next. Sure enough, he lifted my hand to his lips, kissing it. Then he intertwined our fingers. We maintained silence for a few minutes. There were no more meteor descriptions forthcoming, so I assumed the show was over.

"Do you want to sleep out here tonight, Savvy?"

"Yes, I'm tired. Goodnight." I turned away from him, onto my left side. Then I wriggled backward until my body pressed against his.

"Goodnight, my sweet Savannah." He leaned over to kiss my cheek before laying on his side, his arm around my waist.

After a few minutes, I drifted off to sleep, contented.

―⌒―

I studied the ocean, squinting. Occasionally, Ryan's head became visible, a blurry speck, whenever he popped up for air. He'd moved the fish trap to the edge of the shallows. Did he think I couldn't tell? Fury grew in me.

He swam to shore, nothing to show for risking his life. "Nothing in the traps today."

"You went out to the edge of the shallows, just like you promised me you weren't ever going to do again!" I yelled at him.

"Savannah, I'm sorry."

He reached for me, so I took a step back, glaring. "You're not sorry, so don't even bother saying it!"

"I *am* sorry. I didn't mean to upset you. I didn't think you could…"

He cut himself off and looked away.

"You didn't think I could tell you weren't where you were supposed to be? You didn't think I could figure it out? You think I'm dumb as well as sight impaired?"

"No, of course not."

"What then?"

"I have to provide for us."

"Don't you dare blame your decision to risk your life for a fish on me! I'd rather eat plants for the rest of my life than take a one in a billion chance on you being killed by a shark! Don't you know that by now?" I spun and strode away.

Ryan grabbed my arm to stop me. My jaw was tightly clenched, as were my fists.

"Savvy, please. I can't let you go off like this." He moved to block my path. "You're right, of course. I didn't think about it like that. I thought I could catch a better fish out there. I wasn't thinking about what might happen to you if something went wrong and I didn't make it back." He leaned his head against mine.

"No. You still don't get it. That's not what I meant—not at all. I wasn't thinking about what would happen to me. I don't want anything to happen to *you*. I love you, Ryan."

The smile grew slowly. "That's what I've been waiting for so long to hear. Savannah, I love you." He kissed me then, soft, tantalizing, with a hint of salty water. His hands slid to my hips. He gently pressed my body to his.

My hands glided up his bare, wet chest, to wrap around the back of his neck. I returned his kisses with the longing I'd suppressed since we'd been on the island, our hearts growing closer every day. The surging warmth rose inside me in a wave as my mouth desperately sought his, my tongue slipping inside to caress.

He swept me into his arms then, carrying me into the jungle to the place where we'd spent our second night on the island. He lowered us to the ground, then swung a leg over to straddle me as I stretched my arms up to run my fingers through his dripping, tousled hair, then down, over the wet skin of his back as he leaned into me.

Expectation of what was coming had my pulse and breaths rapid.

Ryan moved himself over me, keeping the contact light and tingling. My hands slipped inside his boxers, roaming as far as they could reach. His kisses grew deeper, more passionate, the farther my fingers strayed.

His lips left mine to nuzzle along my neck to my shoulder, over my collarbone and down to the top of my shirt. He leaned away to pull me to a sitting position. I raised my arms to allow him to roll my shirt up and over my head. His fingertips ran down my chest and over my bra, eliciting a moan from deep inside me as my back arched.

Ryan's hands moved to my back, struggling for a moment before unhooking and removing the bra. That allowed him access to cradle my breasts, taking his time in the discovery, sending a cascade of chills through me, despite the hot day. The kisses on my neck came repeatedly, interspersed with a tender, alluring tongue, before he lowered us to the ground. My eyes closed as his lips explored the rest of my body. When his mouth reached my abdomen, my back arched again and he paused to remove the remainder of my clothing, all the while caressing, loving with his hands and mouth.

A quick flick of his wrist had Ryan's boxers in the sand by my clothes. I shifted my legs from beneath him to wrap them around his hips, holding him in place for a couple of minutes, enjoying the building anticipation and the feel of his skin against mine. He pushed free gently, returning his mouth briefly to mine before kissing slowly along my body, lower this time, exploring until he found the sweet spot, which didn't take long. I cried out in repeated, massive upheavals of pleasure, wave upon wave of it, coursing through my body until I begged him to stop before my heart did. But he ignored me, continuing until he left my body limp and trembling, longing for more.

His tongue dragged slowly up my body to my lips, as he slid his body along and then into mine. I found a grip on his muscular shoulders, marveling in his strength. It had been so long, but nothing and no one before him could ever compare. We belonged to each other in that moment, a deep connection between two souls, as we came, together. We were both left heaving for breath.

Ryan rolled over onto his back, holding onto me so that I stretched out on top of him, utterly exhausted. His fingers slowly stroked through my hair. I planted several kisses on his chest as I lightly traced along one shoulder blade.

"We belong together, even all the way out here, in the middle of the ocean," Ryan said.

My head raised and I leaned back just enough to meet his gaze. "With all the people in the world, I can't believe we found each other."

"Considering our situation, I'd say this puts the seal on you being my wife. We're as legal as we can get out here."

My eyebrows rose in surprise as he caressed my cheek. "Legal?"

"There's no one to officiate a ceremony. All we have is God, Dave, and each other."

I smiled. "That's all we need, isn't it?"

"It's plenty good enough for me, Mrs. Buckley."

"Hmm." I hummed. "I like the sound of that." I kissed him, over and over.

Twenty

Contemplation on being stranded with the world's most wonderful man kept me occupied as I sat on the hill a few feet above our cave-port, squinting at the ocean. Ryan's head rested on my lap. My fingers ran absentmindedly through his hair. He must have fallen asleep.

"Ryan?"

"Yes, sweetheart?" He didn't open his eyes.

"I like it so much when you call me that. But I need your eyes for a minute."

He forced drowsy eyelids open. "What?"

"I need you to look at something for me, out there." I pointed to the ocean. "What's that white thing?"

Ryan propped himself up and turned his head, responding immediately with a sharp intake of breath. "Oh my God! It's a yacht–a big one!"

"A boat? We've got to go signal them! Come on!" I got to my feet almost faster than he did.

"Wait, Savvy!" His hand extended to restrain me. "I want you to go up into the northern jungle. We don't know if those people are friendly. Everything's probably going to be fine, but just in case it's not I'm going to get the backpack and bring it to you so you can take it along. I want you to stay up there until I come for you."

That was unacceptable. "No. I'm not going to do that."

"Savvy, you have to. There's no alternative."

"No! What would I ever do without you?"

"Whoever they are, they wouldn't stay here long. You'll be safe to come out eventually. You know how to forage for plants. You can survive on your own, even without your vision." His hands locked on my shoulders.

"That's not what I meant. Do you think I'd want to keep on living without you in the world?"

"Don't think that way. Don't ever think that way. I've got to go light some kind of a signal fire, so they'll see us." He bounded to the cave-port and back, handing me the pack.

"If you don't come back for me, I'm jumping."

He placed the backpack on the ground at my feet. "Don't go pulling a Juliet on me, okay? Promise me. I'm coming back for you."

"I promise."

He gave me a quick kiss on the cheek. "I need you to trust me and do what I tell you. I'll be back as soon as I can. Hide yourself away and wait. I'm sure everything will be fine. Don't do *anything*. Just wait for me. Please."

"I will. Be careful."

"Don't worry, sweetheart. Now go on." He turned and made his way down the hill at a breakneck pace, not pausing to check back for me.

Shouldering the pack, I moved north. My progress was slow. I stopped only once, near the top of the cliffs. There, the vegetation opened. This was where Douglas had his giant birdcage; remnants were scattered around. It made me nervous to be there, especially alone. Irrational fears dwelt here.

Off to the south-southwest, a long tendril of gray curled sunward. Ryan had made it to the beach and gotten a fire going. Now it would be a waiting game.

The cluster of dense shrubs around me prevented discovery. It was an excellent place to hide. Ryan and I should have simply come up here to wait until the people were gone. Although it was likely their boat wasn't even stopping here in the first place.

Logically though, there had been no option. Ryan had to signal them.

Despite my waning patience and mounting nerves, I decided to stay put and listen for his voice. I shouldn't leave my hiding place. After all, I promised.

But the wait dragged on. Where was he? I needed to know what was happening. I crawled out from the bushes and hesitated, listening, wanting to hear Ryan calling me. The only sounds were birds and the muffled crashing of waves.

The top of the cliffs was near, so I decided to climb the rest of the way and have a look around. If I followed them to their western edge, there would be a chance of discerning the elongated white form of the boat again.

The last few feet of the journey were the most difficult, craggy with loose rocks. I remembered that from when Ryan and I carried Dave down after the crash. Caution should rule any exploration here.

Once at the summit, I exhibited that caution. Shifting rocks could easily cost me my balance and send me to the rough surface for nasty scrapes or a twisted ankle. I followed around to the end of the cliffs. If Ryan came, I wouldn't hear him until he was right on me. My ears could detect little over the roar.

I made sure to keep my distance from the edge as I peered over the top of some scraggly shrubs, craning my neck for a better view of the large white smudge on the ocean. A loose rock rolled away, bumped by my foot. That rock in turn hit another, which bounced a couple of times before sailing over the side, less than a couple of feet away and far too close for comfort; I'd never intended to get so near the edge.

"Mrs. Buckley, please!"

I spun, badly startled at the sound of a strange man's voice, with a British accent, no less. Squinting helped me get a fuzzy view of a man about Ryan's size, wearing a white shirt and khaki pants. His dark hair was buffeted about by the winds. He wasn't Ryan, or even Dave.

With my arms extended in front of me, I took a couple of steps backward. "Who are you? Where's Ryan?"

As if in answer, Ryan scrambled up the edge to stand next to the stranger. "Savvy! Stop! I'm right here–everything's fine. They're going to take us out of here. They're happy to help us. Please, sweetheart." He eased toward me with his arms spread wide as though trying to corral a skittish animal.

It took a moment to realize it. I'd stepped away from the stranger and ended up near the precipice–Ryan was afraid I might jump or fall. Glancing over my shoulder, a mass of blurry white foam indicated waves crashing onto the projecting rock formations in the water below.

A single step away from the edge had me safe and two more had me in Ryan's arms, holding on tight.

"It's all okay now, honey. It's over with. We're going home. We're finally going home."

"Would you like me to dial the number for you, ma'am?" the nurse asked, her accent thick.

It might have been the second time she'd said it for all I knew. Or even the third. My eyes were locked to the telephone on my bedside table as if it might jump out and bite me. Picking it up would be as life-changing an event as being stranded on that island in the first place. "Yes, please," I whispered.

She dialed the number then waited, listening for the ring. She passed the receiver over to me. "Okay, it's ringing." She smiled and walked out, pausing in the doorway. "Good luck, ma'am."

I swallowed and took a deep breath. On the fourth ring, Sam answered. My hands shook.

"Sam Dalton."

It didn't seem real to hear his voice. He sounded so confident, so normal. Somehow, I'd been expecting to detect sorrow in his voice, or the sound of a broken man. But then, it had been a long time. "Sam?"

"Yes. Can I help you?"

"Sam it's me, Savannah."

There was a long pause on the other end. "Listen, whoever you are, I don't find this amusing at all. My wife died eight months ago. I don't appreciate what you obviously consider to be a damned joke."

"Wait, Sam! Please don't hang up." I talked fast, before I lost the connection or my nerve. "It really is me. I'm calling you from a hospital. There was a crash. The helicopter I was in crashed on an island. We've been there all this time, trapped. We've been waiting to be rescued and finally, someone came. They found us; I'm coming home."

The pause wasn't as long this time. "Savannah? Is it really you?"

I smiled. "Yes, it's me. I'm so sorry. I can't wait to see you again. How's Samantha?"

"Oh my God. I can't believe it. This can't be possible. It can't be happening."

"Sam."

"Give me a minute, please. I need a minute." His voice had grown tense, even upset.

"Okay, Sam, that's fine; whatever you need. I'll hold on. I'll wait for you." The receiver thumped against his desk as it hit the surface, hard. I never imagined he'd react this way. He'd always been so stoic.

After a pause so long that I'd decided he might have left the office, Sam picked up the phone. "Okay. I think I'm okay now, Savannah. It's just that this is so unexpected—you're alive. We've already had a memorial service for you."

That shocked me. It was something I'd never considered. "You gave up on me?"

"I'm sorry, Savannah. I thought we'd never see you again. There was no trace. Those two hurricanes or cyclones or whatever the hell they call them hit the airport over there hard—it was leveled. There were no records remaining of where the helicopter even went. Those idiots didn't have computers, only paper records. Who even does that? Damned primitives."

"I'm so sorry, Sam."

"They conducted a search in-between the hurricanes and a smaller storm that came after. They didn't find anything. They reported you officially lost at sea. I decided it would be best for Samantha if we moved on. You would've been declared legally dead eventually anyway."

This time it was my turn to pause. "You moved on? What do you mean by that?"

"Nothing. We had the service for everyone's benefit. A lot of people came, including some of the kids from your school and most of the personnel there. The principal spoke. You would've liked it."

"When did you do that?" Something didn't feel right. Was it because the retelling of the story came out as enthusiastic? Could that be a result of discovering I hadn't died or because of how he'd felt when he thought I was?

"Oh, let's see now. It was four weeks to the day after you left us here to go overseas."

"Four weeks? You only waited four weeks? Wait. You couldn't have even known for sure I was missing until at least a few days after my trip was supposed to have ended. That meant they would've spent at least a few weeks searching for us after."

"Savannah, the search was long since over by then," he chastised.

"You didn't try to get them to extend the search? What about my parents?" The thought of what that experience might have done to them had me worried.

"We never had the financial means for a pointless search when you were clearly dead. Your parents were understandably upset but they're better now. They've been coming to visit Samantha a lot more often. She's been staying with them, too. She spent all summer at your parent's condo. It's been helpful for all of us.

"Samantha's in school right now. I'm going to let her stay there; I'll tell her when I get home."

"Okay, if you think that's best. Please don't wait too long." A pointless search? I would have spent my last dime trying to find Sam, despite our problems.

"I won't. How's all this being handled? Do I need to go there, or can you make it here on your own? You said you're in the hospital, right? Are you injured?"

"No, I'm fine. And I'll come to you. You only need to meet me at the airport."

"Good, that helps. Have you made all the arrangements?"

"Yes. The airline's flying me home for free." It had been so good of them to do that.

"They are?" He sounded surprised.

"Yes. I think they're getting publicity out of it. It doesn't matter about that, though. All that matters to me is getting home."

"If they're getting publicity out of this, I guess it makes sense they'd fly you for free. Makes them look better."

What made no sense was that I had no idea what to say to my own husband after an eight-month ordeal. Soon, we'd see each other again, and resume living together. How would I manage that after falling in love with someone else? "Okay, well, I guess I'll see you soon then. The flight's supposed to land at 8:36 tomorrow evening at Reagan National."

"I'll be there. And Savannah?"

"Yes?"

"I'm glad you're alive."

"I can't wait to see you and Samantha. Goodbye, Sam."

"Goodbye."

I replaced the receiver on the most unusual phone conversation I'd ever had. Not that I'd expected it to be anywhere near normal. It took me a moment to realize neither of us said I love you.

"Are you ready to go?" Ryan stood by the curb, waiting for me.

"I'm ready. I don't have anything to carry except my trusty backpack. One of the doctors tried to give me a brand new one, but I turned him down."

"Why'd you do that?" He opened the door of the waiting taxi and took the pack from my hand, standing aside to allow me room to get in and slide across.

"Because I've been through a lot with this one. It holds memories." I took it from him as he settled in.

"Your head's holding the memories, Savvy, not the backpack." He lowered the window so we could wave goodbye to the hospital staff as we pulled away from the building.

"How're those new contact lenses the doctor got for you?"

"They're great! I feel blessed to be able to see everything around me. I'll never take it for granted again." I'd never felt such gratitude for good vision.

"I'm happy you can see, Savvy." He held my hand, interlacing our fingers. "How did the talk with Sam go?"

"He was...surprised." I didn't want to talk about it with Ryan. Or dwell on it too much myself.

"I'm sure. But pleasantly, right?" He squeezed my hand.

"He was in shock."

"I'd be doing cartwheels if I were in his situation."

"Everybody's different." It came out as defensive, but I was unsure why.

"True." Ryan stared out the window.

"What about your parents?"

He turned to me, grinning. "They cried. They're meeting me at the airport."

I smiled at the thought of mine doing the same. "That's good. What about your fiancée? Your almost fiancée, anyway? She has to be thrilled."

"Not exactly. I mean, she was glad to hear I'm alive and well, but she figured I was dead and never coming back. She just got engaged to someone else a few weeks ago. She said it was kind of sudden, but they're in love."

"Ryan! I'm so sorry!" How could any woman let go of this man? Yet, that's what I was doing.

"I'm not. Not really. I would've broken it off anyway."

"Why would you do that?" It had to be my fault. He'd give up happiness with another woman because of me, the woman who was leaving him for another man.

"Come on, Savannah. You know why. Don't make me say it."

A deep sigh escaped my lips as I dropped my head. I didn't know what to say to him. I couldn't let him know I'd fallen so deeply in love with him that I'd never be the same again, that my life would forever be empty without him. It had to remain unspoken. I'd go home to my husband, the man I was legally married to.

How could I possibly be in love with two men at the same time? Were my feelings for Ryan even real, or were they simply a result of circumstance? Was I still in love with Sam? If that were the case, why wasn't I overjoyed to be returning to him? Why was I facing limitless dread at the thought of never being with Ryan again?

There was no reason to share additional information. I don't know why I offered up any of it, but it happened. "Sam gave up on me. He had a memorial service."

"You're kidding? He did that?" Ryan was incensed.

"Yes, four weeks after I left Washington to come here in the first place."

"Four weeks? Good grief. That means only what? Three weeks after he would've received confirmation that you were missing. Are you sure he's going to be glad to see you?"

"Hey! That's uncalled for," I reprimanded. It was a question I had already asked myself, without a logical answer to be found.

"I'm sorry. It just seems a little strange to me, that's all. It worries me for you."

"To be honest, it seems strange to me, too. But like I told you, Samantha is his world. He had to be thinking of her. It probably helped her stop living on the edge, not knowing. She could grieve, get it over with, and move on. That's what I'd guess, anyway."

Ryan lifted my hand to his lips for a brief kiss. He held on all the way to the airport. Once there, he helped me out and offered money to the driver.

"No sir, you've been through enough. This is on me." He waved as a waiting reporter took photos.

"Thanks," Ryan reached through the window and shook the man's hand.

"Thank you, sir," I said.

The driver nodded, waiting for the reporter to approach his window.

"Where did you get money, Ryan?"

"My parents wired it to me."

"Oh."

"You mean Sam didn't..."

"No, he didn't." I cut him off before he could finish. "And before you say anything, no, he didn't ask if I needed any. I told him the airline was flying me for free, so I guess he assumed everything else was taken care of, too. I didn't even think about it myself."

"Sure." Ryan shouldered my bag, took my hand again, and lead me through airport security, back to our gate. We sat in chairs side-by-side, holding hands while we waited, avoiding unpleasant conversation.

Our seats on the plane were together. It was simple enough, considering the flight wasn't at capacity. We were postponing the inevitable. I wasn't sure how to handle the inevitable. Time moved so fast. Too fast.

"Are you nervous, sweetheart?" Ryan asked.

"No, why?"

He grinned. "Because you're gripping that armrest so hard, I think you might snap it off."

I blinked a couple of times then looked at my hands, shifting them to my lap. "I didn't realize."

Ryan clasped one hand over both of mine. "I'm right here. Everything's going to be fine."

"I know. We've waited for this for eight months. We're going home. I thought I was prepared for that. Now that it's happening, I'm not so sure. The readjustment's going to be hard."

He leaned his head in to apply a feathery kiss to my cheek. "If there's one thing I'm sure of about you, it's that you can do anything you put your mind to."

"Thank you. You look different without your beard and your hair being trimmed up. I'd forgotten about that. You're so handsome."

He chuckled. "You go from being worried about fitting back into your old life to finally noticing that I shaved off my beard and cut my hair?"

I smiled. "I'm sorry. I guess I've been rather self-absorbed." I caressed his smooth cheek, and he kissed my palm.

My head rested on his shoulder. What was I doing? Confusion overwhelmed me. How could I ever leave Ryan? We'd each go to a different airplane, returning to our respective homes on opposite sides of the country. How could everything feel so right and so wrong at the same time?

I'd been staring at the people walking past our chairs by the gate of the next flight, mine.

Ryan craned his neck to peer through the window to the waiting jet. "I can't tell if the luggage is on there yet. Are you sure you don't want to close your eyes for a few minutes? I'll wake you up when they call for boarding. You're wiped out."

"I'm just used to those afternoon naps we took on the island every day."

"After we made love. Two weeks' worth of passion." He kissed me, soft and lingering, before I pushed back.

"Ryan, I can't."

"I know. You can't talk about it and I can't *not* talk about it. I can understand going back to your daughter, but... I love you, Savvy. In my heart, you're *my* wife, not his. I want you in my life, for the rest of our lives."

"Ryan, I can't do that. Things are different now. The situation is different. We're back in the real world."

"The real world sucks a lot more than I remembered."

"In so many ways." I took his hand in mine. A large group of people exiting a nearby gate shuffled past, talking amongst themselves. "There are so many people and so much noise. I'd like to find some cotton to stuff in my ears and drown it out."

"If you find some, I'd like a little myself. I'm starting to think I'd rather go back to the island. But only if you come with me." He nuzzled my cheek with his lips.

"You're loyal. You can't be faulted for that. But I have no idea how I'm supposed to live without you now, Savannah. I've spent the last eight months with you as the center of my world. I don't want to give you up. I don't have any idea how to. I love you so much." He closed his eyes, leaning his head against mine.

Just then, first class boarding was announced. My section would come next. A part of me wanted to run away with Ryan. But I had duties and responsibilities, a daughter and husband. I closed my eyes, too.

When it was my turn to board, we moved to the line. Ryan

squeezed my hand repeatedly. My ticket was about to be taken; he couldn't go any farther. I turned to him, but couldn't speak, my eyes filled with tears.

He held my head in his hands, kissing each of my cheeks, then my lips. His kiss was tender and warm and loving. My hands clasped his waist.

"I love you, Savannah. I want to spend the rest of my life with you." His voice broke. "Please, don't go. Come with me instead. Please."

Why did he have to say that? How could I possibly leave him? I glanced to the woman handing my ticket back to me as she hesitated, smiling at us. The woman beside her was also smiling and had a hand to her chest. I couldn't leave my husband and daughter for Ryan. I couldn't do it. It wouldn't be right.

"Ryan, I can't. I wish things were different, but they aren't, and I can't. I don't know how I'm ever going to live without you. But we're both going to have to find out. I'm sorry." I pulled his hands from my cheeks and walked away, sobbing.

Twenty-One

Ryan wouldn't leave my thoughts, not for the entire flight, nor the next. Permanent separation was so much worse than I'd imagined. A heavy weight sat on my chest. It was as if Ryan had died. Certainly, a part of me had in leaving him.

As I shuffled toward the open area where my family would be waiting, conflict hit, a mixture of sorrow and excitement. More than anything, I wanted to see Samantha. The balance tilted.

Emerging past the gate into the waiting area, the cluster of people was impossible to miss. Some held signs welcoming me home, others held yellow flowers or yellow balloons. Off to one side stood a reporter and cameraman, with a bright light that bored into my brain. In front of everyone stood my parents, beside Sam and Samantha. Samantha wore yellow ribbons in her hair and a yellow dress.

Samantha broke ranks, rushing into my arms, nearly knocking me over backward. "Mom! I'm so glad to see you again! I'm so glad you're alive! I missed you so much!" Her tears were uncontrollable.

"Honey, I missed you, too. I love you." I said it over and over, stroking her hair to calm us both.

After a minute, I glanced past her to see my parents, waiting patiently beside Sam. He stood as resilient as I remembered, not a single tear, only a slight smile. He held a single yellow rose in his hand, a long, yellow ribbon tied around the stem. He stood a good four inches taller than anyone else in the group and had put on a few pounds while I'd been away. His bald spot must have grown so large that he decided to shave it all off. I remembered telling him he'd look good that way.

"I've got to go to your dad now, honey." I pushed to my feet, wiping at her tears.

"Okay, Mom," she sputtered, her eyes red.

I crossed to Sam as he extended the rose and accepted it from him. I smiled and reached up, putting my arms around his neck as he leaned down to embrace me, applying a kiss to my cheek, then a light, quick kiss to my lips, like always. Anything more than a simple peck on the lips remained reserved for the bedroom, usually on Saturdays.

His eyes held mine for a moment, as I studied the face I'd almost forgotten, tracing his features with my fingertips, even knowing he didn't enjoy being touched. "I missed you."

"We missed you, too. It's hard to believe you came back."

"I love you," I said, lacking confidence it was true. But under the circumstances, it was expected.

"All these people are here because they love you, too." He moved his head out of my reach, turning me to face my mother.

It took a long time to pass from person to person. There were tears and smiles, and an obligatory, brief interview with the local press. The long-sleeved tee-shirt I wore covered the scars on my wrists, so the question wasn't asked.

My parents were staying at a nearby hotel, promising to come over after breakfast in the morning to spend the day with us. They knew we needed time alone as a family first, and that I needed rest.

By the time we got home I was emotionally drained and still physically exhausted from the long day of airplane rides. Samantha chattered excitedly the entire way, informing me of everything that had happened in her life while I'd been away, with Sam occasionally interjecting a comment or giving her a frown and shaking his head at her in the rear view mirror. As Sam pulled into the driveway, I spotted a giant yellow ribbon around our old maple tree in the front yard, a smaller version on the mailbox.

"Sam, did you do that?"

"Samantha and your parents did it. That's not all. Just wait and you'll see. Hold on and let me get the door for you. I know you're tired."

I waited as he walked around to open the SUV's door. Samantha held my hand, helping me out as though I'd become fragile now, my pack slung over her shoulder.

"Look up and down the street." Sam instructed.

Yellow ribbons adorned the mailboxes, illuminated by streetlights. "Wow. They all did this?"

"Yes. Samantha and your mom handed them out today before we left for the airport. Their porch lights are on for you. Tomorrow's Saturday and we're having a neighborhood cookout in your honor, lasting all afternoon and into the evening. It'll give you time to talk to everyone."

"That sounds...wonderful." And totally overwhelming. Tomorrow would be a difficult day, no doubt. I'd probably have lots of difficult days for a while as I readjusted to the real world. I wished somehow my real world could still include Ryan. It was as though I'd lost a limb. My heart ached.

The porch light revealed a lovely wreath on the front door, made of ribbons and flowers all in yellow. I fingered it. The flowers were fresh.

"This is beautiful," I remarked.

"Your parents had it made for you. They called it in while they were waiting on their flight to depart from Georgia for here," Sam said.

Once inside, additional yellow ribbons graced the curved staircase. When Sam closed the door, the back of it held yet another yellow ribbon, this one festooned with multiple long tendrils flaring from the bow.

I handed Samantha my rose. "Can you put this in water for me, sweetie?"

"Sure, Mom. I'll stick it in the vase with the others."

"The others?"

"Yeah. Dad bought two dozen yellow roses and a huge vase to hold them all. He had to go to three different florists so he could get enough. Do you want to see them now or in the morning?" Her smile dazzled.

"I'll wait until in the morning. Thanks, honey."

"Okay." She dashed off into the kitchen.

I turned my focus then to Sam. "You are so sweet. I missed you so much." I slid my arms around his waist, and he patted my shoulder.

"Come on, you need to go upstairs and get some sleep. You've had a big day, and tomorrow will be another one."

I sighed heavily. "Okay."

"Don't worry. I've made sure everyone knows Sunday's off limits. It'll be just the three of us, all day. Your parents are leaving to go home Saturday evening. On Sunday, we can go wherever you want, do whatever you want."

"How about hanging around the house? It'll be good to see everyone tomorrow, but today was almost more than I could take. It was so quiet and isolated on that island for so long and now I've been thrown back into the real world with all the people and activities and noise."

"I think I understand. We'll keep it as quiet as we can before and after the party tomorrow and on Sunday. How does that sound?"

I smiled. "That sounds great. Thank you."

The next morning, a narrow shaft of sunlight across my face awakened me when I rolled over in bed. I took a deep breath and didn't smell salt in the air. Nor did I hear seagulls squawking in their fight over breakfast. For an instant, I wondered what Ryan would be preparing for us to eat, if there would be more of the fresh, roasted crab. Then everything came back to me in a rush and a terrible pang of loss hit me, stabbing at my heart.

As tears rolled down my cheeks, my nose caught the aroma of bacon. And I remembered that every Saturday morning, Sam prepared an elaborate breakfast. I smiled as I recalled the fun we had, spending time together in the kitchen. Sam and Samantha must be handling it themselves today.

They'd allowed me to sleep late–it was nearly eight-thirty. I gathered some clothes and took a shower. It had been so long since I'd had the luxury of a shower, not counting the cramped little one in the hospital. I stood beneath the water, setting the massage dial to pound on my back. I couldn't keep myself from wondering what Ryan was doing, how he was feeling, if anyone was there to prepare a special breakfast for him.

My head hung as I left the bedroom. I had been given back what I'd missed, what I'd been wishing for. Yet, I'd lost as much as I'd regained. Moving downstairs, the sound of laughter sent my lips curving upward. I paused just beyond the kitchen doorway, listening.

Samantha was going on excitedly about the breakfast they were concocting and the day's coming events, the food, and about her friends coming over. Sam reminded her to put various items on the table and arrange the roses, so they'd be perfectly centered and evenly distributed.

"Good morning," I said warmly, stepping into the kitchen.

"Mom!" Samantha dropped the silverware and napkins onto the table and ran over to give me a crushing bear hug.

"Savannah, why don't you go into the living room and have a seat? You weren't supposed to see any of the preparations. Turn on the television—if you remember how to do that—and relax. We'll get you when everything's ready. It'll be a few minutes. Catch up on some of the news you've missed while you were gone."

"Okay." I patted Samantha's back as she turned away. "And yes, I do remember how to turn on the television, Mr. Smarty Pants. It hasn't been *that* long."

As I settled into the recliner, the two of them giggled as they worked. Nothing on the television interested me, so I watched the weather. When they showed California, it caught my interest. There were no major storms in Ryan's vicinity. Bright, sunny conditions, exactly what he deserved. God, how I missed him. The strength of it overwhelmed. Would this pain and longing ever go away?

On Sunday morning, I awakened about the same time as the day before, but Sam was still next to me, sleeping. I hadn't wanted to go to church. I didn't feel up to facing more people and explaining things over and over again.

There were too many people yesterday, all curious and asking for details of what I went through, how I survived, what I ate. I danced around it as much as I could. Several times I caught Sam watching me or eavesdropping. I hadn't wanted to talk to anyone about any of it and couldn't count the number of times I'd had to say that to different people. I simply told them how good it was to be home and how much I'd missed everyone.

It had been a long time since I'd had Sam's sleeping form next to me, but I needed to readapt to this former life of mine. On Saturdays, whichever one of us had awakened first had held and caressed the other. That led to other things, of course.

Those were things I didn't want to think about yet. And yesterday had been so difficult, so awkward, to get through. Sam told me he knew I still needed time to rest and readjust. I hoped that consideration would carry through to today, at least.

I decided to start my day while Sam slept. He entered the bathroom just as I stepped out. He glanced at me and handed over a towel.

"I'll use the guest bathroom." He walked out without another word.

No sexual innuendo, no caressing or groping, no nothing. That was strange considering how long I'd been gone. He had to be missing the intimacy we'd shared. Didn't he?

The mirror revealed changes. My appearance was the same, except for the tan and longer hair with light streaks from the sun exposure, plus the pounds I'd lost. The tan would fade in time, as would my memories, I suppose. Whether I wanted them to or not.

Sam had always asked me to grow my hair out more. So, I'd leave it long for him. And cuddle with him if he wanted, letting him know I missed him. But anything beyond that was going to be difficult for me.

The day passed leisurely. We watched television and played board games. Sam and Samantha caught me up on various goings-on that occurred during my absence. While we watched a favored movie that afternoon, I fell asleep, my head resting against Sam's arm.

A different movie played in my head. The sound of waves crashing on a beach amidst the raucous cries of seagulls in the movie invaded my slumber. The female character shrieked. That sent me back into the cave, imprisoned, Douglas approaching me with his little brown pill bottle. He reached for my hair.

I screamed and jumped forward, realizing my hands weren't bound. I vaulted over the coffee table and ran. There were manmade obstacles in my path at every turn as I blindly sprinted. I ended up in the kitchen, fumbling, unable to negotiate the locks on the back door and escape the footsteps coming up rapidly behind me. Instead, I grabbed a nearby knife from the block.

"Savannah!"

I turned, holding the knife, yelling a warning. "Stay away!"

Sam's hands extended toward me, his wide eyes calming. "Savannah, take it easy. Everything's all right, you're safe here. Nobody's going to hurt you. Put down the knife." His voice was strong and smooth.

My eyes blinked several times in succession as I tried to figure out where this place was and who stood in front of me. "Sam?"

"Yes, it's me. You're home now. There's nothing to be afraid of. Put down the knife."

My eyes stared to the object clutched tight in my hand and remembered. The terror on the island was long since over. I'd come home. Sam was my rock. I swallowed and shakily placed the knife on the countertop, my body trembling as I reached for Sam.

He took me in his arms, holding me as I cried. "It's okay, it's all going to be okay. Crying never solved anything so stop doing it. I won't have Samantha getting any more upset than I'm sure she already must be. You wouldn't want that, would you?"

I took a deep breath and released it, bringing my tears under control, remembering Sam didn't like crying, ever. Over the years he'd told me I should always be strong, especially around our child. I realized I'd probably frightened my daughter, who had already been through so much.

"I'm okay." I pushed back from Sam. There was little comfort to be found from him anyway. He'd grown cold and distant since I'd last lived with him. "Where's Samantha?"

"I'm here, Mom," a small voice said with uncertainty.

"I'm so sorry, honey," I moved past Sam and extended my arms to her. "I scared you, didn't I?"

"Yes, but I'm okay now if you're okay."

"Yes, honey, I'm fine now. It's just that sometimes on the island it was kind of scary." Instantly, I realized I'd said the wrong thing and needed to cover for it. "It was because I missed you and your dad, and I was afraid I might never see you again." I moved my hands from her back to her shoulders and smiled.

"Mom, I'm not a little kid anymore. I turned eleven before you left on your trip, remember? I'm almost twelve. You don't need to protect me."

I glanced over my shoulder at Sam, who had put his hands on my back, rubbing it in little circles with his thumbs on either side of my spine, the way I liked it. "She's right, you know. It's always best to tell the truth."

"I'd rather not talk about it."

"That's what you said all day yesterday. Samantha, go to your room for a while," Sam ordered firmly.

"But Dad!"

"You heard me. Go on."

"Okay, but this isn't fair." Disgruntled, she left us.

Sam waited until he heard her door close upstairs. "Come with me."

He led me to the living room, turning off the television. I sat on the couch, and he joined me. I avoided him by staring out the front window. I knew what was coming.

"Tell me what happened on that damned island. What did that character do to you?"

I forced myself to look at him then. "I told you I don't want to talk about it. Not yet. It's hard for me."

"What did you say his name was? Brian, Ryan? Is that it?" His voice rose in hostility.

The insinuation became clear. "No! It wasn't Ryan. Ryan saved my life. He saved me, Sam."

"Then what happened? I want an explanation for your behavior, and I want it right now. Not only did you potentially put yourself in danger, but I'm wondering if Samantha is at risk around you. Now, convince me that's not the case."

From his perspective, he was right; and glaringly serious. But I could never hurt my precious daughter.

"We didn't know it at first, but a hermit guy was living on the island. He kidnapped me."

Sam waited for me to continue until his short patience ended abruptly. "And?"

"He kept me chained to the wall of a cave. That's where the scars on my wrists came from, when I tried to pull out of the chains. He punched me in the face and threw me against the rocks. He kept me chained and gagged almost twenty-four hours a day in that dark cave, all alone. Except for the bugs in there that chewed on me. They left those faint little scars around my ankles. He didn't give me much food or water. I made him mad at one point, because he decided to kill me by stopping the food and water."

"What? You must be kidding me, Savannah. Is the demon still there? Where is that blasted island, exactly? Did the authorities go after him or do I need to see to that myself?"

"He's dead, Sam. Ryan found me and killed him."

"Then he's saved me the trouble."

"Sam, please. Don't talk like that. Not right now." A part of me was glad to hear him say it, though. He was at least angry enough to show he wanted vengeance for me.

"Okay, for now. I can't stand the thought of someone doing those things to you, Savannah. It sounds like I owe this Ryan a big thank you. Hang on, I'll be right back," Sam rose, patting my leg.

When he returned, he had a glass of ice water. He placed it on a coaster on the coffee table. "Here, I want you to take one of these. My doctor prescribed them for me to help me relax after you disappeared." He withdrew a small, brown pill bottle from his shirt pocket.

I took in a huge gasp of air as my eyes widened. I shoved his hand back. "No! Get that away from me! Get it away!"

"Savannah, what's the matter?"

"No, and I mean it! Keep that bottle away from me."

"What else happened out there, Savannah?"

The look on his face made me realize I had to tell him everything. "I almost died, Sam. That man wanted to take me to where he slept. I don't know what he had in mind, if anything, but I fought him as hard as I could. That's when he stopped feeding me.

"And he only gave me water a couple of times a day, not even enough for a swallow. He forced me to drink it. He'd grab me by the hair and yank my head back. He always brought the water to me in a little brown pill bottle like that one. And at least twice a day, every day, he told me everything was my fault. The two men who died, the crash, everything.

"I started believing him. Towards the end, after he stopped bringing me even that tiny amount of water, I started hallucinating. I saw people coming by to talk to me and they all blamed me. I felt so worthless, like I should've been the one who died. A little part of me still thinks that, even though Ryan worked hard every day to convince me otherwise."

Sam studied the bottle with new eyes, returning it to his pocket and placing a hand on mine. "You can't think that way, Savannah–not ever. Don't do that to yourself. God, I'm so sorry for what you've been through."

"The last time the guy brought the bottle into the cave, instead of pouring the water in my mouth he threw it in my face and dropped the bottle on the ground. He laughed and never came back. I was almost dead by the time Ryan finally found me. I probably only had a few hours left. Maybe a lot less than that.

"Ryan killed the kidnapper and got me out of there. He nursed me back to health. He saved me twice over that day. And that doesn't even count the other times. He kept me fed and sheltered. I wouldn't have made it if not for him, especially with my bad eyesight. The kidnapper destroyed my glasses. I couldn't see."

Sam had tears in his eyes. But that couldn't be...not from Sam. He slowly inhaled, exhaled, patting my hand. Then he stood. "Well, I'm glad you're okay now. And that you're back with us, where you belong." He walked hurriedly toward the staircase and paused. "I'm going to let Samantha come back down now. She can show you how she learned to make cookies while you were gone."

"Sam, are you okay?" I followed in his wake.

"Yes. I'm glad you survived all that, everything. I'm going upstairs for a minute. I'll be back before Samantha's ready to stir the dough. She's not strong enough to do it for long enough. And you're not ready for that yet, either. So, don't try it, just wait for me." He set his jaw and angled his face away from me, wiping at his eyes.

I watched him ascend the stairs. How could he have left me after I'd poured out my heart to him? Didn't he realize I needed to be comforted? He clearly didn't want me to see him cry.

Twenty-Two

The house was bigger than I'd remembered, lonely with only me in it. I'd wandered aimlessly from room to room, recovering memories. I studied knickknacks, copies of books I'd loved, photo albums, others that held copies of articles I'd written, everything I could get my hands on. It helped, but I looked forward to Samantha coming home from school. Our next-door neighbor had been bringing her home every day while I'd been missing. This time, Samantha would be able to come home to me instead of an empty house.

After I ate a hardboiled egg and a pack of chips for lunch during the noonday news, I turned the television off. Extra noise in the house was unwelcome. I had hoped the voices would help me feel less lonely, but it didn't work. I preferred the relative silence. Instead of the television, I turned on my computer. It wasn't dusty, so Samantha must've used it for schoolwork, since it was the only system tied into our sole printer in the house. I needed to convince Sam to spend the money for an updated system.

I explored science and geography-related news online, then started trying to think of jobs I might qualify for, besides going into the rotation for substitute teaching. There were no open teaching positions for me in the area, my old job having long since been filled.

Unable to stop myself, I searched for news in the San Jose area, anything about Ryan. It took some digging, but I found one entry in an area newspaper with an interview and discussing his amazing survival and rescue, much like what happened with me. Perusing the Internet, I found the telephone number and address of his parents. At least, I hoped they were his parents. I scribbled the information on a scrap of paper and stuck it in a folder in my file cabinet.

I'd be seeing a therapist soon, at Sam's insistence. He said it would get me past the kidnapping. He set the appointments for me, so I wouldn't have to worry about it. It was a good idea, to get everything out in the open and heal. Sam would accompany me to the first session. It had to help things get back to normal.

Not long afterward, Samantha came through the front door, Sam right behind her, surprising me with take out.

"Hey, you're home early, Sam." I said. It wouldn't be as good as the homemade hamburgers from Saturday. Sam made better dishes than I'd remembered. The fresh-roasted crab would never get out of my mind though, no matter what food was in front of me or how hard I tried. And I was trying.

"It's a surprise for you. Come and get it!" Sam announced, carrying the bags up too high for Samantha to jump up and reach, although she continued her efforts as they moved past me into the kitchen.

Their antics made me laugh. I hadn't laughed since my return home. I followed but turned back. "I'll be right there, as soon as I turn off the computer."

"You can leave it on, Mom. I'll use it for homework later unless you need it."

"No, I'm fine, honey. You go ahead." I returned to the kitchen.

"Sit down at the table, Mom. I'll bring you your food." She patted the table in front of me.

"Okay, thank you, honey."

Sam leaned on the back of a nearby chair, giving me one of his knowing looks. "I'm glad I came home early to surprise you and found you on the computer. You've always told me how therapeutic researching and writing articles was for you. I think you need that right now. Once Samantha's done, you need to get back on it and try to write something–anything."

"I don't know about that, Sam." Writing had always come readily to me. Now it seemed foreign. I didn't know how to do it anymore.

"I do. If you want me to, I'll insist on it. It'll be good for you." He moved away to help Samantha get everything ready.

After we'd eaten, Samantha decided to postpone her computer homework in favor of research for a paper. I had a wonderful time sitting next to her, helping her as much as she'd let me. Simply being near her filled a need in me. When it was time for her to go to bed, I got on the machine but ended up staring at a blank page for nearly half an hour.

Sam came to check on me. He walked heavier than normal, probably to give me a heads up that he was nearing so as not to startle me. He rested his hands on my shoulders and his chin on the top of my head.

"I know you have ideas in that head of yours. You always do."

"I don't know how to start. I don't know what to write about."

"Yes, you do. Write about what happened on the island. Tell the story, Savannah. You can do it. Start with something easy or go ahead and do the hardest part first and get it over with. Write what you told me about yesterday."

"I don't think I can do that." I shook my head.

"You can. You said that Ryan guy saved your life. Maybe he did, but you did it, too. You've always been stronger than you think you are. Now start. Just put something on the page. Go ahead." He kissed the top of my head. "I'm going to bed now. You come up when you're ready, but not until after you've at least gotten one page down, and not before."

"Okay."

I started before he left the room. I decided to do as Sam suggested, putting down what I'd told him about yesterday, only in more detail. Yet, it was only a part of what I endured with Douglas.

Multiple pages came from the effort, leaving me drained. I didn't even think to turn the computer off. I climbed the stairs and went to our room after checking on Samantha, who was sound asleep.

"How much did you get? You weren't down there long."

"I did several pages. It kind of poured out of me. You were right. I only hope it doesn't give me nightmares." I withdrew my pajamas from a drawer.

"Don't go talking yourself into anything."

"Rats. I forgot to save the file and turn the computer off."

"That's okay. You go ahead and get your pajamas on. I'll get it. I'd like to read what you wrote if you don't mind," he said expectantly.

"That's fine, go ahead if you want to."

"Okay. I'll be back in a little while. Don't wait up for me."

"All right," I said hesitantly. It shouldn't take him long to read those few pages.

I changed my clothes and waited for Sam in bed, but he didn't come up, so I went downstairs to find him. A viewpoint in the living room revealed Sam sitting in front of the computer, his shoulders hunched. He was wiping at his eyes. I couldn't believe he was crying. Again. I took a few steps toward him but stopped upon seeing the cellphone pressed to his ear.

"I can't. You don't understand. She's been through hell. I can't consider it, not now. We'll have to talk about it later."

I returned to the stairs, scrambling up quickly, climbing into bed. Less than a minute later, Sam was settling next to me.

"What did you think?" I asked softly.

"I think you're even stronger than I thought you were. I can't believe you survived all that." He let out a loud sigh.

"I kept thinking about my loved ones and being back with you again." I placed a hand on his bare shoulder, and he flinched. "I'll write some more tomorrow while you and Samantha are gone. You can read it after dinner if you want to."

"No. I don't want to read any more of it. It's good, Savannah. Honestly, it is. You should finish it. Write the whole thing out. But I can't read it. It's too much for me." He turned away then, facing the far wall.

He didn't even say goodnight.

"Hi, Debbie. How are you?" I forced myself to be chipper. It was difficult to do, but progress came, bit by bit. I'd been home for three weeks and decided to surprise Sam for lunch, on the advice of my therapist. I'd visited the dentist and been to the hair salon this morning and was looking forward to showing myself off to Sam.

"Oh, Mrs. Dalton! It's good to see you! I'm so glad you made it back. How are you doing?" Sam's twenty-three-year-old assistant stood to hug me. The attractive redhead was always jubilant. She could probably cheer anyone up.

"I'm okay, thanks. Is anyone in with Sam?"

"No. Hold on a second." She sat and leaned over to check for his light on her desk phone. "He just got off the phone. Go ahead. I'm sure he'll be excited to see you. He missed you while you were gone."

That made me smile. "He did?"

"Yes, ma'am."

Maybe it was my imagination, but she didn't seem enthusiastic when she said that. I lingered by her desk.

"He was especially unsettled those first couple of weeks while they searched for you. The boss offered to fly him over there, but he turned it down on account of Samantha. Your parents were in town, too, staying at your house and taking care of Samantha and everything else while Sam worked."

A couple of weeks? "Okay, thanks." I proceeded into his office with a light knock on the door. It was easy to smile at the obvious surprise on his face.

"Savannah—what are you doing here?" He rose from his desk to meet me.

"I thought I'd surprise you for lunch. I can see it worked." I hugged him.

"Lunch? Well, okay. I suppose I could do that. Give me a minute, won't you? I need to make a quick phone call. Go ahead and wait for me out by Debbie. I'll be right there."

"Okay." I stepped out, pulling the door along after, but not closing it all the way. Debbie was on the phone with her back to me, laughing softly. I stood just outside Sam's door and felt guilty about eavesdropping, but continued, nonetheless.

It wasn't easy to overhear, since his was voice low. But I caught some of it. He'd been so distant with me since my return. I had to know what was going on.

"There's nothing I can do about it. I wasn't expecting her to show up. She's hasn't left the house much. This is the first time she's gone anywhere alone, except for the doctor and her therapist. I don't know. No. I'll call you later this afternoon. That's the best I can do. I'm sorry. I'll make it up to you later, okay?"

Fearing someone might notice my proximity to the door, I moved a short distance away to wait. Sam emerged soon after.

"There you are Savannah. Are you ready to go?"

"Yes, if you are."

"Let's go then. Debbie, I'll be back as quick as I can, maybe thirty minutes. I've got that meeting."

Her face experienced a moment of confusion, replaced instantly with affirmation. "Oh. Yes, that's right. Enjoy your lunch."

"Bye, Debbie." I managed an upbeat tone.

"Goodbye, Mrs. Dalton."

As soon as the doors of the elevator closed, Sam started in on me. "What in the world possessed you to come here like this, Savannah? You know I don't like surprises."

"Except the surprise that I was alive and rescued," I corrected him pointedly.

"That goes without saying. I think you know what I'm talking about. I have lots of meetings on this job and you know how important they all are."

"Yes, I know. I wanted to see you." I gave a hard swallow.

"Why?"

"I don't know. I just did. I went to the dentist and got a haircut and I wanted to show you how good I look, and that I kept my hair long, the way you've always wanted. Do I need a reason to want to see you?"

"At work, yes. I'd prefer it, anyway. Things are different now. Listen, Savannah. I know it's hard on you trying to readjust to a normal life after everything you've been through, plus, not having a job."

The elevator doors opened, and we crossed the spacious, impressive lobby toward the front entryway leading to the street.

"What I'm asking is that you think about our family first. My work is doubly important since you're unemployed. I'm the sole provider."

"I know. I'm sorry. It's just that I finally had enough courage to try to go someplace on my own and I wanted to share that with you. That and having a meal together, just the two of us." I'd been so foolish in coming here. I wished so badly I hadn't.

"Savannah, I'm proud of you. I am. But from now on, I want you to check with me before you come here, that's all. I had an important meeting I had to cancel at the last minute to be able to have lunch with you. Some days I'll be able to have lunch with you, other days not. Okay?"

"Okay." We hadn't had a meal together like this, just the two of us, since I returned. I'd become a stranger to him. An unwelcome one.

"How about a sub?"

"That sounds good."

"Great. We should be able to get in and out quicker there since it's right next door. I need to get back to work."

"Okay." I would've given anything at that moment if I'd simply fought the urge and gone home. I'd never try it again, not as a surprise.

He opened the door to the sub shop and held it for me to walk through. "Why don't you sit down? I still remember your favorite." He smiled, giving me a gentle pat on the back, which made me feel better.

"Thanks, honey." I grabbed a seat at a booth and watched as he ordered our lunch, engaging in pleasant conversation with the workers.

He'd been at the office most of last weekend. He said it was to give Samantha and me some alone time. Plus, he had work to catch up on. Spending so much time thinking about me had cost him some of his productivity, he said. My instincts told me there was a lot more to it.

Traditionally, Valentine's Day had brought me a bouquet of roses, delivered to me at work, along with a card detailing the affections and desires of my husband. He always liked that day and strove to make it special. The day's end was always the best part, with the two of us in bed together.

This year, our special day was different, starting with a single carnation that had seen better days. Sam said he'd been so busy at work making up for lost time that he forgot what day it was. By the time he got to the florist, the carnation was the only red flower they had left.

The card he gave me was different, too. The printed words were pretty much the same as usual, but he didn't write any of his embellishments this time, only his name. Not even the word love was added. I told him it was the thought that counted, and the single flower was plenty for me, and beautiful. All of which was true, even though it made me wonder.

I'd put my arms around his waist and angled my face up to him. After another of his quick kisses, he said instead of the two of us going out for a romantic dinner, as we'd always done, he wanted Samantha to come along. She was delighted, naturally. We ate at a local chain restaurant. We'd never done that before on a special, romantic occasion, but the three of us had a good time together.

It was fine, only different, like everything now. Sam was distant and we hadn't made love during the six weeks I'd been back. I had chosen to return to Sam, knowing intimacy would be expected at some point.

But he always had an excuse. At first, he worried about my physical condition or about my needing time to re-acclimate. Then came the pretext of needing to readjust to having me back in his life or being tired from working such long, hard hours.

In the weeks since I'd surprised Sam at work for lunch, he'd been unable to find the time to try it again, even though I asked every day. He always apologized for being so busy and kept saying he'd make it up to me sometime. I wore a sexy nightgown to bed one night, as more of a test than any real desire on my part. Sam said he had paperwork that needed to be done and he didn't know how long it would take.

He said he'd make that up to me, too.

So many nights, I'd gone downstairs around midnight to find him on his cellphone, his voice low. I hadn't tried to eavesdrop, even though I'd wanted to. The fear of what I might hear, the fear of what everything was adding up to, held me back.

It was difficult to judge him, considering how my mind often wandered to Ryan. I loved him. But I loved Sam, too. Or at least I convinced myself I did. Sam was my husband, and we made vows to each other. That took precedence over anything else.

Ryan and I went through a series of traumatic events. It was only natural that a man and a woman would become close after something like that. There was no way to find out if it was anything more.

Since my return, Sam seemed engrossed elsewhere. And my suspicions were that his focus was on another woman. I reminded myself there was no proof. At the back of my mind it was a different story, one with an unhappy ending and a broken home.

There had to be a way to prevent it from coming true. We were happy once. Happy enough, until I'd met Ryan and experienced more happiness and fulfillment than I'd ever known. Still though, Sam, Samantha and I were a family. Weren't we?

The night before, I'd been about to walk into Samantha's room to tell her goodnight. Sam was still with her, so I'd listened outside the door, as I used to do before the island trip. I'd always loved listening to their sweet conversations.

This time it was different.

"I don't want you to talk about that in front of your mom. You haven't said anything, have you?" Sam said.

"No Dad. You told me not to."

"Good girl. Your mom wouldn't understand, and she'd get her feelings hurt. She's been hurt enough with everything she's been through. She needs us. It's up to the two of us to protect her, right?"

"Right."

"It's time for you to go to sleep now. Your mom will be up to tell you goodnight in a few minutes."

"Okay."

"Goodnight sweetie."

"Goodnight Dad. But Dad?"

"What?"

"Will we ever get to spend time with her again? I liked her."

"No. I'm afraid not. She was only here to keep us company while your mom was gone. Now that your mom's back, we're focusing on her, remember?"

"I remember. And I'm glad mom's back–she's the *best*. But I still miss Anne."

"It's okay to miss people. We'll both forget about her in time. We've got your mom back and that's the important thing. Now you have to be sure to remember–we don't talk about Anne anymore."

"I won't forget. I promise. I love mom and I wouldn't trade her for anyone else in the whole world."

Hearing that had made me smile, despite the clear meaning behind their discussion.

"That's my girl. I'll see you in the morning."

"Okay, Dad."

I stepped back quickly, allowing me to pretend to have just been walking up, so they wouldn't suspect I'd overheard. The width of my smile covered well enough.

Later that night, after tossing and turning, I surrendered to the futility and crept downstairs. I needed to be alone and think.

The house had been so still that the vibration of Sam's phone stood out. It jittered around from receipt of a text message on the coffee table where he'd left it. The face of a raven-haired beauty appeared. Beneath it was the name Anne. The recognition was instant. Our daughters were friends in school.

I checked through his phone since it still had the same passcode as before I went missing. In it, I found innumerable phone calls between Sam and Anne, since only a few days after the cyclones. The recent ones were either while he was at work or late at night, long after Samantha and I had gone to bed.

With a shaking hand, I checked through his text messages. The majority were between the two of them. And those messages left no doubt about what their relationship was and had been for a long time. Finding that out was a devastating blow. I curled up on the couch to try in vain to sleep.

Twenty-Three

Sam seemed concerned when he came downstairs the next morning, especially since his phone was lying near me. He scooped it up, scanned through his messages, and then looked to me. I simply said good morning, pulled on my robe and went to the kitchen to start breakfast.

Wondering what to do next occupied my thoughts all day. For the first time in my life, I'd written a novel. It detailed my island experiences and had been shipped off to an agent. She called me back soon afterward to say she loved it and had given it to a publisher she knew, who wanted it. I told her I was in the middle of something at home and I'd have to let her handle everything. Whatever she wanted to do with it would be fine with me.

My article in National Geographic would be out over the summer, once they'd finagled the precise coordinates out of the British couple who'd rescued us. They had to recruit a new photographer and were sending out a small scientific expedition, hoping to find a large population of sharks somewhere in the area, playing off the unsuccessful attack on Ryan and me. More sharks would sell more magazines and draw more attention.

The spring would bring lots of changes with it, including a career I'd been dreaming of. But my family dilemma was the sole priority. I didn't care about the book or the article. I had to figure out what to do about my marriage—nothing else mattered. If we divorced, I'd only see Samantha half the time.

I sat at the computer without enthusiasm, reviewing my email for want of something to occupy my thoughts. One of the messages was from Ryan. It took me by surprise, even though I'd figured there was the possibility he might contact me someday.

It was probably the book. I'd sent a copy of the manuscript to his parents at the address I'd found. I included a note explaining who I was, my email address, and asked them to please get the book to Ryan. I wanted to have his consent, after everything we'd endured together. It must have been in his possession for a while now, as I sent it to California and my agent at the same time. I'd given up on hearing back from him, forgetting to check through emails, especially with everything going on with Sam.

I decided to ignore this one from Ryan. I didn't have the capacity to deal with anything else.

The relationship Sam had with Anne seemed intense and deep, like it had been for us once. My decision didn't come without an internal debate, but it was firm and shouldn't be postponed. I needed to confront Sam. I'd been through more than enough in my life already. There was no point in continuing to tear myself up over this.

"What did you want to talk about, Savannah? It's late."

I let loose a big sigh before launching in. "Sam. There's no easy way to say this, so I'm just going to say it. I know about Anne."

"What? Anne?" His face went ashen, his eyes wide.

"Why, Sam? Why didn't you tell me about her? I could've understood that after a few months you probably figured I was dead and never coming back, and you might start to consider moving on, even though it would've been awfully soon after my death. Correction, disappearance."

"Our relationship started a lot sooner than that."

My eyes narrowed, my voice stern. "I know."

He looked at his lap and clearly didn't know what to say. It took him a minute to gather his thoughts. "I'm sorry, Savannah. I never intended for you to know. How did you find out?"

"Does it matter?" I snapped at him. Not helpful, but I didn't care.

"No, I suppose not." He turned his head away, staring at the wall of family photos above the couch. The end tables on either side of the couch held elegant, matching lamps and photos, one of Sam and me at our wedding and another of us holding Samantha at the hospital when she was born.

"How long has this been going on, exactly?" I had my suspicions that he'd had an affair with the woman previous to my disappearance.

"We've known each other for years. Her daughter and ours are friends."

"Yes, I know who she is. She lives down the street."

"She came to offer her condolences after you disappeared. She wanted to help me."

"So, she decided to help by sleeping with my husband. How thoughtful of her shameless ass."

"Savannah. We thought you were dead."

"Only what? Less than a week after you knew for sure I'd gone missing, according to your text messages. No one knew if I was dead or alive. I was *missing*. My God. That's completely unforgiveable, Sam! You couldn't even wait two or three months? How could you do that to me?"

"I don't know. I'm weak. It never should've happened."

"No, it shouldn't have. How in love with her are you? Please do me the courtesy of being honest."

His lips firmed into a line as his head drooped, which told me all I needed to know. Tears filled my eyes and spilled over the rims, racing down my cheeks.

"I love her. She means the world to me. The past months have been so hard."

"Why? Because I came back?" My hands went to my hips.

"Yes, Savannah. I know I shouldn't feel that way, but I do. I'm glad you're alive, for Samantha's sake, but Anne is my soulmate. We just didn't figure that out until late, after we'd already built lives with other people."

"And when were you going to tell me all this?" His words brought back a memory, a dream where Dave had said something similar about Ryan and me. I dismissed it quickly as a delusion brought on by the torture I went through. This was real life, what truly mattered, my family. And it was all falling apart.

"I considered it, but after hearing what you went through, I felt guilty about what I'd done. And you needed me."

"Yes, I did. But you weren't there. You were never there. I needed you so badly. I loved you, Sam. Once, anyway. But you don't feel the same way. You never loved me, not really."

"Savannah, of course I did."

"No, you didn't. You couldn't have loved me and cheated on me like that, too."

"We thought you were gone forever."

"Thought or wished?" The words came out fast.

"Savannah."

"There's nothing more to be said. I want you to leave. Go to her. Wait. Isn't she married?"

"Yes, but she's getting a divorce. Her husband found out about us. We...we started an affair when you were taken to the hospital for your car accident a couple of years ago. The two of them patched things up until we started seeing each other again, after you disappeared."

The shock on my face couldn't be prevented. "You're telling me you had an affair with her while I clung to life in the hospital? That's why you wouldn't stay overnight with me, even when I begged you to, when they were going to operate on me early the next morning? You said you had to stay with Samantha."

"I had the next-door neighbor keep her for me. Anne said she needed me, that she loved me. And I needed to be comforted because of my fears you weren't going to survive the operation. It was touch and go for a while there." He truly seemed to believe he'd been justified in his actions.

"You didn't consider how I felt, alone in the hospital with surgery looming? Stay away from me as much as you can. I should've known, even back then. You're a monster, Sam.

"We'll have to put the house up for sale, because I certainly can't afford it on my own, on a teacher's salary, and I wouldn't want to stay here even if I could. And we'll have to work out a custody agreement for Samantha."

"We don't have to sell the house. I make plenty of money. More now than before." He paused.

"Before I disappeared?"

"Yes. More than I ever let on. I've been helping Anne financially since you disappeared. We spent time together, having lunch and sometimes dinner, just as friends. Well, mostly as friends. And I bought her an engagement ring a couple of months after we thought you'd died. She couldn't wear it in public until you'd been declared legally dead."

"Mostly friends? And you bought her a ring? You never even bought *me* an engagement ring. Said it was a terrible waste of money. Did you dance on my grave, too?" How could I not have seen this before? How could I not have realized what kind of person I was married to?

"Savannah, be reasonable."

"Reasonable? You don't have a clue. You're a terrible person, Sam. I don't want anything to do with her, you, or your money."

"I'll keep making the mortgage payments. You don't have a job yet."

"I'll find one, somehow. I'll figure something out. But I can't stay here long, not with the memories of *our* family everywhere I look. As soon as the house is sold, I'll go. But I won't give up my child just because you gave up on me a few days after I disappeared and cheated on me. Even before then, I guess. I'll never understand any of that as long as I live, Sam. You never loved me, not doing something like that."

"We can't talk about this anymore because I can't take it. I'll find an attorney tomorrow. You can sleep in the guest room tonight. I'm assuming you'll move in with that—with your—*whatever* she is, tomorrow. You need to go. And keep Anne away from me. If she comes anywhere near me, I swear I'm going to punch her in the face and break her dainty little perfect nose, no matter how much money her poor husband invested in it."

I moved slowly upstairs. I laid in our bed, unable to sleep all night. There were too many memories in the room. They'd been good ones, at least for me, until I took that fateful trip. I wished to God there was a way to turn back time, so I'd never gone. But then, did I ever have Sam's love in the first place? Apparently, it would have ended between Sam and me anyway. I had no idea what to do next.

How much longer would the torment from that ill-fated trip continue? How much more would I have to endure? It seemed my punishment would never end.

It had been weeks since Sam moved out. I needed to write again, since I had free time between substitute teaching stints. But it was difficult. There was nothing in me except anger and frustration and those emotions blocked me. I had no idea how to make them go away.

Instead of continuing to push myself, I checked through my overload of emails, deleting most of them unread. I opened one of a dozen from my agent, asking when I'd be ready to go out on promotional tours for my book, plus all the book signings.

The book was selling fine without any of those efforts on my part. I responded briefly, saying I didn't know, that I'd get back to her soon, whether it was true or not. I couldn't think about the book, or the island that caused me so much grief. My marriage had been destroyed because of what happened to me and the last thing I needed was to think about that place. A book tour was out of the question.

Indications were that it would continue to sell well enough to change things for me, to allow me to achieve my dream of writing fulltime, just as a novelist rather than a journalist. It would allow me to spend more time with Samantha.

A new email popped up while I was busy thinking of other things. It was from Ryan. I closed my eyes for a moment and sighed. I'd forgotten the message he'd sent before, however long ago that was. My life had been so turbulent since then. Not ready to communicate with him yet, I opened his message anyway.

OMG, Savannah! Your book is AMAZING! I love it. Parts of it were difficult for me to read, of course. It brought back a lot of memories I've suppressed since we've been back in the United States. I've been trying hard to let you go. I still think of you as my wife and I love you with all my heart. I doubt that will ever change.

The company I worked for filled my position while I was gone, which was completely understandable. They think they'll have something coming open in their Maryland office soon, but I'm not sure about accepting, even though it would be a substantial promotion.

I'm reluctant because I don't know how you'd feel about me being so close to you, geographically speaking. I've been missing you so badly, Savvy, and I don't know how I could keep myself from trying to see you if we lived that close to each other. I've fought hard against the temptation, even living here in California like I do.

I'm sure your husband wouldn't like it, even if all we did was get together in a public place for lunch. We could invite him to come, but I'm sure he'd be able to see how I feel about you. Given all that, I'm leaning toward declining the position.

Instead of worrying too much about work, I'm taking this time to complete the renovations to my house and yard. I'm going to make it what I've been envisioning for so long. I had a great income and saved a lot of money, so not having a job right now is fine for me. The construction work is letting me get out a lot of frustrations.

Anyway, I'm telling you all this over email, because you need to know about it, I think. I'm assuming since I haven't heard back from you that you aren't planning to attend the funeral, so I just wanted to say goodbye. I don't want to cause you any difficulties, Savvy. I won't try to contact you again.

I see that you've published the book—you never needed it, but you have my enthusiastic permission. I've even bought a copy for the collection of your books I'm starting. I've got a whole shelf ready and waiting, as I'm sure there will be many more to follow. I'm so proud of you. I'll never forget you. I hope your life is everything you ever dreamed it would be.

Goodbye and please know I'll always love you,

Ryan

Funeral? What funeral? I wracked my brain, trying to think of who could've died. Could it have been one of his parents? I closed the message and scrolled down to his original email. My stomach was in knots from reading what he wrote, knowing he still had feelings for me. It was a hard fight to push my emotions down. I opened the first email.

Hi, Savannah. I found your email address on the note you sent. I hope you don't mind my contacting you this way. I figured it would be a lot easier on both of us than a phone call, even though I'd give anything to hear your voice again. I'm going to start reading your book as soon as I finish writing this email. I can't wait.

Anyway, there's something important I thought you'd like to know about. I'm traveling with Dave's brother back to the island to supervise the disinterment. We'll be bringing Dave's remains back to the United States for a proper burial. We're having a ceremony in his hometown of Wichita, Kansas at two o'clock in the afternoon on the first day of spring. His mom wanted it that way. She said that was his favorite season.

We've got some members of the Coast Guard who'll be at the service to honor him, too. I'm sure Dave would have liked having you there if you can make it. Your whole family's welcome to come, by the way, if that will make it easier for you to attend. I'd like to meet them, especially Samantha.

Just let me know and I'll make all the arrangements. I'll get you a hotel room and I can pick all of you up at the airport, too, if you'll tell me when your flight will be getting in—wait a second—didn't you tell me your husband was afraid to fly? I know you're not too keen on it yourself now. If you decide to drive, be safe. I can still make that hotel reservation for you either way.

I hope to see you soon.

Ryan

A glance at my desk calendar showed the time for Dave's burial had nearly arrived, only a few days away, on Friday. Today was Wednesday—I almost missed it. I'd been wallowing in remorse and self-pity instead of getting my life back on track.

I immediately picked up my cellphone and booked a flight to Wichita. It would have me arriving at ten fifteen on Friday morning. The next step was a hotel room, which was easy enough. I had no intentions of leaning on Ryan for anything. This was hardly the time.

I rushed upstairs to check through my closet. I had a slinky, black cocktail dress that would have to do, even though it wasn't what I had in mind. If I added my black sweater with its dark abalone buttons, and conservative black flats, the outfit would be appropriate enough.

Suddenly, it was good to be unemployed—there was no boss to request time off from, especially on a new job. Most employers probably wouldn't be understanding of the situation or forgiving. I went downstairs to sit on the couch as I placed a call to Sam. It was intercepted by Debbie.

"Mrs. Dalton. Hi. Um, did you need to speak to your–to Mr. Dalton?"

"Yes, Debbie. That's why I'm calling him. It's important."

"Well, he has company now. I mean, he's in a meeting."

"A meeting, huh? Do you mean to say he's in his office with Anne?" I pronounced her name with a razor edge to it.

"Yes, ma'am. I'm sorry. They just returned from a long lunch."

I held my tongue. After all, it wasn't Debbie's fault. "Like I said, this is important. I need to speak with him. It'll only take a minute."

"Okay, hold please."

The wait was nearly a full minute long, testing my patience sorely. I'd gone from tapping my foot on the floor while sitting on the couch to pacing.

Sam cleared his throat. "What can I do for you, Savannah?"

"Don't worry, Sam. I won't keep you from your lunch date, even though you told me a while back you didn't have time for those. At least, not with me you didn't. Of course, she's your lover, not your wife, so I guess that makes all the difference, doesn't it?"

"Savannah."

"Listen to me, Sam. Something's happened and I'm going to need you–*not* Anne–to come by the house tomorrow night to pick up Samantha a day early. You'll need to get her sometime Thursday after you get off work."

"Are you starting a tour for your book?" He sounded suddenly interested. He'd been wanting details of my book sales and had suggested a financial advisor. I'd told him to mind his own business.

"No. I have to go to a funeral out-of-state."

"Oh–I'm sorry to hear that. Who was it?"

"No one you knew." I hadn't expected him to be nosey. My life was no longer any of his concern.

"Then who was it?"

I gave a loud sigh to indicate my annoyance with him. "It was Dave Rodgers, the pilot of the helicopter. He saved our lives in the crash."

Sam was silent for a moment. "I remember you telling me about that."

"They went back for his remains. He's being buried on Friday afternoon in Kansas. I'm flying out Friday morning and coming back late Saturday afternoon. It was the best the airline could do on such short notice."

"You just now found out about it?"

"Yes. Someone sent me an email several weeks ago, but today was the first time I've checked my email since—well, in a long time."

He hesitated so long it seemed the call had been dropped. "Will he be there?"

"Will who be there?" All he had to do was say yes, he'd take care of Samantha an extra night. This was his weekend with her, after all. I didn't care to talk to him any more than I had to and there was no doubt my tone conveyed that.

"You know—that guy you were with on the island. Ryan."

"Ryan? Yes, I'm sure he'll be there. He and Dave were best friends. Closer than that, even. Why? What difference could that possibly make?"

"Well, I was thinking..." his voice trailed off.

"About what?" I stood on the verge of failing in my attempt not to verbally take off his head.

"Well, I was thinking that maybe you could give him a message for me."

What in the world was he talking about? "A message?"

"Yes. Please tell him thank you from me—for saving your life, I mean. And for bringing you back to us, to Samantha. If it's not too much for me to ask of you, Savannah." He sounded sincere.

"Sure. I'll tell him." He'd surprised me so that I scarcely knew what to say.

"I'll be by to pick up Samantha at seven o'clock Thursday. That way, you two will still be able to have dinner together."

"Thank you, Sam." How could he be so considerate?

"You're welcome. And you have my condolences on the loss of your friend."

"Thanks. Goodbye Sam." It was difficult to know what else to say.

I'd been a jerk for how I'd spoken to him, but I didn't know how to apologize for it.

"Goodbye Savannah. I'll see you tomorrow evening." He hung up.

I watched until the image of his face faded away with the light of my phone. Then my thoughts shifted. The last person in the world I wanted to see now, aside from Anne—who would eternally be number one on that list—was Ryan. I had no idea what to say to him or how to handle this encounter.

At least the trip would be mercifully short. My flight out of Wichita left at eight o'clock Saturday morning, with a lengthy layover in Atlanta. A later flight with a brief layover had been possible but getting out of there sooner rather than later seemed wise.

The last thing I did before forcing myself to eat lunch was respond to Ryan's email. I simply let him know I would come alone, I already had a hotel, the time of my flight's arrival, and that I'd be fine getting to the funeral if he couldn't pick me up. I also lied, saying I had too much to take care of to check my email anymore before leaving for the airport Friday morning.

I turned my computer off, without waiting for a response. If for some reason he wasn't at the airport when my plane arrived, I'd take an alternate mode of transportation. But I had little doubt he'd be there waiting for me.

Twenty-Four

My little black dress wasn't quite as tight as I'd remembered it, but it fit well enough. Of course, I lost weight on the island and whatever I might have put back upon my return was shed again by my lack of appetite once I found out about Sam. My tan had faded, as had most of my scars, thanks to modern medicine. Even the emotional ones had dramatically improved.

It was both difficult and silly, but I wore my wedding band. Hopefully, that would save me from having to talk about something painful, embarrassing, and uncomfortable. I wasn't ready to tell Ryan. He never even had to know. This would be the one and only time we'd see each other. He wasn't taking the job in Maryland, and I doubted he'd ever contact me again after this. A ball of nerves kicked at my stomach from the thought of seeing Ryan.

What we had was simply a result of circumstance. It would take me a long time to get over Sam's betrayal and having my family destroyed. I couldn't imagine ever wanting to be in another relationship. It wasn't that I missed having Sam in my life, because for the most part, I didn't. Rather, my trust in other people had been shaken.

Walking into the airport waiting area, I shouldered my backpack and immediately spotted Ryan. He was dressed in a dark suit with a long, dark overcoat. The occasion was somber, but he was so striking it lifted my spirits. I couldn't help but smile as the rush of emotions swept over me.

He stepped forward to greet me with a huge smile, embracing me warmly. I had forgotten what it felt like to be in his arms, the heat and comfort. It was as though we'd been apart years instead of months.

"I've missed you so much, Savvy," he said by my ear, rubbing his hands slowly up and down my back. "You look amazing in that dress. Of course, I've always thought you looked amazing no matter what you wore."

I swallowed hard, ignoring both his compliment and the somersault performed by my stomach. It would be unwise to get caught up in anything with him. Logically. "It's been a long time, hasn't it? How've you been?"

I couldn't think of anything else to say and felt like an idiot for it. Looking into those blue eyes, at the tempting lips, it was difficult not to latch onto him with a kiss. I remembered so clearly what his kisses felt like, what they did to me.

"Fine, I guess. You?" He looked at my face, his fingers brushing my cheek. "I'm glad there's no scar. It's been so long since I've been able to see you and touch you."

Using a firm hand, I removed his fingers from my cheek, though what I wanted to do was nuzzle against them. I applied a quick kiss to his knuckles instead. "Why don't we get going? I think we need some lunch before the funeral. I know I do, anyway. Something light would be good."

"Okay. What about your bags?"

"There aren't any. I managed to get everything I needed into my backpack."

"Just a backpack?"

"Yeah, that's all. I've got a change of clothes and shoes and some toiletries. That's all I needed. I like to travel light."

"I remember. Here, let me take those for you." He removed the coat from my arm and the backpack from my shoulder before any protest could come from me.

"You bought a new one? I thought you wanted to hold onto the old one for the memories." He sounded disappointed, as though I'd rejected him somehow.

"You were right. The memories were in my head, not the backpack. I threw it away when I was cleaning out the house a few weeks ago. I threw a lot of things out. I've decided to live my life more minimalistic."

"I guess you got used to that on the island, huh?"

"I guess so."

"Not much mattered there besides basic survival. And each other." He put a hand on my lower back, guiding me as we made our way toward the exit.

"So, is your book a best seller yet?" Ryan asked while we waited for our lunch order.

"I don't know. I've asked the agent to handle everything. It was therapeutic to get it out, but I don't want to be involved any more than I absolutely have to."

"Bad memories, I know. There were some good ones, too."

I flashed him a quick smile. "That's true." I didn't want to talk about it, but soon we'd be headed to Dave's service, which would bring those memories even more to the forefront. "So, how is Dave's family handling everything?"

"Well, I think I've sold them and the local news media on the fact that Dave died a hero. And then when everyone reads your book that'll just reaffirm everything I said. You did a great job, Savvy. Dave would've been proud."

I nodded my head. "Can we talk about something else, please? I don't like thinking about it. This is going to be hard enough for me as it is when we're there."

I hung my head a moment. "I'm sorry, I didn't mean that to come out the way it did. I know it'll be even harder on you, and on Dave's family. Speaking of which, I don't mean to be selfish or anything, but will you be able to be with me while we're there, or do you need to sit with Dave's family? I'll be okay if you need to sit with them instead. I didn't mean..." I collected the napkins I'd grabbed from the holder on the table and began twisting them absentmindedly.

"It's fine, Savvy. I've already told them I'm going to be taking care of you. They're fine with that; they understand. Besides, I'm staying with them while I'm here, so we're spending lots of time together."

"You are?" That was bound to cheer Dave's parents. The corners of my mouth tugged upward.

"Yes. I've been here for the past couple of weeks. They insisted I take Dave's old room. His brother's there, too. It's helping them to get through everything by having a full house."

"I'm sure it is. I'm sure they're glad to have you around."

"They are. I am, too. So, what hotel are you in? Your email said you got one on your own."

"I'm staying at the Best Western near the airport. That way, it'll be convenient for me when I leave in the morning."

"Tomorrow morning? You're leaving tomorrow morning?" The shock on his face was evident, almost as though I'd reached across the table and slapped him.

"Yes. I couldn't afford to stay long; I still don't have a fulltime job yet. I need to get back home." I hadn't intended to say anything about money and work, not wanting him to pick up on clues and ask questions. This was proving to be much more difficult than I'd imagined it would be. My heart was overcoming my supposed sensibilities.

"I know you need to get back to your daughter, but I'd hoped you and I would have some time together."

"We're spending time together right now." Thankfully, he missed the whole money reference. He was more concerned about spending time with me. He was such a sweet man and as the minutes ticked by, I realized how much I'd missed him and how much better life was with him in it.

"But we'll only be together less than a day," he said.

"That reminds me. Sam wanted me to thank you for saving my life and bringing me home."

"Really? You can tell him he's welcome." Ryan took my hands across the table. "I'd do anything for you, Savvy, including leaving you alone. Your life is with your husband–your legal husband. And your daughter, of course, which is how it should be. I'll respect that, don't worry. After I take you to the airport in the morning, you won't hear from me again."

My stomach twisted into a pretzel. I'd never see him again. It was so much easier to think of it from a distance than it was to face it in person. My eyes brimmed with tears. "No. You won't see me in the morning. My flight leaves at eight. I'll be taking a shuttle over. It's not far. You stay with Dave's family. They need you." Seeing the waitress approaching, I slid my hands out from beneath his.

She deposited our food before Ryan could respond. It was better this way. Ryan could build a new life in California near his family, and I'd figure things out for myself eventually. I never should've come here. But I had to, for Dave. I owed him that much.

Sam, why did you leave me? Did you ever love me at all, to have abandoned me so quickly and all those years ago for *her*?

All too soon, we were at the cemetery. It was lovely, as far as cemeteries went. The sun was shining in a cloudless sky, the day cold.

Ryan and I sat on the front row, beside Dave's brother, Mark, who had an arm around his mother's shoulders. He bore a remarkable resemblance to Dave in almost every way, making everything far more difficult than I'd anticipated.

Everything the minister said was a blur. Dave was a wonderful son, brother, friend, a brave man who served his country well and died a hero. I bit my lip until it came to the verge of bleeding to prevent myself from crying. At the conclusion of the ceremony, Dave's mother was handed a folded American flag. In my hands, I twisted and strangled the dark blue handkerchief Ryan had given me before the service began. I jumped badly each time the guns were fired in Dave's honor, even when Ryan clasped one of my hands tight in his.

Mark handed a white cardboard box to Ryan, who nodded solemnly before holding it between us to slowly lift the lid. Inside was a large red flower, shockingly like the flowers I had used to decorate Dave's burial spot on the island. My hand covered my mouth and my eyes darted to meet Ryan's.

As I reached in to reverently lift the flower out with trembling hands, the first of many tears rolled down my cheeks. Ryan passed the box back to Mark and held my arm to steady me as we stood together.

The family must have heard the story of the flowers from Ryan, aware of his plan. Silence reigned as all eyes focused on the two of us as we approached the coffin. I kissed the flower and placed it on the coffin, tucking it beneath the red, white, and blue ribbon wrapped around the burnished box holding the physical remains of our friend.

Thoughts of all the comfort Dave's spirit provided me with on the island, whether it was real or simply my imagination, flooded my mind and I lost my composure. I turned to Ryan and let him hold me while my body was racked by deep sobs. The family stood and Dave's mother came to us, reaching around Ryan to pat me on the back. I turned from Ryan then and embraced her as Mark took the flag from her grasp.

"It's okay, honey, it's okay. My son is in a much better place now and we'll all be back together again someday in Heaven."

"I know," I nodded. "I miss him so much. He saved my life."

"That's my Dave. He was always a hero."

I nodded again but couldn't speak. She turned to the arms of another relative and I returned to Ryan. He held me and kissed my cheek. This experience was far more difficult than I'd imagined. I rested my head against Ryan's shoulder. I couldn't have gotten through the funeral without him. I had no idea how to get through the rest of my life without him.

Everything was ready to go. I'd eaten breakfast in the hotel and packed away my toothbrush. That was the last thing to go in. All that remained was to find the shuttle driver to take me to the airport. The lady at the front desk said he came in around six on Saturday mornings. It should be nice and easy.

I'd told Ryan goodbye last night after dinner. I kept it brief by telling him the flight and the funeral had worn me out, physically and emotionally, which was true. We'd kissed each other on the cheek before he left my room. He'd insisted on escorting me up and checking over the room first, to be on the safe side. He was still protecting me.

Yet, no one could protect me from the blow of losing my family. I lost Sam on the island, but I had Ryan then. I'd lost him before the island, but I had the shield of not knowing. Now he was gone for good, but I didn't want anyone else, not now anyway.

I didn't know how I'd ever be able to get past this. Losing Sam wasn't by choice, but I had chosen to lose Ryan, twice over. How much pain could one heart endure?

Every time I looked at myself in the mirror, confusion stared back. Comprehending how my life had changed so much in such a short period of time eluded me. Everyone in my situation must think the same about themselves. Divorces were terrible things to go through.

Sighing, I knew I'd better leave. My watch was reading a few minutes past six o'clock. I put on my coat, picked up my backpack, and opened the door to find Ryan standing there, his fist poised to knock.

"Ryan—what are you doing here?" My eyes were wide.

He smiled warmly. "Ryan's taxi service has arrived, ma'am."

"I told you I was taking a shuttle." I couldn't keep a smile from my lips.

"I know. But I can take you as good as they can; better, even. I'm going to take you inside and wait with you until it's time. It'll be the last chance I have to spend time with you."

My hesitation lasted only for a moment, my resolve melting away as I peered into his bright face. "How could I possibly refuse you?"

"I have no idea. Here, let me carry your luggage for you." He shouldered my backpack.

"Thanks."

"Do you need to check out?"

"No, I took care of that earlier this morning. I just need to stop by the front desk and turn in my keycard." I pressed the button to call the elevator.

"What about breakfast? You didn't eat much at lunch or dinner yesterday. Even with all the people around us at dinner, I noticed," he admonished.

"I couldn't eat much then. Everything was too upsetting for me. As for breakfast, I already ate something downstairs. What about you?"

"I grabbed a banana on my way out the door and ate it on the drive over. What did you have?"

"A bowl of oatmeal," I said matter-of-factly as we stepped onto the elevator.

"Oatmeal? That's all you ate?"

"Yes. It's what I wanted." I didn't want to tell him it was also all my stomach could handle. And as it was, I had no idea how to pay for the airline tickets and hotel once my credit card bill came. They'd have to wait for the next royalty check, which I hoped would beat the bill.

The first checks that come in had covered car repairs, insurance, the electric bill, and groceries. And a mortgage payment. It seemed Anne needed Sam's money for a down payment on an expensive trip to Tahiti for a two week honeymoon a year from now. It couldn't possibly have waited.

"That doesn't sound like much food. I still worry about you, Savvy. You don't look like you've put on any weight since we've been back. I've put on ten pounds. It's mostly muscle, but still..."

"I'm fine. I can take care of myself. There's nothing for you to worry about."

"I can't help it. We went through so much together. I can't just let you go like that. It's not that easy; not for me."

"You don't need to worry about me anymore and you didn't need to pick me up."

"Yes, I did. Everything that's happened since we went our separate ways tells me one thing."

I dreaded what might come next. "And what's that?" I asked softly.

"After this morning at the airport, I'm never going to see or hear from you again."

He stared a hole right through me. I couldn't bring myself to meet his gaze, but I felt him looking. "You're probably right," I whispered.

His body responded with a subtle slouch. "That's what I figured. It was why I knew I had to come and see you one last time, Savvy. We went through so much together on that island. And in my heart, you're my wife and I'm your husband. For a while there, I was sure it was going to be the two of us living out the rest of our lives on that island. I just can't believe it's ended up like this."

"Me, either." The changes in my life had been so dramatic, so astounding, so senseless.

The elevator doors opened, and I handed my keycard to the

woman behind the counter, mumbling a quick thank you as we left.

Uncomfortable silence governed the short ride to the airport; there wasn't even small talk. It continued even once we got inside, waiting for my flight.

The need to sort out what had happened with Sam seemed more important than telling Ryan what had gone on in my life. If Sam still loved me, if he'd waited for me and been faithful, or if I'd simply never discovered his long-term affair, what would I be feeling for Ryan? Was I experiencing old feelings for him just out of loneliness? That wouldn't be fair to Ryan.

He couldn't be second best; he deserved so much better. I couldn't tell him about the divorce until I came to a mental and emotional resolution about it. Even though I knew by the time I managed to figure everything out, Ryan might very well be with another woman and lost to me. Could I take a chance on that happening? I wished it was already time for my flight to board, to escape the lingering confusion.

"Did you decide for sure what you're going to do about that job offer? The one in Maryland, I mean," I asked, thinking perhaps conversation would help pass the time.

"Yeah. I'm going to call my old boss as soon as I've gotten you on your plane. He wanted me to take some more time to think about it."

"Are you going to accept it?"

"No. Even though it's a great company, I'm going to try to find something in California with a different firm, I guess. That way, I can stay near my family."

"I'm sorry. It's because of me, isn't it?"

"Of course. I told you it would be too hard on me, being close to you and not being able to see you. That's become crystal clear in my mind now that I've seen you again. Your husband wouldn't like us seeing each other at all and I certainly don't ever intend to cause you any problems, especially with your husband."

He lifted my hand to kiss it tenderly. "I'll always care about you, Savvy; and I don't know if I can ever stop loving you. I hope your husband is smart enough to appreciate you and treat you right. He's a damned lucky man."

There was no way to hold myself together any longer. "Excuse me." I shoved up from my seat to dash to the nearby women's restroom. Inside, I slammed the stall door shut and let myself cry; keeping the sobs soft so no one would overhear. The last thing I needed was to attract any unwanted attention.

I pulled off a sizeable quantity of toilet paper to wipe my eyes with. I'd totally blown it. There was nothing to say to Ryan to explain my behavior, except the truth. He'd probably be upset I hadn't told him before this. I had to pull myself together before going back out there.

Once my breathing returned to normal, I blew my nose. As I washed my hands, I critiqued my appearance in the mirror. There was no way to conceal I'd been crying my eyes out. Not without staying in here for another fifteen minutes or so. Then I'd end up having to explain that instead.

There was no option. It was time for the truth. I only hoped he wouldn't be too angry with me. I grabbed another handful of toilet paper, took a deep breath, and returned to my seat.

Ryan stood as I approached, his brow furrowed. "Savvy, are you okay? Are you sick? If you're sick, you probably shouldn't fly, you know."

He steadied me as I sat, not that it was necessary. It was simply what he did for me. I took another deep breath and put a hand on his, where it rested on my forearm.

"No, I'm not sick, Ryan. There's no easy way to say this." But the words refused to come.

"Oh my God—you're pregnant, aren't you? You and Sam."

"No! No, I'm not pregnant, thank God." That would've made my life infinitely more complicated.

"Then what is it? You know you can tell me anything. I'm here for you whenever you need me, Savvy. I mean that."

"I know." I paused to inhale and blow it out, nice and slow. "It's Sam and me. We're getting a divorce." I watched closely for his reaction.

His eyes widened with shock. "A divorce? Why?" His expression changed then. "Savvy—it wasn't because of anything that happened with us being stranded together on that island, was it?"

"No, it wasn't because of that. It was because of Sam. Right after I didn't come back from the trip, he started dating someone. To be accurate, he started sleeping with her before the authorities even called off the search for us. And he told me he cheated on me with her back when I had the auto accident that nearly killed me, while I was in the hospital, begging him to stay with me because I was so afraid of the coming surgery. If only I'd known back then..."

Ryan's expression darkened, his jaw muscles hardening, eyes narrowing. "You're kidding me. You must be joking, Savannah. He cheated on you under those circumstances? And he didn't wait for you when you were declared lost at sea? He gave up on you and moved on, just like that? How could someone do that to the person he supposedly loved more than anyone else in the world? To his wife?"

"I don't know." I sighed heavily. "I've been trying to figure that out for myself. I know what he's told me, but still..."

"There's no excuse; none. You were off fighting for your life–and mine." He shook his head. "He's a damned fool, that's all. The worthless idiot."

"That's certainly true," I responded with a little laugh. It had been a long time since my spirits felt so light.

Ryan leaned over to rest his head against mine. "I'm so sorry, sweetheart. I do mean that. Is there anything I can do to help you? Anything at all–just name it."

"No. There isn't anything anyone can do. I need time to figure out how to deal with it and rebuild my trust in people."

"That's understandable." He slipped an arm around my shoulders. "I'm here for you, Savvy–always. Even from the other side of the country."

"I know you are. Thank you for that."

"You don't have to thank me. We're friends and that's what friends do. We're more than that even, Savannah." He kissed my cheek then nuzzled it affectionately.

"I never thought anything like this would ever happen to me. I don't know what to do, or think, or how to act. I even wore my stupid wedding ring so I wouldn't have to tell you, because I didn't know how. I'm mad and sad and frustrated, all at the same time."

Ryan sat back. "I've had a couple of friends who went through divorces and felt the way you do. Then, they met someone special and decided the gamble was worth taking.

"You've got to give yourself some time. You're a great person with so much love to give. That's clear from how you were with Dave on the island, and me. Sam wasn't worthy of you. I can't believe he didn't know what he had. How could any man be so completely clueless?"

"Thanks, Ryan."

"Did I help you feel better?"

"You always do."

He kissed my cheek again. "Give me your cellphone for a minute."

I fished it out of my backpack and handed it over, watching as he programmed his number in and took a selfie to link it to. "Now, anytime you're feeling blue, I want you to call me, day or night. I'm serious about that. Or send me a text or an email. Okay?"

"Okay. You won't get tired of hearing from me all the time, especially if I'm sad or upset? I don't want to depress you." The smile I sent him didn't come out well.

"That's impossible. You have no idea how hard these past few months have been for me, Savvy. Not hearing from you at all, aside from the brief message that you were coming to Dave's funeral. It's been terrible, not knowing how you were or what was happening in your life, or if you were well and happy. I got used to watching over you. I couldn't let go. And now I find out what you've been going through without me. I want to help you as much as you'll let me.

"If I thought for one second you were ready for it, I'd ask if I could move in with you. You have to at least allow me to be there for you from a distance. You can tell me anything. I thought you'd know that by now," he chastised.

"I guess I was embarrassed."

"Embarrassed? You don't need to feel embarrassed. You haven't done anything wrong. He has. He's the cheating idiot who left you. He's got no clue. He doesn't even deserve you. He doesn't know what true love is, or devotion. He..."

"Okay! That's enough—I get it." I held up my hands to indicate my surrender. "I'll call you, or text or email or something. I will. I'll lean on you as much as you can stand."

"I'm a strong guy. I can take it." He squeezed my hand and gave me a wink.

"I know you can."

"As soon as you think you're ready, I'd like to visit you. Maybe you could show me around the National Mall like you promised me." His finger traced my lips as he spoke.

"We'll have a great time. Could you come soon?"

"Naturally," he said with another kiss to my hand. "I'm calling my boss to accept the Maryland job as soon as your plane is in the air. I'll be there in a week, once I get my California house rented out and a mover set up. They'll need to take my car, too. It'll get me to you faster if I come by plane. We can see each other every day unless you want to hold off because of Samantha."

I leaned into him, nuzzling my face against his neck, applying several soft kisses as his arms wrapped tight around me. "She's living parttime with Sam and his fiancée already. You're a way better role model than that woman is. Why don't you move in with me as soon as you come for your new job?"

"Perfect." He kissed me. "All I need is your–or I guess that's *our*– home address. As soon as the divorce is finalized, I want to make our marriage legal, Savvy."

"Umm, good," I purred, winding my arms under his so I could snuggle into him. "Then I'll officially be Mrs. Buckley."

"And maybe we can give Samantha a baby brother or sister."

"Or two." I laughed in delight as he moved to kiss me.

Twenty-Five

During the drive to school, Samantha peppered me with questions about Ryan, excited about meeting him six days later. The prospect of having two sets of parents appealed to her. I supposed that meant Sam and I were handling the transition as well as could be expected.

On the drive home, I noticed a black sedan behind me that I didn't recognize. They'd been there for the past few miles, even turning into my neighborhood and my street. Whoever it was would simply have to slow down. I didn't like people speeding through my neighborhood.

My neighbors had been too good to me for that, even though the yellow ribbons had been a lifetime ago. I tapped my breaks and gave a signal so the driver behind me would back off enough to let me make my turn. I pulled into the driveway, past the for sale sign in the front yard.

It might be time to have the sign removed. Give it some time, living in the house with Ryan. The master bedroom needed a complete change, all the way down to the paint on the walls. Make the place *ours*. Ryan wanted to handle the renovations.

As I parked, the sedan pulled to the curb in front of the house with a squeal of tires against the curb. Another person searching for a house now that spring had arrived. They'd ask if they could take a look inside, just like the last few.

The day before, it'd been a pristine white Cadillac sedan. I'd been friendly to the elderly couple it carried. But the answer would always be call the realtor, that's her job.

In my mind rested the fear that Sam needed primary custody to keep Samantha in her school. Unless Ryan and I kept the house. Samantha didn't need her life disrupted by a school change. Sam and I moved to this area for the schools. Only the best for our baby girl.

As I closed my car door, two men exited the black sedan. They didn't look like typical home buyers. They were both about the same height, dressed in dark suits and sunglasses. The scene felt like something out of a mafia movie.

I met them at the edge of the driveway, since I couldn't get into the house before they'd reach me. Here, we'd be out in the open. Many of the neighbors had one or more cars in the driveway, indicating someone at home. There always seemed to be eyes on the street. In a good way.

"Can I help you?" My stance was wide, hands on my hips. My voice issued a loud challenge, not a question. Hopefully someone else would overhear and be curious.

From farther down the street, a black SUV approached, heading out for work. That gave me confidence, being well-acquainted with the vehicle. Sam's.

The men didn't speak until they stood in front of me. "You're Savannah Dalton, aren't you?" the driver asked.

The hair on the back of my neck stood at full alert. I'd caught a glimpse of a gun strapped under the driver's jacket. "Who's asking?"

"Martin Wainwright," the driver said.

"Who?" My brow furrowed. "What's this about?" I took a step back as the passenger stepped toward me, reaching for my arm.

"We need to have a conversation," the driver said. "It won't take much of your time, ma'am."

The SUV braked hard, squalling its tires. It stopped at a sharp angle in the road behind the sedan. Sam emerged, running around the front of his SUV, brandishing a handgun.

The men in front of me shared a concerned glance.

Sam strode up. "What the hell is going on here?" He cut an imposing figure. Sam meant business since he'd removed his gun from the glovebox. It took a lot for him to do that.

The driver cleared his throat. "We were told this house was for sale, but it isn't what we were looking for, though, now that we're seeing it in person. Come on Phil, let's go check somewhere else."

"What I'd suggest is that you stay the hell away from my house and my wife. If I ever see either of you again, I'm liable to shoot first and ask questions later. Do I make myself clear?"

"Yes, sir. We meant no harm to your wife. We apologize." They nearly fell over each other in retreat. Sam watched until the sedan was out of sight, which didn't take long as fast as they were going.

"Are you all right, Savannah?" Sam interjected. He came to me, placing his free hand on my shoulder.

"Yeah, I think so. They scared me."

"Who were they and what did they say?"

"They asked if I was Savannah Dalton. They were already following me before I turned into the neighborhood. from dropping Samantha off at school."

"They knew your name? Are you sure you don't know them?"

"I'm sure, Sam. I don't have any idea who they are. They said something about Martin Wainwright."

"Martin Wainwright? I've never heard of anyone by that name."

"You came up before they could say anything else. Thanks for stopping to help me." I twisted my hands around repeatedly.

Sam seemed not to have noticed. "Whatever it was they were after, I don't like it. Savannah, I think Samantha should stay with me for a while—beyond this weekend. Until we figure out what's going on, I mean. Why don't you go to Georgia and stay with your parents?"

"Just because of a couple of random weirdos? You're trying to take my daughter away from me because of them?" Any remnant of fear in me was immediately replaced by fury.

"No, that's not it. It's a precaution, nothing more." His eyes shifted to the house. "I'll move my SUV into the driveway. You wait on the porch where I can see you. Don't go inside yet."

"Okay." At the front door, I watched Sam on his phone as he walked to the SUV.

When Sam came, he still brandished his gun. "Savannah, I want you to lock this door and stay right here while I check the house. And call the police. I want someone to come out and have a look around."

"Sam, I don't know if they'll do that or not. After all, those guys didn't threaten me or anything."

"I saw that one guy try to grab you. I should've shot his lousy ass."

"He scared me. I'm so glad you were coming by when you did." My lower lip began to tremble, so I bit down to make it stop. I shouldn't cry in front of Sam.

He moved closer and hugged me. "It's okay. I'm here now and they're gone. I'm going to call the home defense people and see if they've got any ideas for beefing up security here. Everything's going to be fine. Call the police as the first step. I'll be back once I've gone over the house thoroughly."

I watched him walk up the stairs with his gun. I seriously doubted an intruder was inside. Still, I locked the front door and made the call.

Twenty-Six

Ryan picked up right away when I called him the next day. "Savvy." The voice was smooth as expensive chocolate, deeper than I'd remembered from yesterday. It comforted.

"Listen, Ryan, I need to tell you about something. When I drove home yesterday, a strange car followed me and parked in front of my house." I hesitated. "Two men got out of the car and confronted me."

"What? Are you all right, Savvy? Did they hurt you? What happened?" His voice escalated in its urgency with each question.

"I'm fine, Ryan. Sam was driving by. He stopped to help me."

"Tell me what happened."

Glancing to my friend Rebecca, I noted she'd moved to a booth filled with colorful pottery. One finger tapped at her chin as her dark eyebrows rose. Something had caught her imagination. A good friend and a fabulous decorator.

"They knew who I was. They called me by my name, but I've never seen either of them before. And they said another name, Martin Wainwright."

"Who's that? How'd they know your name?"

"I don't know who he is or who they were. Sam's been checking into it, but there're lots of them, all over the place. It doesn't make any sense."

"Where are you now?"

"I moved in with a friend and her family."

"Are you in that much danger?"

"No, no. It was only a precaution." If he couldn't be calmed down, he'd be on the next plane. "Sam wanted me to stay away for a while, just in case. I'm with my friends all the time. You don't need to worry."

"I'll rent a car at the airport and meet you at your house on Sunday. But I'm only willing to wait until then if you promise you'll be with other people all the time, and when you're outside, you'll stay in a crowd."

"I will and am, in fact. I'm out right now. There're tons of people around."

"Okay. I'll take your word. You have to stay safe. We'll be back together Sunday afternoon. And just so you'll know, I'm not going to leave you again. Especially not with what you've told me."

"I love you, Ryan."

"I love you, too. Look, I'm going to get a flight out as soon as I can, today if there's one available. I'll go visit Dave's family on the way. Where're you staying now?"

"I'm at a friend's house. Her name's Rebecca. She teaches at the school I did."

"Husband? Gun in the house for extra protection?" He rattled off the questions. Savannah interrupted before he could finish.

"Yes to both. And her husband is a policeman. Practices martial arts for fun. Nothing to worry about. Seriously."

"Good. I'll text you so you'll know the plane schedule. I'll see you Sunday. Guaranteed."

"I can't wait. I've missed you." I disconnected and turned back to Rebecca.

We resumed our leisurely stroll in pursuit of knickknacks and decoration Rebecca didn't need but couldn't pass up. But I couldn't shake the feeling I'd had since we went to the movies last night, no doubt rooted in paranoia. The crush of people around us made it hard to be sure.

But I'd swear someone was watching.

Ryan's absence on Sunday brought out my suspicions right away. He'd never have stood me up.

I paced the living room floor as I dialed the number of the last place I knew he'd gone. "Hi, Mark. It's Savannah Dalton."

"Savannah! Hi, it's great to hear your voice. How're you doing?"

"I've been better."

"Well, I hope Ryan's taking good care of you. We're disappointed he didn't get to spend time with us on his way to you. Not that I blame him. Can I talk to him for a minute?"

"You could if he was here." This was just as bad as I thought.

"He's not with you?"

"No. He was supposed to arrive early this morning and rent a car for the drive to my house, but he never showed. And he didn't make it to you, either. He hasn't answered his phone, or the texts I've sent. A friend of mine found out Ryan bought a ticket but never got on the plane in California. I called his parents because of a bad feeling."

"The same feeling's hitting me right now. He told me what happened to you. Are you safe, Savannah?"

"Yes, I think so." Now I was beginning to wonder. But concern for Ryan took precedence.

"What did his parents say?"

"Ryan told them he was heading for the airport to go to Wichita. They checked after I called and found his car at the airport, but like I said, Ryan never boarded that plane. None of his friends or family have seen him. Oh, God, Mark. I don't know what to do."

"Ryan wouldn't just not show up. Not for us and definitely not for you. He talks about you nonstop. He loves you."

"I know," my voice broke. "I've got to find him. I'm going to California."

"Do me a favor and stay put for now. Let me do some checking, okay?"

"I don't like not doing anything, but I'll give you a day. Thank you, Mark."

"Don't thank me. Ryan's a brother to me now, like he was to Dave. I'll call you back soon. Keep the doors and windows locked and if you see or hear anything strange..."

"I know. I'll call the police."

"That's right. And call me, too. Hang in there. We'll get this figured out and find him. Try not to worry."

Instead of just waiting around, I did some checking. None of it made any sense. Sleep wouldn't come. So, I turned to my computer to search for any missing persons reports or kidnappings witnessed at the airport Ryan went to.

There wasn't any luck, which in a way was good. It had to be a kidnapping. But why? I didn't know the details of his life, but after spending eight months alone with him, I knew enough. He was liked and well-respected.

Who would've held a grudge against Ryan intense enough to kidnap him? The only person was Douglas, but he was dead, with Ryan cleared of all charges by the local police and government there. He'd even been hailed as a hero for dispatching an unwelcome and highly dangerous squatter.

That's when it hit me. Word had gotten out about what happened on the island. Not from Ryan. He hadn't been broadcasting what he did. He hadn't needed to. I inadvertently did it for him.

I immediately began searching for the name Martin Wainwright. There must be a connection between the men who approached me in my driveway and Ryan's disappearance. Something was there, I just had to find it.

An idea came to me then. Instead of continuing with Martin Wainwright, I searched for a connection with a wealthy man who died under mysterious circumstances ten years ago, the body never having been found. Douglas. There on the screen was the answer. Douglas' father was Martin Wainwright, an incredibly powerful and wealthy man, complete with a family photo that included a brother and mother.

Douglas was right all along. It was my fault. I never should've written that book.

At the Wichita airport, I waited, drumming my fingers on one knee. Where was he? There was no connection to Mark in all this. Surely, he hadn't been kidnapped.

As if in response, a tall, dark, and handsome man threaded his way through a large group of people on his way to me. I smiled and released the breath I'd been holding. I stood and waited for him to reach me.

"Savannah." Mark extended his arms to hug me.

"I'm so glad to see you. I was getting worried." The embrace was just what I needed. I wasn't alone in this.

"I'm sorry about that. There was bad traffic. Let's go, we've got less than fifteen minutes to reach our gate. Did you get something to eat while you were waiting for me?" He took me by the hand as we executed a fast walk through the airport.

"No. I'm not very hungry. My stomach's in knots."

"You can't do that, Savannah. You need to eat so you can keep your strength up. We'll get something when we get to the next airport. We've got to be ready for anything, since we don't know exactly what we're getting ourselves into."

I scowled. "I think I do." There was no fear, just anger. I had help for the upcoming confrontation.

Twenty-Seven

"Are you okay, Savannah?"

My arms hung over the railing of the small ship, watching the neighboring boat move into position beside us. We'd been waiting almost a day for them to arrive. The water was a beautiful blue, calm and peaceful. An illusion.

I probably did look a little green. The salt air wasn't having its usual soothing effects on my system, due to nerves and scary memories. "I'm okay, Mark. It's just where we are. I never wanted to come back here ever again."

"You didn't have to come, you know. My friends and I can handle this ourselves." He rested a hand on my shoulder.

"We both had to come, and you know it. No option."

"Captain sent me to get you. We're going to sick bay for something to help us relax. We need at least a few hours' sleep before sunset. Captain's orders. Otherwise, we'll be staying here and missing all the action."

"I don't know if they've got anything strong enough to make me sleep."

"Come on. I've always hated shots." He led me through the ship.

"They don't have pills? Wait, you hate shots? A big guy like you?"

"Yeah. Doesn't everybody?"

"I'm not a fan, but I've never minded them much. Is the doctor giving us shots to knock us out?"

"No, they're for being out of the country, and only for me. You don't need any since you got yours something like a year ago. She's giving us a pill for the sleeping part. Do you think you could hold my hand while they give me the shots?" Mark winked.

"I'd be happy to. Do you think maybe she'll give you a lollipop if you're a good boy?" I managed to work up the slightest of smiles.

"Ooh, let's go find out!"

I knew he was being silly on purpose to put me at ease. That was impossible. I'd never done anything remotely like this before but having Mark around helped. It was almost like Dave was back.

Staring into the mirror, I tugged on my shirt to straighten it. A loud knock at my door startled me. I opened it to find Mark in his Navy camouflage. Even though he told me earlier it'd been five years since he'd worn it, he hadn't lost much of his form.

I smiled in greeting. "Hey, you look great."

"Thanks, Savannah. It's a little snug in a few places. You ready to go?"

"Yep. Let's get this show on the road." I followed him down narrow passageways.

"Are you sure I can't talk you out of this? We've got a good plan, but we've got someone to stand in for you. I don't like you being involved to this extent, and it's for sure Ryan wouldn't approve. You haven't had enough training and it'll be rough on you emotionally. You've been through enough already, I think."

"I know." I stretched my strides to keep up with his longer ones. "Remember what I said. If I don't go in with you, I'll find a way to go in without you."

We stopped outside in the relative darkness.

"Hang on. I've got a present for you." Mark withdrew a short necklace from a shirt pocket. He fastened it around my neck, arranging it to his liking.

"Keep it just like that. The beads are miniature cameras, and two of them are microphones. We'll be monitoring so we can go in as soon as you show us the layout. Get over by Ryan and both of you get low. That's a requirement to be sure you two are out of the way in case of gunfire. They're going to try to avoid that at all costs, considering we don't know if the bullets might ricochet."

"So, this is spy stuff?" I was so far out of my league I didn't know what else to say.

"Old. We bought it surplus. This isn't a government sanctioned mission, after all. Not counting the local government help."

"Okay. I'll see you in a few hours." I wagged a finger at Mark. "Be careful."

"I will. You be careful yourself. Don't take any unnecessary chances." He enveloped me in a bear hug. "I'll have your back all the way to the summit."

"I know. Bye for now," I pushed back from him and swung over the rail, onto the ladder leading down to a lifeboat that would shuttle me to the small yacht nearby. There were no lights on the lifeboat and few in the other two larger craft, even though we were a long way from the island and on the opposite side of it from the cliffs.

The two men in the lifeboat, both friends of Ryan from his time in the Coast Guard, helped me find my footing and sit in a secure spot. Then we rotated away from the ship to head for the yacht. My nerves attacked again, making me regret the early breakfast I'd gotten down a half hour ago.

―⁂―

Dawn hinted at its arrival through the portal window. The three men waiting with me were volunteers, accompanying me ashore. They passed along amusing stories about Ryan and assured me this was going to work. Ryan had good taste in friends.

"Okay, let's see what you remember. Has your food had enough time to settle? I don't want to have to clean up a mess in here if you get sick," Wes teased.

He was nearly Ryan's height but with a leaner build, and medium brown hair and eyes. He'd been friends with Ryan since their time in the Army. He knew Dave, too. They all used to hang out back in Kansas.

"I'm fine. I might make you lose yours, though."

Soft chuckles came from the other men in the room.

Wes' eyebrows rose. "In that case, let's see what you've got, *Savvy*."

"How'd you know about that?" I shot him a scowl and assumed the preferred defensive posture Wes had shown me the day before.

"What? You mean your little nickname?" he teased again, a big grin on his bearded face.

I kept my cool, moving with him as he rotated around me, searching for an opening. All three of these men had been working together to teach me some interesting techniques for self-defense. Just in case.

"Ryan told me. No, wait, I think it was Mark. Doesn't matter, 'because everybody knows about it now. Why? Are you sensitive about it or something? Am I hurting your feelings?" He lowered his defenses, as the other guys snickered.

One corner of my mouth lifted slightly. Since he thought I couldn't, I wanted to wipe that smirk off his face. Not too much, just enough to make a point. "Nope. Think about Captain Jack."

"Who?" The question mark was written on his face.

"Aw, come on, Wes. You have to know who she's talking about," Chuck said in a chastising tone. Chuck was a couple inches taller than Wes, with a medium build and brown hair and eyes, much like Wes, but no beard. "Captain Jack always comes out on top. My money's on her."

"Mine, too," Douglas, who thankfully went by Doug, agreed. Doug was African American, about Chuck's size. He'd regaled me with all kinds of crazy stories about Ryan, Dave, and the rest of their little gang, even pulling a couple of giggles from me.

Wes' eyes darted to his friends at their comments. That was it. I dropped quickly, bracing myself with my hands as I swept my legs across his with sufficient force and surprise to take Wes' equilibrium before he could respond.

He stumbled, nearly falling backward to the floor. The wall caught him, but he still dropped to his hands and knees. He allowed a resounding series of expletives to escape his lips, his face red with embarrassment. His friends laughed as if it was the funniest thing they'd ever seen.

Good enough for me.

"Okay," Wes said through gritted teeth. "Not bad. It looks like you're good to go. Unless one of you other guys have enough balls to go through a round with her." He stood and ran his hands through his hair; then straightened his shirt.

"Nope. I think I speak for both of us when I say we surrender," Chuck said, attempting to stifle his laughter. Doug couldn't catch his breath enough for words. Wes lead the way to the bridge.

The island loomed large. I did my best to focus on the plan, reviewing it over and over in my head. And what I intended to say once I came face-to-face with the father of the monster.

It was vital to focus on rescuing Ryan and the fact that he needed me. Thinking too much about where we might find him would be unproductive. Too much to handle, especially as the island loomed.

"Everything's ready to go, sir. Lifeboat's set," Chuck reported.

"Understood," the captain stated. He called for a halt to the engines, for the anchor to be dropped. He picked up the radio. "This is Crumley, Captain of the Lotus. We're ready to deliver the target to you, over."

"This is Wainwright. My men are standing by to receive you, over."

At the sound of his voice, so much like my captor, my stomach tightened. I looked to the captain expectantly. My hands clenched repeatedly.

"Try not to worry, Savannah." Chuck didn't smile, all business now, like the rest of them.

I clutched at his hand like a lifeline, took a deep breath, and nodded. We exited, preceded by Wes. Outside, the sky was clear blue, the temperature warm. Several seagulls flew overhead toward the cliffs. Old habits must die hard. I refused to take it for a bad omen.

We descended the yacht's ladder to the waiting lifeboat. I took another deep breath as Chuck pushed off from the yacht. No going back.

Twenty-Eight

The men carried automatic weapons. I gripped the side of the boat, my heart pounding. We skimmed the waves, our speed making for a jarring ride. Wes cut the engine at the right moment to coast in on a wave that carried us in.

Chuck and Doug exited first, steadying the boat as it rose from the lifting of their weight. Wes followed.

"Stay put," Wes instructed me, his boots splashing through the water.

The three men drug the boat until it was clear of the ocean's reach. Wes helped me out, gave me a solemn stare followed by a quick wink. Five men waited near the jungle's beginning. Waiting to swallow me up.

My first steps wobbled as my brain adjusted my legs from sea to land. Wes held onto me until I steadied. Doug and Chuck moved ahead of us, their weapons held for all to see.

"It's okay. I've got it now," I whispered with lowered head. Act like the defeated, frightened, and helpless female, they'd told me, over and over.

Wes didn't verbalize a response. He simply removed his hand from my arm as he moved ahead to meet Wainwright's men. "Here she is. Now where's that reward money we were promised?"

One of the five moved past Wes and the others, stopping to stare at me. It made me nervous. More nervous. He withdrew a photograph from his shirt pocket, holding it to my face for a comparison. He nodded over his shoulder to his companions. "It's her."

Another of their number spoke into a walkie-talkie. "Got her. Savannah Dalton, confirmed."

"Bring her up here," the voice crackled.

The man beside me took a firm grip on my arm and got two steps before Wes blocked him. "Reward money." Chuck and Doug trained their weapons on the other four. The moment shifted into a stare down.

"Your money's in the account you gave us yesterday. Have

someone check it. It's not my problem anymore."

Wes called our rented yacht and received confirmation. "Okay, guys, the money's all there." He turned to the man holding me. "It's been nice doing business with you."

The man grunted, escorting me past. Wes' lips pursed.

"Next time you need someone brought to your boss, we'd appreciate the first crack at it. We're good at what we do," Wes said. No response was given.

Play the victim, don't forget to play the victim. I lowered my head again, rounding my shoulders, shuffling my feet. As they led me from the beach into the jungle, I threw in a few stumbles, and made sure to whimper as they pulled me upright.

Three men were left on the beach to watch the lifeboat leave.

The plan was for two bad guys to return to the yacht on the lifeboat. Unconscious or dead, they'd be rigged with special gear to sit up and appear lifelike to anyone who might be watching the departure through binoculars. The third bad guy would also be incapacitated. There were a substantial number of good guys hiding in the jungle.

My trek wasn't scary. Somewhere nearby, watching our every move, was Mark. He assured me he'd be close enough to touch my arm if he wanted to. The jungle was sufficiently dense that he could pull it off. My confidence in Mark's presence ran high.

The journey grew steep behind the cliffs. One of the men climbed up and the other passed me along to the first. Thick, leathery leaves slapped about our bodies.

We drew closer to the summit. I tried convincing myself of how simple a thing it was to calm down. Logically, I knew my survival odds were high. A former Navy Seal was already in the cave with Ryan, posing as a hired killer. I'd have no way of knowing which man he was until it was time.

With each step, my mind rebelled, telling me to run, to save myself. The memories and emotions crept in from the dark places. They'd never left me.

Emerging from the vegetation, we stood atop the stark, rocky cliffs, waves crashing below. The wind gusted at my hair. Even though it was warm, a strong shiver ran down my spine. How many times would I find myself staring at the terrifying view below? The stuff of my nightmares.

The men motioned me along the top toward where we'd make the climb down. I continued obediently, as the first man picked his way down. The second man remained at the top. But not for long. Mark was coming.

As we descended to the ledge below, I focused on each foothold along the way, keeping my mind occupied with the task. We exercised a healthy dose of caution. The man accompanying me put a hand against my back to steady me as I took the last step down to the ledge. He led the way forward.

My prison cell was only twenty paces ahead. Each step came slower and shorter than the one before. I wanted to see Ryan, to save him. I truly did. But by the time we were near the bathroom area and the doorway to my cell, an elephant sat on my chest.

On the inside, my heart pounded like a drum, so loud it reached my ears. That made it impossible to hear anything else, even the pulverizing waves below. The sheer terror flooding through me overwhelmed everything, completely out of control. I'd been a fool to have imagined myself capable of handling this, to play the part Ryan needed me to play.

The next step, the one to give me a glimpse of my cell's interior, simply wouldn't come. It was as though an invisible wall blocked forward progress and the horrors waiting inside. I couldn't move.

The man turned to stare at me. My uncontrollable trembling was noticeable, sweat trickling down my temples. I spun around and tore along the narrow ledge toward the carved pathway leading up. The man grabbed me as I reached it. I struggled to no avail. Both my training and the mission were forgotten in blind panic.

"No! He tried killed me in there! No!" I screamed, hoping that somehow, someone or something would stop this senseless ordeal and my descent into madness for the second time.

The man pinned my arms to my sides from behind, lifting me off my feet. In spite of the danger presented by the certain death beyond the precipice, I thrashed against him wildly.

"No! No! No!" I continued screaming as he forced me into the narrow tunnel. I used the walls to brace myself with hands and feet, to prevent him the inevitable. I lashed out so violently it was difficult to see anything. But when the space opened up, I headbutted his chin.

"Son of bitch!" he yelled, letting go to cradle his chin as he strode outside.

Another man took his place, restraining my arms from behind.

"Shut up!"

I froze. Lanterns provided illumination. Ahead was the man who must be Martin Wainwright. He was the one who'd yelled. My chest heaved from my futile battle.

He stepped forward to smooth back the hair from in front of my wild eyes. As he brushed aside the last strands of hair, I bit him, snarling like a captured wild animal. He yanked his hand away and cradled it.

"I'll get you, you crazy monster!" My struggle began anew, as I kicked out at the elderly man. My efforts succeeded this time. Not in contacting Wainwright. Instead, I broke free from the man restraining me.

"Put that animal down," Wainwright ordered, cowering by a wall.

A different man stepped in front of me. He grabbed a fistful of my shirt and maneuvered me backwards. "You know why you're here. Stay down!" He ordered, one hand clamped on my shoulder as he gave me the smallest of nods. Something in his expression, his words, caught my attention.

His fist swung at me as Ryan yelled a warning from nearby. I hadn't even seen him. In my utter panic, I'd forgotten him. The punch hurt, but it pushed my head aside and moved my body, rather than delivering a crippling blow. My body twisted and fell near the back wall. I played dead.

My mind raced, trying to process what happened. The Navy Seal hit me. My cheek stung, but nothing was broken. He put me out of harm's way, near Ryan, where I was supposed to go on my own.

The plan had gone wrong. My fault, like Douglas said. My mind had leapt back in time to my imprisonment. It rushed over me in a wave, shoving away who I was, leaving me in a panic, forgetting my friends, the plan, and even Ryan.

My hair landed across my face, concealing my open eyes from notice. I faced the back wall of my prison cell.

There, chained to it as I'd been, was Ryan. But another man shared the rusted iron ring embedded in the wall and a set of shiny new chains. He kneeled on the bare rock, as did Ryan. How long had they been here?

The stranger's face in the light of the multitude of lanterns, told me who he must be—Douglas' brother. But why?

"I'm going to find a way to kill you for hitting her." Ryan stared at someone I couldn't see.

"You're not intimidating him. Keep your mouth closed or I'll have you gagged. Then I'll have that man hit your woman again," Martin dismissed.

I remembered the gag and the torture that accompanied it.

Getting to Ryan would clear the rest of the cave for the Navy Seals to step in, overwhelm and intimidate. The risk of gunfire had been deemed too great. That was the original plan. My scrambled mind was no longer following it. And may have ruined it.

I needed a new plan, fast. Where were the other Navy Seals? I lay near Ryan, low to the floor, well clear. Why hadn't rescue come? Most likely, it was because Ryan hadn't been warned and had no protection. That was my fault, too. And they hadn't gotten a good view of the scene inside from the cameras I wore.

"Martin." A woman's silky voice dripped with controlled anger.

A new player had arrived, someone unexpected, judging from the gaping mouth and wide eyes of Douglas' brother. I was in a position where I couldn't see her. This must've been why the rescuers hadn't entered the cave yet.

"Adeline. What're you doing here?" Martin asked, surprise clear in his voice.

"I could ask you the same question, but I already know the answer. You're carrying out your obsession for revenge over Douglas' death."

"That doesn't explain why you're here."

"I'm here to stop you from murdering your own son. Desmond, don't you worry. I'm getting you out of here."

It made twisted sense to kill Ryan and me. But his only remaining child? Could this woman have tipped the balance against us? She wouldn't have come alone.

I thought briefly of attracting Ryan's attention but dismissed the idea. Desmond might notice. Ryan's wide eyes were focused on the confrontation. Everyone seemed to have forgotten about me.

"He's as responsible for what happened to my precious boy as surely as these other two. He started it by taking Doug away from me. All these years." The voice was petulant.

"You're insane." Light footsteps approached my location. "So, what happened here? Is this the untalented little writer? Did you kill her? I wanted to do that myself." She nudged me with her foot, rocking my body back and forth a few times. I moved with her.

"She's alive. She went completely insane. The girl belongs in a sanatorium. She bit me like a rabid dog."

"Oh, really? Well then, perhaps she's not so bad after all. But I'm not going to bite you, Martin. That's what the bullet's for."

Ryan and Desmond drew back. The woman must've pulled a gun. The place was crowd with people. I'd flailed around so much I didn't get a good look at them. The cameras I wore probably didn't help the rescuers at all.

"You're not going to shoot your own husband. You'd never do anything like that, and we both know it."

"Do you? Do you?" Her shrill voice rose. "You were going to kill my son!"

The gun discharged. No more time to waste. I shoved over and up, then charged. It was a short run but unexpected, like the gunshot the others were reeling from. No one had considered the unconscious basket case on the floor.

Lowering my head, I collided with the nearest man, propelling him into Adeline Wainwright, who dropped her handgun from the force of the man's body impacting hers. The three of us piled into the wall near Martin's immobile form. The man I'd hit reached for his sidearm, but he was off balance, pinned against a struggling Adeline.

My hands darted quickly over his, shoving the gun hard against him. Sam's insistence that I learn how to use a gun came in handy.

274

THE STRANDING

The weapon discharged, the bullet striking the man's thigh. He screamed in pain, releasing his hold on the gun, falling, and taking Mrs. Wainwright with him. Inadvertently, he'd pinned her to the floor.

Everyone else in the cave was engaged in a fierce brawl.

I yanked the gun free from its holster and sidestepped away from its owner. I remembered the warning about shooting in the cave. A body by the tunnel entrance wasn't moving.

Everything happened fast after that. The Navy Seal who'd struck me delivered an amazing kick to send one man airborne into the crates of food, still stacked against the far wall. Other good guys, men and women, stormed in.

Two rushed past me to Ryan and Desmond. The Navy Seal who'd punched me approached, extending his hand for a firm shake. "Nice work. Sorry about your jaw. I had to get your attention and put you where you were supposed to be."

"You did the right thing. I lost control for a few minutes there." I managed a smile.

He moved to Martin, fishing through pockets until he found a set of keys. "Here you go." He tossed them to a woman and pulled zip ties from his pocket. Adeline was in a seated position, her hands secured behind her back.

When I turned, Ryan was free, rushing to me.

He kissed me quick and stepped back to check me over. He slipped the gun from my hand. "Are you okay, honey?"

"I'm fine now that I've got you back." I loved him and could've so easily lost him. Time was precious.

"Savvy are you all right?" a voice called from the entrance.

I turned to see Mark pushing his way past people to get inside. "Mark!" I opened my arms to him, wrapping them around his neck when he reached me.

The bear hug was warm and welcome. "You had me worried. I heard gunshots in here. You'll have to show Wes you how well you learned."

"Hey, what about me?" Ryan sounded annoyed.

"You can wait. This is a once-in-a-lifetime moment for me, with

275

the exception of your official wedding day," Mark told Ryan as he leaned down to kiss my lips.

"Okay, okay. That's enough, break it up." Ryan pulled me toward him, his other arm extended to push at Mark. He didn't grin until he'd successfully separated us. "It's my turn."

"To kiss Mark or me?" I said with a grin.

"Very funny," Mark said, but Ryan grabbed him and planted a loud kiss on his cheek.

After a roar of laughter, Mark and Ryan slapped each other on the back.

"I should've known you'd come, big brother," Ryan said. "How'd you find me?"

Mark nodded in my direction. "Savvy's the one you can thank for your rescue. She figured it out fast and got ahold of me. We worked together to round up a cavalry composed of veterans. Come on, we've got a boat to catch."

Ryan and Mark each held one of my hands as we walked out in a single-file chain through the tunnel and into the sunshine.

THE END

If you'd like to follow the progress on upcoming novels, you can follow the author on Amazon: https://www.amazon.com/A-L-Nelson. Or you can grab a free novella that is a prequel to Dangerous Offer (a new series) when you sign up for the author's newsletter at: https://alnelsonauthor.com/newsletter. If you don't see the free novella as an offer for signing up, please check back because as of early January 2022 it was nearly complete.

Additional novels by the author are available on Amazon:

The Chaperone
Winning Wonderland
Dying for a Family
Dangerous Offer

A note to the reader:

You have the power to increase the reach of my books. If you enjoyed this book, please consider recommending it to your friends, mentioning it on social media, and especially by leaving a review on Amazon. It is amazing the power those reviews carry for authors, and it just takes a couple of minutes of your time.

Only a sentence or two for comment is needed or you can leave some stars. It not only helps me, but it increases the visibility of the book, which earns more money for the charitable organizations supported. Likewise, if you didn't enjoy it, you are also free to review! Thank you so much for purchasing this book.

Sign up for the author's newsletter and stay up on all the latest book news, because there are more novels to come, including some freebies. And follow her on:

Website: alnelsonauthor.com
Facebook: ALNelsonAuthor
Instagram: a.l.nelson
Twitter: ALNelson13
BookBub: a-l-nelson
TikTok: alnelsonauthor

ABOUT THE AUTHOR

The author writes romance and romantic suspense/thriller novels. Her characters work to overcome near-impossible odds. She lives with her husband, two children, and a dog afflicted with a joyous case of the zoomies in sunny Florida. When she isn't working at her fulltime job to pay the bills, she enjoys spending time with her family, writing, swimming, and searching beaches for treasures.

Profits from her novels go to charity, with information about these on her website. So, buy a book to enjoy and help a good cause in the process.